TRAPPED

SAL MASON

ISBN: 978-1-9164743-1-4
2nd edition
Rapid River Publishing

Cover by render/compose
Edited by Ayers Edits
The text type was set in Adobe Garamond Pro

For more information or to sign up to my newsletter, visit
www.salmasonauthor.com

Trigger Warning: This story includes relevant social topics such as
anxiety, self-harm, and depression, as well as references to rape/abuse. Do
not read if you find any of these topics disturbing. They are not meant to
upset anyone but to raise awareness.

*To my daughter who always told me to
hold on to my dreams*

Prologue

The blanket around my shoulders doesn't provide any comfort. My teeth are chattering like there is no tomorrow and my insides are frozen to ice. I stare at the wall, my brain barely registering the sounds of the occasional nurse tiptoeing around me. Every time I move, pain throbs through my body, but I'm so used to it by now that I hardly notice. Something hot drips on my skin and I realize that I have started to cry again.

A hand claps down on my shoulder and I jump, almost falling off the chair.

"I'm sorry, Kelsey, I didn't mean to startle you. My name is Detective Larouge."

I narrow my eyes to focus on his face. He is an older guy, maybe the age of my father. A badge is stuck to his belt, which signals "friendly," but my mind still cries caution—he is a man who can hurt me. There is movement behind him and I strain to make out a young woman with a wide, fake smile.

"I know this is difficult for you, but can we ask you a few questions?"

I want to scream at them to leave me alone. "I already told the other officer what happened."

He gives me a crooked smile. "I know, but we have to go over a few points again."

I glance around for my mom and Roy, hoping for them to rescue me, but they're still not here. I shake my head to get the fuzziness out of my brain before I turn back to Larouge and the woman.

He lowers himself on the empty cot next to me while she pulls up a chair at a much safer distance. I try to control my trembling hands when I tuck the blanket tighter around me.

Something is pushing on my chest and I'm having trouble breathing.

"Kelsey, you told the officer at the police department intake desk that two men abducted you?"

I nod.

"And do you know who they were?"

I close my eyes and Jed's face flashes in front of me. The memory of his cynical laugh before he bends down to forcefully kiss me turns my stomach into tight knots.

"One of them was Jed Edwards." My voice is hoarse and no longer recognizable. I sound like a broken robot.

"Are you absolutely sure?"

Stupid question—Jed tormented me every single day for three months and his face is forever burned into my mind.

"Yes, I'm sure. He and my brother were in the same year together, and kids in school used to pick on him."

"What about the other one?"

A sorrowful sob escapes my throat when I remember the night he took my innocence.

"I don't know." Tears stream down my face. "I was always blindfolded when I was with him and he never spoke. I have no idea what he looks like."

The two officers exchange a glance.

"Do you have any idea how old he is?"

I bite down on my lip when my mind screams to stop the questions. The dull pain in my head pounds so hard that I'm about to lose it. All I want is to go home—hide under my blankets—and not be stuck in this hospital with a bunch of strangers.

"He was very strong with firm muscles," I say with a slight quiver in my voice. "I don't think he was that old."

"Anything else you remember that could help us to identify him?"

Trapped

With a sigh, I close my eyes. I just want to forget, but they force me to dip back deep into those horrible memories I try to block out.

"Kelsey? Do you remember anything else? We need you to tell us everything."

I open my eyes and realize that I have been silent for a while. Larouge wants to hear everything. The words are pulled out of me by an invisible force that knows I have to cooperate if I ever want him to leave me alone. "One night, he untied one of my hands and made me jerk him off." A shudder runs through me and I choke on the words when bile rises in my throat. "He had a scar, I mean down there, on top of his inner thigh. It wasn't big, like a small slash."

"That's very helpful, Kelsey. You're doing great."

I give him a weak smile.

"Now, let's get back to Jed—"

A scream from the doorway interrupts him. "Kelsey, oh my god."

I turn toward the voice, the whole room blurred from my tears. "Mom!"

I missed her so much and want to run to her, but my legs are no longer under my control. My arms fly up when she squats down next to me and pulls my head against her shoulder. I weep, feeling halfway safe for the first time since this whole ordeal started.

"Shh, honey, everything will be all right now. You're alive, that's all that matters." The words are muffled by her tears.

"I'm so sorry, Mom, that I didn't listen to you."

"Don't worry about a thing, honey. No one blames you." A cry escapes her mouth. "I thought I lost you forever, Kelsey. I love you so much."

"I want to go home."

She strokes my hair. "Can I take my daughter home?"

I raise my head and turn to Larouge with pleading eyes.

He can't even hold my gaze. "I'm sorry, Joan, but there're still a lot of questions we need to ask her."

Roy huffs. "Can't this wait till tomorrow? As you can see, Kelsey is exhausted and in shock. I really want to take her home."

I manage a small smile. Just as usual, Roy is my hero. Since he and my mom married about ten years ago, he has always been there for me. With his son, Luke, we're just like a smaller version of the Brady Bunch.

Larouge's face twists, but then his head begins to bob back and forth. "I understand. We can postpone the questioning, but I'm afraid that Kelsey has to remain at the hospital until the doctors complete her physical examination. As you know, we have to preserve the evidence."

Roy takes in a sharp breath. "I presume . . ."

As his words trail off, my mother's hand clutches over her mouth. All eyes are on me with pity. I must have the word "RAPE" written all over my forehead.

Larouge clears his throat. "We'll likely make an arrest in the next few hours and need Kelsey to make a positive ID in a lineup."

Roy nods, his eyes determined. "That won't be a problem. I will make a few calls to ensure the bastard won't make bail. Who is it?"

"You know I can't tell you in an ongoing investigation." Larouge squirms when my stepdad rolls his eyes.

"Come on, Nick, we're talking about my family here. Don't give me this bullshit. We have been friends long enough that you know you can trust me."

Larouge glances at the lady cop, who takes the hint and excuses herself with some mumbled words under her breath.

Trapped

They wait until the door closes behind her before Larouge speaks again.

"It's Jed Edwards."

A frown wrinkles Roy's forehead. "Isn't that the kid who lives out there in the woods by the creek?"

"Yes," my mom jumps in. "His parents died a few years ago and he hasn't been around much since."

Roy huffs again. "I always knew that boy was trouble." He squeezes my shoulder. "Don't worry, Kelsey, I'll make sure he's locked up for a really long time. He'll never be able to hurt you again."

I put all my hope and trust in him in this moment, certain that my tormentors and rapists will go to prison and rot there for eternity. In the end, justice will always prevail—because that's how it is supposed to be.

Chapter 1

The wailing screech of the electric guitar almost rips my eardrums when Slash performs one of his guitar solos. I used to despise heavy metal until I discovered that the shrill sounds numb my mind to a point of total oblivion. The plugs of the Beats in my ears are turned up to full power while I lie rigidly on the bed, waiting for the next guitar solo to shoot throbs through my brain. This is better than getting freeze shocks from eating large mouthfuls of ice cream.

When Slash is just about ready to strike again, a hand tears me out of my heavy-metal world, making my heart jump into the air. My eyes fly open as my heart rate doubles, just to be mocked by the sight of my mother. False alarm—no need to get upset.

I'm still in a rotten mood. "What the hell are you doing? You scared the living daylights out of me." The hissing sounds rolling off my lips are far from the image of the respectful daughter I ought to be.

Her eyebrows knot together in response. "I screamed at you at the top of my lungs, but you didn't even flinch. That music is too loud. It's bad for your hearing. One of these days, you're going to end up deaf."

I'd heard it all before. "Yeah, Mom, I know, but you still shouldn't invade my privacy like that. What do you want?"

She looks like a lost puppy. "I just wanted to remind you that it's time for your walk."

I eye the gaps in the curtain, thinking of an excuse not to go. Why couldn't it just be raining? "I don't feel like leaving the house. It's way too chilly."

She doesn't go for it. "It's beautiful outside. You could even wear shorts."

Trapped

I glare at her. Why would I want to do that? Shorts mean exposed skin, which in turn could give the impression in someone's perverted mind that I might be interested in anything other than being left alone.

My mom continues her lecture. "Dr. Stromberg said that those daily walks are important."

Everything Dr. Stromberg has ever prescribed is of utmost importance for my recovery, but except for those pills that help with my depression and give me a buzz, I generally disagree with her opinions.

"Maybe tomorrow, Mom. I have a headache."

"No." She pulls away my cover, exposing my pj's with the white and red skulls on an all-black background—my absolute favorite. Everything symbolizing death and destruction is totally noteworthy. "You will get up, young lady, and take a shower for a change. Then you'll get out of this house and enjoy the sunshine."

I moan, trying to recover the blanket, but she is relentless.

"And when you come home, you will join us at the table for dinner and not just disappear in your room again." She underlines her words by jutting her chin at me. It's her "don't challenge me" look.

My moans grow louder. "Mom, please—"

She cuts me off with a pointed finger. "Don't *please* me, Kelsey. You're making yourself sick and it has to stop."

I pull my pillow over my head to block her out and hide the oncoming tears. "I *am* sick, Mom. In case you haven't noticed, I'm a total nutcase."

She sits down on the bed next to me and strokes my back the way she used to when I was little. "I know you're still hurting, but it has been three years. It's time for you to at least make an effort to get your life back into some type of order."

I mumble something inaudible into my sheets.

"What was that, honey?"

I fiercely fight the tears. "Nothing, Mom. I'll get up in a minute."

It's an empty promise and she knows me too well. We have been here plenty of times before. "I'm not leaving until you are in the shower."

With a growl, I jump out of the bed and stalk into the bathroom, slamming the door behind me. Why in God's name can't people just leave me alone?

Ten minutes later, I have showered and even washed my hair before dressing in saggy black jeans and an oversized black sweater that reminds me of a huge tent. Some grungy old sneakers complete the ensemble. My damp hair is pulled up in a messy bun with a plain rubber band after I don't even bother combing it in the first place. I used to wear makeup but not anymore.

I grab the offered apple from my mother's hand before heading outside, no longer in the mood to argue. I toss it in the next garbage bin I pass on the street. My steps are heavy as I stroll along without any particular destination.

My mom was right; it is the perfect May afternoon. The warm sun dances on my skin whenever I step out of the shadows, an occasional breeze playing with a few loose strands of my hair. When I speed up, a thin layer of sweat soon covers my back. I should have worn a short-sleeve shirt, but the risk of someone noticing my little acts of indiscretion is just too high. Rumors spread through Stonehenge like wildfire and there is no need to fuel my reputation as the town's wacko even more.

Somehow I end up downtown by the park and find myself on a bench away from the main sidewalk but still within visual range of the high school. It's almost four, and when the bell rings, students begin to file out. I gasp when I notice Justin by the gate, leaning against a light post.

Trapped

A sharp pain stabs at my heart as he wraps his arms around Cynthia Tranton, of all people, who looks like a total slut in her little cheerleader outfit. They kiss passionately and I can practically see their tongues colliding. My soul is weeping—he used to kiss me like that before I became damaged and used. The pain worsens when the little green devil claws into my heart with cruel laughter.

No one wants the raped girl, he spits in my face.

I lower my gaze, wondering how long they've been together. Cynthia is a year younger than me and will graduate in a few weeks. After that, she's probably off to some West Coast college on her parents' dime. I've never even stepped foot outside of Maine, one of the least crime-ridden states of the country, yet I'm the one abducted and raped. Figures!

Someone slumps next to me on the bench, and I am just about to karate chop him into his temple, like I learned in my self-defense class, when I realize it's Luke. I nudge his shoulder harder than intended.

"You jerk, scaring me like that."

He rubs his arm with a grimace. "I didn't know you lost your eyesight overnight. Didn't you see it was me?"

"I was deep in thought."

"I suppose that's a good thing. Usually, all you do is sulk, so I guess animating those brain cells is an improvement."

My eyes linger on Justin and Cynthia, who have been joined by a few of their friends. Justin is laughing and Cynthia hops excitedly from one foot to the other. She looks absolutely silly. It's Friday night and they probably plan to have a party out by the lake.

Luke rests his arm on my shoulders. "Are you okay? Maybe we should leave."

I can't tear my eyes off them. "How long have they been together?"

"I don't know, but I think it has been a while. The jerk moved on pretty quickly." He squeezes my shoulder. "It's his loss, you know. He'll never find someone as special as you."

Tears blur my vision. "You're the only one who thinks that and only because you're my brother."

"Don't do this to yourself, Kels. You'll see—one day, you'll find someone who loves you just the way you are."

I have my serious doubts but don't debate with him. He always wins anyhow. His arguments are usually solid and sharp—he's just like Roy in that respect. I guess like father, like son.

He reaches into the side pocket of his backpack and produces a tall paper cup. "Here, I brought you something."

I grin from ear to ear, touched by his gesture. "Starbucks. Is it the caramel latte with cream I like?"

"Yep."

I reach for the cup, already tasting the sweet whipped cream on my lips, but he pulls it out of my reach. "Only if you kept your promise. Let's see your arms."

I grit my teeth, staring at the coffee. "Come on, Luke. Give it to me." It seems so close, yet still so far.

"Show me your arms."

His piercing eyes stir my bad conscience, and with a groan, I roll up my sleeves, knowing I have lost. The coffee cup lands in a nearby bin, the brown liquid spilling through the wire mesh and soaking into the ground. Only a little bit of cream and sprinkles are left behind. He stares ahead with pursed lips, the disappointment oozing from his body.

I shrink in my seat, feeling incredibly worthless and despicable. "It was only a small cut."

He refuses to play my game. "A cut is a cut, Kels. You know how I feel about self-harm. It's stupid and won't solve any of your problems."

Trapped

A cold claw clenches my chest. "It makes me feel better."

"I understand that it's a coping mechanism, but it'll never erase your real pain. You might think you feel better for a little while, but that's just an illusion. Causing more wounds won't help to heal those scars in the end."

I don't want to talk about it anymore and punish him with silence. He doesn't seem to mind, leaning back on the bench with his eyes closed, enjoying the sunshine. My focus returns to the school gate, but Justin and Cynthia are gone. Most of the area in front of the building is deserted. Only a few guys are throwing a football.

A boy is sitting in the grass, his back resting against a tree. His eyes follow the football jocks with a smirk. He absentmindedly pulls a pack of cigarettes from his pocket and lights himself a smoke. I'm baffled by his open display of defiance—the school has a strict no-smoking policy. He'll be suspended if caught by a teacher.

He inhales deeply and blows the smoke in the direction of the boys with the football. His "don't care" attitude is annoying. I eye his stereotypical bad boy outfit with a wrinkled nose—black jeans, biker boots, and a black muscle tank that highlights his wide chest. A leather jacket is tossed casually in the grass beside him—what an idiot. His rebellious appearance might work up in Lewiston or maybe even down in Portland, but not here, in the sheltered community of Stonehenge. In this town, most boys and girls are churchgoing goody-two-shoes with parents who do not approve of guys like him. He must be a fairly new arrival who has yet to learn the error of his ways.

"Hey, Luke, do you know that guy?"

His gaze moves in the direction of my pointed finger. "Yeah, that's Finn. Don't you remember? He's Andrew Walker's nephew and used to come up here in the summer with his brother. We went to kayak camp together a few times."

I vaguely remember. He ran in a different crowd, already a troublemaker back then. "What's he doing here?"

"Oh, he just moved from Connecticut. Apparently, he got into some trouble back home and they kicked him out of school. Rumor has it that he is on his second attempt of senior year, but Maya said he's likely not going to make it. His grades must be terrible and he cuts a lot of classes."

I chuckle and almost feel sorry for him—Finn has probably no idea that he is the center of the town's juicy gossip. Maya, the sister of Luke's girlfriend, Rhonda, is the biggest newsmonger around and will keep everyone diligently informed about any of his mischief.

Luke stretches. "We should get home. Rhonda and I want to catch a movie up in Auburn tonight." He winks at me. "Care to tag along?"

"Nope. I have plans of my own."

"Do those involve leaving the house?"

I glare at him. "What do you want from me? I already took a shower and this stupid walk. Isn't that enough to prove that I'm trying?"

"Don't expect a medal from me, Kels. It has been three years and hiding in your room is not the answer."

Not again. Why can't he and my mom understand that memories don't just fade away because a certain time frame has elapsed?

I glance one more time at Finn, who flips the football jocks a bird, causing some shouts to float our way. One guy is turning red in the face while Finn laughs off his insults. I just silently shake my head. Somebody needs to put him in his place with that type of attitude.

I follow Luke to his truck and slide into the passenger seat, buckling up. As we drive by the high school where Finn and

Red Face have advanced to pushing each other, the words "fuck you" assault my ears. I frown—what a jerk.

Halfway home, Luke pulls into a gas station and fills up the tank. Just when he is about done, his phone rings. He hands me a twenty-dollar bill. "Could you run in and pay? I need to get this."

I grab the money and stroll inside, thirst suddenly bubbling in my throat. The clerk has his back turned as I walk in, his nose stuck in a magazine. The cooler is right beside the door and I study the selection of drinks before reaching for a peach iced tea.

"Excuse me, do you also have this in lem—?" A small yelp springs from my lips when the clerk turns around to face me. The bottle escapes my hands and crashes onto the floor. When the cap pops off, iced tea splatters all over my shoes and pants, but I barely notice the mess.

The clerk sneers. "Oh, hey, honeybun. Haven't seen you in a while."

An invisible force wraps around my throat and I gasp for air, cold sweat spilling from every pore of my body. Before I can faint, my hand reaches for the water cooler to steady myself. My eyes are fixed on him like a mouse on a snake while I continue to breathe heavily. All my mind registers at that very moment is one single thought. What in the hell is Jed Edwards doing here?

Chapter 2

I stare at Jed with an open mouth. My mind screams for me to run and hide—anything to get away from him—but my legs refuse to move. When tears pool in my eyes, some of my brain's commands finally reach their destination. In a daze, I slap the twenty-dollar bill on the counter and dart from the store.

Luke's truck seems to be at an unattainable distance, and I don't even make it halfway there before breaking down on my knees. The sting in my chest is unbearable when my lungs come up short of oxygen with every breath I take. I feel I'm about to choke. My arms wrap around me as I rock back and forth, sobs mixing with low whimpers.

Luke's hand weighs a ton on my shoulder when he squats down next to me. "Kels, what's wrong?"

I point at the store while struggling for air, black dots dancing in front of my eyes. My lips form silent words, but no sound escapes. As I have so many times before, I curse my worthless body. He tries to pull me into his arms, but I slap him away, unable to stand his touch.

Finally, I manage to croak the word "Jed" in between tear spurts.

He goes rigid, sucking in a deep breath. "Is the jerk in there?"

I nod, digging my fingernails into his sweater when he slowly rises. "Don't."

He ignores my plea and marches toward the store with a stony face. Crazy thoughts race through my mind, imagining all kinds of impending doom—Luke hurt in a physical altercation or even shot. I force myself back on my feet and follow him with slumped shoulders.

Trapped

The situation is already hairy when I step through the door. Jed is pinned against the wall, Luke right in his face. "What the hell did you do to my sister?"

Jed, who doesn't seem fazed at all by Luke's assault, offers him a smug smile. "Nothing, man. I just said hello and she totally freaked out."

"What are you even doing back in town, asshole?"

Jed snorts. "It's a free country. I can live wherever I want and I just really like it here."

"Well, that was a big mistake." Luke raises his fist. "No one wants you here."

"Luke, don't," I cry in a feeble attempt to stop him. "You know what happened the last time."

Jed's eyes come to rest on me. "Yeah, listen to your sister, man. If you beat me up again, I'll press charges, and this time, you won't get away with community service."

Luke's face is full of struggle. When his gaze falls on the camera above the counter, his arm drops. "I swear this is not over, Jed. If I were you, I would get the hell out of town before someone jumps you from behind in a dark alley. You have a lot of enemies around."

"Sure I do." Jed's tongue runs over his lips as he gives me a good once-over. "But that doesn't change the fact that I'm walking around a free man while your sister here is still screwed." He laughs. "And I mean that literally."

I lower my eyes when a few tears trickle down my cheeks, my breath heavy again. "Please, Luke, let's just go."

With a growl, he releases Jed and grabs my hand. I allow him to whisk me away after glancing one more time at my tormentor. Jed's glare burns into my back as I walk to the truck. The fact he knows what's underneath these clothes and would probably love nothing more than to tear them off stabs painfully at my insides.

On the way home, I fight the nausea while Luke rants and rages about the injustice. Most of his words fall on deaf ears. I'm captured in my own little world, thinking back to the moment when I first woke up after my abduction.

It was dark, the scent in the air musty. A shudder ran through me when a cold breeze hit me, goosebumps covering my body. I realized I was naked. My throat was raw and it hurt every time I swallowed, a foul taste coating the inside of my mouth. A pounding headache overpowered the rest of my senses.

I turned my head toward the screeching door and instinctively curled into a ball when a dark figure entered. The light came on and I blinked. My eyes teared from the sudden brightness.

"Good, you're awake."

My heart cringed in my chest at the slyness in Jed's soft voice.

"Why did you bring me here?" I bit my trembling lip, trying to give my words some firmness. Though I wanted to scream, my instincts told me that getting myself all worked up wouldn't get me anywhere.

He lowered himself onto the bed next to me and ran his fingers down my back. I recoiled from his touch, sickness cramping my stomach.

"I'm sure you know the answer to that, honeybun." His eyes were greedy when they wandered up and down my frame. "You're a terrible tease, always parading around in those short tight skirts and flirting with guys any chance you get. You drive me crazy, but all you've ever had for me was ridicule. Whatever happens, you brought this on yourself."

Trapped

Tears dribbled from my eyes. "I'm sorry, I never meant to upset you. Please, Jed, just let me go. I swear I won't tell anyone that you kidnapped me."

He clicked his tongue. "Kidnapping is such an ugly word. You should see it more as an invitation to an extended party." He tried to roll me on my back, but I hugged my knees with such force that he couldn't break my grip. He laughed wickedly. "If you continue to be such a prude, I'll have to tie you down."

His words were like a fist, punching into my stomach. "Please, Jed, I'm still a virgin. Don't do this."

His thumb caressed my wet cheek. "Don't you think I know that, honeybun?" He sighed. "Unfortunately, I lost the coin toss, so my friend will do the honor. He'll be over later." His eyes filled with darkness. "If you're a good girl and let me take a peek, I'll bring you some food and water."

I didn't move, my head spinning. Somehow, I needed to escape.

"Suit yourself. Just so you know, you're underground and there's no one around who can hear you scream. The door is solid metal with three different locks. You're trapped, honeybun. You can either make this a whole lot easier and cooperate, or fuss and learn the hard way that we mean business."

When he walked toward the door and had his back turned, I seized the opportunity and jumped him. Luke had shown me a few self-defense moves when we were wrestling out back for fun, but my feeble attempts were no match for the number one lightweight contender in the state. One punch knocked me out cold. I didn't wake up until later with my arms and legs tied to the bedposts, my head bursting from pain.

I screamed for help at the top of my lungs until my voice was hoarse and reduced to a whisper. As Jed predicted, no one came to my rescue. I was trapped and at their mercy.

When Luke's hand brushes over my arm, I almost jump out of my seat.

"You look really upset." His eyes are filled with worry. "Do you want to talk about it?"

I lean back in my seat, trying to calm my ragged breath. "Talk about what?"

"You've never told anyone what actually happened and keep everything bottled inside. Maybe if you confided in someone, it would help you to process the trauma."

I roll my eyes—Dr. Stromberg is already constantly on my case about opening up. Last thing I need is his probing. "I was raped, Luke. What's more to say?"

"Well, how do you feel about it now?"

I glare out of the window with empty eyes. "You can search the Internet about the experiences of rape survivors."

"I don't want to know about a bunch of strangers." The words are sharp with a hint of anger. "All I care about is my sister. Why are you even fighting me here, Kels? Don't you know I'm in your corner?"

"I'm just not ready, Luke." I pinch the bridge of my nose, trying to fight the oncoming headache.

He opens his mouth, but I cut him off.

"And don't tell me again that it has been three years. I need more time and I'm tired of people trying to rush me."

He sighs. "Fair enough." His hand comes to rest on my lower arm and squeezes gently. "Just promise me that you won't do anything stupid in the meantime. No more cutting or other form of self-harm."

I avoid his searching eyes. "I swear," I say—damn well knowing that this is not a promise I intend to keep.

When I get home, I dash into my room, just to be ordered back downstairs by my mom.

Trapped

"Kelsey, dinner is almost ready."

I know she won't give up and will insist on me joining the happy family get together. Her plans apparently include an all-night torture—Roy is just starting the grill when I step onto the porch. Luke breaks out the old badminton set from the garage and approaches me with a wide grin.

"Come on, grouchy, let's play."

I just shake my head. "I don't feel like playing. Didn't you have plans with Rhonda tonight?"

"Not anymore." He starts to bounce the shuttlecock on the string bed. "I cancelled after, you know . . ."

He allows his words to trail off and I eye my mom and Roy.

"You didn't tell them, right?" My mom would freak out again and I can't handle that right now.

"Nope, I didn't say a word"—he catches the feathered ball—"but I will if you continue to be such a whiner."

I can't believe he is blackmailing me, but I am not prepared to take any chances. With a small growl, I grab the racket and soon we're bouncing the shuttlecock around. The basics come back to me quite quickly and I actually find the game a little fun. With every hit of the racket, a little piece of today's memories is pushed further and further to the back of my mind.

"I saw that." Luke laughs.

My eyes narrow. "What?"

"That little smile you were trying to suppress."

I give him my best impression of Grumpy Cat. "Oh, shut up."

We continue our game until the aroma of grilled meat taunts my nostrils. My stomach grumbles. I'm famished for a change and toddle into the kitchen to help my mom. As I cut the tomatoes for the salad, Luke sets the table, chatting away with his father about some upcoming baseball game. For a moment, my heart aches with nostalgia—that's how it was almost every weekend before my abduction. Back then, I had stupid fights with my mom half the time and didn't even appreciate my easy-going existence.

When the steaks are done, we gather around the table. I pile up my plate with meat and corn on the cob. The food is delicious and the light atmosphere continues until almost the end of the meal. That's when Roy returns me to my harsh reality.

"Detective Larouge called today to inform me that Jed Edwards is back in town."

Luke gives me this "should I tell them, or will you" look.

"We ran into him at the Easy Mart," I fess up. "He works there."

"Oh my god, what if he takes Kelsey again?" My mom's hand is clutched over her mouth. "You have to do something, Roy. Can't you file a restraining order?"

"Unfortunately, I can't. Since the charges were dismissed, there's no basis. Unless he threatens Kelsey, the law is on his side." His fingers wrap around my mom's hand. "Don't worry, honey. Nick agrees that the chances he will kidnap Kelsey again are slim to none since everyone would immediately point the finger at him. Not even he is that dumb."

"I still want Kelsey to be careful." Her lips have that overprotective poutiness to them that I used to hate. "One of us should be with her when she leaves the house, and hopefully, he'll disappear again soon. Don't you play tennis with the owner of the Easy Mart? I mean, if Jed lost that job—" Her gaze drops when she meets her husband's frown. Usually, Roy is straighter than an arrow and only calls in these types of favors when he absolutely has to.

"Okay, I'll talk to him," he says when her eyes fill with tears.

Trying to ignore the growing unrest in the pit of my stomach, I pick at the last pieces of my salad to distract myself. With my mom's worry, my daily walks will most likely be suspended, something that would have been beyond thrilling just hours ago. The prospect that I could bump into Jed at any given moment is nerve-racking. On top of that, her smothering will become unbearable.

Roy's clearing of the throat finally breaks the uncomfortable silence that has fallen over the table. "Did anything else happen with Jed I should know about?"

Luke stuffs the last piece of steak in his mouth. "Nothing," he says while chewing.

Roy's eyebrows quirk. "That's not what I heard. Jed called the station and claimed you threatened him."

"It's unbelievable that he can complain and we can't," my mom pipes in with a huff. "It's so unjust."

"I know, honey, but that's just the way it is." Roy pats her hand without taking his eyes off his son; he is obviously still waiting for his side of the story.

Luke and I exchange a glance. "He was way out of line, Dad, and really upset Kelsey. I swear I didn't touch him."

Roy gazes at me and I confirm Luke's story with a nod.

"Okay, Luke, but I don't want any further trouble. Any more run-ins with the law will negatively impact your bar admission once you graduate law school."

Luke grabs a beer from the cooler. "I promise, Dad, I'll behave."

I'm sure he is just as insincere with his words as I was earlier. Hopefully, he won't encounter Jed alone on the street. Jed looked just as sturdy as he used to and has probably continued with his boxing training, even if he hasn't performed in public since the scandal. Luke could get seriously hurt.

I dart from the table as soon as dinner is officially over and hide back in my room. My mood is thoroughly ruined and I stretch out on the bed, staring at the ceiling, which has been my favorite activity over the past three years. Jed's nasty insinuation about me being screwed sliced deeper into my soul than I want to admit. It seems like no matter what, he has always been on the winning team.

After he got off on a technicality, Luke took a couple of swings at him and broke his nose. Jed had nothing better to do than run to the cops and cause a big stink. The prosecutor was Roy's friend and Luke got away with forty hours of community service. When he turned twenty-one six months ago, he had his record expunged, so his criminal conviction was luckily gone. Yet the unfairness of it all rattled not only my world, but my belief in justice in general.

The pain hits me head on—everything that happened is really my fault. My mom had warned me not to walk home alone after the party, but I thought I was invincible and didn't listen. I almost ruined Luke's life when he fought my battles. Now, I drag the whole family down with my constant whining and impossible mood. Ultimately, I'm poison for everyone who cares for me.

Driven by a sudden undeniable urge, I hop off the bed and stroll over to my desk. The razor blade is hidden on the bottom of my wastebasket. I remove the tape holding it in place before finding myself in front of the bathroom mirror. With a grimace, I stick out my tongue. Dull eyes respond with a frown and I hold the blade next to my cheek. I'm sure if my face had been totally disfigured, I would never have been abducted. Maybe Jed will never look at me again if I do it now.

I picture how the blood would pulse out of me like red rain and drip into the sink— how the pain would surge through my body and overpower my pitiful existence. Cutting myself is like an addiction these days, the one thing that always makes me feel better. The physical agony is so powerful that everything else around me is numb. The adrenaline does the rest. It's a high which allows me to forget—the burning pain the only sensation that has a total grip on me—even if it's just for a few moments.

My hand moves farther down, running the blade over my skin just below my breast. Maybe I should slice it off? No man would ever be interested in me and a lot of heartache could be avoided. I run the edge over my belly, but know deep down that I would never have the guts to end my life. It is one thing to cut myself, yet another to call it quits for good. The latter is something I could never see through. Death would be the easy way out, but would leave my mom and Luke in shambles. They don't deserve that, just so I could be taken out of my misery. I don't even think I want that respite—not forever, anyway. The small escapes that I get from cutting are enough for now.

The razor ends up on my lower arm, which is already decorated with several scars. My last night's despair cost me my coffee today. I only scratched the surface of the skin—it hardly even bled; the satisfaction ever so slight. Tonight, I need a real kick to forget the pain of the past. I will have to slice deep.

I squeeze my eyes shut and hold my breath when I finally slash into my arm. The pain spreads up through my shoulders and below into my fingertips. My hand shakes when I move further down to repeat the exercise. After my third gash, I move over to my other arm. My hand is trembling so hard that I almost drop the blade, but I manage three more cuts before my legs buckle.

I slide to the ground. The blood pulses from my veins and I'm stunned to see so much more than usual. It sprays everywhere, the white tiles next to me soon coated with crimson streaks. Nevertheless, I indulge in the pain as hot and cold flashes run through my body, balling my fists to stop my arms from shaking. When my eyelids grow heavy, I'm pulled into the depths of a bottomless ravine.

Chapter 3

A monotone beep soaks through the layers of fog surrounding my mind. I stir, trying to scratch the burning spot on my arm, until a throbbing pain radiates into my shoulder. Squinting at the bright light, I'm halfway expecting to be back in my underground prison and my heart beat accelerates. When the brightness burns in my eyes, I squeeze them shut again.

The scent in the air reminds me of latex gloves and gives me a headache. The last time I smelled something similar was on the night of my rescue when they took me to the hospital to perform those dreadful tests. In some ways, it was almost as bad as being raped. Strangers dug around in my insides, trying to scrape up any possible DNA evidence before pictures were taken of every bruise on my body. Everything was out in the open. The nurses stared at me with pity, while talking to each other behind shielding hands.

I finally pry my eyes open and scan the room. It's painted in soft pastel colors, but without any pictures or other decorations. The blinds on the window are white and sterile. There are no curtains. This is definitely a hospital room and the annoying beeping sound from the monitor is probably my heartbeat.

My lower arms are covered in bandages. A tube runs from the crook of my elbow to an IV bag, which hangs on a metal rack right next to the bed and holds a clear liquid. Pain shoots through me every time I twitch.

I turn my head with great effort to examine the rest of the room. A nurse is sitting next to my bed, staring with blank eyes at a tree outside. She almost looks like a statue. When I croak out an indefinable sound, her head snaps around.

"Oh, you're awake." A smile spreads on her lips that doesn't hit her eyes.

To be polite, I force the corners of my mouth to raise some. One point to her for being so observant.

She checks the drip. "Are you in any pain?"

"A little." My throat scratches when I talk. "Why am I here?"

"Your parents admitted you when they found you." She doesn't elaborate further and injects a liquid in the IV bag. "This is for the pain."

"Will it knock me out?"

"No." She strokes my hand. "You don't have to worry about a thing. You're safe here and everyone has been taking good care of you."

I sink back into my pillow when the room starts to spin. "What did you give me?"

She strokes my hand again. "It was a shot of Ketorolac, which we routinely give for muscle pain. You might feel a little woozy, but that's normal. You don't need to worry about a thing."

I almost roll my eyes at her. She sounds like a broken record with her repeated assurances. My tongue licks over my cracked lips when the thirst becomes unbearable. "Can I have some water?"

"Everything you need it administered intravenously." The smile has yet to leave her lips—she's almost creeping me out. "I'll have to clear it with the doctor before I can give you anything to drink."

I grumble something under my breath to show my resentment, still struggling to believe my mom had me admitted to the hospital. "How long do I have to stay here?"

"Your doctor and your parents will explain everything to you. They're meeting with the head of administration but should be back shortly. Unfortunately, nurses are not allowed to discuss medical information with a patient."

I exhale slowly, shaking my head in my mind. "Whatever." If they want to keep me in the dark, so be it. It's not like I can go anywhere and it's the same to me if I lie here or in my bed at home.

When I move my hips, something pulls between my legs. To my horror, a small plastic tube comes out from under the blanket. It's filled with a yellow liquid and ends in a bag.

I shudder. "Am I on a catheter?"

"Yes. It's standard procedure when you are on a drip and can't get up. Don't worry, it won't be there for much longer." Her voice has a cheerful *cling clang* to it. She's probably just trying to make me feel better without even realizing how much she is getting on my nerves.

After that, she at least keeps her mouth shut, the beeping of the monitor the only thing that breaks the silence. With a sigh, I close my eyes, utterly exhausted from our little chat. The blanket weighs a ton but still protects me, though I feel stuffy. My legs are tingling from the tension. I want to get up and walk around. The stillness becomes nerve-racking, and ultimately, a shower is the only thing that could relax me. Hot water running over my skin has always had a soothing effect on me.

My mind drifts to the morning after the longest and worst night of my life. Come to think of it, I felt a tiny bit like I do now—my throat was raw from all the screaming and begging. Every inch of my body throbbed, my insides on fire whenever I moved. Yet it was so cold and my body shivered; I was naked and unprotected with my arms and legs tied to the bedposts in a spread-eagle position. A blindfold blocked the light. I strained my ears for any sound; other than my own breath and rhythmic heartbeat, there was nothing but absolute silence.

That day, I would have been happy to have a catheter, my bladder so full that it almost burst. I felt so sticky down there and I was determined not to soil myself even more. When I was just about to give up, the key in the door turned. My body tensed, halfway expecting my tormentor to have returned to violate me even more.

When warm fingers stroked over my belly, I winced, my heart pounding in my throat. The hands moved alongside my neck and up my cheek before stopping under the blindfold. Heated fingers removed it with one pull. I gazed into Jed's ebony eyes, which viewed me with a mixture of hunger and curiosity.

"Good morning, honeybun." There was a wide grin on his face. "Enjoyed your night?"

I turned my head when my insides revolted at the sight of his cheerfulness. "Can you please untie me?" My voice was so hoarse that the words were barely audible. "I really have to use the bathroom."

"You promise not to attack me? I don't want to have to knock you out again."

I nodded.

He loosened the ropes enough for my wrists and ankles to slide out before pointing with his chin to a pot on the floor. "You can pee in there."

I froze for a moment, but my urges were overpowering. When I tried to stand, I wobbled and his arm slid around my waist to stabilize me. His touch brought tears to my eyes. I recoiled, which only tightened his grip.

My feet stumbled forward until I was next to the pot. With blurry eyes, I gazed at Jed. "Can you at least turn around?"

He hesitated before giving in and facing the wall. I went down on my knees, the pot between my legs. As my bladder emptied, a soft moan escaped my lips, yet the pee burned terribly as it left my body. The stench was nauseating. I only took small shallow breaths until I was done.

When I stood up, I realized Jed did not keep his end of the bargain and was watching me intently. I instinctively covered myself with my hand and wrapped an arm around my chest. My eyes dropped to the floor.

"You look different," he said.

My stomach clenched. I had always wanted my first time to be special. A few hot tears dripped to the ground, splattering on the dusty floor. His friend destroyed everything pure in me.

All of a sudden, I had an urge to cleanse myself. "Can I take a shower?"

His gaze wandered to my thighs and I noticed they were smudged with blood.

"Later," he said. "I have to make sure the house is secured first so you don't run off on me."

Maybe if I had some water, I could at least get rid of the sticky feeling. "I'm really thirsty." My voice was small and sounded like that of a nagging child.

"I'll get you a drink and something to eat, too." He chuckled. "After all, you need your energy. It's my turn next."

His words went straight to my core, all my muscles clamping together. Tears trickled down my cheeks as he gave me a final once-over before slamming the door shut behind him. This time, he kept the light on, making me realize just how dirty I truly was.

Mumbled voices mix with my horrid memories and I blink toward the door to make out a group of people with Roy in the lead. He's accompanied by my mom and Luke, a woman in a white coat walking next to him. That's probably the doctor.

She is the first to speak. "Good morning, Kelsey. I'm Dr. Lestrup. How are you feeling?"

I roll my eyes but give her a smile regardless. "Fine, I guess."

"The nurse told me that you have a lot of questions."

I just glare at her—who wouldn't after waking up in a hospital bed with her arms all bandaged up?

"Well, you were admitted after you lost a lot of blood since you hit a major artery during your suicide attempt."

I suck in a deep breath, trying to keep myself from screaming. "I didn't try to kill myself." My eyes beg when I turn toward my mother. "Please, Mom. You know I would never attempt to take my life."

"I'm sorry, Kelsey, but I don't know what to believe anymore. You've been shutting me out and I have no clue what's going on in your head. Even Dr. Stromberg isn't sure if you didn't subconsciously want to end it all."

I tilt my head back with a small growl. This is ridiculous. "What will happen next?" I want to go home, but they will probably force me to stay in a mental ward for a few days.

My mom confirms my suspicion. "There is this new clinic in Sabattus right by the lake. We think it would be good for you to stay there for a while and get some help."

I've heard about the place. It's a modern loony bin for people with serious mental health issues. "I don't want to go there. I swear I'll work harder with Dr. Stromberg."

Uncertainty is on my mother's face when she looks at Roy with confused eyes.

I sputter, "*Please*, Mom, I promise I'll be good. No more cutting."

Luke snorts. "It's getting old, Kels. No one believes you anymore. You're out of control and need some serious help."

My jaw drops when I stare at him. He has never stabbed me in the back before. "Luke, you know—"

"No, Kels, not this time. We're worried sick about you and you're getting worse. You were lucky that I checked on you or you would've probably bled to death. Jed being back in town might push you over the edge. I love you too much to let him destroy you. This place will be good for you."

I adamantly shake my head. "No, it won't." I raise up my chin. "And I won't go. You can't force me."

Roy jumps in and delivers the final blow. "We filed court papers, Kelsey, and the judge signed an order for involuntary committal. I'm afraid you don't have a choice in this matter. Even your dad agrees."

Tears pool in my eyes—I have never felt more alone. They just abandon me when I need them the most and send me away like an unwanted puppy who has become an inconvenience. "For how long?"

"Four months."

Those two words are like a punch in my stomach. "That's the whole summer." A wailing sob escapes my lips. It sounds like an eternity.

Luke lowers himself next to me on the bed. "Trust me, it's for the best."

My anger flares up. He has no clue what he's talking about. It's already bad enough that I feel trapped in my own mind all the time, but now, they are even going to take away the little bit of freedom I have left. "Go to hell, Luke." My words are muffled by my tears. "I hate you." I gaze at my mother. "I hate all of you. Don't think I'll come home after this. I'll leave Maine and you'll never see me again."

This threat is my last attempt to blackmail them into reconsidering this outrageous idea, but none of them budge.

My mother's eyes are glazed with tears. "I'm sorry, honey, but this is the end of the line. Our decision is final."

I turn my head away. In that moment, I actually wish I had died. "Get out."

My voice is shrill and I gasp for air, rattling the bed when my fingers wrap around the rails. The pain shooting up my arms numbs the feeling of rejection. My lungs burn as I try to retain the oxygen, yet my body shakes uncontrollably from the tears that keep spilling from my eyes. As my mouth opens and closes like a fish on land, I catch an occasional shallow breath, which doesn't seem to make it past the rising bile in my throat.

"She's having an anxiety attack." Doctor Lestrup's statement breaks through my mind like a big joke. What did they expect?

Luke rubs my shoulder, which irritates me even more and I tear away. Loud rapid beats from the monitor echo in my ears. My heart jumps around in my chest when blood begins to rush in my head like a rapid flowing river. A warm tingling sensation spreads up my arm from where the IV needle pierces my skin before the room spins. Darkness once again closes in on me, taking me mercifully away from my treacherous family.

Chapter 4

When the orderly wakes me in the morning, my response is to throw a pillow in her direction. It has been three days since I arrived at Oakwood House and I have yet to venture from my room. I blew off four appointments with the psychologist and have refused to take part in meals at the mess hall, boycotting my family's plan through and through. They can force me to stay here, but not to play ball with the other kids.

I swing my legs out of bed and graze the floor with my toes. The mint green linoleum is still cool from the night. It takes me a while before I get motivated enough to peel myself out of my blanket. I toddle to the window to take a peek outside.

The sky is bright blue with the sun glancing through the treetops. It's another beautiful summer day in the making with Sabattus Pond sparkling mockingly under my nose. A small growl escapes when my eyes fall onto the wall that separates the garden from the small pebble beach. I'm a damn prisoner, allegedly for my own good. It's just plain annoying.

With scorching eyes, I scan my so-called realm, which can't be much better than a jail cell. Although the bed is comfortable, the mattress is covered in plastic, likely to protect the precious fabric from vomit and pee. The pillow is flat and hurts my neck. The only good thing about the whole setup is the fluffy blanket with a big "fireproof" label in the middle, undoubtedly to blight any horrific ideas to set myself on fire with imaginary matches.

There is no TV and everything with cables has been confiscated, including my laptop, iPhone, and iPod. I even had to turn in the belt of my night robe. The hospital administrator promised I would get my stuff back once I earn privileges and can be trusted again, so I am not very hopeful. All these things would require my cooperation, which is out of the question. Quite frankly, they can all kiss my behind.

With played up drama, I rattle the chair that has been bolted to the floor together with the table. They probably imagine I would stake myself with a chair leg if given the opportunity. It is absolutely ridiculous—my teachers even trusted me more in preschool. The only other living thing in the entire room is a small palm tree, planted firmly in a pot that has also been bolted down and has proven indestructible to my kicks.

During the morning, the sun moves behind the building. It gets quite dim in the room. Yet the bright fluorescent light from the ceiling bites my eyes and gives me a headache, so even reading is no longer an option. I never liked artificial lighting, but since my abduction, it drives me insane. It's cold and makes me feel naked all over again.

My fingers run along the cream-colored walls. I want to claw them to mess up the smooth pattern. Unfortunately, they manicured me down to the skin since I could hurt myself with those sharp "weapons." It's as though they thought of everything to ruin any fun ideas I could come up with, which enrages me further.

It won't be long for my body to adjust to the new antidepressant medicine that keeps me halfway in check. Then the pain will start again. This time, there is no tool around to help me fight it, so I'm screwed. The thought alone clenches my chest.

Nature is calling and I make my way into the bathroom, which is maybe the only part of my room I remotely like. It's small and cozy; my only refuge when I try to get away from the nurse or the psychologist who stops by at random times during the day. A knock on the door and I take cover, claiming I'm not feeling well. I am not sure how much longer they are going to buy this, but so far, they have left after a five-minute rapid word exchange through the closed door, during which I usually only grunt yes-and-no responses.

To help me get rid of the fuzziness in my brain from my sleep and medication, I turn on the shower and step under the stream without checking if the water is the right temperature—just like I did the day after I was violated for the first time. Today, it burns my skin. Back then, it was so cold, it hurt.

I remember how hard my teeth were chattering while I desperately tried to adjust the levers, until finally, some warmth surrounded me. I turned my face upward to allow the water to pelt down on me like a gush of rain on a sticky summer's day, letting the liquid run into my mouth and down my throat. It felt good, my thirst slowly fading, though the salt from my tears still mixed with the heavenly bliss.

Soft foam lathered my body just moments later and I scrubbed with a sponge until my skin threatened to be torn off my bones. The ultimate feeling of cleanliness was still not there, and I washed myself between my legs over and over again. I still felt dirty. The hands of Jed's friend kept touching me in my mind and my stomach heaved.

I made it out to the toilet and threw up, but my gut was so empty that only foam came up. I choked dryly, my skin still wet and freezing cold. Shivers ran through my body while my hands desperately clutched the toilet seat, my knees soon aching from the hard floor. When I was finally done, my face was streaked with tears—not only from the effort, but also from the ultimate revelation of what I had lost.

I leaned my bare back against the cool wall tiles as sobs raged through my body, a sad wail resonating from the depths of my throat. My face was buried against my thighs until a towel was forced around me.

"You'll catch a cold down there, honeybun."

My head rose and I gazed at Jed through my tears. "Why?" My voice grew louder. "Why me? What did I ever do to you and your friend to deserve this?"

His eyes were fixed on me and he stroked a strand of hair from my face. "You're beautiful, Kelsey. We both wanted to own you for so long, but you never even looked at us. I was nothing more than dirt under your shoes." A small smile tugged on the corners of his lips. "I bet you feel different now. Now you wish you didn't call me all those names."

More tears pooled in my eyes. "We were nothing but stupid kids, Jed. You were the smelly boy with the filthy clothes that no one wanted to play with. It's wasn't just me who made fun of you."

A shadow crossed his face. "Yes, but you were the girl I loved and who hurt me the most. I never cared what the others thought of me."

My hands enclosed his. "If you love me, you don't want to hurt me." Hope was pounding in my heart. "Please, Jed, just let me go. I won't tell anyone what you and your friend did."

He pulled out of my grip, his fingers running alongside my cheek. "You don't get it, honeybun. Those feelings are long gone—now all that's left is hate." He grabbed me by my shoulders. "Up you go. It's time to return to your bunker."

I pulled the towel closer around me to shield myself from the cold while trotting behind him. My body was still frozen to the bone. The floor was chilling under my bare feet and the ragged towel barely covered my upper torso. As we passed through the kitchen, a whiff of scrambled eggs and sizzled bacon teased my nostrils. My stomach growled in response. I hadn't eaten in at least three days and was absolutely famished. For a moment, the room began to swim. I held onto the table before I fell.

Trapped

Jed's arm wrapped around my waist as he came to my aid. Our lips were only inches apart and he pulled me closer against his chest. His frame was still small compared to most men, but the muscles he developed from his boxing days flexed firmly under his shirt. His arousal pressed against my inner thigh. I turned my face with a frown just as he tried to kiss me. His lips landed on my cheek, turning my stomach into knots.

He caught my chin and forced me to look at him. "Don't fight this, honeybun. This can be fun for the both of us if you want it to be."

My palm smacked him hard in the face. "Your friend raped me and you are touching me against my will. It's disgusting. I will never enjoy being with you."

"Suit yourself, but if you want to get some decent food, you better start behaving."

He grabbed me roughly by my wrist and pulled me outside. A warm breeze caressed me as soon as I stepped onto the heated porch, the sun tickling my skin. It was a beautiful early summer day, the scent of fresh-cut grass in the air. I glanced around, amazed by the stillness of the forest, which was surrounding the small log cabin. The peacefulness was so contrary to the violence I had suffered these last days.

My bliss didn't last long. The trap door in the ground was only fifty feet away, right at the edge of the tree line. From the rumors in town, Jed's dad had been some militia freak and had built the bunker in case the FBI ever raided the place. There had been talk that he had stored explosives around the house, but so far, I hadn't even seen a rifle.

Jed pulled up the wooden board. "After you, honeybun."

The hole in the ground was dark and menacing. I went down on my knees and grabbed the top of the ladder, my feet searching downwards for the first rung. The edges were sharp and cut into my skin. I slowly made my descent, the light and sun disappearing from my vision as dampness and darkness closed in.

When my soles touched rough soil, I knew I had reached my destination. Jed arrived right after me and opened the door to my dungeon. With a welcoming gesture, he ushered me inside. To my surprise, the bed was made with fresh sheets and covered with a patchwork blanket.

He closed the door behind him and fumbled with his shirt. With a wide grin on his face, he pulled it off, exposing his scarred body. "Okay, honeybun. Ready for round two?"

With a gasp, my mind returns to reality. The water in the shower has turned chillingly cold. My arms hug my knees as I cower under the stream in a fetal position, the only way I still feel safe. With a sigh, I stand up and turn off the water. My hair is matted since I haven't washed it in over a week, but my appearance is of no importance to me. I'm not planning on leaving my room today, so no one will see me anyhow.

The towel is soft and thick, covering me all the way to my knees. I indulge in the scent of lavender which must be a byproduct of the softener. I tuck the edges firmly under my armpits before glaring at myself in the mirror.

My eyes are bruised from the lack of sleep and I'm paler than a ghost. The golden brown tan that I used to keep all year around has totally vanished, left behind with a worry-free existence. My mom would complain that I would get skin cancer from the tanning booth; now she only hopes I still make it through today. How ridiculous were our fights back then, yet I wish again for that life almost every single moment. If I could turn back the clock, many things would be different.

The second I cross the threshold back into my room, a yelp escapes my lips. I almost drop the towel. An unexpected visitor is leaning over the palm tree. As he slowly turns around, his eyebrows knot together like I am the intruder. I squint at him. He looks somewhat familiar.

"You scared me half to death," I hiss. "What the hell are you doing in my room?"

"Sorry." He holds up a watering can. "The warden sent me around to water the plants."

It finally clicks in my head. It's the Finn guy from the high school. "What are you doing here? You can't be one of the patients."

"Community service." His eyes wander slowly up and down my frame with puckered lips.

My anger flares, overpowering my initial apprehension. If I didn't have to hold onto the towel, I would have smacked him. "That doesn't give you the right to just waltz in here unannounced. Didn't your parents teach you any type of manners?"

He is not fazed by my rude remark. "I knocked, but there was no answer and I didn't think you wanted me to join you in the shower."

My eyes send daggers his way, which he finds amusing. With a chuckle, he turns back to the plant. "I'm almost done."

"You need to leave." I suck in a sharp breath. "NOW!" My voice is three octaves higher when I spit out the last word.

He raises his free hand in defeat. "Hold your horses, lady, I'm going."

He strolls right past me and my tapping foot, close enough for me to take in a mixture of smoke and peppermint. In the door frame, he gives me another glance. "You know, people are totally right about you. You *are* crazy."

I growl, looking around for something to throw in his direction, but the pillow is out of reach. "That's a mean thing to say."

"Yeah, maybe, but if you didn't act like a total brat all the time, you might actually find some sympathy. Those tantrums don't suit you, though your eyes do look pretty when you're mad."

My jaw drops as he leaves me standing there, feverishly thinking of a smart retort, but his audacity caused a brain freeze. His words sting more than I want to admit—deep down, I know he has a point. I don't like the person I have become either.

Chapter 5

Three hours later, I'm ready to blow a gasket. My last book is finished and I have taken a nap, but when I wake up, there is an inner unrest that forces me to pace back and forth in the room. Boredom is holding my body hostage. I cuss at the walls, which seem to be closing in. The window is cracked open and the shrill song of a bird fills the room. The sound chips away at my nerves. I long for loud, harsh music to numb my mind, or better yet, a nice blade to slice into my skin to take off the edge.

My eyes fall on the window and an idea takes over. They will probably put me in a straightjacket after this, but at least I will have satisfied the need to hurt myself one more time. My feet shuffle over the linoleum until I reach the open window. My elbow slams hard against the glass, but instead of the expected cracking sound, my funny bone resonates in my arm. A dull pain radiates up into my shoulder. After a minute of recuperating while relishing the throbbing pain, another attempt yields the same result. I realize that the window is shatterproof. This time, the "F" word rolls easily off my lips.

With bubbling rage, I gaze outside, my eyes scanning the garden. A group of residents are gathered under a tree, probably for a therapy session, and a couple of guys play boccie by the basketball court. Some more women are scattered throughout, either sitting in the shade in little lounge chairs or on the grass with a book in their laps. Everyone seems to be outdoors with something to do except for me. I bite my lip. There is this urge in my legs to join them, but that would be admitting defeat.

My eyes scan over the wall before resting on the small gate with the security keypad. When the administrator first showed me around, she pointed out the door, highlighting that most residents could take walks by the lake once they jumped through some hoops and made progress in their therapy. I still can't believe that almost every patient is here voluntarily, happy to have their liberties infringed upon without protest. Luke told me his dad is paying a fortune for my stay; apparently Oakwood House is the "it" designer rehab place for Maine's elite.

A small hum of an engine captures my interest at the other side of the garden where flowers sway softly in the wind. A truck has pulled up and Finn jumps out, walking to the back. His shirt is casually tossed aside before he drags a big bag of mulch over to an unkempt area, which is partially hidden by the laundry annex. I have to admit he has a nice body when measured to the current beauty ideals. There are some hints of a six-pack and his shoulders are proportionate to his waist. Some female residents are practically drooling at the sight. I wrinkle my nose in disgust. What a show-off! He purposely causes a spectacle to draw attention to himself.

My pride is still hurt from him calling me a brat and I decide to give him a spoon of his own medicine. Those poor women out there are all in a weak mental state—he should not taunt them like this. With invisible steam pouring from my nose and ears, I march through the building and over the adjacent lawn until I end up in front of him.

He has started to loosen the ground with a shovel, his body covered in sweat which glistens in the sunshine. In a former life, I would have considered him hot.

I toss his muscle top in front of his feet. "Put that damn shirt on."

"Why? It's scorching out here." His lips twitch; he must think this is funny.

"This is a hospital and not the beach." My teeth clench together so hard that my jaw hurts. "You don't walk around half naked."

He chuckles, picking up the shirt. "Admit it, my body is turning you on." He starts to shake invisible dust off the fabric, pushing out his chest for me to admire.

"Wrong, buddy. I don't even like guys."

"Oh." His eyebrows arch, yet there is disappointment in his eyes. "Are you a lesbian?"

If the steam from my nose was real, it would have robbed me of my vision. "Nooo." My voice is shrill. "I just find guys disgusting."

With a smirk, he pulls the shirt over his head. "Well, I don't want to cause you any distress." His arms find the holes. "Out of curiosity, what did my kind do to you to get you so wound up?"

Tears rise in my throat. "I was raped," I blurt out before I can help myself.

The smile vanishes from his face. "I'm sorry. I didn't know."

I'm expecting the typical pity expression that is always in everybody's eyes when they find out, but he doesn't even flinch. His foot drives the shovel into the ground and transports a pile of dirt to a nearby corner.

There is nothing left for me to do but return to my prison. I spin around and storm off. I don't even make it ten feet before his voice stops me.

"Hey, care to help me?"

I slowly turn, my brows knotted together. "Why would I want to help you? I hate gardening." It's a total lie. I have always loved spending time in our backyard, helping my mom plant the flowers for the summer season.

"I thought it would be something for you to do. You must be dying of boredom up there alone in your room, but then, maybe not . . ."

He returns to his work, probably just trying to be nice because he feels sorry for me after all.

"I don't need your sympathy," I snap.

His eyes find mine. "Look, if you're out to cry on someone's shoulder, I'm the wrong guy. I just got out of my own hell and don't need anyone else's baggage."

I fold my arms in front of my chest, curious. "Is that why you have to do community service?"

"Yep." The pile of dirt is tossed with more force than the last.

"What did you do?"

"I beat up my mom's boyfriend."

I snicker. "Did he ground you or something and you didn't like it?"

"He molested my little brother." His lips press together in a thin line as he rams the shovel deeply into the ground.

A sudden anger rages through me. How can all these sick people in the world live with themselves? I want to scream and punch the walls, or at least rant a little.

The prospect of returning to my lonely room is no longer appealing, and I get the second shovel from the truck. Five minutes later, my blouse clings to my back when I ram the shovel into the ground again, the loose dirt hurled into a corner with all my might. Every bit of energy which is poured into the task is like a loud shout that cleanses my soul. The more force I use, the better it feels.

Jed's face appears in the dirt, and I cut it in half with the sharp edge of the shovel. His chest is next and I dig deep into his scarred skin. Tears trickle down my cheek. My bad conscience had always eaten me up after what Justin did to him, but Jed got triple payment with interest. For him, it was always about revenge, and getting his needs met was just an added bonus. His friend was different. He only wanted my body and tore away everything beautiful inside me.

With fury, I stab at the ground, sweat pouring down my face. My throat is raw from thirst, but my anger battles any physical need. I want to hurt Jed—and I want to hurt his friend. Driving the shovel into the ground is the best I can do. It's liberating to cut into his imaginary body over and over again. When I lift up the dirt, it's like tearing him apart and tossing away his malice.

An iron taste in my mouth mixes with the salt from my tears and sweat as I silently weep. I'm completely captured in my assault of the ground so that the cold water hits me with total surprise. I squeal, my eyes darting around for the culprit.

Finn laughs loudly when he aims the spurt of the garden hose right at me.

"Get that away from me," I shout.

In response, he tilts the hose upward, shielding the harsh gush with his thumb. Drops pelt down on me like a soft rain shower. I turn my face toward the sky, savoring the coolness of the water on my heated skin. A laugh escapes my throat and scares me to death—it has become such an unfamiliar sound.

I have had just about enough when he diverts the water toward the flowerbed. There is a wide grin on his face. "There're some drinks in the cooler by the truck in case you're thirsty."

I stroll over to the car, slightly shivering under a gentle breeze. My clothes are absolutely soaked. I pull my hair to the side into a ponytail, wringing out the water. The cooler is on the passenger seat and holds quite a selection—soda, water, and a six-pack of Hanfill beer. My fingers run over the chilled metal of the cans before enclosing one of the beers.

I quickly scan the area to ensure no one saw me before my eyes settle on the open garden shed that is fully hidden from view by the laundry annex. Strolling over while casually glancing around to keep an eye out for a nurse, I lower myself on the sun-flooded steps of the shed. The beer can is safely hidden behind the wooden wall. I take a quick sip, halfway expecting a scolding, but the area is so secluded that I doubt anyone will hassle us here.

Finn soon slumps next to me onto the other side of the steps, his beer can concealed in the same manner as mine. He fishes a pack of cigarettes from his back pocket and offers it to me.

"Want one?"

I have never smoked in my life. "Sure."

He lights mine before his own, inhaling deeply.

Watching how the smoke escapes through his nose and the corners of his mouth, I dare to take a drag. My lungs are on fire. I choke, coughing until tears run down my cheeks.

There is a twinkle in Finn's eyes. "First time?"

I nod, unable to speak.

"Hold the smoke in your mouth like this and swirl it around." He pulls his cheeks in, resulting in a silly grimace.

I giggle before I push myself to try again. The burning sensation is bearable when I hold my breath before exhaling. A few drags later, I slowly get the hang of it.

He opens his beer can, taking a few sips, and I dare to gulp down more of my ice-cold brew. We sit in silence, the sun playing on my bare arms and face. Every time I move, I realize how sore I am from the heavy work. My back is killing me. Finn leans against the door frame of the shed, soaking up the sunshine.

"What ever happened to your rapist?" he asks out of the blue.

"He got off. There was a second one, but they never even caught him."

A deep wrinkle spreads on his forehead. "How did he get off?"

I finish the rest of my beer, trying to drown the resentment I have felt since the day Jed walked away a free man while I was left in shambles. Yet the wound that was left behind by the injustice is still wide open and throbs like hell.

"When the police arrested him, they searched his house without a warrant. His lawyer filed a motion to suppress, but the cops swore on the stand that Jed gave them permission. Turns out, the bastard secretly taped the whole encounter. When the judge heard his loud words of protest, he threw out all the evidence from the search. After that, there was nothing left to prosecute him with other than my word, and I wasn't stable enough to testify. That's when the DA dropped the case." The bitterness of my words runs like venom over my lips.

"Figures." He takes another mouthful of his beer. "Wasn't there any DNA evidence?"

I shake my head. My insides recoil when I remember all those tests they performed at the hospital, which made me feel violated all over again. Not even one of them yielded any result. "Before I escaped, I had my period and Jed didn't touch me. His friend always used a condom and the doctors were unable to find any useful DNA traces."

Finn lights another cigarette. "Did they have a suspect?"

"Everyone in town has always believed it was Drake Whitmer. He and Jed were as close as brothers since kindergarten and he disappeared a few days after I escaped. Since Jed never confessed or pointed the finger at him, the suspicion alone wouldn't have been enough for an arrest anyhow."

"You know, that's really fucked up." Finn's smoke escapes with a sigh. "Do you think it was Whitmer?"

I shrug when a knife slices into my heart. "I honestly don't know. I was blindfolded when he was with me and he never spoke. His build matched Drake's height and weight, so there is a high probability it was him."

In my mind, I had replayed the times with my tormentor over and over for any type of reassurance, but the memories were so horrific that they usually triggered an anxiety attack before I could come to a conclusion. Even now, the thought is so painful that my insides weep.

My finger runs along the empty beer can. A satisfied shudder runs through me when the edge cuts into my skin. The burn spreading in my knuckles feels divine. "Question is: why would he have disappeared if he had nothing to hide?"

"I guess." Finn flicks the ashes of the cigarette onto the grass. "How long did they hold you?"

"Three months." My hand balls instinctively into a fist as something presses on my chest.

He lets out a surprised whistle. "That's a long time. Must have been tough."

That is the understatement of the year—it was like a trip to hell and back. "Yep." I suppress the oncoming tears, mad at myself. I shouldn't have told him. He is a total stranger, after all, who just happened to catch me at a good moment. Talking about my kidnapping only causes incredible heartache.

He must have sensed my distress, a sad expression spreading across his face. "I'm sorry. I didn't mean to upset you."

I want to change the subject. "What about you? Did they convict your mother's boyfriend for what he did to your brother?"

Before he has a chance to reply, a furious voice disturbs our break.

"What the hell are you both doing?" Luke's eyes are dark when he glares at the beer can, the cigarette butt next to my knee also in his direct line of vision.

"Relax, we're just chilling." Finn extinguishes his cigarette in the dirt.

"You provided alcohol to a minor." Luke's finger shoots angrily in Finn's direction. "That's a crime, my friend, and my dad told me you're already on probation for attempted murder. This will have some serious consequences."

I tug at his hand. "Come on, Luke, it's not a big deal. It was only a beer."

"It's a huge deal." He frowns at me. "You're on medication and alcohol is dangerous. I can't believe how irresponsible you are." His eyes zoom in on the cut on my finger. "And bravo, another self-harm injury. Even when you're locked up, you still find ways to hurt yourself."

Tears spill from my eyes. "All you ever do these days is criticize me. I was actually having a really good day and you had to spoil it." I jump to my feet, ready to take off.

He tries to pull me into a hug. "Look, Kels, I—"

I push him away. "No, Luke. Just leave me alone." My gaze turns to Finn, who has also risen and watches the drama with narrow eyes. "Both of you."

My legs carry me away as fast as they can while sobs shake my body. I hate them so much. My life sucks, thanks to those geniuses who always believe they know what's best for me. In reality, no one does. I am not even sure myself, but talking about my ordeal over and over again sure won't kill the nightmares. They will probably never stop. That thought scares me more than anything.

As the pain builds up in the depths of my soul, my breath fails me. I gasp, my lungs burning in agony. I can't keep the air retained within me, so I take quick shallow breaths, yet nothing seems to help. My mouth opens, but no sound comes out and tears stream down my face. A nurse's firm hands reach for me when my legs finally buckle, but I slap them away. The entire time, an invisible claw continues to squeeze the oxygen from my lungs.

Something wet and cold rubs across the crook of my elbow before a needle pierces my skin. When warmth spreads through my arm, the pressure on my chest finally eases. The sound of a rapid flowing river takes over my brain as black dots start to swim in front of my eyes. Footsteps approach, resonating in my skull like a jackhammer.

"I got you, Kels." Luke's words bounce around in my head with painstaking precision.

I try to block them out. My arms want to complain when he scoops me up, but they are too heavy to fight him. Everything feels surreal, and then the river sucks me in.

Chapter 6

As my mind slowly drifts back to reality, a cool breeze brushes over me, followed by a rolling thunder. The booming sound tears away the rest of the fogginess surrounding my brain. To battle my dry throat, my tongue, which feels more like a ball of cotton wool, wiggles around in my mouth. I lick my lips before opening my eyes, fully prepared for irritating bright light to aggravate my senses.

Yet it is obscure in the room—only Luke's Kindle shines dimly in the darkness, giving his face a surreal glow. He is captured by his book, not realizing that I'm awake. For a moment, my heart cringes. We used to be so close, and I don't like this new distance between us.

"What time is it?"

His gaze finds me. "After eleven already. How're you feeling?"

"Alright, I guess, for someone who was knocked out."

He edges the chair closer to the bed. "About that." His fingers brush over the back of my hand. "I'm really sorry I upset you."

I can't stand to look at him, painfully remembering the scene he caused in front of Finn.

"Look, I know you're mad," he continues. "And I really get why. I was just worried and can't stand the guy. He's nothing but trouble with his fuck-the-world attitude."

I glare at him. "You don't even know him."

"I know exactly how he ticks, Kels." He laughs with bitterness. "Remember, I used to be just like him."

I chuckle. How could I ever forget? Luke Franklin—the poster guy of a bad boy when he was still in high school. Smoking, drinking, sleeping with any girl who was willing to spread her legs. He changed after my abduction. The ordeal marked the end of both our carefree childhoods.

"He only tried to cheer me up. If you make a big stink about the beer, he could really get into trouble." I suck on my lips, my throat burning. Every word is an effort, but at least we're talking.

He squeezes my arm. "I won't. Our fight made me realize that I've been a real jerk these last few days."

I open my mouth to protest, but his raised hand stops me.

"No. Let me finish." He grimaces. "I feel I haven't been listening to you. I was so shaken up with you almost dying that all I could think of was getting you safe, but I shouldn't have tried to rush you with your recovery. If you need more time, so be it. I still believe this place is good for you, but I want to help you, not be your enemy."

His eyes are so sincere that I almost forgive him. "I just don't like to be locked up, Luke, and forced to participate in this circus." I sigh. It is so hard to make him understand. "Healing takes time, and truthfully, I was stunned that you, of all people, sided against me."

"I agree. I should've been more supportive, but trust me, your mom's mind was made up. There was nothing I could've done to change that." Exhaustion lingers on his face. "It is what it is and you are here now. Can you please just give this place a chance?"

I moan. What choice do I have? "Okay."

He raises a brow. "Just okay?"

I stare at the ceiling, another crack of thunder breaking through the night. "I promise." I haven't kept my word on so many occasions this past year, it's not even funny. "Is that better, Luke?"

"I guess that's the best I can ask for." A slow smile spreads across his lips. "Are we good?"

Trapped

I have never been able to hold a grudge against him for long. Ever since our parents married and he became my stepbrother, he has always been my best friend, and sometimes, fights just happen. "Yeah, we're good."

The air escapes through his lips when he exhales, the wrinkle on his forehead smoothing. I can relate. I hate when we argue.

A cold gust slams the window wide open. I jump, the cover almost slipping off the bed, which makes him laugh. My eyes ogle him with played venom, causing him to laugh harder. I have always been easy to spook—the pranks he used to play on me at Halloween were legendary. One year I peed my pants when he pretended to be a ghost, making scary noises from inside my closet.

Of course this didn't stop me from walking home alone in the darkness on the night of my abduction, having long learned that bold behavior guaranteed a certain respect from my friends. I was the fun-loving tough girl, always ready to accept a dare, and had come up with plenty of wild ideas of my own.

When Jed approached me in the van that night and asked if I wanted a ride, I never thought twice about it. My mom had warned me not to roam the streets after midnight alone, but being the typical stubborn teenager, I ignored her words. I felt she was just overprotective—we were in Stonehenge, of all places, and who would have ever wanted to cause *me*, the most popular girl in school, any harm.

Luke closes the window. The rain beats hard against the glass. A flash lightens the sky, followed by a loud clap of thunder.

"I better go before the storm gets worse." He stretches. "Do you need anything?"

My tongue still feels heavy. "I'm really thirsty."

"I'll tell the nurse to bring you some water." He bends over me and kisses my forehead. "Sleep tight, Kels. I'll stop by tomorrow afternoon."

"Can you bring me Starbucks coffee?" I give him my best puppy dog eyes.

"I will, but you'll only get it if you finally talk to your psychologist and make a therapy plan."

"Always making me work hard for my coffee."

"Anything to get you motivated, sis."

I miss him the second he closes the door. After clearing the air between us, it seems like I have my old brother back.

When thunder booms again, I pull the blanket closer around me, shivering all of a sudden. Even underground, I was able to hear those summer storms, curled up on my bed in a ball of nerves, paralyzed by the horrid anticipation of what was to come right afterward. As soon as the storm passed, Jed would pick me up for a walk. He had said he loved the woods when the trees were still wet after a good rainfall. It made him feel the life of the forest.

The first time he came to my dungeon to announce we were going on a stroll and held up the dog collar, I thought he was joking. It was the choker kind with little teeth that tightened when the owner pulled on the leash. He ordered me to slide it around my neck.

"You're kidding, right?" I stared at him incredulously with my mouth open.

He grinned with a vicious sparkle in his eyes. "I'm not, honeybun. Bitches belong on a leash, something your boyfriend should've remembered before he let his dog loose."

"You know I tried to stop him."

He snorted. "That's a half-ass excuse. That dog listened to you, but not once did you try to call her back when she mauled me." The words oozed with bitterness and his voice grew louder with every syllable he spat out. "You stood idly by until my body was a bloody mess and your boyfriend got scared that he'd land behind bars!"

A shudder ran through me—it was a day in my life I had wanted to forget. Justin and I had been walking his Doberman and had run into Jed by the lake. Justin hadn't liked the smoldering look Jed had given me.

"That nasty fucker needs to be taught a lesson," he had said before he had sent the dog after Jed.

I had begged him to stop, but he hadn't listened. Roxy had always been quite aggressive and had totally lost it when she had tasted warm blood. She would've never listened to my command. When Justin had finally come to his senses after realizing that Jed could actually die, he had pulled Roxy off and called an ambulance.

Four months and several surgeries later, Jed had been quietly paid off by Justin's father to avoid a lawsuit. His face had been restored in the fifteen months since it happened through reconstructive surgery, but his body had been too damaged to get rid of all the scars. Roxy had been put down after Justin and I had sworn to the cops that she had attacked Jed for no reason and had been totally out of control. It broke my heart since I have always loved dogs.

I had cried for a week straight and had felt terrible about Jed's torment, but on Roy's advice, I'd never gone to the hospital to apologize. Jed could have pressed charges against me or sued my mom if he had had any proof, and Roy didn't want to take any chances. He had ordered me to stay away from Jed and I had gladly obliged. Not having to face him had been the easy way out. Or so I thought.

Looking into Jed's eyes as he dangled the dog collar, I was not so sure.

"Put this on now, honeybun, or I'll force you and your pretty face might get damaged. Either way, you'll be on a leash under my command during our little walk."

The collar was snug on my neck and tightened further when he attached a long chain right after I had made my way up the ladder. With a wide grin, his hand extended toward the small pathway cutting through the woods.

"This way."

I stumbled across the soft ground, the moist dirt sticking to my bare feet. The air was fresh and crisp, the sun, which was hidden behind the thick forest tent, only taking a peek through the treetops once in a while. My body was covered with goosebumps and I tried to control my chattering teeth. A couple of days ago, Jed had given me a pair of panties and a bra, but otherwise, I was naked.

The first jolt on the chain took me by surprise. The metal bit into my skin. I tripped and fell on my knees, the collar tightening around my throat. A whimper escaped when my fingers tried to relieve the choking pressure, but I didn't manage to loosen the restraint. My fingertips were soon raw and covered with blood, the pounding pain in my neck and hands excruciating. I gasped desperately for air while Jed continued to yank the leash. His cruel laughter rang in my ears.

"How do you like this, honeybun?" Another jolt forced tears to spill from my eyes. "That's how it feels when you're at the total mercy of someone else."

As my torment continued, the metal teeth clawed deeper and deeper into my skin. Breathing became impossible. The pain continued to rage through me as my pleas and screams were replaced by my sputters for air. I gazed at Jed, my eyes begging for him to stop. My expression had to have been similar to the one he had the day Roxy's jaw had ripped into his flesh.

When my body finally buckled, he loosened the leash. My fingers tore the teeth out of my nape as my lungs soaked up much-needed oxygen. I rolled onto the ground, my cheek resting on the damp forest floor. My eyes found Jed leaning against a tree, watching me with a twitch around his lips. When my ragged breath slowed, he was ready for round two.

"Slide down your panties and get on your hands and knees," he ordered. "You'll get what a little bitch like you deserves."

When I tried to protest, a jolt of the chain convinced me to comply. My cries were muffled when my face was pushed into the soft grass after he mounted me. What followed was almost as bad as when his friend had stolen my innocence.

A knock on the door drowns out the terrifying memories. My fingers trace the scars on my neck, which were left behind by the dog collar, tears dripping off my chin. I quickly wipe them away with my blanket. I expect the nurse, but instead, Finn pokes his head in. Despite my distress, I can't help but snicker.

"What're you doing here?"

He quickly walks in, silently closing the door before turning on the light.

I squint at him while my eyes adjust.

He looks tired. "I feel terrible about your anxiety attack and wanted to make sure you were okay." His lips curl to a crooked grin. "And since I didn't want any more beef with your brother, I waited until he left. I hope I didn't wake you."

Though he means well, I feel a little stalked and would prefer him to leave. "I wasn't sleeping, but the nurse will be here any minute." I wonder how he even managed to enter a secured mental health facility in the middle of the night. "How did you even get into the building at this hour?"

He lifts a badge hanging around his neck. "I have janitor credentials which gives me access to the building twenty-four seven." He shuffles his feet. "I'd better go. You need your rest."

I realize how rude my behavior is; after all, he waited the whole night just to talk to me. His clothes are still soiled from this afternoon's yard work and his hair is messy—he didn't even go home to take a shower.

"Thanks for checking on me, I'm fine." I force a small smile. "Luke promised he won't give you any hassle about the beer, so don't worry about your probation."

"Main thing is that you're okay."

There's an awkward silence.

"Well, goodnight, Kelsey."

I call him back at the door. "Finn, thanks for today. For all it's worth, I had a really good time this afternoon."

He nods slightly. "If you have the urge to cut yourself again, punch a pillow real hard and imagine it's Jed's or Drake's face. It doesn't come close to the thrill of a pain rush, but it at least takes off the edge."

I raise my eyebrows askance, and in response, he pulls up the leg of his jeans. His whole calf is covered in scars, clear leftovers from cutting.

"I didn't think it was cool if anyone knew, so I never used my arm."

"How did you get over it?"

"I beat up my demon and almost killed him. It's not what I'd recommend, though, so better stick with your therapy."

It's the best pep talk I've had in years. "Maybe I'll give it a try."

His hand reaches for the door, but I'm not ready for him to leave.

"Finn."

Trapped

He spins around, amusement in his eyes. "Girl, if you carry on, you'll get me caught by the nurse."

One question has been on my mind since the afternoon and I need to get if off my chest. "Your mother's boyfriend— he didn't only molest your little brother, did he?"

He silently shakes his head, a single tear trickling down his cheek. There is so much pain when our eyes interlock that my heart winces.

"You have to fight them, Kelsey, or they'll ruin the rest of your life. Don't give them the satisfaction of completely breaking you."

Chapter 7

For once, I keep my promise to Luke and see the psychologist the next day to make a therapy plan.

He insists on completing our first one-on-one session straight away during which we go through the basics but stop before we reach the abduction. Afterward, he also gets me to agree to daily group counseling sessions, luckily not to start until the next morning.

My mom had dropped off a couple of new books and I get lost on Mars in a new dystopian novel while getting comfortable in the shade on the grass. All afternoon, I keep an eye on the garden, but there is no sign of Finn or his truck. I had hoped to talk to him again. He's the first person who gets exactly how I feel. He also made me laugh, which happens so rarely these days.

A sting of confusion mixes with disappointment—why am I even interested in spending any time with him? Bad boys are usually not my thing, and just because he confessed to cutting himself in the past doesn't make him trustworthy. We had a good time in the garden, but there is nothing special about him that would warrant me getting to know him any better. Luke is probably right—Finn will be trouble in the long run.

My brooding is interrupted when my brother appears with my coffee and a wide grin. He must have talked to the psychologist to confirm my compliance.

"I'm proud of you, sis," he says, kissing my forehead. "You'll see, if you work hard, you'll be out of this place in no time."

I grimace at the thought of having to endure all this therapy, yet the smell of the coffee makes today's efforts worthwhile. He asked for an extra shot of caramel and the cream melts on my tongue while I slowly sip my treat. There might be girls who kill for chocolate, but my soft spot has always been flavored lattes.

"How was your day?" I ask when he continues to beam at me. He's practically exploding to share some news.

He lifts up an envelope. "Got my LSAT results today."

My heart plummets into my stomach. Judging from his good mood, he must have done well on the standardized test required for admission to law school, which means he will leave Maine as soon as he graduates next summer. Harvard, Columbia, and Yale Law were all previously discussed and are still within driving range, but I know that Luke favors Stanford. He could just as well be going to Mars—as soon as he moves to California, he will be out of my life. I'd be lucky if he comes home once a year for Christmas.

"And?" My finger runs over the rim of the Starbucks cup so I don't have to look at him.

"One seventy-four."

The excitement in his voice makes me cringe. I should be happy for him, but instead I'm fighting with my tears.

"I spoke to the admissions counselor at Stanford today and the average score is one seventy-two," he carries on. "Together with my four-point-oh average, I have a really good chance to be admitted."

A treacherous tear lands in the coffee.

"Kels?"

I ignore him.

"Kels, look at me."

With a clenched jaw, I shake my head. Any eye contact and I will totally lose it.

He catches my chin and forces my head in his direction. The valves open; my tears begin to flow like a waterfall. He pulls me against his shoulder, stroking my hair without a word. He knows what's going on. We have always understood each other without the need for words.

"I'm sorry, Luke," I say between sobs and hiccups. "I know I should be happy, but I'm just so scared to be alone. You're the only one I've got."

His leaving Maine had once before been on the table just after my abduction, when Roy insisted that Luke attend Penn State, his alma mater. Only after I threw tantrums and cried many tears did he give in and allow Luke to attend the University of Southern Maine in Portland instead. I was thrilled, though I have always known that it was just prolonging the inevitable. Since he was a child, Luke has wanted to move away. In his opinion, small places like Stonehenge are suffocating.

He continues to stroke my hair until the tears finally subside, yet my face stays buried in the comfort of his chest.

"You know, sis, you could always come with me to California."

I chuckle with bitterness. "My mom would never allow it."

"It's still a full year and you're only a few classes shy of your high-school diploma. You could easily get your GED and enroll in a community college when you get there."

I finally leave the comfort of his embrace and gaze at him with big eyes. "What about money?"

"You could apply for financial aid or get a part-time job. Besides, my dad will pay for an apartment and we'd be roomies. Your mom might even chip in if she sees that you're really trying. It could be a new start and might be good for you."

The idea, which sounded outrageous just moments ago, is slowly growing on me. "You really think I could do it?"

A small smile softens his face. "You can do anything you put your mind to, Kels. All you have to do is stop being the victim."

"You know, Finn said something similar."

His eyes narrow. "Finn?"

"Yeah. He stopped by my room last night and told me I should fight to take back my life."

"When was that? I was here the whole time."

My smile is crooked. "It was after you left."

He clicks his tongue, anger burning in his eyes, but he doesn't comment.

"You know, he has been through a lot and is really not as bad as you think."

His fingers massage his forehead the way they usually do when he tries to break bad news to me. "I really didn't want to tell you this, but there's a lot more to his conviction. He not only almost killed a guy by beating him with a baseball bat, but he also raped his little brother. That guy is sick, Kels, and you need to stay away from him."

My eyebrows knit together. "That's not what he told me. He said his mother's boyfriend molested him and his brother."

"All I know is that he pled guilty to attempted murder and sexual assault. My dad found out because he's required to register under the Sex Offenders Act. He lied to you, Kels, probably because it's a challenge for him to get you in the sack. He's not your friend and you really should be careful."

Everything inside me is numb. How could I have been so mistaken about Finn? Like a fool, I spooned up his bullshit without even questioning it once. His story didn't fit his behavior at all—he is a desperate show-off and troublemaker and God only knows how he got those cuts on his leg.

Yet a part of me can't believe my instincts could have betrayed me. There is something genuine about him, like the pain reflected in his eyes. The same pain looks back at me in the mirror and I don't think anyone could fake that. Maybe there is a logical explanation for all of this. Finn deserves that I at least listen to his side of the story before passing judgment.

For the rest of Luke's visit, I pretend to listen to his detailed account of the new *Jurassic World* movie without soaking up even one word. My mind continues to be with Finn. Since he is the only one who can answer those tough questions, I plan on confronting him about his crimes the next time I see him.

~~~~

My next encounter with Finn is much sooner than expected and in a manner I never imagined. I'm already in bed with my lights off when a thump almost makes my heart jump out of my chest. I pull the covers over my head.

Another thump, a little louder. I squeal softly, cuddling further in the dark comfort of my bed. My heart beats so loudly in my ears, at twice its usual speed, that I almost miss the whistle. Another thump follows, making the glass of the window vibrate. I finally realize that these are the efforts of someone trying to make contact with me.

I slide out of bed and toddle over to the window. Moving the curtains aside, I peek outside. Finn is crouched next to his truck, his features obscured by the surreal light of dusk. I tear the window open and am just about ready to give him a piece of my mind for scaring me when he cups his hand over his mouth to silence me. He flails about, pointing at the building from time to time. My forehead wrinkles in a frown—what does he want from me? I have no idea what his secret Navy Seal type message means.

Trapped

He continues on, whirling his arms around, until it finally dawns on me that he wants me to come downstairs and meet him at the side door. For a moment, I hesitate, but then give into my curiosity. Who knows when I will see him again? The only way to put my mind at ease is to face him and get to the bottom of things. What better place is there than a secured mental health facility with plenty of people around who will hear my screams if he tries to pull me into his truck?

I'm about to go down in my night robe, but it is quite short and exposes too much of my legs. It could give him the idea that I am interested. I slide into my jeans and one of the airy summer tops my mom recently bought me. A critical look into the mirror and my hands pull my ruffled hair into a messy bun. In the last moment, I have the urge to apply some lip gloss, though it's totally silly. It's just Finn, for crying out loud, and I am not exactly planning on going on a date with him.

I tiptoe downstairs, careful not to draw anyone's attention to me. The hospital is quiet; just the voices of some television show hum in the distance. My watch reads not even ten o'clock. In a way, this 9:00 p.m. curfew for the residents is ridiculous. Even at fourteen, I was allowed to stay out longer during the summer.

When I get to the side door, I rattle on the doorknob until the door is shoved open.

"Shh, be quiet," Finn hisses. "You're going to alert the nurses."

"So?" I glare at him. "What do you want?"

"I'm taking you out."

"Out where?"

"Out to Portland, silly. I thought this would cheer you up."

My arms fold in front of my chest. "I'm not going anywhere with you until you've answered some questions." I give him my best evil stare to underline my words.

He hops from one foot to the other. "Can we please talk about that in the truck? I'm not working today, and if they find me here, they'll probably call the cops."

I shouldn't—I don't even know him. He could even be a serial killer at heart. "How do I know you're not trying to rape me?"

That gets a chuckle out of him. "Kelsey, please." He pushes his chest out with his hands on his waist, his muscles flexing under his tight shirt. "Do I look like a man who needs to trick a girl into having sex with him?"

He has a point. I know at least a dozen girls in Stonehenge who would gladly spread their legs for him if he appeared on their doorsteps tonight. The town is full of horny teens on the lookout for the next bad boy to sweep them off their feet.

For a second, Luke's disapproving scowl flashes in my mind—he clearly told me to stay away from Finn. Yet he also said I needed to stop being a victim. Not being afraid all the time would be a good start. So far, Finn has been nothing but supportive and I haven't had a reason to doubt his sincerity.

"Okay, but if I don't like what you tell me, you have to take me back immediately."

He nudges me. "Deal."

I follow him to his truck, my heart racing all of a sudden. This is so wrong but exciting at the same time. My mom would have a hissy fit if she knew I was leaving the hospital and my dad would probably spank me despite my age. He has always had a quick temper—one of the reasons my mom divorced him. He has also never gotten along with Luke and calls him a "smug ass," so Finn will definitely not meet his approval. If we are caught, we both will be in a boatload of trouble.

Finn doesn't open the door for me, and I slide in after giving him a nasty look.

He shrugs. "Hey—you're not my girlfriend. Don't expect the royal treatment, especially after implying there won't be any sex."

I stick my tongue out with a giggle. "You're such an ass."

He bows before starting the engine.

Still laughing as he takes off, I'm tempted to roll down the window and just scream into the growing darkness, but this could seriously sabotage our escape. To my surprise, he swerves off the main driveway just behind the building, taking a dirt road toward the lake. I bump up and down while he seems to drive through every possible pothole. When he glances at me with a sparkle in his eyes, I realize he is doing it on purpose.

"Stop that. I'm getting sick."

He smirks. "I'm trying to knock some sense into you."

I try to shoot daggers his way, but my eyes probably betray me, showing him just how much I am enjoying myself. We continue in silence while my fingers clutch the seatbelt. I hope that, at least, I won't bump my head. The truck carries us alongside the fence until we finally get to a small gate. He jumps out and opens it, fumbling for a lock on the backseat as soon as we are on the other side. After he secures the gate, we are on our way. The truck makes a sharp turn onto the main road toward Lewiston.

"What was that all about back there with the gate?"

"Well . . ." A sheepish smile crawls on his lips. "I didn't want to take the main entrance and had to kind of pick the lock."

My jaw drops. "Isn't that breaking and entering?"

"Since I'm not intending to steal anything, it's only trespassing."

I roll my eyes. "It's still a crime."

"Yeah, but only a misdemeanor." He smiles at me. "Don't worry, they won't put you in jail for a first offense."

"That's comforting."

He turns on the radio. Rap music with lots of profanities fills the truck. When I send him a scolding frown, he turns the volume down. "So, what did you want to talk to me about?"

My smile is crooked as I ponder how to best approach this delicate situation without totally spoiling the mood. Yet there is no easy way to say it. "My brother told me that you were also convicted of sexual assault."

His body tenses while his eyes stay fixed on the road. "That's right."

A chill runs through me. He is a sexual predator. I want to jump out of the truck and run.

His hands grip the steering wheel so tightly that his knuckles turn white. "But it's not what you think. When all this stuff happened with my mom's boyfriend, he claimed that *I* was the one who molested my brother. Bastard swore he walked in on us and that's why I beat him, though it was the other way around. My brother was totally intimidated and feared for his life, so when the police questioned him, he didn't tell them the truth."

"Then why didn't you take it to trial?"

"I could have and even had a good public defender, but they would've tried me as an adult. With the attempted murder charge, I was looking at life. I didn't want to take that chance."

I squint at him. "So you just pled guilty?"

"I did beat him up and almost killed him, so that charge was going to stick no matter what. They offered me a juvenile conviction in delinquency lockup until I was nineteen and two years' probation afterward if I pled to both charges. It was the best deal I could have gotten. After my release, my mom didn't want me, but luckily, my uncle took me in and I was able to transfer my probation. That's how I ended up here."

There is a huge lump in my throat when I gaze at him. His jaw is clenched and his eyes glisten with tears. "It must have been hard, losing your family like that." His mother is either really dumb or a total bitch.

Wetness glistens in his eyes. "I couldn't care less about my mom. She has never given me the time of day, so I didn't really expect any different. What really gets me is that my brother is still living with them and that asshole is probably raping him day in and day out like he did me. He's only thirteen."

I can't even imagine what he must be going through. "What's your brother's name?"

"Cameron." He wipes his cheeks with his sleeve. "I swear, once I'm off probation, I'll go back and get him out of there, but for now, there's nothing I can do. It's driving me nuts."

There is again this pain in his eyes when he glances at me. I'm sure he's telling the truth; there's no way that anyone could act that convincingly.

"What about your uncle? Can't he petition for custody now?"

"He could if he believed me." Finn sighs. "At the moment, he's still trying to figure things out. So far, my mom has always sided with her boyfriend and claims I'm full of crap, so he doesn't know what to believe."

I want to comfort him but am lost for words. "I can't tell you how sorry I am."

He nods. "Let's just forget about all this—just for tonight. No more talk about Jed, my brother, or anyone else. It's just you and me having a good time out of town, like two regular teens." His eyes are pleading. "Let's go dancing. Would you like that?"

I haven't been to a club in years. "Yeah, but there's one problem. It's Thursday and there're no underage discos open."

A small smile tugs at the corner of his lips. "I was talking about a real club, not some kiddie party."

I already have an idea where this conversation is going, but with one last-ditch effort, I try to hold on to my moral turpitude. "Last time I checked, you had to be twenty-one to get in."

The smile gets wider. "You're in luck. A friend of mine sells the best fake IDs in the state for only twenty bucks."

When our eyes interlock, it is settled. There's no stopping us now.

Chapter 8

An hour later, we stop in front of a house in a rough neighborhood. It is dark now, the remains of broken bottles and scattered garbage only dimly lit by a couple of working streetlights. We stop behind a raggedy old Buick. When we get out, I notice a brand new SUV parked in the driveway—whoever this guy is must be living in this area by choice and not lack of money.

A couple of thugs and a girl in a dress that barely hides her cleavage, or her butt, are out on the porch, sharing a cigarette. The girl looks totally wasted with her mouth hanging open, her eyes in another world.

A big tall dude opens the door for us after briefly nodding at Finn. "What's up, man?"

Finn pushes right past him without the benefit of even a glance. I choose to ignore him as well when he eyes me from top to bottom. A tingling sensation spreads down my scalp—the whole situation is kind of creepy. I would prefer to just leave and forget the whole ID business, but Finn has already disappeared in the depths of the house.

With reluctance, I step over the threshold. The interior is worse than expected. Most of the furniture has seen better days; broken toys and candy wrappers litter the ground. A musty smell hangs in the air, mixed with the sweet bite of cigarette smoke. When laughter drifts from somewhere in the back, I follow the sound of muffled voices and low rap music.

The living room is packed with people who would have me running for the hills if I had my own car. A giant leans back on a couch with his arms and legs spread open. A girl on her knees in front of him is just zipping up his pants. From the look of things, we interrupted them at a bad moment. Another couple is on a chair in the corner, totally oblivious that more guests have arrived to their party. After the guy unhooks the girl's bra, I avoid glancing in their direction at all costs.

Finn has made himself comfortable on the small love seat. "Kelsey, this is my friend Tyrone and his girl, Daliana. Say hello."

"Hi." I blush when Tyrone gives me a good once-over. His hard, dark eyes give me the creeps. Half the buttons of his shirt are undone, exposing a broad chest over his beer belly roll, thick gold chains hanging around his neck. From all the stereotypes I know, he has drug dealer written all over him.

"She's adorable, man," Tyrone grumbles. His lips are barely moving as he talks to my breasts. "Maybe I should get to the countryside more often and get me one of these."

My cheeks burn while I just stand there, unsure what to do. A heavy stone forms in the pit of my stomach while his eyes travel south. I halfway expect him to ask me to turn around, so he can inspect my behind. Daliana's neck is extended to get a good glimpse at her boyfriend's object of interest. Her pupils are dilated and her face is flushed—she is definitely high.

Finn finally takes me out of my misery when he pats the space next to him. "Come on, Kelsey, have a seat and relax."

"Want a beer?" Tyrone asks, smacking his lips.

Finn's arm slides around my shoulders. "Sure thing."

I go rigid, but he doesn't seem to notice.

Tyrone snaps his fingers and Daliana is on her feet. As she rushes out, I notice a big bruise on her upper arm. What the hell did I get myself into?

There is a moment of silence while Tyrone shifts his heavy body around on the couch until he finds a more comfortable position. "What do you need, man?"

"Fake ID."

Trapped

A grin spreads on Tyrone's face. "No problem, but the price went up. It's forty now. If that's too much, your girl can pay me in kind."

When a chuckle vibrates through his body, my stomach clenches. My eyes travel to the big bulge between his legs—he is totally disgusting.

Daliana returns with three cans of Hanfill and hands one first to her man before offering the others to Finn and me.

"Get Marcel down here, woman. I have a job for him."

She trots out like a good lapdog who is sent to fetch the paper. Finn opens the beer and takes a mouthful while beaming at Tyrone, his arm moving straight back into position around my shoulders when he is done. I feel like a prized possession he wants to protect from harm, which mirrors the ever-growing mountain of ice in my stomach. Everything about Tyrone screams danger. I cannot wait to get away from him.

Tyrone rummages around the table and tosses a small bag to Finn. "Here, some new stuff I got yesterday from Jamaica. It's strong, man. You'll like it."

The bag contains a leafy substance reminding me of oregano. "How much?" Finn asks.

"It's on the house since you brought her around." Tyrone winks at me, sending some bile up my throat. "I always like meeting new people, especially cute ones."

It finally dawns on me that the bag contains some type of drug, probably marijuana. It looks just like the picture they showed us in school during Drug Awareness Week. All of a sudden, I am glad Finn's arm is cradling me, but my comfort doesn't last long when he begins to fish around in his pockets for a pack of rolling paper.

With the tips of his thumb and index fingers, he spreads a little of the bag's contents on one of the thin papers, rolling it up tightly before moistening the edge with his tongue to stick it all together. After he lights the joint, he takes a drag, holding the smoke in his lungs with his eyes closed. A satisfied groan runs over his lips at the same time the smoke finally escapes through the corners of his mouth.

A small cough follows. "Boy, that's some good shit." He holds the joint under my nose, the sharp scent making me dizzy. "Here, have some."

I want to decline, but his eyes scream caution. I realize that Tyrone will likely get upset if I reject his welcoming gift. My hand trembles as I carefully tuck the joint between my fingers and bring it up to my lips. My lungs are on fire as soon as I fill them with smoke, a cough battling me until tears run down my cheeks.

When I finally settle down, two sets of ridiculing eyes stare at me. Tyrone has been joined by a guy who is the exact opposite of him—short, firm muscled, and clean. His head is shaven while Tyrone's strings of hair keep obscuring his vision. Everything about him chills my blood. Next to him, Tyrone is like a cuddly teddy bear.

"I'm Marcel," he introduces himself. "You need a fake ID?" There's a hint of a southern drawl in his voice.

All I can do is nod—his glare paralyzes my vocal cords.

He picks up a camera off the table. "Stand over there by the wall."

I hand Finn the joint, who takes another drag, and stumble over to the spot Marcel has pointed at. The noises around me sound surreal while the blood pulses in my ears. I blink a few times to focus while my picture is taken before finding my way back to the couch. My face and neck are burning up, a foul taste lacing the inside of my mouth.

"This'll only take a few minutes." Marcel disappears just as the joint is offered again. Daringly, I first down half of my beer before taking another drag. It burns less, but still throws me into a coughing fit. Finn squeezes my shoulder, which sends a shiver down my spine. I snuggle against him while a lulling feeling caresses my mind.

Daliana passes around another round of beers while a new joint is lit. The smoke hangs heavy in the room. I lose total track of time as I sip from the can, taking more drags of the joint whenever Finn offers it to me. My mouth dries up, which I battle with big gulps of Hanfill. The beer is ice cold and runs down my burning throat like soothing balm. As soon as a can is empty, it is replaced by another.

The rushing in my ears gets louder as the air shimmers in front of my eyes. It is almost like I am floating around outside my body. Finn's hand rests heavy on my shoulder. Every time his fingers twitch, a hot flash lights up my insides. I cuddle closer, enjoying the warmth of his body.

His breath grazes my neck. "Slow down."

I pout. "Why? I'm having an excellent time." My fingers trace alongside his chiseled chin. He really is gorgeous. "Don't I deserve that for a change?"

His lips meet mine in response. His kiss is soft, and when our tongues intertwine, a shudder runs through me. Heat wallows in the depths of my belly, turning into a bubbling volcano as his teeth nip at my bottom lip. When his hand moves under my shirt, the tingles left behind by his fingernails gently cutting into my skin draws out a moan.

The magical moment is broken by a small voice. "Where's my mommy? I'm thirsty."

A young girl of maybe five stands in the doorway. She is really cute with dozens of braids framing her face, yet her eyes are dull without any joy. Her pink pajamas are two sizes too small with brown stains all over. Both her arms are wrapped around a big white bunny in a tight embrace.

I giggle. She reminds me of Alice in Wonderland.

"Oh hey, Cherry," Finn says. "What's up?"

More giggles float from my mouth—she is named after a fruit.

The girl eyes us with a frown. "Your girlfriend's silly."

This makes me laugh so hard that tears run down my cheeks. Finn's fingers play with strands of my hair while the girl continues to glare at us until her free thumb moves between her lips. With glistening eyes, she lowers her gaze.

"Come on, I'll get you something to drink, sweetie." Daliana pulls the girl behind her out of the room.

I wish Finn would kiss me again, but he has struck up a conversation with Tyrone over some rapper who is supposed to be an Oreo. The expression makes me snicker again. Almost every other word he utters is totally hilarious—he is such a comedian. Even Tyrone has a funny side to him. My stomach soon hurts from all the laughing. My earlier apprehension has totally evaporated as the weed and alcohol cause chaos in my bloodstream.

At some point, Marcel resurfaces and hands me my brand new ID, which still smells like burned plastic. I'm now Jenna Brooks from Florida, born February 12, 1995. And at twenty-one, I am allowed to legally consume alcohol. The driver's license looks totally genuine, although I have never seen one from outside of Maine and have no comparison. Two crisp twenty-dollar bills change owners before Finn pulls me to my feet.

"Got to go," he announces, his arm sliding around my waist when I begin to take wobbly steps toward the door. "Great seeing you, man."

Tyrone waves us goodbye. Daliana is already back on her knees, fumbling with his zipper. The other couple has vanished. I didn't even notice when they left.

Trapped

I keep tripping over my feet on the way to the truck, giggling nonstop while Finn drags me along. One time, we almost fall over after my laughter catches. When we get to the car, we are both out of breath.

I lean against the door. "Kiss me again."

He rolls a strand of my hair around his finger. "I don't think that's a good idea. You're totally high and I don't want to take advantage of you."

I frown. What the hell is he talking about? For once, I am happy and enjoying a man's company. He looks like a delicious apple I want to devour. My hand lands on his groin and slowly rubs over the fabric.

He exhales sharply as his head tilts backward, a groan shaking his frame. I triumph, certain I have convinced him that this is a good idea after all, but just as his body reacts, he catches my wrist.

"Let's just go dancing, okay?"

His lips are only inches away. I lunge forward, but he turns his head and my mouth collides with his chin. Before I can protest, a loud growl resonates from my stomach.

I'm all of a sudden starving. "Can we get something to eat first?"

He smiles. "Sure. What would you like?"

"French fries." Drool forms in my mouth at the thought of soft, velvety ice cream melting on my tongue. "And frozen yogurt." The urge for something salty teases my senses. "And maybe butter popcorn." Something is missing and I hop from foot to foot. "And caramel, too."

He chuckles. "I guess we stop at a convenience store and stock up on snack food before going to McDonalds. Sound good?"

I nod enthusiastically. He briefly squeezes my hands before opening the truck door for me. "Okay, let's start phase two of our night out."

That makes me giggle again. So far, phase one was a total success.

Chapter 9

The sounds, colors, and movements blend into one as I groove to the music with hooded eyes, my arms and legs in harmony with my swaying hips. I'm burning up with a constant buzzing in my head, the world around me vibrating in a surreal dancing light. As a matter of fact, everything appears surreal. It's like I've traded in the troubled, haunted Kelsey for the fun-loving and laid back girl I used to be before my abduction. It's dreamlike and I love every minute of it.

I have also discovered a new favorite—golden tequila. Together with lime and salt, those are the best shooters ever, and Finn and I have almost killed our first bottle. The fake ID has worked magic. We had no issues getting into the club and the bartender has not once raised an eyebrow when I demanded a refill. I never even imagined that it would be that easy to fool people about my age.

Finn's fingers intertwine with mine as I continue to sway to the music. Deciding to move in, I tilt my head backward and close my eyes as I grind against him to the rhythm of the song. He plays along, his arm cradling my back when he pulls me closer. He is such a tease. The volcano in the depths of my belly erupts once again as his body reacts to mine, matching the lust in his eyes. He wants me badly and for the first time in three years, I don't mind at all. Breaking down his reservations and getting laid has become the ultimate goal of the night.

The nausea hits me unexpectedly and I almost barf all over the floor. With a crooked grin, I spin around and head in the direction of the restrooms. Ignoring the snide remarks of the other girls waiting in line, I squeeze through an opening in the door just as someone is leaving.

The strong scent of perfume and toilet bowl cleaner sends me over the edge. My insides rebel as I lunge into the stall, ignoring more angry mumbling from the other patrons. Before I can even lock the door, my stomach contents begin to leak into the toilet. When the retching stops, I lean back, my whole body shivering. Rapid changes of hot and cold flashes battle through me while I catch my breath. My throat is raw and on fire, the foul taste in my mouth almost making me gag again.

I must have dozed off. When the stall door slams against my feet, I'm startled. A girl stands in front of me, her features blending in and out of focus. I squint, trying to figure out what she wants.

"Hey, are you okay?" Her brows knit together in a critical frown.

I feel judged.

"Your boyfriend is out there, going nuts, because you've been in here like an hour," she says. "Do you need help?"

I have no clue what she's talking about. I don't even know how I got here. "I don't have a boyfriend." And then the truth hits me. It must be Jed or his friend, trying to recapture me. This terrible fear has been constantly in the back of my mind ever since I escaped.

My arms wrap around the girl's calf. "Please, don't leave me. This guy is trying to kidnap me. You have to call the police."

She tries to free herself from my grip, but I hold onto her leg for my dear life. She is the only one who can save me.

"Are you crazy?" she hisses when she finally gets out of my clutches. "Call the cops yourself. You're totally wasted."

She storms out just as my eyes fall on the window. It's wide enough for me to squeeze through. I fiddle with the handle until it finally pops open. A warm night breeze brushes over me. The sweetness of lavender in the air makes me sick again and my stomach heaves, but the fear and unrest that cause my heart to beat triple its speed drives me forward. I won't allow them to drag me back to Jed's cabin.

I almost make it. My head is already hanging down, my arms stretched out to reach for safety. The sidewalk is close, only inches away, when someone pulls on my legs, inching me back toward danger.

I squeal, kicking. "Leave me alone."

Colorful curses assault my eardrums when my feet find a soft target. The pulling stops, but my efforts prove too stringent on my body. Vomit spills from my mouth again. I end up a trembling mess, just as my assailant resumes hauling me back into the club, despite my growing protests.

"HELP!" I scream at the top of my lungs. "HELP! He's trying to abduct me."

A sharp "What're you doing, dude?" makes my heart rejoice. Finally, someone is coming to my rescue.

"My friend had too much to drink and is freaking out. I'm trying to get her inside. She doesn't even realize she's on the second floor and will get seriously hurt if she falls."

No, no, no—he's totally lying. The sidewalk is right under my nose, even if it is a tad blurry. I start to kick again, but another set of hands comes to my attacker's aid. They restrain my legs from causing any more damage and also bar my escape. I can't fight them both. After one joint pull, I find myself back inside the bathroom.

I immediately change strategy and punch the air in front of me. The room is spinning. I'm dizzy, but stand my ground until two strong arms wrap around me.

"Kelsey, stop. It's just me—Finn."

"NO," I yell, my shrill voice almost splitting my eardrums. "You're him. You're Napoleon and you're only nice to me because you want to rape me again."

"Hooo." The guy next to Finn raises his palms, taking a step back. "That's getting too heavy for me. I'm gonna call the cops and they can figure this out."

Finn releases me. "Hey, she's totally high and doesn't know what she's talking about." His hands run through his hair. He looks like he is about to cry. "I'm on probation, man. If you call the cops, they'll arrest me. She's underage and you'll be in trouble as well for serving her alcohol."

I get sick again, throwing up right on the floor. Finn jumps back, but is still hit with a generous amount of half-digested food and tequila. Good.

"Goddammit," the guy cusses. "You better get her out of here. I swear if you're not gone in the next five minutes, I'll have the bouncers beat the crap out of you." He extends his hand. "And before you get any ideas, gimme your car keys."

Finn's eyes go wide. "Are you crazy? How'm I supposed to get her home?"

"Not my problem. You're both drunk and you'll probably kill someone if you get behind the wheel. The club will be sued and I'll lose my job on top of all this." He adamantly shakes his head. "No, dude, not happening. And I swear if I find out you touched her tonight, I'll personally crack your skull. Now get out of my sight and don't think of ever coming back here again."

"Please, I don't want to go with him," I whimper.

The guy just shoots me a nasty look and leaves. A large group of girls gawks at me, but no one even lifts a finger. Each and every one of them lowers their gaze when my begging eyes meet theirs.

Finn's hand gets ahold of my wrist. "Come on, Kelsey. We've to go or we'll both be in trouble."

I tear my arm away from him. "NO."

He grabs my shoulders and shakes me violently. "What's wrong with you? I'm not Napoleon. I don't even know who the hell that is!"

Tears roll down my cheeks. "Please don't hurt me."

He catches me just as my knees buckle. I stagger through the club, hanging onto his neck. I can't fight him anymore. My head swims and a jackhammer is moving in. Thirst burns in my throat while I desperately fight the nausea. The sound of the music explodes painfully in my skull as we seem to crawl over the dance floor toward the exit.

We finally make it outside, and as the cool night air hits me, I barf again in a corner next to a dumpster. When I'm done, I pant, too weak to remain on my feet without support. I double over and sink to the ground, cradling into a ball. My eyes twitch from exhaustion.

Finn squats next to me. "Kelsey, you have to get up."

I grunt, tiredness slowly luring me under its spell. The humming of my blood in my ears is soothing. My eyelids become heavy.

"Luke," I mumble. "I want Luke."

"Okay, I might as well call him to pick us up since I can't get ahold of anyone else. What's his number?"

With a last-ditch effort, the numbers slur from my mouth before my mind goes totally blank.

~~~~

I awake when the car swerves and I'm almost tossed off my seat. It takes me a minute to realize that I'm squeezed in the back of a moving vehicle. The slight scent of coconut suggests it's Luke's truck. He's always been a fan of those air fresheners you hang from the rearview mirror and coconut is the flavor of the month.

"What the hell were you thinking of taking her from the hospital?" Luke's voice trembles with fury. "That was totally irresponsible."

"Look, all I wanted was for her to have a break for one night. I never thought she would freak out like this." Finn's words are whiny, reminding me of a small child.

Luke huffs. "What did you give her?"

"We had a few joints and some shots."

Luke clicks his tongue and the temperature in the truck drops by a few notches. "That's just great. Mixing shit like this is fucking genius." The sarcasm oozes from his voice. "No wonder she freaked out. If you paid any attention in class, you would've known that mixing alcohol and weed can cause anxiety attacks and paranoia. You were just lucky that she didn't try to cut herself."

Finn's head hits the back of his seat. "God, that would have been awful."

Heavy silence falls over the truck. I almost drift back to sleep from the even humming of the engine when Finn clears his throat.

"Who's Napoleon? She thought I was him."

Luke sucks in a deep breath. "That's Jed's friend who also abducted her."

"I thought his name was Drake something."

"Well, yeah, that's what everyone thinks." The car makes a left turn before speeding up. "But there was never any real evidence that it was him. It could have been anybody. Napoleon was what Jed called him."

"That's stupid."

"Oh yeah, and why is that, genius?"

"Napoleon's character was highly influenced by his height. He was very insecure because of that, which made him so vicious. I doubt the abductor was really short, so the nickname isn't really fitting."

Luke snorts. "I guess you do pay attention in class when you want to. And yes, I agree. It was a stupid nickname, but then, Jed isn't really smart. The few brain cells he had were destroyed in the boxing ring. He's dumber than a brick."

The nausea crawls up my throat again when the car makes another turn. "Hey, I'm really sick."

Finn peeks over the passenger seat. "Do you need us to stop?"

"Uhum," I mumble before my hand clutches my mouth.

The car slows. I jump out before it has fully stopped. My stomach heaves and I gag. Finn holds my hair back as my ordeal continues while Luke strokes my back. In that moment, I swear I will never touch another drop of alcohol—or smoke a joint for that matter.

Luke produces a bottle of water which I down in one go before climbing back into the truck. My throat is still raw, my head pounding. The water settles my stomach, but I'm still not convinced I will be able to keep it down. The humming of the engine soon lulls my mind as we continue our journey in silence.

"Luke," I whisper just before drifting back to dreamland.

"Hm," he grumbles.

"Please don't tell anyone about tonight. I don't want Finn to get into trouble."

He lets out an exasperated gasp. "Kels, I can't just ignore—"

"Luke, please. Do it for me. He's my friend."

An annoyed sigh escapes his lips. "Okay, as long as this stays a one-time thing. I won't cover for you guys again."

"Thanks." A small smile tugs on my lips when the Sandman knocks on my door. Luke really is the best big brother any girl could ask for.

There are three more stops until we finally get back to the hospital. Finn shows Luke the back entrance, and while cursing, my brother commits a misdemeanor to end our little adventure. A sweep of Finn's employee card allows us access to the building, which is covered in total silence. I'm snuggled into Luke's arms while he carries me upstairs to my room and tucks me into bed.

He kisses my forehead. "Good night, sis. You'll feel worse tomorrow morning, but that'll be a good punishment."

"Thanks for coming to my rescue, bro."

There are tears in his eyes. "Nothing will ever make up for me not coming to get you that night of the party. If I had only picked you up, you would never have been kidnapped. It's all my fault. I will never forgive myself."

"Hey." I grab his hand. "Don't beat yourself up. If it hadn't happened that night, it would have been some other time. Jed and Napoleon planned for months—he told me so himself."

He gave me a crooked smile. "Yeah, maybe."

"Tonight you were there for me and that's the most important thing. I'm sorry I messed up."

"I guess we're both experts when it comes to that."

I close my eyes, battling more nausea. "Yes, I guess we are."

"Sleep now." He tucks the blankets closer around me. "I'll take your friend home and make sure he gets his truck back tomorrow."

"Thanks." My eyelids flutter. "I love you, Luke."

"I love you, too, sis."

Chapter 10

For the rest of the summer, there are no more excursions outside the hospital—it is one of Luke's imposed conditions to keep his mouth shut. At first, he also insists Finn stay away from me, but that sanction is lifted after a few days when he realizes how miserable I am. Though Luke hates to admit it, Finn gets me to open up to him. Since both Finn and I went through a traumatic experience others can't relate to, I feel connected to him. He empathizes with my vulnerability without judging me and that is the one thing Luke doesn't get. It upsets him, but is something he grudgingly learns to accept. He even agrees that this is the first big step I have taken toward my recovery.

I meet my obligations and attend group and individual therapy but only go through the motions. I don't like Dr. Malcolm, the psychiatrist, and talking in front of a group has always terrified me. Yet, according to the clinic, I'm making progress. As a sign of goodwill, I even allow my mom and Roy to visit me in the beginning of August. After all, I can't hold a grudge forever. It's an awkward situation when they also drag my dad along, and for an hour, we sit under a tree, making small talk. I'm thrilled when they finally leave.

I expect for Luke to stop by afterward to smooth over the waters, but he is busy with his summer job in his dad's law firm and his visits have become a rare treat. It's irritating since he has always been there for me, no matter what. Now it almost seems he is excluding me from his life, especially since Finn has been coming around.

My sulking is cut short when Finn pulls his truck next to the garden a couple of hours later. He was finishing a project for summer school in the last few days and I'm dying to catch up with him. When I join him by the flowerbeds, he is just starting to fumble with the garden hose.

His face lights up when he sees me. "Hey, Kelsey. What's up?"

"Not much." I lean against the truck. "How did your project go?"

"I'm sure I aced it. It was history, something I particularly like." He turns on the water, spraying the flowers that we planted a little over a month ago. They are flourishing. "Just my finals left in two weeks and I will have officially graduated high school."

In many ways, I envy him. It has always bothered me that I just quit before the end of my junior year. After the kidnapping, I dragged myself to classes every day for a few months but could not stomach the stares and whispers behind my back. When Justin broke it off after I had refused to be affectionate with him, I stopped going altogether. The pain of losing him was the final straw and I felt punished all over again. That's when the cutting started.

"I'm glad you don't have to repeat your senior year again," I say.

"It's not that I had that much of a choice." He grimaces. "My probation officer was going to violate my probation if I didn't get my act together. After the summer, I'll work in my uncle's shop, which will hopefully shut him up."

"What about college?"

He chuckles. "College isn't for someone like me. No one in my family has ever even graduated high school. My mom is third-generation welfare."

"So the way it was at Tyrone's house, that's how you grew up?"

His face darkens. "No, Tyrone's place is like paradise in comparison. There's always enough money for food and he doesn't allow any of the hard stuff in the house. My mom's a major crackhead and would sell her kids for a fix. Luckily, I don't have any sisters or that boyfriend of hers would have probably sent them hooking."

"That must have been tough. How do you even know Tyrone?"

His forehead wrinkles. "What's that supposed to mean?"

I flush, shuffling my feet. "I thought he was your drug supplier."

For a second, I fear I offended him, but he laughs instead. "I was never into drugs and only smoke weed from time to time. I bunked with Marcel's nephew in juvenile lockup. When I came to Maine, he helped me out with money a few times. I met Tyrone through him."

"Oh." I can't believe he likes to hang around people like that. "So Marcel is your friend? I felt he was a little creepy." I grimace, once again not sure if I put my foot in my mouth. All this talk about shady characters is new to me. People like Tyrone and Marcel don't tend to walk around in places like Stonehenge.

Finn is a good sport about it. "Marcel just looks scary, but all in all, he's a nice guy." He turns off the water. "Tyrone is the dangerous one—he has connections to the Colombian cartels and is not someone to double-cross."

I wrinkle my nose, glad I got out of that house alive. Truthfully, I wouldn't mind if I never have to see any of them again.

When I am just about to ask Finn what he has planned next, a nurse approaches us, an Amazon package in hand.

"Here, Kelsey, this was delivered for you. It's a book."

A small smile automatically appears on my lips. It's probably from my mom. She told me earlier that she had ordered me a few novels.

"Thanks."

When I pull the book from the package, it takes a few seconds for the title to register in my brain. It's *Messenger of Fear* by Michael Grant.

The book goes flying and I shriek as hundreds of little legs run across my skin. I try to shoo them away, but my lungs are crushed at the same time. I gasp for air, my voice shrill as I slap my body, trying to get rid of the crawling feeling.

Two strong arms enclose me. I punch my assailant, my screams so loud that they almost split my eardrums. I struggle as tears run down my face. The tingling sensation is everywhere on my skin, my breath caught in my throat.

"Kelsey, concentrate on your breathing. You can get through this." Finn's voice is muffled through the heavy fog surrounding my mind that has stolen all sense of reason.

I fight harder as the small legs continue their assault until a piercing pain in my upper arm takes me away into darkness.

~~~~

As I slowly wake up, I keep my eyes squeezed shut when I hear Finn's and Luke's low voices.

"And you have no idea what made her freak out like this?" Luke asks.

"No clue, but it must have been something about the book." Finn exhales heavily. "Did you see the gift card with the get-well message from Jed?"

"Yeah, pretty sick." Luke's voice is full of fury. "That bastard must have figured out where she is. I could kill him. In one afternoon, he destroyed two months of therapy just like that. Why can't he leave her alone?"

"It must have triggered some horrific memory. As soon as she saw the book, she totally lost it."

"But she got you pretty good." Luke chuckles. "That black eye is class."

Finn snorts. "My probation officer won't like it and will probably think I got into a fight. I can already hear his lecture."

"That sucks."

Silence follows Luke's words and I ponder whether I should let them know that I am awake. They will likely ask for an explanation, but that is one memory I never wanted to relive.

I was already in captivity for over a month when Jed showed up one morning with the book. My whole body was throbbing from an especially hard night with Napoleon, who had punched me a few times in the ribs when I didn't remain still in my shackles.

"Here, honeybun, I brought you something. Your voice is lovely, so I want you to read it out loud."

My throat was raw from all the screaming and crying. "I need water, Jed."

He got a bottle from the shelf in the next room. "For every page you read, you get a few sips."

So I read the book, page by page, so that I could get some relief in between. It was a story about a bully meeting the Messenger of Fear, who brought justice to people who wronged others. They had a choice—play a game or face their greatest fear. Yet, if they lost their challenge, they had to face their fear regardless. The book wasn't very long and we were finished after a few hours.

"Well, honeybun, since you're also a bully, let's just pretend I'm your Messenger of Fear. Do you want to play the game or face your biggest fear?"

I stared at him. "You can't be serious."

"Oh, I am." His smile was smug. "The challenge is not very hard. I hid ten things around the house and all you have to do is find them."

A sickening sensation spread in my stomach. There was no way it would be as easy as he claimed.

I really had not much of a choice. "Yeah, I'll play your stupid game."

"Great. You'll see, it'll be so much fun."

He allowed me to put on panties and a bra before ushering me aboveground to the cabin and handing me a list. "You have twenty minutes. Good luck."

I stumbled through the cabin, trying to find random items. A bar of chocolate, a condom, a pair of shoes. The sight of the bracelet my mother had given me for my sixteenth birthday brought tears to my eyes, but it was the DVD that cost me most of my precious time. He forced me to turn it on when I located it in the player.

With trembling lips, I watched Jed raping me while I was screaming at the top of my lungs. It must have been recorded a few days ago, just after Napoleon left me.

"You sick bastards are taping me," I yelled as tears rolled down my cheeks.

"We're thinking of putting it on VideoTube. You could be an Internet sensation, honeybun."

I bit the inside of my hand to hide my horror. The humiliation would be for everyone to see. Yet I wasn't able to take my eyes off the TV screen even though it was blurred through my tears. Utter disgust raged through me.

Jed finally turned off the recording. "Only a few minutes left. You should hurry."

I remembered the game and realized I still had three items to find. It was a losing battle. Jed grinned from ear to ear when he informed me that I had failed.

Trapped

"Time to face your biggest fear, honeybun."

I pleaded all the way back to the dungeon. "Please, Jed. I never meant to bully you, I just wanted to belong. You know how it is. Please, we were just stupid kids." The whole time, my heart clamped in my chest in terror and fear.

The words fell on deaf ears. He dragged me along, threatening to throw me into the hole when I refused to climb down the ladder. As soon as we were back in the room, he made me strip and secured my hands and ankles with cable ties.

His eyes were glinting with malice and excitement when he approached me with a large bucket. "Ready, honeybun?"

Before I could even respond, he poured the contents over me. Hundreds of little spiders began spreading over my skin. I had always been deadly afraid of anything that crawled and I screeched until the air was totally pressed from my lungs. The assault continued, but my arms and legs were safely secured. I couldn't even fight back. Bile rose in my mouth, mixed with salty tears and blood from my lips, as I begged for him to make it stop in between my shrilling shrieks.

Jed laughed the entire time, at some point taping my ordeal with his phone. Soon, the crawly spiders were in my ears, nose, and mouth. The skin on my ankles and wrists was torn off my bones where I tried to loosen my restraints, my lungs burning in agony as I fought with all my strength. There was no relief. I was totally helpless as thousands of little legs used my body as their personal playground.

"Now you know how it feels, honeybun, when something terrifies you and you can't do nothing about it."

When my voice was reduced to a croak, Jed finally showed mercy and poured water over me until the crawling stopped. Soon after, I drifted into a deep sleep, totally exhausted, though I woke up every so often when my muscles twitched. It was one of the times during my abduction where I would have preferred death over life.

I snap out of my horrific memory when Luke's deep voice penetrates my mind.

"You want half an apple?"

"Sure," Finn says.

Luckily, they haven't noticed that my hands are curled into tight fists. It takes all my effort to continue to lie still, my skin crawling from the vivid memory. I want to itch myself badly, but only dig into my palms with my newly grown fingernails to stop myself from tearing off my skin.

They munch, an occasional crunch from a bite breaking the silence. I still don't want to talk because I fear their intrusive questions. My breath stays even. I have pretended so many times that I was asleep when my mom checked on me at night to avoid her noticing my tears that I manage to fool them.

When the door opens, rescue is near.

"Excuse me, gentlemen, but visiting hours are long over. You really need to leave. She could be asleep for a few more hours and you should check back in the morning."

I hear the guys get on their feet.

"No problem, ma'am." That's Luke. "Just make sure you take good care of my little sis."

Something drops in the bin beside my bed, probably the leftovers of the apple. The door closes with a low click. The room falls quiet. I finally dare to peek and confirm the coast is clear. The small lamp by my nightstand is still on, covering the room in a dim light. I sit up and rub my eyes before shaking off the little bit of heaviness in my head.

My gaze scans the nightstand and my heartbeat accelerates in delight—I just hit the jackpot! Luke's Swiss pocketknife has been carelessly left behind, next to a small apple stem.

Trapped

I bite my lip when my trembling hand reaches for the knife—I will kill the rampant pain in my chest with the best medicine there is. Tonight, I will be able to sleep without nightmares or haunting memories. My heart dances in my chest as I unfold the blade and allow the tip to gently scratch my skin. A shudder shakes my frame as an ache spreads alongside my arm.

Without the slightest hesitation, I slice deeper, indulging in the pain as it radiates in small waves throughout my body. The blood oozes from my arm like red rain, washing away the deep-rooted agony left behind by Jed's torture. Tears run down my cheeks as I sink back into the pillow, this time controlling my breath to stay conscious.

When the imminent pain is suppressed by the adrenaline released into my bloodstream, I cut myself again, repeating the exercise in shorter and shorter intervals. My body's survival instincts cause the throbbing pain to flare, demanding me to stop, yet nothing can compete with the incredible urge to soothe my tormented soul.

Chapter 11

After three days in the closed psychiatric ward, I am released back into the general population. My cutting is not ruled a suicide attempt this time since I didn't cut as deep, but my relapse still promises me plenty of additional sessions with Dr. Malcolm. Overall, it's a total drag, and for the first time, I doubt that the short relief I felt was actually worth it.

Finn had disappeared from the face of the earth which causes further distress, especially since Luke is also miffed that I used his knife to harm myself. His long lecture is literally drowned by my tears when I turn into a sobbing mess on his shoulder.

"I'm sorry, Luke, I don't know what has gotten into me."

"Hey." He strokes my back. "I shouldn't have been so careless, but I really thought we were past this cutting business."

A fist clenches my heart at the disappointment oozing from his voice. "If it hadn't been for the book—"

It's a lame excuse and he doesn't persuade him. "It has to stop, Kels, or you'll never get out of this place."

My eyes narrow. "What do you mean?"

He doesn't respond but stretches out in the grass, turning his face to the sun with his eyes closed. We are back under our usual tree in the garden. It is a beautiful afternoon with record high temperatures for Maine. A light breeze is cool, but otherwise, it's a perfect day for the beach. I'm sure he is less than thrilled at being stuck here with me instead of spending time with Rhonda or his friends.

"Luke, is there something you're not telling me?" I try again while my fingers comb through the long grass.

"I overheard your mom and my dad talking and they think you should stay longer at the hospital."

I take in a sharp breath. "Can they do that?"

He rolls on his stomach and finds my eyes. "Probably. Androscoggin County has a small law community and my dad is real chummy with all the judges. I'm sure he could get another court order signed if he tried."

Tears pool in my eyes. "I don't want to stay here. Please, you have to talk to them."

"Truthfully, I'm not sure if I disagree with them. You did get better for a while when you were trying."

My head is spinning and I fall on my back, staring into the sky. A few puffy clouds are scattered throughout, drifting softly toward the sun. One reminds me of a dragon who could carry me away, another of a dog snout which makes me shudder. For a second, Roxy's teeth flash in my mind as they tore into Jed's skin. The thought makes me sick to my stomach.

I close my eyes, trying to clear my mind but fail. Luke is right. I am still a loose cannon and will probably end up dead by Christmas if I don't finally accept some help. It's just so hard and painful, having to deal with those inner demons.

"Can I still think about whether I want to stay or not?"

He plays with the stem of a dandelion. "For how long?"

It's not a decision I'm prepared to make without some further advice. "I want to talk to Finn and see what he thinks."

In the hopes of changing the subject, my finger begins to draw the outline of the dragon cloud in the air.

"That might be a problem. Finn is in jail at the moment."

My head snaps up. "WHAT!" There must be some type of mistake. "Are you sure?"

"Yes." His eyes avoid me. "My dad is representing him. He and a friend beat someone up."

I stare at him, my fingers massaging the bridge of my nose as pain spreads rapidly across my forehead. "Who?" I can't believe Finn could be so reckless—he must be looking at some serious prison time.

Luke ignores the question and observes another dandelion like it is the most interesting plant in the world. "Did you know that these are actually edible?"

I couldn't care less about the nutritional value of flowers. "Who did he beat up, Luke?"

His face twists into a grimace. "Jed. He was really mad about the book, so he and this guy jumped him the night after he found out you cut yourself."

A groan runs across my lips, the guilt eating at me. "Please tell me he didn't." I can't bear the thought that Finn could go to prison because he tried to protect me.

Luke's fingers stroke the back of my hand. "I'm sorry. Hopefully, he won't have to do much time since the DA is really after his friend who works for this big drug dealer."

Tears drop into the long grass, the desperation crushing my chest. First, Luke got into trouble with the law after I was rescued, now Finn, and if he squeals on one of Tyrone's men, there might be additional repercussions. Yet the one who really deserves to be locked up instead of walking around without a worry is Jed—he, of all people, seems untouchable. It's unfair, but what is worse is that every time I confide my feelings to anyone, they pick my battles and end up in harm's way.

"Can you tell Finn I'm sorry?" I sob. "I feel so terrible about this."

"He just wants what's best for you. I'm sure he'd also agree that you should stay here until you're better."

"You think?"

His eyes soften. "We all love you, Kels, and just want you to be alright. Don't make your mom go to court again. It's not fair on her."

Just agreeing to stay and get with the program might really be the best under the circumstances. "Okay, and I promise I'll work even harder this time."

"That's my sis." He tucks a loose strand of my hair behind my ear. "You'll see, things will be so much better afterward."

All of a sudden, I have the urge to get back to my room and sulk. This whole situation is royally screwed up and I am the one who is to blame the most—but the worst is that I will not get a chance to apologize to Finn, even if he should not have risked everything for me. Beating up Jed was really stupid.

~~~~

Fate is finally kind and I get a chance to talk to Finn when he returns to the hospital a few days later. From the outset, he is in an awful mood, his face flushing when I confront him about Jed.

"I still don't get why you just went ahead and beat him up without even talking to me. I could have told you that you'd get into trouble. Jed might be dumb, but he knows his way around the system."

"He had it coming, Kelsey." Finn is rummaging with the garbage cans, dragging them toward the large space out back behind the kitchen where the truck always picks them up. "Guys like him only understand one thing and that is a good punch in the mouth. Otherwise, they'll never shut up."

I glare at him—that is the dumbest argument I've heard in a long time. "Violence is never the answer, Finn. Jed won't stop torturing me just because you beat him up. To the contrary. He'll probably pull another stunt just to prove to you he can. Fighting him was totally pointless and look where it got you."

His eyes are blazing. "I did what needed to be done and don't regret it. Having that bastard bleed for a change felt great, even if I have to do some time. It's a guy thing. I don't expect you to understand."

"It's a *guy* thing?" I cannot keep the mocking from my voice. "Please, Finn, that's ridiculous. How much prison time will you get for being tough?"

The steam is practically pouring from his nose. "You see, that's exactly your problem. You allow people to beat up on you and then you feel all vulnerable and helpless, but instead of standing up for yourself, you feed on your misery and fault those who actually do something about it."

I stomp my foot. "I never asked you to fight my battles. Beating up Jed was really immature and stupid."

"Oh yeah." His mouth curls into a sarcastic smirk. "But cutting yourself is a real mature way of handling things? You should listen to how hypocritical you sound."

Tears roll down my cheeks—how can he be so mean all of a sudden? He used to cut himself and knows it's an addiction which is hard to beat. "I thought you of all people would understand me, but I guess I was wrong. You don't give a rat's ass about my pain and what I'm going through."

He runs his fingers through his thick waves with a sigh. "Look, if you're so unhappy, do something about it, but stop waiting around for someone else to save you." His intense eyes burn into my skull. "Move away and start fresh, or find Jed and cut off his balls—anything—but stop being such a crybaby. We all have a lot of shit to deal with and your whining is getting on my nerves."

I glare at him in disbelief. He just turned into the same patronizing asshole as Luke when he yelled at me after my alleged suicide attempt. I want to push past him, but he blocks my way.

"Please, Kelsey, I didn't want to fight. Not today."

Trapped

He reaches for my hand, but I pull away, my whole body shaking with anger and disappointment. I can't even stand looking at him while the tears keep spilling from my eyes. He will never know how much his words sliced into my soul.

"I'll be locked up for four months." His voice is rough and laced with despair. "With good time, I should be out by Christmas. I promise I'll contact you then and we'll talk without the pressure we are both under at the moment."

I raise my head and find his eyes. "Don't bother. As far as I'm concerned, I never want to see you again."

His mouth contorts like someone just punched him in his stomach, but he gets out of my way when I take a step forward. I run right past him and up to my room, falling onto the bed while heavy sobs battle my body. The tears keep flowing and flowing until I have a bad hiccup and am barely able to breathe through my nose. I hate him, the way I hate everyone else—I am more than a fricking crybaby. After everything I've been through, I've earned the right to be miserable.

~~~~

When Luke finds me a few hours later, I'm still in shambles, feeling absolute pity for myself. The fight with Finn upset me more than I want to admit, but I am convinced that I was right and he was wrong. I don't understand how he could just blow up the way he did after everything I confided in him.

My face is buried in the pillow when Luke lowers himself on the bed next to me.

"Are you okay?"

"Yes," I grumble. "You were right about Finn all along. He's a conceited and selfish bastard."

Luke sighs. "There's something I have to tell you and you won't like it."

I roll on my side and look at him sullenly. "Not sure if I'm ready for any more bad news today."

His eyes squeeze shut; it is something that will make me angry. "Finn actually didn't beat up Jed with his friend, but with me."

"WHAT!"

He grimaces. "When it first happened, Jed ran to the cops and swore it was me. We were wearing ski masks, but I had no alibi, and with my track record, the police were going to arrest me. A friend of my dad's tipped us off, so Finn decided to step up to the plate and turn himself in. He knew the cops were after his friend for the longest, so he implicated him to get them off my back. If he hadn't done that, I could forget going to law school."

I lie still while the truth settles in. Finn must be under an unbearable pressure. "Who was his friend?"

"Some guy called Marcel Brown. He's a real big fish in the Portland drug gangs and I don't have a clue how Finn even knows him. Apparently, the feds have been after him for years, but never had anything on him until Finn pointed the finger."

My stomach turns to knots. Marcel will kill Finn for this, and if he doesn't get the chance, Tyrone will do the deed as soon as Finn gets out of jail. "What happened to him?"

Luke leans back in his chair. "Surprisingly, not much. He hired some hotshot lawyer from Portland who was even better than my dad, and since it was his first offense, he plea bargained the charge down to a misdemeanor and ninety days' jail." He shakes his head with a small sigh. "I still don't know why this guy stayed quiet. He could've easily taken this to trial, and if he had won, I would've been screwed since the cops would've started to investigate again. Finn must have had something on him. He really came through for me."

Trapped

I watch Luke through hooded eyes. "Marcel is really dangerous and I'm sure he'll make Finn pay for lying to the cops about him."

No wonder Finn was so worried—this stunt was even more reckless than beating up Jed. The thought of Finn and Marcel being together at the Androscoggin County Jail terrifies me and I feel awful about our fight. He should have told me about my brother's involvement.

I massage the bridge of my nose. "I have a bad headache and honestly need some time to digest this."

"I totally understand but wanted to tell you the truth about Finn so you won't be mad at him anymore."

I'm still upset about his hurtful words, but I would like to clear things up. "Could you tell him to come by tomorrow so we can talk?"

"As far as I know, he's going in right after his finals in the morning. His exams are the only reason the judge let him out in the first place. I'm sorry, but you'll have to wait until after you leave the hospital."

I will have to make this work—there's no way I want to be in here when Finn gets out of jail. Hopefully, he'll still want to talk to me after I told him I never wanted to see him again. My heart gives me a good knock on the head with a bat. I brought this on myself. For the next few months, I really need to get my act together and figure out what to do with the rest of my life.

Chapter 12

Over the next few weeks, I grit my teeth and get on with my therapy. My individual sessions with Dr. Malcom progress well, but I still struggle with my group therapy, staying quiet as a mouse. I just can't relate to the other patients, most of them deeply depressed women twice my age whose successful husbands cheat on them, or burned-out managers going through midlife crises. The younger patients, who had been around during the summer, have departed with the beginning of the new school year to return to their respective colleges. Their parents had used the hospital as a kind of boutique summer camp for individual character growth.

When constant rain starts battling the state in late September, my mood drops to an all-time low. Only the thought of Finn at the Androscoggin County Jail gets me up in the morning. Most of my spare time is spent staring at an almost empty piece of paper while chewing on a pen, pondering how to start out my apology. Only the words "Hey, Finn" stare back at me, and after the second week, I doubt they'll be joined by any more of my creations.

After an especially bad group session in which I snap at the counselor to leave me the hell alone, I am summoned to Dr. Malcom's office. Sure to be in trouble, I slump into the chair across from him, conjuring a rueful smile to show him that I am sorry.

"Well, Kelsey, Mirabelle told me about what happened at group therapy today. Apparently, things haven't been going so well."

My smile turns crooked. "Yeah, it's been tough."

Trapped

"Why do you think you struggle so much?" His smile is open and he has that fatherly tone that he always uses when he tries to dig around in my feelings.

"I guess I just don't have anything in common with the other patients. Their problems seem so—" I search for the right word but can't come up with one. "Odd," I finally mutter.

"Odd?" He blinks at me with a hint of irritation.

"Yeah, I just don't understand most of their problems." I giggle to get over the awkward hump when he frowns at me. "I mean, I'm not even married and I don't have a job. Their problems are like a foreign language to me."

His smile become wider; he likes my answer. "I think it shows that you really thought about this. That's good."

"I guess." I return an eager smile to show him that I'm trying my best here.

"In your case, Mirabelle and I actually agree that the group is not a good fit for you."

His statement surprises me, but I keep my poker face. If I play my cards right, maybe I get out of the group therapy in lieu of a few more individual sessions, which will definitely be a plus.

"However, in your therapy phase, group counseling is imperative," he continues.

I bite my lip to hide my disappointment.

"So that's why I've discussed with your parents sending you to a group specializing in teens outside this facility." He smiles when my jaw drops. "How would you like that?"

The prospect of leaving the hospital, even if only for a few hours, is amazing. I still haven't gotten the code for the keypad and have been feeling like a prisoner more and more.

"I think that would be great."

"Excellent." He pulls his calendar closer. "A former employee of mine runs a youth group in Portland twice a week in the evening. He has a space available and would welcome you to join them."

My temporary excitement is stalled in its tracks. "How do I get to Portland? I don't drive."

"Oh, your brother will take you. Your parents said he's available on those nights."

I grin. This is the best news I've had since I got admitted to this place. Luke had enrolled in fewer classes this semester to ensure he could visit me more regularly and this works in our favor. Riding down to Portland twice a week with him would be fun and make the whole ordeal of group therapy worth the effort. This could actually work.

~~~~

Three weeks later, I'm no longer sure if this group therapy has been such a good idea. The group is tough and most of us don't want to be there. We are twelve altogether, most of the others forced to attend as part of some court-imposed sanction. During every session so far, at least two girls have gotten into a fight, and Reggie, the counselor, has had his hands full to keep people in check. If Luke had not diligently dragged me here and stayed around the whole time, I would have ditched the group on more than one occasion.

The atmosphere during tonight's session is relaxed for a change. Everyone is slouched in their chairs with an eye on the clock over the door. The seconds are dwindling down in snail speed. I yawn behind my raised hand, staring sullenly at the rain-spattered window. It's surprising that the state hasn't drowned yet in a big water puddle.

I wonder what Finn is doing right this second. Luke told me that most inmates watch TV all day since this is apparently the only thing to do at the county jail. It will be torment for him, knowing how much he loves to read. On top of that, Marcel is in there, probably plotting how to beat him up. The thought is terrifying. Finn must be on edge, having to watch his back all the time.

When someone clears their throat, my head snaps around. This girl Hallie stands in front of me, holding up the stupid talking stick. It means that it's my turn next. Hallie is actually really nice, one of the few participants who is here voluntarily. Her parents died a few months ago and she's really struggling. Most of the time, her words are drowned out by her tears. The other girls roll their eyes at her, calling her a crybaby behind her back. The word struck me. There's a connection between us, even if only by the mere fact that Finn used that exact same phrase when we had our fight.

I gaze at the talking stick. "Pass," I mutter, grinning at Reggie to see his reaction.

"Sorry, Kelsey, but you already got your three free passes. Time's up. You need to share something with the group."

A sigh is stifled when my fingers wrap around the stick. "Fine." I glance around as Hallie returns to her seat, and to my dismay, most of the other girls have changed from disinterested to fully focused. Judging from the curiosity in their eyes, they've been trying to figure out what's wrong with me. This will be excruciating.

"Well." I suck in a deep breath, trying to hear my words over my sudden pounding heartbeat. A mouthful of air is swallowed down to help with my breathing. "A few months ago, I was admitted to the hospital after I cut myself. The doctors thought I tried to kill myself, but that's not true. Doing better now." My gaze meets Reggie's. "That's pretty much all there's to know about me." My eyes are pleading. Surely I made enough of an effort.

His smile is mild. It's his "I'm just getting started" face. "So why do you cut, Kelsey?"

I shrug. "Don't know."

"Man, cutting is so stupid," one of the other girls jumps in. "It doesn't solve anything."

"It kills the pain." I toss her a dark look. "Not that you'd understand."

"Now, now, no fighting, girls." Reggie raises his hand to take some of the sparks out of the sudden explosive atmosphere hanging over the room.

"What's the pain you want to kill?" he asks next.

All eyes are on me. My cheeks are burning when I lower my gaze, studying the patterns of the linoleum to fight my sudden rising tears. "Three and a half years ago, I was kidnapped and raped. I just don't seem to be able to move on. Every time I breathe, it hurts. I look at myself in the mirror and all I see is this dirty and used girl. So I cut. In that moment, it's like all that pain in my heart is lifted, the physical pain so strong that I feel alive again. I breathe because I have to, but it doesn't hurt anymore. It just feels good."

Silence hangs over the room. When I raise my head, most girls are avoiding my gaze. One girl is crying. All of a sudden, Hallie pushes up the sleeve of her sweater, exposing several scars.

"I cut," she says, her smile timid. "It helps me forget."

"Me, too." With a sigh, the girl next to me leans back in the chair.

There is general nodding around. An awkward laugh sucks up some of the pressing tension.

"Okay." Reggie's eyes dart around the room. "Show of hands. Who is or has ever engaged in any type of self-harm?"

Hand by hand goes up and for the first time, I don't feel alone. We might all come from different backgrounds and have different problems, but on the inside, we have more in common than what's on the surface. Only the girl who called me stupid is left in the end before grudgingly admitting that she used to binge eat chocolate and throw up to deal with her own problems.

"Well, I guess over these next few weeks, we'll be exploring how we can beat these inner demons that drive us to harm our own bodies." Reggie glances around. "What do you think, guys?"

His suggestion is met with more nodding. The scent of a general fighting spirit is in the air. I grin from ear to ear, knowing Finn would be proud. I'm on the right track.

~~~~

If I had thought my recovery would get easier, I had something else coming. Though group therapy is no longer a total drag, revisiting the past proves incredibly painful. Nightmares are battling my dreams almost every night, leaving me in a constant state of exhaustion. I dread falling asleep, afraid of Jed's eyes in the dark. Keeping the light on all night helps a little, but I still wake up at least once from my own screams.

Dr. Malcom claims that this is just a phase which will disappear again, though I have my doubts. His answer is a stringent exercise plan to keep my mind occupied on other things, draining my body of its remaining energy to help me sleep better. Roy hires a fitness trainer who shoos me around the hospital grounds every morning until I'm ready to throw up. After finally getting the combination for the keypad, afternoon strolls on the pebble beach around the lake are added to the program together with Pilates sessions in the early evenings to "cleanse my soul." Surprisingly, it works and I feel better about myself than I have in a long time.

Reggie assigns us buddies like they do in AA who we are supposed to call in case we have the urge to self-harm again. I get paired with Hallie and after I get my phone back, we settle on a few Skype calls to get to know each other better. Though I enjoy chatting with her for short periods of time, I realize we have very little in common. She is the typical carefree fifteen-year-old, busy with school and crushing on this new guy she met. The envy burns that she is so easily regaining control of her life while I still battle with my nightmares and haunting memories.

Unable to relate, I withdraw in my shell again, my need to prove myself to Finn my only driving force. Deep down, I know I should be doing these things for myself, but I figure that the spark will eventually catch. As long as I am getting better, who cares about the reasons? Luke is also thrilled with my progress, and so is my mom, which gives me another boost.

One night when we drive back to the clinic from therapy, he brings up California.

"I should hear from Stanford soon. Have you given it anymore thought if you want to come with me?"

"Yeah." My walks had given me plenty of time to think, but I'm still undecided. "Truthfully, Luke, I just want to make it through this therapy and get out of the clinic before making any decisions about the rest of my life." I omit that I also want to talk to Finn, not sure if I should leave him behind if we rekindle our friendship. Though Hallie and the therapy group are great, he's still the only person who ever understood what I've been going through.

"You know I'll always have your back," Luke says, giving me this look like he knows exactly what I'm thinking about.

"You shouldn't base major life decisions on advice of someone you hardly know."

"I promise I won't." My fingers stroke alongside his arm and he tosses me a sweet smile. "I just want to look at things from different angles, that's all."

"I understand." Though the smile is still on his lips, the temperature in the car has dropped a few degrees, like he's angry. "I just feel I'm losing you and I don't like it."

"You'll always hold a special place in my heart." I laugh when he wiggles his eyebrows, nudging him hard in his shoulder. "I mean as a brother, you moron."

"I'm just worried about you, Kels. The thought of not being able to see you whenever I want to so I can make sure you're okay, is just"—he clicks his tongue—"daunting, I guess."

My head snuggles against his shoulder as far as the stretching seatbelt permits. "Have I told you that you're the best big brother ever?" I gaze up at him from under my eyelashes, snickering when his lips start to twitch.

"Let's see." He rubs his chin, tossing me a playful smile. "About a million times."

I snicker again. "I guess we should invite my mom and your dad for dinner when I'm back home and thank them that they got hitched."

"I suppose we should."

I close my eyes, shifting my head around until I find a comfortable spot on his arm. He hums along to the song on the radio. It's just like old times. Going to California with him might ultimately turn out for the best. There is no way I could ever imagine a life without my big brother in it.

Chapter 13

They finally let me out of the hospital the week before Thanksgiving. The discharge papers confirm that "the patient has been sufficiently stabilized to no longer present a danger to herself or others," but this opinion is qualified with the recommendation that I should "continue with further therapy under the supervision of a trained health care professional." This means that I will get to see Dr. Stromberg again and continue with my group therapy sessions in Portland, which moves California further up the list. A new start could also mean a drastic cut in therapy sessions.

While I was gone, my mom and Roy took the opportunity to search my room for possible self-harm weapons with the result that the razor blades and other sharp objects were removed. My walls were repainted with bright, cheerful colors, and a vibrant, fluffy comforter covers my bed. If optimism is not something that comes naturally to me at the moment, they will make sure to shove it down my throat. Everything is set for me to resume an easy and untroubled life, yet the turmoil still bubbling inside me is unwittingly ignored since I have been doing "so much better." Maybe they hope that if they close their eyes to my true feelings, they'll evaporate in thin air together with my memories.

I sulk around the house for a few days, hoping for Luke to show, but he's staying with a buddy in Portland to work on a big term project that is due after the holidays. Roy is busy with a murder trial and hardly home, so it's only me and my mom for a change. A few times, she tries to reach out to me, but I'm still holding a grudge that she had me committed to the hospital. Her mother-daughter bonding efforts fail.

Trapped

After all the exercise I endured at the clinic, cabin fever gets the better of me in the end. I venture outside after agreeing with my mom on a new check-in routine since Jed has still been sighted around town on a few occasions. She insists on hourly phone calls with an additional call if I spot Jed or feel threatened in any way, which includes anxiety attacks. Though I feign disapproval, I'm secretly thrilled about the extra layer of protection.

It's a crisp winter's day with a bright blue sky, the distinct smell of snow in the air. A light breeze bites the tip of my nose and my eyes water from the chilly wind. When my fingertips get numb and my toes start to prickle uncomfortably in the woolly socks, I come to the conclusion that I've had enough exercise for today. With a sigh, I am about to turn around when my eyes fall on the Ice Princess. It's by far the best ice cream parlor in town. It also sells a killer hot chocolate with loads of whipped cream all year around.

The sudden urge for a special treat hits me and I stroll across the street without hesitation. The café is warm and cozy, but also packed with kids from the high school. They stare at me, some with their mouths open, as soon as I enter. For a second, I want to spin around and run, but my newfound determination to not allow even the smallest challenge to trip me up prevails. Proud of myself, I head toward the counter.

I avoid glancing around the diner when I order. "One large hot chocolate with marshmallows and cream to go, please."

Eyes burn into my back from every table. I begin to twitch under the stares while I wait, folding a five-dollar bill into a small square before unfolding it again. More than once, I curse myself for even stepping foot into the place in the middle of the afternoon, but there is no backing away now. It will only be a few minutes. I desperately swing my mental pom poms, my gaze fixed on the money in my hand.

Someone leans against the counter next to me. "Hey, Kelsey, what's up?"

I don't even give him the benefit of a glance. "All good, Justin. How about you?"

"I'm great. Working over at the plant and taking a couple of courses at the community college."

I feel his eyes drilling into the side of my skull.

"Good for you, Justin."

A girl giggles beside him. "Ask her," she mumbles and I recognize Cynthia's voice.

"My girlfriend wants to know if it's true that they locked you up in the loony bin?" His tone is taunting; he can barely stifle a laugh.

My face is on fire as I begin to fold the five-dollar bill again. "Not sure how this is any of your business."

He chuckles. "Come on, Kelsey. You can just admit that you're a total nutcase. We all know."

Chuckles follow his words; everyone must've been listening. I quickly wipe my eyes to prevent a tear from getting loose—the hot chocolate is totally not worth this humiliation. Ready to take flight, I am about to push past him to get to the door when a calm voice comes to my rescue.

"Yo, I hope y'all not givin' my friend a hard time."

My head snaps up and I find Marcel right in front of me, glaring at Justin. Sober and in broad daylight, he appears even more menacing than at Tyrone's house. Though he is at least half a head shorter than his opponent, his shoulders are probably twice as wide, and solid muscles bulge under his shirt. A long scar I didn't notice before runs from his right eyebrow to the middle of his clean-shaven skull.

Justin glances around as a few of his friends slowly rise from their seats. With a triumphant grin, he gazes at Marcel.

"And who are you?" There are a few snickers and he gains momentum. "Kelsey's new pimp?"

A small smile plays on the gangbanger's lips. "Man, you really have no clue who you're dealin' with." Casually, he raises his shirt by a couple of inches, exposing the grip of a gun. "Sure you're ready to play with the big boys?" His voice is so cold that the temperature in the café drops by at least a few degrees.

All color leaves Justin's face. "I'll call the cops if you threaten me again."

That gets a chuckle out of Marcel. "Y'all little country boys think you're so tough, but y'all don't know what's out there in the real world." He eyes Cynthia from top to bottom. "Fuck with me or Kelsey again and I'll smoke you before showing your girl here what a real pimp looks like."

When he takes a step forward, Justin jumps back, knocking hard against the side table next to the counter. The sugar basket develops a mind of its own, soon decorating the floor in white and pink packs, and is quickly joined by the stash of napkins. Justin's face flushes when he bends down to gather up the mess.

Though I should probably be appalled by Marcel's behavior, I can't help but gloat. Justin got exactly what he deserved. His face could compete with any tomato, and judging from the glint of fear in his eyes, Marcel made an impression. Cynthia's gaze is glued to the floor, a few droplets dripping off her chin and splattering on the tiles.

The waitress sets my hot chocolate on the counter. "Look, sir, I don't want any trouble and must ask you to leave."

"That's no problem, ma'am." Marcel gives her a beaming smile. "I'll go as soon as this douche apologizes to my friend." His attention returns to Justin. From the now grim expression on his face, there's no doubt that he's done playing. A physical altercation will be next if he doesn't get his way.

Justin avoids my eyes. "I'm—I'm sorry, Kelsey." His voice is trembling.

I decide he has suffered enough and reach for the hot chocolate.

Marcel places a ten-dollar bill on the counter. "For your troubles, ma'am. Keep the change."

With his hand on my elbow, he guides me toward the door. All eyes burn into my back just the same way as they did when I arrived, but this time, they feel different. There is a smell of fear which I relish. Marcel might be a violent drug runner, but in this moment, he is my hero. No one is mocking me—there is nothing but respect with him around. For a second, I wonder how it would be to be his girlfriend before I discard the idea with horror.

When the cold air hits me outside, I come to my senses. He thinks I'm Finn's woman and likely in Stonehenge to take revenge. He probably just rescued me from Justin so he could harm me instead.

I wiggle myself free from his grip. "What are you doing here, Marcel?"

He takes a step back, throwing up his hands. "Hoo, I expected a thank you, not this attitude, girl."

I remember the gun in the waistband of his pants. "Sorry, I'm just surprised to see you."

His gaze is intense. "You're afraid of me. Why?"

"For starters, you're carrying a concealed weapon and threatened the life of my ex-boyfriend." I hug my chest, wondering if he would shoot me in the back if I ran. "Finn got you to spend time in jail and you must be absolutely pissed. Wouldn't you be scared under those circumstances?"

He actually laughs at me. "I guess, but you got this wrong. I'm not pissed at Finn."

I arch an eyebrow. "You're not?"

"No. When this stuff happened with your stepbrother, he rang me and called in a favor. Tyrone wasn't thrilled that I had to spend some time in jail, but he got over it, so that's it."

"So you don't care that you went to jail?"

"Nope." He gives me a small smile. "Finn and I go way back and he helped my nephew out when he was in a bind. I owed him."

Stunned by such loyalty among thugs, my respect for him rises a few notches. "So what are you doing here?"

"I was on my way to Finn's uncle's to find out if there's any news about Finn's condition. The cops have him all locked up in the hospital, and since I'm not a relative, I can't get any information from the doctors."

I frown. "Why is Finn in the hospital? I thought he was in jail."

He sucks in a deep breath. "You don't know." It's not a question. When his eyes find me, his gaze is full of pity.

My heartbeat almost comes to a standstill. "Marcel, what's going on? Is Finn alright?"

If something happened to him, it's my fault. He was only in jail because of me. If I hadn't cut myself because of the book, he would never have beaten up Jed and gotten into trouble.

Marcel sighs. "While I was at the jail, no one dared to touch him and all was good. Last week after I got out, the guards let it slip to the others that he was a convicted sex offender and had raped a young boy. Guys in jail don't like that type of stuff, so they beat him up."

My stomach turns to knots as tears fill my eyes. "Is it bad?"

"He's still in the ICU and they don't know." As my tears begin to fall, he shuffles his feet. "I'm sorry, Kelsey."

"Why didn't the guards help him?" I ask between sobs.

"That's not how it works in jail. When it comes to sex offenders, everyone looks the other way. They're considered scum."

I still don't understand. "But Finn never raped anyone."

"He pled guilty"—he grimaces—"so for them, that's good enough."

We stand out in the freezing cold while I continue to weep in the middle of the street like a big baby, but for once, I don't care. Let people think what they want to think—I need to grieve for my friend until I feel better. The warmth from the hot chocolate is comforting, and with anger, I toss the cup into the bin. I don't deserve a treat. If I had just stopped and thought of anyone but myself for once, Finn would probably be right here with me.

Marcel just lets me be. I'm sure he is at a total loss about how to soothe a crying woman. He must think I'm either crazy or pathetic. When I finally settle down, I wipe my tears away with the sleeve of my coat before fumbling in my pockets for a tissue to blow my nose.

"Can you call me later and let me know how he is?"

"Sure thing."

I give him my number and he programs it right into the phone. Just before he takes off, I call out to him. "You should really be careful with that gun. This is a small town and the cops focus on outsiders. You could end up in jail again."

"Don't worry, I have a concealed weapons permit." He laughs at my dumbfounded face. "I work officially as a PI."

My jaw drops. "Seriously?"

"Yep, no joke. Got my license a couple of years ago."

"What about your conviction?"

"That don't matter. Only felons can't own firearms under federal and state law. Tyrone owns half the police force on top of that, so no worries."

Trapped

I grin. Why am I not surprised about this latest revelation? I hate to admit it, but if Marcel wasn't a gangbanger, he could potentially grow on me. In a sense, it's scary that I currently prefer the company of criminals over regular folks.

My steps are heavy on my way home, my hands buried deep inside the pockets of my coat. The wind has picked up and I battle against the arctic air with every step. It numbs my brain and in a way, that's a good thing. Emotions rage through me—guilt, confusion, and disgust—not only for what happened to Finn but also about myself. I don't deserve a friend like him.

When I get home, I hide in my bed under the bright comforter, which doesn't lift my spirits. My heart is aching. I'm so worried that I am sick to my stomach. Nothing seems to distract me—neither the music I begin to blast nor the movie I start to watch on the laptop. Finn's angry eyes, the way they were the last time I saw him, scorch my mind like a flame of vengeance.

Finally, Marcel's call comes in. His voice is muffled by the engine of a car. He must be on his way back to Portland.

"Good news. Finn's out of the ICU and the doctors said he will fully recover. He should be out of the hospital before Christmas. The jail will probably let him go straight away. Tyrone will sue their asses and they might even throw some money at him."

I can breathe again without the guilt. "Thanks, Marcel."

"Don't mention it."

I cut the line and sink back into my pillow. The room is spinning and the knots in my stomach slowly unravel. The elation that Finn will be okay burns in my heart. Now I can only hope that he'll be able to forgive me.

Chapter 14

It has started to snow. I sit in the window seat that my father built for me when I was little, watching the snowflakes whirl around as they slowly cover the dirt with fresh whiteness. I used to hate snow. It meant being stuck in the house for days during a bad storm and ruining my shoes the minute I ventured outside again. The hat my mom made me wear never worked well with my hairstyle, and the warm sweaters I forced myself into scratched my neck until the itch drove me nuts.

Now I love the snow. It allows me to hide in my room without having to make excuses. The therapy sessions have been suspended until the new year and my mom doesn't expect me to leave the house or help with the groceries. She usually warms up some precooked meals from the freezer and we can eat whenever and wherever we like. This gives me even more opportunities to stay in my room and sulk.

The guilt and worry about Finn have been consuming me. A few times, I've started a new letter and even considered calling his uncle to beg him to take me to the hospital to see him, but my fear of rejection always prevailed in the end. That would be a setback from which I wouldn't recover easily and not contacting him keeps the hope alive.

I lean my cheek against the cool glass of the window, my warm breath fogging it up. In a forgotten time, I used to draw little hearts with Justin's and my initials on the smooth surface. It seems so long ago that we were crazily in love. Back then, I never imagined that he'd become such a bully or that my other friends would just turn their backs on me. Now, the only one left is Luke and maybe, if I'm lucky, Finn.

The soft sound of Christmas music floats up from downstairs, accompanied by the sweet scent of freshly baked cookies. I love the chocolate chip kind, especially warm from the oven, since my mom uses those big morsels that melt deliciously in my mouth. My stomach growls just at the thought of them. I can't believe it's only three more days until Christmas Eve. Maybe I should try to be a little bit more social this year. My constant foul mood has been hard on my mom and Roy, and at least for one day, I could make an effort to be part of the family again.

The ping from an incoming email startles me. I eye the laptop with frustration. Deep down, I hope that Finn is out of the hospital, trying once again to cheer me up, yet there is always the chance that it's just another spam message. In any event, I will have to move to find out. That alone is an unappealing thought. After a few minutes of glaring at the screen in a desperate attempt to open the mail with telekinesis, I decide that I will never develop paranormal abilities and get up with a sigh.

My hand rattles the mouse to wake up the computer when I slump into my chair. There is a little red "one" next to the inbox. I click on it repeatedly with a low growl to determine if my latest physical exertions are justified. Squinting at the email heading, I frown. Some unknown sender, not Finn, claims to have "An Early Christmas Present" for me. Disappointment washes over me as I bite back the tears—he's probably still mad at me.

For a moment, I consider just moving the new email to the trash folder, but something makes me click on it. It has a link to a private VideoTube video and might be one of those electronic greeting cards. Maybe Finn remembered after all.

My heart beats in my throat and a few butterflies in my stomach even make a fleeting appearance while the video buffers. I fully expect to see some singing Santa giving me a cheesy holiday greeting, but my insides freeze when the video begins to play. Tied up on a bed, Hallie stares back at me with wide terrified eyes, her makeup smudged from her tears. Sobs shake her fragile frame, a gag in her mouth preventing her from screaming. Bruises cover parts of her body, but I can't see any blood.

My stomach heaves; I can hardly keep in the bile. Images of me, lying in a similar bed, invade my mind before a huge claw gets ahold of my chest, squeezing hard. When I start to gasp for air, my hand flies toward the mouse to stop the torture just as the video ends with a message.

You can save her, honeybun—just give me a call. 207-555-4502. Don't involve the cops or she dies. Merry Christmas.

Nausea finally prevails and I sprint into the bathroom, retching into the toilet. When I'm done, I lean against the wall, my whole body shivering. Tears drip onto my bare legs. I try to fight the oncoming terror by sucking in short gasps of air, but the oxygen is hard to retain in my burning lungs. What if the nightmare begins all over again? With a low wail, my forehead comes to rest on my arms.

Pictures race in my mind of me crying in pain while Jed thrusts himself inside me, followed by my shrill pleadings that are muffled when Napoleon wraps his hands around my throat. The images melt together like a horror movie. A scream runs over my lips while I fight for air again, a spiral of darkness closing in on my mind.

I force myself on my feet and stand by the sink. This is where I used to watch how the blood oozed from my veins when I cut myself, but not this time. To spite me, the room spins faster and faster. I splash cold water into my eyes so I won't faint. Pain throbs through my head, but my breath becomes more even. It is not enough. The pictures still flash rapidly in front of my eyes and I need them to stop. The only way to battle them is pain. Hoping to snap myself out of my nightmare, my fingernails claw into my palms as my teeth begin to dig into my skin.

This time it works. I close my eyes and breathe in deeply, letting the air slowly escape through the corners of my mouth. After I count to ten and reopen my eyes, the room comes into focus. Burning pain radiates through my arm into my shoulder and I laugh. It feels good to have some control again. My shirt sticks to my back and I shiver, but I realize that my body reacts to the cold and not the panic.

I wash out my mouth and splatter more water on my face before returning to the bedroom. Squatting down in front of the desk, my eyes glare at the laptop. Sharp pain stabs at my heart at the thought of replaying the video—I should tell Roy or at least Luke. They'll know what to do, but in all likelihood, they will also insist on involving the authorities. Roy is close friends with Larouge, who still holds jurisdiction in my old case. He never got over the blow with the warrant and would probably itch to get something on Jed. Knowing him, he will get Hallie killed within a matter of minutes.

The grandfather clock on the wall keeps ticking monotonously while I try desperately to figure out what to do. If Jed kills Hallie, her death will be on my hands. I alone have the power to save her. Every day during my captivity, I prayed that someone would come for me and take me home, but no one ever did. It was a horrible feeling. I can't just let Hallie go to her slaughter without at least making an effort to help her.

With a new determination, I grab my phone off the nightstand before rewinding the video just far enough to get the phone number.

Jed answers on the first ring. "Hello, honeybun. It's nice to hear your voice."

His snarling words almost make me drop the phone.

"What do you want, Jed?" My stomach is in knots, yet I'm surprised by the calmness in my voice.

He chuckles crudely. "I want you, honeybun. Napoleon and I bought you a great Christmas present and are eager to spend the holidays with you. I mean, you can't blame us. Of all the little bitches around, you're still the best in the sack."

Nausea crawls up my throat as my breath accelerates. I close my eyes, forcing myself to focus. "Please Jed, just let her go. Haven't you caused enough misery for everyone?"

"Forget it, honeybun. You have thirty minutes to get to my house, and if you don't show, Hallie is dead. Don't bother bringing the cops with you—she ain't there. She's with Napoleon, and if I don't call at certain times, he'll kill her. It's all up to you. If you cooperate and do what we tell you, we'll let her go."

He cuts the line and I sink to the floor. I can't do this. I sob into the crook of my elbow, wishing I was dead.

I don't know how long I dwell in self-pity before the truth finally hits home. This will be my one chance at redemption, the one way to get my revenge. The anxiety is still keeping a grip on me, but the force that used to hold onto my own free will so tightly and crippled me in any possible way has eased. I can almost think clearly—for the first time in over three years.

A fuzzy memory enters my mind when Finn's words break through: *If you're so unhappy, do something about it, but stop waiting around for someone else to save you. Move away and start fresh, or find Jed and cut off his balls—anything—but stop being such a crybaby. We all have a lot of shit to deal with and your whining is getting on my nerves.*

Back then, I could have slapped him, but now, I understand what he meant. Bad things happen to good people all the time and you can either allow your demons to destroy you or fight back. It's time for me to crawl out of the hole I dug for myself and do what I should have done a long time ago—put Jed Edwards in his place and not allow him or anyone else to run my life. It's time to stand up and say e*nough is enough.*

~~~~

Fifteen minutes later, I am in the woods on my way to Jed's cabin. Roy and my mom were in the living room, decorating the Christmas tree, when I snuck out the back door. I left a note on Luke's pillow with some bullshit story that I need some time to myself to work things out. At first, I was going to tell him the truth, but I was scared that Jed will find out. Roy has always figured that someone from the Stonehenge Police Department had tipped Jed off about the warrant, and if he truly has a friend on the force, Hallie will be dead. Luke hopefully knows me well enough to realize that something is wrong when he finds the letter and it won't take much to convince my mom to call the police once I disappear without a trace.

The night is freezing. I cuddle into my warm winter coat, my eyes fixed on the foggy breath streaming from my mouth. At the last minute, I grabbed a screwdriver from the garage as a weapon, which is buried deep inside my pocket. My fingers curl around the handle as my walk turns into a jog. With every step, my grip tightens as I imagine ramming the metal through Jed's eye. That's what Finn would do.

It has stopped snowing, but the wind has picked up, biting at the tip of my nose and ears. I wish I put on a hat and a scarf. My eyes wander to the sky when I pause at a clearing to catch my breath. There are hardly any clouds and hundreds of stars twinkle above, a full moon hanging lazily over the trees like a big fat orange. This is so cliché—the perfect night for one of those werewolf or vampire encounters. A chill runs through me when I ask myself what I'm even doing here. This is not me—

I'm a chicken. As I spin around to head back, Hallie's scared eyes flash in my mind. I grit my teeth. I can do this.

The creek gurgles in the distance as I get closer to Jed's cabin. This path is full of bad memories. I hold my breath before exhaling with a small groan. Fine mist temporarily steals my vision and blurs the picture of Jed walking me here for my exercise when I was hooked up to the dog chain.

I force myself to continue, my heart pounding heavier and heavier with every step. I fight the oncoming anxiety attack by focusing on the image of Hallie on the bed. If I lose my sanity, she'll be dead.

"I have to go on," I mumble to myself, repeating the words over and over to drive myself forward. The snow crunches under my feet. I'm almost startled to death by the barking howl of a coyote. One last turn and the woods open up to the familiar sight.

The cabin lies peacefully in the darkness. There are no lights other than the moon from above. I hesitate for a moment before stepping out of the protection of the forest, almost running when I close the gap between the tree line and the porch of Jed's home. By the time my fingers wrap around the porch rail, I'm out of breath.

"Jed, where are you?" I try to keep the fright out of my words, but my voice still trembles. My hand fumbles with the handle of the screwdriver—I am ready for him.

"I'm right here, honeybun."

Every part of me turns numb when he slowly approaches from behind. I am glad to hold onto something, or I would have collapsed. My grip around the rail tightens until my knuckles turn white at the same time my fingers clamp around the screwdriver. A hitch in my throat cuts off my oxygen supply— who am I fooling? I'm so not ready.

His warm breath grazes my neck when he halts behind me. "I knew you'd come." His voice is hoarse and full of longing. "I can't tell you how much I've missed you, honeybun."

I'm frozen, my stomach revolting when he leans in and nibbles my ear. His hand glides into my free coat pocket and pulls out my phone, which disappears into his own pocket.

"You should be more careful." His words are scolding. "I followed you all the way from your house and you didn't even notice. There're some crazy folks out there. You should really glance over your shoulder once in a while."

His hand moves over to my other pocket, jerking on my arm to free my hand. This is my last opportunity.

With a low growl, I turn, my arm rising with the screwdriver in my hand. The sharp metal tip glimmers in the moonlight before I stab at his face. Without any effort, he blocks my blow, his reflexes still as impeccable as they were during his boxing days. He chuckles when two of his fingers dig into the soft centers of my wrist like pincers. I cry out, letting go of the screwdriver as pain shoots up my arm. He doesn't loosen his clawing grip until after his feet kick my weapon far away into the snow.

"That was really stupid of you," he hisses. His arms wrap around my waist, holding me firmly in place when I try to wiggle free. The angry glow in his eyes reminds me of burning coals. "I should call Napoleon and tell him to punish Hallie for this stunt."

"Please, Jed, I'm sorry."

His fingers run alongside my jawbone. "Swear you'll behave. I promised Napoleon I'd deliver you undamaged, and it'd be such a shame if I had to break my word."

A few tears spring loose and trickle down my cheek. "If I come with you, do you swear you'll let Hallie go?"

"I do, honeybun." His tone is soothing. "Don't worry about a thing."

Even though I have my doubts, my chances to overpower him without a weapon are nonexistent. For the moment, all I can do is play along.

His arm supports me while we make our way to his van. I stumble along with wobbly knees, my legs barely under my command. He buckles me in before kissing my cheek.

"Smile, honeybun. The party is just starting."

Smiling is the last thing on my mind; I'm about to throw up all over the car. As the engine starts and the van sways forward, the feeling of total helplessness spreads once again in my chest before this incredible will to live takes over. I have two choices—die or fight to retake my life. On second thought, I fully intend to go with the latter.

Chapter 15

As we drive through the night, the icicles in my stomach multiply with every passing minute. I try to keep my mind off what is ahead, glaring out of the window to avoid looking at Jed. Soft Christmas music plays on the radio. When the song "I'll Be Home for Christmas" comes on, I bite back the tears. There won't be any holiday cheer for me—not this year.

A few times, Jed's eyes fall upon me. "You okay, honeybun?"

The nerve to even ask that question. I choose to ignore him, though I would have liked to flip him the finger.

When we get to the highway, he heads north.

"Where're you taking me?" Once again, I'm stunned by the calmness in my voice, so contrary to the raging fear that chills every fiber of my body.

"Tacoma Lakes. It's real pretty up there."

It's a popular vacation spot just north of Lewiston, maybe about a forty-five minute ride from Stonehenge. The area consists of five lakes, connected by small water passages, which are surrounded by nothing but dense woods and swamps. In the wintertime, it is totally deserted since most of the cabins are not suitable for all-year occupation. It will be a tough place to escape from.

Roy took the family up there a few times when I was younger to go canoeing. We barbecued on the shore and roasted marshmallows by the fire. The entire waterfront is private, but his brothers own a couple of houses up there where we spent a few long weekends on Jimmy Pond. Fond memories—soon to be replaced by new, horrific ones.

Jed turns up the heat in the van. Usually, the humming of an engine puts me right to sleep, but tonight, my heavy heartbeat thumping painfully against my rib cage keeps me awake.

"You comfortable?" Jed asks.

I don't want to think about it and refuse to respond.

He takes his right hand off the steering wheel. It lands on my thigh. I go rigid, but he doesn't stop there. Caressing the inside of my leg, his fingers move toward my crotch until my own hands stop him.

"Don't."

He exhales with a huff. "I told you to behave. Don't make me stop this car and tie you up. I swear you'll regret it."

When I turn my head to look at him, my vision is blurred from my tears. "Please, Jed."

"What did you expect? Did you think we'd all just have a Christmas ham and go home? Come on, honeybun. Just don't fight it."

Of course I knew that coerced sex would be on the program, but I had hoped that I would at least have a few days to adjust. This would've given me time to come up with an escape plan, or at least, provide me with an opportunity to mentally prepare myself for what is to come. Yet I doubt that anyone can ever prepare themselves for rape.

Luckily, he doesn't start again and we continue our ride in silence. The highway has been cleared from the snow, but he still drives well below the speed limit. Luke told me once that cops are on the lookout for any unusual behavior and cautious drivers are flagged since they are often drunk. When the siren wails behind us, I'm not even surprised.

Jed shoots me a warning look. "One wrong word and Hallie is dead." He pulls over in the breakdown lane with the trooper right behind him. Fumbling in the glove compartment for his paperwork, he lowers the window at the same time to talk to the officer who is cautiously approaching.

"Good evening, sir." The trooper tips the rim of his wide-brimmed hat when his eyes fall on me. "Ma'am."

"What's the problem, officer?" Jed asks, his fingers tapping the steering wheel. "I know I wasn't speeding."

"You swerved back there," the trooper claims. "Could I see your license and registration?"

Jed hands him the required documents.

The trooper inspects them closely. "Have you been drinking tonight?"

"No, sir." Jed gives him a winning smile as he grabs my hand, squeezing it gently. "My girlfriend is not twenty-one yet, so we don't do that stuff."

I stare ahead, afraid that the cop will notice the unrest which is spreading in my body like wildfire. If Jed gets arrested, Napoleon will kill Hallie. I have to stay calm and not show panic, yet my right eye twitches the way it usually does when I'm anxious. My chest tightens under the growing tension. I suck in a deep breath to relax. An anxiety attack is the last thing I need.

"Are you okay, ma'am?" The trooper must have been watching me closely.

I finally turn to him with a wide smile. "Yes. Everything's fine."

He wrinkles his forehead, but his attention focuses back on Jed. "Where're you heading?"

Jed is thrown off for just a second. "To Bangor to visit my aunt for the holidays. She just lost my uncle and is all alone."

The trooper's face softens—he's actually buying Jed's bullshit story. "Well, that's nice. It's rare these days that young kids like yourself still worry about family." He hands Jed his license and registration and tips his hat again. "Have a safe journey and Merry Christmas." With that, he turns back to his own car.

Jed closes the window and chuckles. "What an idiot. Did you see his face? He almost cried when I told him that crap about my aunt. Old people really crack me up."

I couldn't help but giggle in a high-pitched tone the way I sometimes do when I'm really nervous. He does have a point, although the trooper wasn't that old—maybe in his early fifties like Roy.

He takes my laughter as a sign of comfort and squeezes my hand again. "You know, honeybun, if you hadn't dated Justin, I would've probably asked you out. You and I would've made a great couple." His eyes find mine and deep longing pools within them.

For the first time I realize how lonely he must be.

"You can be great fun and are really smart," he continues. "Too bad we didn't get to know each other under different circumstances."

I break eye contact by staring out the passenger side window. His words totally creep me out. "That was your choice, Jed. You didn't have to kidnap me."

He starts up the car. "That was actually Napoleon's idea. I just tagged along for the fun."

I glance at him; this is my big opportunity. He seems in a chatty mood and might spill the beans. "Who is he? Napoleon, I mean."

A small smile twitches on his lips as he pulls back onto the highway. "Oh, it's someone you know."

I figured that much. "Is it Drake?"

"Maybe." He laughs softly. "Who else do you think?"

"Dunno." There has always been one suspect on my mind, but it is just too gruesome to imagine. "Justin perhaps."

The suspicion first formed during the aftermath. After my rescue, Justin was distant, like he didn't care if I was safe or not. All he wanted was to score with me, and he refused to accept that I couldn't stand being touched. When he broke it off, he even told me that he didn't understand my problem. I wasn't a virgin any longer, so sex shouldn't be a big deal. His words hurt me to the core and made me feel totally worthless.

Jed's eyes stay fixed on the road. "Interesting guess. What makes you think that?"

I search his face for some kind of sign which would confirm my hunch, but he doesn't even flinch. "Well, he told my brother and all the other guys that I was a total prude and that he couldn't wait to take my V-card. Maybe he took matters into his own hands to speed things up."

The smile is back on Jed's lips. "Interesting. I'm surprised your brother let him get away with it, being your big protector and all."

Luke had been furious and put him in his place. "He gave him a black eye."

Jed snorts. "That's your brother all right." His jaw is clenched so tightly that his teeth are grinding together. "There's just one problem with your theory. I absolutely hate Justin's guts. What makes you think I would even give him the time of day, let alone kidnap a girl with him? He sent his fucking dog after me and almost killed me."

This has always been the flaw in my premise, but not to a point where it has erased my suspicion. "Desperate times make for the strangest allies. Look at World War II when Roosevelt joined forces with Stalin. It happens."

There is an amused twinkle in his eyes. "You do know your history. That's certainly something you and Napoleon have in common."

"So is that a yes?"

"You know, there's someone else you haven't considered."

I frown. "Oh yeah. Who's that?"

"Your new friend, Finn."

"Finn didn't even live in Stonehenge when you kidnapped me."

"True." I can tell he's having fun with this. "But he and his brother visited their uncle in the summer all the time, even came up here during some of the other school vacations and on long weekends. Finn and I used to work in Andrew's shop together, fixing up old cars."

I gasp.

There's triumph on his face. "I guess he forgot to mention that little detail."

For a moment, I'm totally thrown off course. I recall the conversations I had with Finn about my ordeal. He genuinely seemed shocked and appalled. There's no way this could have all been an act.

"If he was Napoleon, why would he beat you up?" I counter, convinced of Finn's innocence.

Jed even has an answer to that. "It could've been a diversion." When I go rigid, he adds: "I mean, I'm not saying it's Finn. All I wanted to show you is that Napoleon could be anybody. Since he'll never reveal his true identity, you'll never know."

The fact that I will likely never have closure brings new tears to my eyes. As long as Napoleon is a mystery to me, I will never 100 percent trust a guy.

"He's just a coward," I mutter, my voice slightly trembling.

"Don't be upset, honeybun." Jed's fingers brush my cheek. "This was supposed to be a fun game."

I recoil under his touch. "You know what, Jed? You're just a total pervert. I hate you."

His hand withdraws as he chuckles. "Don't be a party pooper, or this will turn into your worst nightmare yet. I'll torture you again like the last time. The dog leash is still around and I can dig up plenty of crawly things around the lake." There is a cruel smirk on his lips. "Napoleon also has some pretty crazy ideas of his own. After we're through with you, you're gonna stay at that loony bin till you're old and wrinkly, so be good."

His threat hangs over the car like an angry storm cloud. My stomach turns into a solid knot. Suppressing the rising tears, I glare out of the window, my hands balled to the tightest fists. My fingernails cut into my palms, leaving a sharp pain behind which keeps me halfway sane.

I will survive this! It is a statement I repeat over and over in my mind to drown out the incredible fear that is attempting to bubble to the surface. Deep down, I know that this time, there's a good chance they will kill me. It has always been hanging over my head during my first abduction, knowing that Jed wouldn't have revealed his identity if he wanted to let me go. Only Napoleon's continued secrecy had put me at ease, though I'm still not sure if I wasn't lying to myself.

When I gaze at Jed, who is humming to the Christmas song like he's trying to get into the holiday spirit, my anger seethes. He doesn't deserve to be happy; as a matter of fact, he doesn't even deserve to live. My torment will never stop unless he is dead. In a moment of total insanity, my hands ball to fists. I'm ready to take a swing at him until the rational part of my brain takes back over. We are in a moving car, driving close to fifty miles an hour. If I lunge at him and he loses control of the van, we will both die. On top of that, Napoleon will kill Hallie. No, for the moment, gritting my teeth and playing his game is all I can do.

I lean back and close my eyes, controlling my breath to calm my nerves. We continue to drive through the night. He leaves the highway at the Sabattus exit, actually passing the hospital before turning onto Route 197 toward Tacoma Lakes. He turns onto a bumpy dirt road, which is narrow and fully covered by snow that crunches under the tires. Hanging tree branches curve across like a solid roof, robbing me of the sight of the pale winter moon.

In a curve, the van swerves to the right, but Jed gets it back under control before he hits a snowbank. A short while later, he speeds down a gentle slope, coming to a halt at the end of the road.

A log cabin lies in the moonlight. The property borders on one side with the lake, but is otherwise only surrounded by trees. It's rather small with an elevated deck out front that faces the water. It's a typical summer holiday home. I wonder whether the owners know that their vacation paradise is used in the commission of several felonies.

Jed ushers me up the wobbly steps that lead to the deck. With a welcoming gesture, he holds the front door open for me. "Home sweet home, honeybun. I hope you like it."

The place is actually quite cozy and quaint. A light scent of pine emits from the wood paneling that covers the walls all the way up to the cathedral ceiling. Large windows open up to the deck and the lake; the view in the daytime must be stunning.

A fire is crackling in the open fireplace and the cabin holds the heat well. It's almost roasting. The whole downstairs is an open floor plan. I can see the kitchen out back to the right and part of a bedroom through a cracked door on the left. A set of stairs leads to a landing and another room upstairs.

"Where's Hallie?" I hiss, hugging my arms around my chest.

He points at the landing. "She's up there." Invitingly, his arm swings toward the sofa. "Come on, get comfortable. I'll get you a drink. What would you like?"

"Well, I don't believe you." I glare at him. "If she's here, I want to see her. You swore you'd let her go."

His laugh is vicious this time. "Well, I lied. She ain't going anywhere and you can say hello in the morning. For now, she's asleep. Napoleon knocked her out when he left."

I can't believe I was that gullible. "If you don't let her go, I will—" The sentence hangs unfinished in the air. There are not really any believable threats I can make.

"You'll do what?" His voice is full of amusement.

"I'll kill you," I blurt out. The words sound like a joke even to my ears. Who am I fooling? I don't have a weapon, but even if I did, he is a championship boxer who can fight off any attack without even breaking a sweat.

His eyes darken before he slaps me hard across the face. "You'll behave, or I swear I'll take it out on Hallie." His finger points at the sofa. "Now sit your ass down before I drag her downstairs and pop her cherry right in front of you."

My body shakes uncontrollably when I lower myself onto the couch while Jed disappears in the kitchen. The metallic taste of blood is in my mouth. My cheek stings like hell, but the pain is nothing compared to the dull ache drilling into my heart like an auger. How could I have been so stupid to ever believe him? I should have known better.

Stifling heat chokes me, but I'm shivering from cold sweat at the same time. My chest is so tight that I can barely breathe. The rapid pounding of my heart drowns out every other sound in the room as tears begin to fall. I bury my face in my hands, focusing on my breathing.

Don't lose it, I tell myself. *Not in front of Jed.*

When I look up, he's right in front of me, watching me intently. A steaming cup of tea is in his hand, which he places on the table right in front of me. "You can sleep on the couch tonight since I'm exhausted. The door is locked with a deadbolt and all the windows are nailed shut, so there's no way out." He sets a razor blade right next to the tea. "Here, in case you want to feel better. The bathroom is to the left of the kitchen. Sleep tight, honeybun."

After the bedroom door closes behind him, my fingers run over the razor blade. Maybe once he's asleep, I can take him out. If he disarms me again, there will be serious repercussions, not just for me, but Hallie as well. It might be my best option to end this ordeal quickly, though. When the key to the bedroom door turns, my shoulders slump. So much for that idea.

An incredible pain washes over me, which robs me of my breath. The razor blade is teasing me, the urge to find a quick relief overpowering. Just one more time will give me strength. Trying to battle the growing urge, I replay Reggie's words during the last group session before the break. *It takes courage to fight the addiction.* I want to be courageous so badly, but my newfound strength is dwindling. I just want to go to sleep without the pain.

Ten minutes later, I give up the fight. With my back against the wall, I slide onto the bathroom floor after making three quick parallel cuts in my forearm. The searing pain from the red rain spilling from my veins lulls me into a total sense of oblivion. With a deep sigh, I indulge in the hot and cold flashes, and for just one brief moment, I forget all the things that keep me from breathing without the pain.

Chapter 16

When I awake at the crack of dawn, my throat is raw, a dull ache pounding in my head. In some ways, it feels like a bad hangover from a drinking spree gone astray, even if the underlying act was nothing more than self-mutilation. I lie still on the couch, feeling like total crap, while trying to ignore the throbbing pain in my lower arm. I curse myself for the relapse.

My eyes are still closed when a warm body cuddles into me. I know instantly that it's Jed from his aftershave.

"I saw the blood in the bathroom. Did you have a good time, honeybun?"

His question makes me feel even more despicable. "You knew this would happen, didn't you?"

He wipes a strand of hair from my face. "Of course. I didn't use to get why you cut yourself, but Napoleon explained to me that it's like an addiction. You can't help it. It numbs the pain you feel inside you. Intriguing, when you think about it. Inflict more pain to kill the other. It sounds ridiculous, but it must work since quite a lot of people are doing it these days." He bends forward and his breath tickles my neck. "Tell me, honeybun. Did it make you feel better?"

I fight the urge to push him away, opening my eyes instead. His dark orbs are like liquid gold as they pierce into me. I detect a hint of glee. When I realize that our lips are only inches apart, a shudder runs through me. He must be getting ready to kiss me. I turn my head away.

"It didn't help," I lie. My voice is feeble and absolutely not convincing.

His fingers run over the bandage I found under the sink in the first aid package after the freezing bathroom floor became unbearable. "I should take a look at that later. We don't want you to get an infection." He grabs my chin and forces me to look at him. "But first of all, how about some early morning fun? Let's begin by you kissing me, and I mean, really kissing me. Like you mean it."

I laugh bitterly. "Fat chance. That'll never happen."

"Oh, it will, honeybun," he says in a husky voice. His thumb traces my bottom lip. "If you don't make me happy, I'll take it out on Hallie. For the moment, she's safe. Since I'm not attracted to her, I won't touch her. I want you, honeybun, but not like the last time. I realized last night that I went about it the wrong way. You have to give yourself freely to me."

The whole concept makes my stomach turn. "What is this, Jed? Some wishful thinking that I'll become your girlfriend and we play house. You kidnapped me—again—and I'm your prisoner. That's not really a strong basis for a love affair."

His eyes darken as he clicks his tongue. "Maybe not, but then I suggest you become a really good actor. I want this. If not, I'll make Hallie suffer and have you watch every step of the way. It's all up to you. As I said before, only you can save her."

The thought that he will tear her innocence away right in front of me drives tears to my eyes. That night when Napoleon took my virginity, something died inside me. I don't want to have Hallie experience the same. After she already lost her parents, this could break her. "How do I know she is even here? You lied to me before. Maybe Napoleon took her."

Jed sits up and stretches. "You're right, honeybun. I'll prove to you that she's here, but let's make breakfast first. She hasn't eaten in a couple of days and sure must be starving."

I wonder if he allowed her to use the bathroom or whether she also had to pee in a pot right in front of him. With some reluctance, I follow him into the kitchen, which is a standard vacation home setup. Small stove, single fridge, and just big enough to have a person turn around while working. Padlocks are on all the cabinets and the fridge, which is another blow. There is no way for me to get a knife or another weapon.

He unlocks the fridge. "Do you want bacon with your scrambled eggs?"

I will need all the strength I can get to pull through this. "Yes, please." My stomach is queasy, but I'll force myself to eat. My eyes fall onto the bathroom door. Nature is calling. Without asking for permission, I walk inside and slam the door shut.

"There is a spare toothbrush in the cabinet under the sink," he calls from the kitchen.

While I relieve myself, I scan the room for possible weapons. The mirrors, which would have been my first choice, have been removed and there is nothing sharp I could use to stab Jed with. The razor blade I left on the sink is gone, together with any sign of my self-harm efforts. Jed must have scrubbed the place clean before waking me. The distinct scent of bleach is still in the air.

I check under the sink, but there is nothing other than the first aid kit, without the required scissors, and a new toothbrush. Toilet cleaner, bleach, and other chemicals could have worked to cause some serious damage, but Jed thought of everything. He totally baby-proofed the place, which also comes in handy to keep kidnapped victims confined.

When I step back into the kitchen, he portions the eggs onto three plates. "Eat up, or Hallie will get cold breakfast."

The smell of the food proves too much. I rush back into the bathroom before my stomach heaves. I haven't eaten or drunk anything since lunch yesterday and only manage to choke up dry air. Continuing to gag, I feel totally helpless while doubled over in front of the toilet. Every muscle in my body convulses as minor explosions set off in my head every time I retch. Desperate whimpers mix with the gurgling sound resonating from my throat. When my stomach finally settles, my skin is covered in cold sweat.

Jed hands me a small wet towel. "I'd better fix you some tea."

All I can do is nod while leaning against the bathroom wall. My mouth is laced with the bitter taste of bile, competing with a fire that burns in my throat. I fight with the continuous nausea as the blood pounds in my temples, wishing for nothing more than some aspirins and my mom's milk toast. Thinking about her brings fresh tears to my eyes. Now I'm sorry that I was such a bitch to her lately.

When I stumble back out of the bathroom, Jed has moved the breakfast into the oven and is fixing some tea. A light trace of ginger emits from the steaming cup he sets right in front of me.

"Here. My sister used tea to battle morning sickness when she was pregnant and swears it's really good when you're nauseous."

I didn't even know he has a sister. "Where does she live?"

"St. Louis."

"And how old is she?"

"You ask a lot of questions." Judging from Jed's face, they do not get along.

"Does she know you and Napoleon have been kidnapping girls?"

His finger shoots in my direction. "Do yourself a favor and shut up. I don't wanna talk about her."

I file this bit of information away in the back of my mind. If I ever need to wind him up, this will be a way to do it.

The tea is hot and offers instant relief. I sip slowly, rolling it around on my tongue to get the nasty taste out of my mouth.

"Do you have any painkillers?"

Trapped

He unlocks a kitchen drawer and tosses me a couple of ibuprofen. I get a good look at the other contents before he slams the drawer shut and locks it again—it holds various medicine bottles and a small knife. Picking that lock would definitely give me access to some treasures. I could probably knock Jed out if I grind up the pills and mix them in his food, or I could stab him with the knife.

By the time I finish the tea, my stomach has settled down, yet the food still doesn't look appealing. I nibble off small pieces of the bacon while Jed devours every bit of his breakfast. He is a fast eater and the whole affair doesn't take longer than five minutes.

After he scoops my leftovers into the bin, he grabs the last plate. "Well, let's go and see Hallie."

"How do you even know her?" It's a question that has been bothering me the whole night.

A smile curls his lips. "I've been watching you since you were admitted to the hospital. Your brother is as careless as you and never even noticed I was following you guys. A few times, you and Hallie walked out together and seemed really friendly. I followed her one night to find out where she lives. Napoleon figured you were close enough that you would come to her rescue."

My stomach cramps again at the thought that he has been following me around this whole time. This is so creepy. Wiping the sweaty palms on my pants, my legs carry me automatically up the steps, my apprehension growing. I'm mad at Hallie for getting herself kidnapped, but my sympathy prevails in the end. She must be scared out of her mind.

There is only one room upstairs and it's padlocked. Jed fumbles with the keys while I drum my fingers on the banister. When the door finally opens, I push past him just to stop in my tracks at the appalling sight in front of me.

Despair lingers over the room as I take in her shivering, almost naked body, which is covered with bruises and small cuts. Her ankles and wrists are raw from the tight ropes which hold her in place in a spread-eagle position. Fortunately, there is no sign of blood on her thighs, and I'm relieved that Jed was not lying with respect to her V-card.

With no heat in the room, it is freezing. A cold breeze floating in from the cracked window makes matters worse. Despite the ventilation, a strong stench of urine irritates my nostrils. I scan over the various-sized stains on the mattress, which causes anger to flare momentarily. Those bastards must not have allowed her to relieve herself away from the bed. I can only imagine how terrible and dirty she must feel.

I lower myself next to her and fumble with the gag in her mouth. She gazes at me with utter confusion. I pull on the knot but can't get it loose. My fingernails are too short.

"Cut this off her," I finally hiss at Jed with frustration. "And get a blanket." I want to help her so badly and assure her that everything will be okay again.

He has been watching me intently but doesn't move. "I told you before—you'll have to be nice if you want to help her."

I huff. "What do you want?"

"For now, a kiss. A real one."

I massage my forehead, totally at a loss. I don't want to play Jed's sick game, but I have no clue what else to do to help Hallie. My knees almost buckle as I stand up. Without resistance, I allow him to pull me into his arms.

When he used to kiss me, his lips had crushed down hard on me, and he had forced his tongue into my mouth. This time it's different. He is gentle, letting me take the lead while waiting for my signals. Maybe he really believes somewhere in his twisted mind that we could become a couple and perhaps even fall in love. He's so totally clueless, it's not even funny. All I'll ever feel for him is loathing and hatred.

When I allow him access, he pulls me even closer, his hand moving to the small of my back. It takes all my effort not to break away. A soft groan escapes his mouth as he continues to explore me with his tongue, totally oblivious that I have gone rigid in his arms. When he finally releases me, I face the wall to hide the tears in my eyes. Every fiber in my body burns with disgust.

Jed seems satisfied and removes the gag before leaving us alone.

"Why are you here?" Her voice is hoarse and breaks under her tears.

"They showed me a video of you and threatened to kill you if I didn't surrender myself."

Her gaze is filled with bewilderment. "So this is all about you?" There is a hint of blame in her voice.

The guilt that I got her into this mess finally hits me. Jed and Napoleon would never have kidnapped her if it wasn't for me. I owe Hallie her life back without permanent scars.

In that moment, Jed returns with a quilt. His chin points at the plate with the breakfast. "Feed her."

I cover her body loosely with the blanket and her grateful look makes up for that slimy kiss.

"Just untie her. I'm sure she has to use the bathroom, too."

He chuckles. "You don't get it, honeybun. For every privilege I give her, I expect something in return." His lips purse. "Let's see. I'll untie her if you show me your boobs, but for her to use the shower and bathroom, I expect the full package."

My hand rises to slap him across the face, but his boxing reflexes kick in. He catches my wrist before I can cause any damage.

"You're a despicable human being." My voice trembles as I spit the words out with venom. "Go to hell."

He slowly walks to the door and locks it. "Let me show you what'll happen if you disobey me."

Sudden fear consumes me from the vicious glow in his eyes. I dash to the window, tearing it open. The roof slope is steep, but the gutter is down far enough for me to jump. I would definitely survive and would probably not even get hurt that much.

My leg is already on the windowsill when he pulls me back by my hair. With a fluid motion, he backhands me. The force throws me against the wall. Warm blood trickles down my cheek as the sting spreads across my face all the way into the depths of my skull. When he twists my arms back, I wince. A minute later, my hands and legs are secured with cable ties. I am deposited in a corner of the room with a front-row view of the bed.

"Now this is on you," he yells, his finger pointing right at me. "All I asked you to do is play nice, but no, you had to be stubborn."

Hallie's face is streaked with tears. She recoils when he approaches her like a menacing monster.

"Please . . ."

The word is soft and spoken with so much fear that it tears my heart to shreds. What have I done?

Jed exposes his teeth to a wide grin, reminding me of a vicious wildcat before the kill. "This is gonna be good. I always wanted to get myself a virgin." With one swift move, he tears away the blanket before ripping off her panties.

Hallie's pleas mix with my sobs as Jed slowly unbuttons his pants. After he shakes them off, they are tossed in my direction with a cruel laugh. "This could have been avoided, honeybun."

I bury my face against my knees. My stomach cramps as the thumping of my racing heart with the rushing of blood in my ears combines into a raging river. When the foil pack of the condom tears, all sounds are drowned out by Hallie's loud cry. "No, please—"

"Stop." My voice breaks through the commotion.

Silence falls over the room.

"Did you say something, honeybun?" Jed squats down next to me, his breath grazing against my neck.

I raise my head. "Whatever it is you want me to do, I'll do it."

A sadistic smile curls his lips. "Is that so?"

I want to shake my head, but my mouth develops a mind of its own. "Just leave Hallie alone."

His fingers lift my chin to force eye contact. "So you swear you'll cooperate?"

I'm having second thoughts, but once again, my mouth betrays me. "Yes."

Triumph spreads across his face. "Okay, I'll give you a second chance." He glances at Hallie before his focus turns back to me. "Don't screw this up again, or I promise that taking her virginity will be the least of your worries." He cuts the cable ties around my wrists and ankles with his knife. "Now feed her and then come downstairs. I'll get everything ready. After we've had our fun, I'll even give you girls some privacy."

He slams the window shut, pulling out a key to lock it. This bars my last hope of escape. With a last lingering look at my cleavage, he leaves the room. Yet his eyes said it all—welcome to my own personal hell.

Chapter 17

I am totally numb by the time Jed collapses on top of me, his body still shaking from his climax. He took his time, extending the last bit as much as possible. His face was laced with an expression of total ecstasy until he got lost in the heights of his lust. Luckily about halfway through, he neither noticed that I had totally stopped moving, nor the few stray tears that were rolling down my cheeks.

"Boy, that was amazing." A small sigh follows his mumbled words. His heated breath warms the nape of my neck before he covers my shoulder with soft kisses. "You see, honeybun. This can be fun after all."

I battle the nausea and the tears. The feeling of being totally dirty and worthless is stronger than ever—at least before, I fought for my body. Now that bastard actually believes I'm having a good time.

The thought sends a shudder down my spine and I suppress a small sob. My insides wince in total agony when I try to move, yet worse than the physical pain is the throbbing ache in my heart. There's nothing left of my self-esteem—I am totally despicable.

"Can Hallie use the bathroom now?" I whisper, hoping he doesn't break his word again.

He rolls on his back. "Sure. I have some things I've got to do around the house, but will be close by if you need anything." His head points toward the closet on the right. "There are towels in there and you may want to put a sheet on the mattress. I'll spray some disinfectant on there. Hopefully, that'll get rid of the smell."

Since I'm still naked, I don't want to give him another eyeful of my body. I pull the covers closer around me when he slides out of the bed.

"What about some clothes? It's freezing up there in that room."

He glances at me. "You'll have to earn those later. For now, all she gets is a bath and a dry place to sleep."

I turn my head, sick at the thought of being his willing sex toy just to get the smallest of things for Hallie and myself. At some point, this whole ordeal might prove too much. All of a sudden, I have a craving for the razor blade, but I would rather have my head cut off than ask Jed about it.

He brings Hallie downstairs and ushers her into the bathroom. I follow with a couple of towels after getting redressed. At least he had been gentle and there are no bruises on me, though I'm sore when I walk and my stomach is cramping.

I fill the tub with water. It burns my fingertips when I check the temperature. With a small hiss, I withdraw my hand before turning the cold lever to full. I scratch the reddened spots with my nails. The dull pain gives me a quick but short-lived buzz.

"Are you okay?" comes Hallie's small voice from the toilet. She is wrapped in a towel and watches me with huge puffy eyes. Her lips are bleeding and swollen.

I stare at her. What do I answer to that? Jed just forced me to share my body with him, an act that should only be reserved for couples to demonstrate their ultimate love for each other. It is supposed to be a wonderful experience to bring them closer together and at some point during their joint journey in life, it should produce a child as a decisive sign of their union.

Yet for me, sex has never been about love. It was forced on me from the start, and now, I even have to pretend I like it to prevent Hallie from getting hurt. No matter what I do, it is what it is, and there's no need to scare her or make her feel guilty.

"I'm fine," I say, giving my words an extra firmness to make them convincing.

Her soft eyes fill with tears. "But—"

"Don't go there, Hallie. It's alright, really."

My gaze drops so she won't notice the distress on my face. My statement is followed by pressing silence. I add bath gel to the water and recheck the temperature.

"All set. You can get in."

She bites her lip despite the blood. "Don't you want to go first?"

No matter how hard I would scrub my skin, it won't make me feel better. "You go ahead." I grimace when I look at her matted hair. "You need it more than me."

For five days, she has been in captivity and has not even been allowed once to wash her hands or sprinkle water on her face. They made her lie in her own urine, but at least they kept her food and water intake to a minimum to avoid her soiling herself too often.

Her face cringes when she slides into the water. "Ouch, that burns. Must be the cuts."

I take the sponge and soak it up before squeezing the water over her shoulders. With a sigh, she leans back, almost disappearing under the mountain of soft foam.

"I never appreciated a bath so much." Her eyes cut into me. "It will get worse, won't it?"

I shrug. "Honestly, I couldn't tell you. I have no clue what Jed's plans are for you, but I hope that as long as I play along, he'll leave you alone."

She can't hold my gaze. "Why do you do it?"

Trapped

When I frown, she continues. "I mean, we hardly know each other. You don't owe me anything, so why do you allow him to touch you? Why not just save your own skin?"

I play with the sponge in my hand. "I'm already damaged, so why should I put you through the same ordeal? No matter what I do, I'll never get my virginity back. I'm always gonna be the second-hand girl who's dirty on the inside."

She stares at me. "You know that's not true."

The sponge is chucked into the water as the anger seethes under the surface like a bubbling volcano. The fact that I was "broken in" and no longer in the "new" category has always bothered me the most. "It's what I know. My boyfriend broke up with me because he felt that someone like me shouldn't be picky. His exact words: 'Someone who's been tapped should be ready at all times, or they'll dry up and no one wants them anymore.'"

She rolls her eyes. "That guy is just a jerk. You shouldn't listen to him. What you did for me today was heroic. I'll be forever in your debt."

"Forget it. You'd do the same if you were in my position."

It's something I have to believe to carry on and she doesn't counter. Instead, she dunks to get her hair wet. I get the shampoo bottle off the shelf. After lathering twice, I get the brush to comb out the rest of the knots.

"So how did they snatch you?"

New anger flares up at her stupidity to get herself kidnapped and she winces when I tear on her hair too hard.

"I was on my way to a friend's house to spend the school vacation with her and her family in Vermont. They have a cabin up there and I was even gonna go skiing. I always wanted to do that. It was a present for my sixteenth birthday." Her voice trembles slightly as she tells her story.

I'm surprised that she would spend the holidays away from her sister. In therapy, she had always stressed how close they are. "And Donna just lets you go away over Christmas?"

She avoids my eyes. "She's a nurse and has to work over the holidays this year, so my friend's parents thought it would be a nice treat. I don't know if I told the group, but it's my birthday the day after Christmas."

I reach for her hand. "I'm so sorry, Hallie." Hopefully, half the state is already searching for her. "Maybe the police will find us before then and it'll be all good."

She shakes her head, the tears now spilling from her eyes like a waterfall. "Jed put a gun to my head and made me call my friend's parents to tell them that my sister got sick and I couldn't go after all. Yet *she* thinks I'm gone with them, so there isn't even anyone looking for us."

My jaw almost drops, but I try to stay calm. If no one filed a missing-person report, we're screwed. Hopefully, at least Luke caught on that my letter was nothing more than a bunch of crap.

"So did you see Jed's friend?"

"No." She uses the sponge to scrape the dirt from underneath her fingernails. "Jed pulled me into the back of a van and I never saw the driver. Since I got here, he's also the only one who checks on me. I never even heard his friend's voice."

So this is another dead end. I had hoped that Napoleon wouldn't be as careful around her and she could help me to finally lift the secret. All this must have been well planned, probably already since I first started those therapy sessions in Portland. Who could have known that the few hours of respite away from the hospital would turn into a new nightmare?

Trapped

Fifteen minutes later, Hallie is all cleaned up with damp hair, wrapped tightly in a towel. I eye her dirty underwear, not sure what to put on her.

"Wait here."

I walk out into the living room, looking for Jed. He is outside, chopping wood, and I watch him through the window. Dressed only in a tank top and a pair of jeans despite the cold, his body glistens with sweat as he raises his arms with the axe in his hands. His muscles flex with every blow he takes. I can't help but think that most women would probably find him hot. Yet I only see his ability to hurt someone with all that strength. There is nothing attractive about him.

I knock on the window and he looks up, waving. He grabs a towel off a small rack next to the chopping block and wipes his hands and face before turning toward the house. I mark the spot where he disappears from my vision. If Hallie and I ever make it outside, it will be important to stay hidden from his prying eyes while finding an escape route.

"What do you need, honeybun?"

"Hallie's clothes are all dirty. I need something else."

He puckers his lips, his eyes on my disheveled appearance. "I tell you what. Since you haven't had your bath yet, let me really spoil you."

"Jed, please." I can't hold his gaze. "We just had sex."

He pulls me into his arms and squeezes my butt. "Yeah, but everything in this world costs something. Do we have a deal?"

I nod against his shoulder, my stomach queasy. I'm upset that I won't even have a minute of privacy. In hindsight, I should have taken Hallie up on her offer and had my bath first.

"Okay, let me see if I can find her some clothes."

He strokes my back before releasing me and I return to the bathroom in total defeat. If he continues like this, I'll be a nervous wreck by tomorrow.

He soon joins us and hands Hallie a pair of sweatpants and a T-shirt. "You can get dressed upstairs. I got the room ready."

Hallie hesitates, staring at me with tears in her eyes. "Please, I don't want to be up there alone and be tied up again. Can't I stay down here with Kelsey?"

A small chuckle runs over his lips before his arm slides around my waist. "Kelsey is my girlfriend, so it's different for her."

I almost choke on his words. How can he even think for one second that we are a couple? He is totally delusional.

With her head lowered, Hallie follows him. I empty the tub and rinse it out before filling it again. The water has reached about the halfway mark when he returns. A vanilla-scented candle is in his hand, and soft flute music drifts through the door even after he closes it. Maybe this is his idea of romantic ambience.

"Come on, hop into the tub."

I feel self-conscious all of a sudden. "Can you turn around while I get undressed?"

He laughs. "Honeybun, I've seen you naked a hundred times before, so don't be a prude."

His words stab like a dagger into my heart. What he doesn't realize is that none of those times have ever been my choice. It is still something I struggle to accept.

"Come on, let me get that for you," he says when I begin to fiddle with the button of my shirt.

He takes his time, unhooking every single button with agonizing slowness. When he is finished, his hands linger on my breasts before moving down, stroking my belly. His finger draws circles around my bellybutton.

"God, honeybun, you're beautiful. Your skin is flawless and you're just so soft."

I search his face, but to my surprise, there is no desire, just the same longing I noticed last night. Yet his facial expression changes when he peels me out of my shirt and unhooks my bra. The burning need in his eyes causes my chest to tighten.

With a low growl, he spins around. "Get in that tub before I change my mind and take you right here on the bathroom floor."

He doesn't have to ask twice. I slide off my pants and panties and immerse myself in the water, the foam hiding me from sight. The warmth is an instant relief to the aching tension that is clenching every muscle in my body. The thought that his hands will be all over me again is unbearable.

I tilt my head back and close my eyes, wanting to forget that I'm not alone at my own home for just one minute. The scent from the candle lingers in the air and mixes with the almond fragrance of the bath gel. The music is lulling my senses. I exhale, totally relishing the moment. I have always loved taking a bath—it was the only way to find some relief other than cutting.

When I reopen my eyes, Jed is seated on the toilet. He stares at me with glowing eyes. When he clears his throat, I know my time is up.

"Let me scrub your back, honeybun."

I rise just far enough to keep my body below my waist hidden by the suds. He warms his hands by scooping up some water before squirting soap on his palms and rubbing them together. Slowly, he applies the gel to my back in a rotating motion. Despite his gentleness, the touch resonates painfully throughout my body.

"Stand up," he demands when he reaches my lower back.

His voice is hoarse and laced with craving, making my heart thump in my throat. I would give anything for him to stop. Yet I have no choice but oblige. If I refuse, he will either turn violent or take it out on Hallie.

He lathers my legs and the tears begin to roll as soon as he reaches my thighs. I bite my lip hard to prevent the sobs from ratting me out. Yet, at some point, I can't prevent a shudder running through me, leaving goosebumps all over my body.

"Turn around, honeybun."

I do what I'm told and meet his eyes while he is looking up at me. The tears are still rolling down my cheeks. I feel so exposed and helpless. Since he knows I am truly rejecting him, he'll probably punish me.

"You aren't enjoying this at all, are you, honeybun?"

I don't respond and lower my gaze. "If you really want *us* to work, Jed, you have to give me time."

He stands up and cups my head into his hand, softly kissing my forehead. "I can't promise I'll be patient for long, but for right now, I'll give you some space."

To my amazement, he leaves the bathroom. I sink back underwater. Trying to relax, I close my eyes again, but in my mind, his hands are still all over me, forcing intimacy against my will. I shift and try to get comfortable, but the feeling persists.

When my teeth chatter after the water has cooled down, I give up and begin to rub soap all over me. Shudders battle my body with every scrubbing motion. Even after I rinse myself off three times, the dirty feeling sticks to my skin like superglue.

As I wrap myself in the thick towel, my eyes fall onto the candle. With a sigh, I pick it up and hold it over my arm. Slowly, I allow the hot wax to drizzle onto the fresh cuts from last night that have hardly formed a scab, breathing deeply in and out as the pain crawls toward my shoulder. My hand shakes when the pain intensifies, but I keep pouring the wax onto my skin. I can't get enough of the sudden buzz that calms my frayed nerves.

When there is nothing left to give me comfort, I extinguish the flame with my fingertips, digging my incisor teeth into the sore flesh to prolong the high. After the pain subsides, I run into the bedroom and slam the door shut. As I hide under the covers, my whole body shakes from my sobs. I weep until my tears dry up.

Exhaustion is finally merciful by releasing me into a deep slumber, yet my nightmares are just around the corner. It seems that there is nothing I can do these days to escape my inner demons.

Chapter 18

For the next two days, Jed allows me my space and even sleeps on the couch. I hear Hallie walk up and down the stairs a few times to use the bathroom. Relieved that he doesn't force her to soil the bed anymore without expecting payment from me, I stay mostly hidden under the covers, only venturing outside the room for my own potty breaks or to quickly choke down some leftover food in the kitchen when Jed isn't around.

On the morning of Christmas Eve, I am awoken by a loud thump, followed by some colorful cursing. I halfway expect Jed to call me for help, but the commotion dies down after a few minutes. I lie silently in the bed, still a bit foggy from my sleep while soaking up the noises in the house. A harsh wind howls outside and rattles angrily at the shutters every so often.

At some point, the aroma of coffee and sizzling bacon conquers my senses. My stomach growls loudly at the prospect of a big breakfast. The scent of fresh toast kindles my imagination. I can already taste melted butter on my lips.

There is a soft knock on the door. "Can I come in, honeybun?"

I admire his restraint and civility, although I am sure that the next explosion is probably seething under the surface. Someone with his track record doesn't just turn nice overnight. "Yeah, it's okay."

He pokes his head around the door. "I fixed some breakfast and I'm going to get Hallie. Since it's Christmas Eve, I thought we could spend some time together."

I've missed Luke and my mom more than usual over these past few days and crave for some company. "That would be nice."

His face lights up. "Hurry up or the food will get cold."

Trapped

As soon as the door closes, I slide out of the bed. My clothes are dirty by now and I rummage through the drawers until I find an old football jersey and some sweats I can tighten in the waist. The floor is freezing. I curl my toes, choosing a thick pair of wool socks from Jed's underwear drawer. My hand runs over his boxers before I grab a pair. The thought that he may have worn them before raping me is disturbing, but the need to have clean panties prevails in the end.

Hallie already sits on a barstool at the kitchen counter, her hair damp and pulled up in a messy bun. She smells like the almond cream shower gel and I'm glad that Jed must have allowed her to take another bath. Some of the bruises have faded. Her face almost appears relaxed when she smiles at me.

"Morning, Kelsey."

I briefly squeeze her arm as I climb onto the stool next to her. "All good?"

"Yeah. How about you?" Her eyes stay on the scabbed cuts on my forearm. Some accountability partner I am.

"I'm fine," I reassure her, though I'm still fighting my inner unrest. This all seems too perfect. It's just a matter of time before Jed rears his ugly head.

He has gone all out with the selection of breakfast food. Besides the bacon and toast, there are eggs and even chocolate chip pancakes. As soon as a plate is empty, second helpings are piled up. I stuff myself until I'm ready to burst. The food is washed down with orange juice.

"I got us a Christmas tree," Jed remarks while sipping his coffee. His eyes dash constantly back and forth between Hallie and me. "I thought you girls could decorate it after breakfast."

I can't shake the feeling that this is his idea of a harmonious holiday, and since he seems to be in an exceptionally good mood, I allow the question to run over my lips that has been burning on my mind since I got to the cabin. "Will Napoleon be joining us today?"

He considers me with narrow eyes. "Why are you asking, honeybun? Do you miss him?"

A slight hint of jealousy is in his voice, which surprises me. "No, of course not."

He takes another mouthful of coffee before responding. "Napoleon has other commitments. He'll be here after the holidays."

Once he is back in the picture, it will be harder to escape. "Actually, I'm glad."

That gets a chuckle out of him. "Admit I'm a much better lover than he is."

Rape is rape no matter how you twist and turn it, but I play to his ego. "You know you're best."

The longing glow in his eyes is back as his fingers graze my hand. He must seriously think that there is hope for us. The thought is so ridiculous, it's almost scary.

The tree has been erected in a corner of the living room and must be at least eight feet tall. Boxes with ornaments and lights are piled up next to it, with a small ladder leaning against the wall.

We get busy. Jed helps with the lights before stretching out on the sofa.

"I point, you hang," he instructs, his eyes focused on my crotch.

I realize he wants me up on the ladder to get a good eyeful of my curves. There's really not much I can do. I feel his gaze upon me the entire time, causing my nerve ends to constantly twitch in anticipation of his next move. Hallie hands me the ornaments, which I hang on the various branches according to Jed's instructions. A few times, I pinch my fingers on sharp edges, a welcome distraction.

When we are finally done after adding the star to the top, the tree looks pretty decent.

Jed suggests a tea break. "And afterwards, we can play Monopoly." His eyes twinkle with excitement.

Hallie and I get comfortable on the couch while he rummages in the kitchen.

"Why is he doing this?" she whispers.

"I think he's lonely, and in his mind, we're like his family."

She grimaces. "That's absolutely crazy."

"Yeah, but still better than being locked up and hurt."

We fall quiet when he joins us with a wide grin, placing a tea set on the table. "Here we go, girls."

I notice he stays away from alcohol, probably remembering the last time. In a drunken stupor, he passed out next to me on the bed, which ultimately led to my escape. He had staggered into my prison that night, babbling incomprehensible words before falling next to me on the mattress. It didn't take much to convince him to loosen my restraints so I could give him a massage. After rubbing his shoulders for a few minutes, he fell into a comatose-like sleep.

In my haste, I forgot to lock the door behind me, something that would ultimately prove fatal in getting him convicted. If I had only confined him that night, the blunder with the tape recording would have probably never happened. I still partially blame myself that he got off.

Over the next hours, we play board games: first Monopoly, then Trivial Pursuit. As dusk settles, he turns on the Christmas tree and lights a few candles.

"Let's watch a movie," he announces. "I'll make pizza."

He got an assortment of Christmas flicks from the video store and we start with *The Santa Clause*. While he is busy in the kitchen, I signal Hallie to keep an eye out for him.

"I'll check out the locks," I whisper before tiptoeing to the front door. My heart plummets into my stomach—two deadbolts and a separate lock. Without the keys, there is no way out. Wiping my sweaty palms on my sweats, I turn toward the window. Just like the one in the bedroom, it has been nailed shut. The only option is the small hatch in Hallie's bedroom, but that could still be locked.

"Kelsey."

Hallie's hissed word makes me jump. In panic, I spin around, but it's too late. Jed appears next to the couch, squinting at me. "What you doin', honeybun?"

My heart pounds in my throat as I watch him, my mouth dry as cotton wool. Heat burns my face. I must look like a ripe tomato.

His brows rise in challenge as he waits for an answer.

Finally, my eyes fall onto the fire pit. "I was hoping to start a fire. It's so cozy and I'm a bit chilly." I bend down to pick up a couple of logs that are stacked between the door and the window, carrying them over.

He doesn't miss a beat, tension in his face. "Hey, let me get that. That's guy's work."

If I wasn't still so shaken up, I would have rolled my eyes at his sexist remark. Any child can start a fire if someone shows them how to stack the logs correctly. As I get out of his way, he catches my wrist and pulls me into his arms.

"I know what you were doin', honeybun." He nuzzles my neck. "Don't let me catch you again, or I'd be forced to end this little party. It'd be such a shame for Hallie, having to spend Christmas all by herself."

I am frozen in his arms, trying to hide the shivers running through me. "I'm sorry, Jed."

Trapped

He squeezes my butt. "I'll forgive you." His lips graze my chin. "After all, it's Christmas. Now be a good girl and sit down."

Like a trained puppy, I follow his instructions. Hallie's eyes are wide when she mouths an apology. It's not her fault. The house is too small to get away with deceit and I shouldn't have tried to check out an escape route that openly. Now Jed is not only suspicious, but will lash out for sure if I step a toe out of line again.

He starts the movie as soon as the fire is blazing, disappearing into the kitchen again to check on the pizza. This time I don't move, sitting motionless on the couch next to Hallie, who is wrapped tightly in a blanket. The longing for my mom breaks my heart in two—I have never missed her more. Christmas Eve has always been our special night. There's not one unhappy memory I can recall.

It has been difficult over the last three years, but that was mostly my own fault. Instead of sulking, I should've been thankful for the family I have and not fought them every chance I got. They were not the enemy and didn't deserve my foul mood. In the end, all they ever tried was to help me.

When I look at Hallie, she's crying. I know she feels the same. After losing her parents, this must be an even bigger nightmare for her. I wonder if her sister has figured out yet that she was kidnapped. If we are lucky, she will call Hallie's friend to wish her a Merry Christmas and the whole abduction will be discovered.

She quickly wipes her tears away when Jed reappears with two large plates stacked with different pizza slices.

His head motions her to move to the chair. "Scoot over. I wanna sit next to my girl."

After glancing at me and receiving a small nod, she obliges.

Jed gets comfortable on the couch, his arm landing on my shoulder. "Dig in, honeybun. Let's have a nice dinner."

I nibble on the pizza and manage to choke down two slices before my stomach gets queasy. Sitting next to Jed, who has positioned me in a way to force my body to lean against him, makes every single one of my muscles clench. His fingers caress my shoulder and my neck, playing with my hair every so often. He's totally engrossed in the movie, laughing at every silly joke. I don't find it at all amusing; I'm ready to barf and barely able to hold back my tears.

The ordeal continues with *Christmas with The Kranks.* I try to focus on the movie but keep thinking about my mom and Luke. What are they doing right now? Even if they believed my story that I needed a break, they are likely just going through the motions while worrying sick about me.

Moving on, my mind drifts to Finn. He is probably spending the holidays with his uncle or Tyrone and has forgotten all about me. That thought brings fresh tears to my eyes.

Jed strokes my cheek. "You okay, honeybun?"

I nod, unable to speak. One word and the tears would be rolling. He cuddles me closer against him. The tightness in my stomach triples. I'm sure he wants to have sex at the end of the night.

As soon as the movie is over, he announces that it is time for bed. It couldn't be past ten, but I still feel exhausted, the tension and pressure slowly eating away at my very substance. Jed ushers Hallie upstairs while I venture into the kitchen. All the drawers are locked and I start the kettle.

"Want more tea?"

His question startles me. "Yeah. I hope that's okay."

"Sure." He unlocks one of the cabinets. "Chamomile or something. It might help you sleep."

Trapped

I hate chamomile tea. My mom used to force it down my throat when I was little and had a stomachache. "Do you have mint?"

"Yep." He passes me a tea bag and a cup.

I add some sugar. "What about you?"

"I have some man tea." He laughs, filling up a small glass to the rim with whiskey. "One should be fine, don't you think?"

As far as I am concerned, he could have the full bottle. Even if I don't make it out of the house, his passed-out body wouldn't want to force sex on me.

I sip my tea in silence, too well aware that he is staring at me the whole time.

"You miss your family, don't you?"

A few treacherous tears trickle down my cheek. "That's a stupid question. Of course."

"Me, too." Sadness burns in his eyes. "Since my parents died, I've spent every single Christmas alone."

Under different circumstances, I might have felt sorry for him, but now, it just makes me angry.

"They died a little over four years ago," he says. "I was only seventeen. Social Services wanted my sister to take me, but she refused. I ended up being emancipated to avoid going into the system. Fortunately, my parents left me enough money to take care of myself."

I refuse to look at him. "Is that supposed to make me feel bad?"

His fingers stroke the back of my hand. "It wasn't my idea to take you before the holidays. I wanted you to spend Christmas at home, but Napoleon insisted. He said it would tame you."

My head snaps up. "Why do you allow him to call the shots?"

His face twists in a pained expression. "You don't understand. Every time I try to defy him, he wins. There's just no stopping him."

I narrow my eyes. "Who is he, Jed?"

He shakes his head rapidly. "I can't tell you. He'll kill you if you ever find out his true identity." His fingers wrap tightly around mine. "Please, honeybun, whatever you do, don't test him. He's really violent. I saw him once almost beat a man to death—he has no conscience." His eyes pierce into mine. "Please, honeybun, you have to promise me to do whatever he wants."

My scalp prickles. "He's coming for me, isn't he?"

"Yes, after Christmas."

My hand clutches over my mouth as a small whimper escapes my throat.

He allows me to cry in silence, rubbing my back the entire time. "Shh, it'll be okay," he mumbles over and over.

I don't believe him; my nightmare is never going to end.

When the tears finally dry up, I'm so tired that I stumble as I slide off the barstool. He catches me just before I fall.

"Please, Jed." My voice is hoarse from all he crying. "I don't want to have sex tonight."

"That's alright, but I'm scared you're gonna hurt yourself again, so I'll sleep in the bed with you."

When my lips twist in agony, he quickly adds, "In my clothes. It's really just for your own protection."

It's the first time that I believe he is genuinely concerned about me. Though he keeps his word, I can't fall asleep as I lay there in bed, scooped up in his arms. The memory of Napoleon's hands on my skin is too vivid to get him out of my mind. In not even forty-eight hours, my time will be up.

Chapter 19

Fresh snow is falling on Christmas morning. I sit in the rocking chair by the window for a long time, staring outside with vacant eyes. Every so often, my gaze wanders to the clock on the wall. In my mind, I'm counting down the minutes to tomorrow night, my mind drifting back to those times I was with Napoleon before.

While sex with Jed had already been horrifying, it was even worse with his friend. Napoleon had always gotten physical and hurt me one way or the other, seemingly enjoying my screams and pleas for him to stop. I felt weak and unprotected, hating to be tied up and blindfolded. It added to the fear to be totally at his mercy.

In the months after my escape, the police asked me hundreds of questions—from a special scent I might have picked up to any other bits of information that could have helped them to identify him. I picked my brain, which almost always came up blank. All I could remember was my pounding heartbeat, my dry mouth, and the smell of my own sweat. I still shudder every time I imagine his breath grazing over my skin or his hands wandering over my naked body. Those memories overpower the rest.

I am torn from my sullen thoughts when the door opens with a small squeak. My eyes close as Jed begins to rub my shoulder. I wish desperately for someone to comfort me who I truly care about. Having him around doesn't make it any easier.

"I fixed breakfast," he says softly.

My stomach is in knots. "I'm not really hungry."

"Hey"—he squats down next to the rocking chair—"it's Christmas. Let's get Hallie downstairs and try to have a nice day. I even have a surprise for you that might cheer you up."

A celebration is the last thing on my mind. "I'm sorry, Jed, but I'm not in the holiday spirit."

His lips twist in disappointment. "I shouldn't have told you."

A desperate breath flares my nostrils. "No, I'm glad you did. Gives me time to prepare."

He nods and squeezes my knee. "Is there anything I can get you?"

A razor blade would be nice, but after last night, I doubt he would go for it anyhow.

"No." I give him a crooked smile. "But you could fix a cake for Hallie or something. It's her birthday tomorrow."

He plants a kiss on my forehead. "That's what I love about you. You've changed so much for the better in the last few years, always thinking of others first."

I would like to agree, but it's really his misconception. Over these past years, I have been mostly selfish, thinking of nothing other than my self-pity. Yet, this second abduction has been a real eye-opener and things will be different if I ever make it out of here in one piece. My fear and my memories will no longer destroy me or hold me hostage. I owe that to myself.

He quietly leaves. I resume to stare out into the snow. There's only one way to avoid the inevitable and that is to escape. It would be easier if I left Hallie behind. Since I know now where Jed is keeping her, I could alert the cops, but the risk that they will kill her straight away is just too high. I could never forgive myself.

In my mind, I change strategy. Playing along and celebrating Christmas will distract Jed and give me more time with Hallie. If we somehow make it outside and into the forest, the trees would give us shelter. Not having any shoes or coat is a real hindrance, we both wouldn't make it far with the freezing temperatures outside. That's still something I will have to figure out.

My scheming is interrupted when the door opens again. I sigh, expecting Jed to bother me again, but instead, I only hear a low pitter-patter. A warm, wet tingling on my calf almost startles me to death. I squeal, but then my eyes fall onto a small puppy. It's the cutest thing I've ever seen.

He or she looks like a golden retriever and can be no more than a few months old. My heart swells. I've always begged for a puppy, but my mom didn't want the dirt in the house.

My fingers stroke through the soft fur. "Hey there. Where did you come from?"

The puppy pushes its nose into my palm. The tickling sensation when its rough tongue licks over my skin makes me snicker.

"You can pick her up. She won't break."

My gaze darts to the door where Jed is leaning in the frame, a sparkle in his eyes.

His excitement catches.

"You got a puppy?"

He breaks into a wide smile. "She's for you, honeybun. I thought you might like some company."

I squint at him. "How did you know I like dogs?"

He walks over and sets the puppy into my lap. "Lucky guess."

I stroke the small retriever behind her ears. "What's her name?"

He chuckles. "That's, of course, up to you. She's my Christmas present for you."

It's the nicest gift anyone has ever gotten me. "Thanks, Jed." I lift up the puppy and hold her in front of me. Her small tongue shoots out, trying to get to my nose. I tilt my head. "I think she looks like a Maisie."

Jed allows for the puppy to chew on his fingertips. "Maisie is a nice name." He purses his lips, cooing at the puppy. "Do you like that name?" The retriever is suckling his finger in response, like she is giving her consent.

I cuddle the puppy on my lap and rock lightly. She squirms around, licking my hands all over and nudging me with her head. I rub her belly, enjoying her warm body pressing against me. For a moment, I forget all about my kidnapping and Napoleon.

Jed smiles. "I'll let you two get acquainted."

An idea forms in my head. "Can Hallie and I play with the puppy in the living room?"

His eyes light up. "Sure."

So far, so good. At some point, Maisie will need to go outside for a bathroom break, and hopefully, Jed will allow us to take her. It might be our one chance to escape.

Hallie adores the puppy. We soon have a little game going, rolling a small ball back and forth between us while sitting on the floor by the tree. Maisie scampers about, halting from time to time to demand a tummy rub. Jed is sitting on the armrest of the sofa and watches us with glee in his eyes. He has this stupid grin on his face like he's Santa or something, obviously enjoying the success of his present.

When Maisie gets tired, I put phase two of my plan into action. "I think we should take her outside before she pees in the house."

Jed, who moved into the chair before dozing off, awakes with a startle. "What?" He rubs his eyes, trying to comprehend what just happened.

My chin points to Maisie. "She has to use the bathroom."

"Yeah." His voice is still thick from his sleep. "Why don't you take her?"

Trapped

I wiggle my toes in the woolly socks. "Where did you hide our shoes?"

He waves at the closet by the door. "In there. Put on a coat and a hat, or you'll freeze to death. The windchill is brutal today."

Hallie and I slip in our shoes before putting on the warm winter coats. Hallie finds her hat stuffed inside a sleeve. I grab a spare beanie off the rack.

As Jed unlocks the door, he shoots us a firm look. "I'll be watching you. Don't try anything stupid."

The arctic air chills me to the bone the second I step outside. It must be well below zero. The snow has stopped. There is not a cloud in the sky and the sun shines brightly above, which even offers moments of comfort when the freezing wind takes a short breather.

I stumble down the stairs, holding on to the banister. A few times, my feet almost slip. With worried eyes, I watch how Maisie wobbles down the steps, landing in a big pile of fresh snow. She shakes her little head, sneezing, her ears flopping from side to side. She is adorable.

Jed remains on the porch, pulling a cigarette pack from his coat. Squinting against the sun, he lights himself a smoke before taking a deep drag. As he exhales, he tilts back his head, letting the sunrays play on his face. I continue to watch him out of the corners of my eyes, luring Maisie away from the house. Hallie catches on and trots behind us.

I scan the area to find an escape route. The lake is right in front of us and even though it is covered with a layer of ice, it is not a viable option. To our left is the end of the dirt road with Jed's van parked close to the gate. Without a key, the vehicle is useless. The only other option is a large open space to the right, ending by a tree line about two hundred yards away. It's quite a distance to cover. Still, it's our only chance.

I signal Hallie with my eyes before picking up two handfuls of snow, forming a sturdy ball. Tossing it at her boisterously, I move a few steps in the direction of the forest. Soon, a cloud of snow is heading my way as she uses her hands as shovels. Maisie toddles along, oblivious to our efforts to disguise our escape as harmless play. I laugh loudly in between, pretending to have a lot of fun, while edging closer to the tree line.

We make it about halfway there when a loud "hey" indicates that Jed must have caught on.

"Run," I shout.

Hallie takes off after scooping up Maisie in her arms.

I'm right behind them, my muscles pumping. Despite my latest exercise efforts, my breath is ragged and my lungs burn after only a few yards. I push forward, ignoring the sudden surge of fear that threatens to cripple my legs. My eyes are fixed on Hallie's back and the trees. She seems to be flying which gives me motivation to sprint faster.

Sweat sticks to my forehead as my breath mists the air in front of me for brief moments until I break through the foggy wall, just to build a new one right in front of my eyes. My heart is pounding loudly as I find a rhythm, my arms and legs moving in unison. The wind bites at my nose. I ball my chilled hands to fists, continuing to push my body to its limits. In my mind, I count down the distance—forty yards, then thirty. The snow scrunches under my boots. Other than that, all I can hear is my breath and the howling of the wind, rushing by my ears.

Hallie has almost reached the forest when I'm tackled from behind. Something cold pierces my skin. Pain throbs through my neck before something warm trickles down my throat. A few ruby drops fall into the white snow that has broken my fall.

"Don't move, honeybun, or I swear, I'll cut your throat."

Paralyzed in fear, I stop struggling under Jed's body. The blade presses lightly against my thyroid. When a whistle echoes across the field, Hallie halts in her tracks. She spins around, her eyes wide.

"Come back here, or I'll kill her," Jed yells, the threat resonating painfully in my ears.

There is not the slightest hesitation as Hallie reverses her path, walking slowly back in our direction. As she approaches, tears stream down her face. Her gaze is laced with terror.

"Please don't hurt her," she whispers when she reaches us.

The knife is withdrawn. I'm lifted to my feet before a shove sends me back in the direction of the cabin. With my eyes glued to the ground, I trudge back through the snow until I get to the stairs. Jed is on my heels and nudges me in the back of my head.

"Move." His word is nothing more than a growl.

I can tell he is furious. There's no doubt that some form of punishment is imminent. When I step through the door, warmth from the fireplace greets me. The air in the cabin is still filled with the scent of oranges and cinnamon, but all traces of the light atmosphere are gone. I find Jed's eyes. His face is contorted in rage, his bottom lip trembling.

"Get upstairs"—he hisses at Hallie—"and take that dog with you."

She juts her chin at him. "What are you gonna do to Kelsey?"

"That's none of your concern." His eyes narrow. "Now. Move." The last two words are spit with so much venom that they give me the chills.

When Hallie still doesn't show the slightest inclination to oblige, I give her a small nod. "Go."

She finally storms up the steps. Maisie is curled up in her arms, staring at me with her big dark eyes. She must sense that something is terribly wrong.

Jed darts up the stairs and locks her door before returning downstairs. I glance at the open bedroom, pondering whether to make a run for it, but I don't even have a key to lock myself in. One hard push and Jed would be able to pry the door open.

He grabs my wrist and drags me behind him, ignoring my small yelp. With one shove, he tosses me on the bed as soon as we are over the threshold.

My wrist pulses. I rub over the sore spot to ease the pain.

"You were a very bad girl," he scolds in a loud voice, an angry finger pointing right at my nose. "I fucking trusted you and that's how you repay me. Why did you have to ruin everything?"

Tears spill from my eyes as I stare at him, unsure how to respond. I have never seen him angrier and don't want to aggravate him even more.

When I stay silent, he drops his pants. I know what's coming next. Towering over the bed, both of his hands grab strands of my hair, forcing my mouth closer to him.

I struggle, my scalp stinging from the assault. "Please, Jed." I gaze into his eyes. "You know how much I hate it."

His laugh is cruel. "You should've thought about that before pulling this stunt."

When he tightens his grip, I whimper, fighting to tear away.

He lets go of my hair and squats next to the bed. "Now listen, honeybun. If you don't do this, I'll take it out on Hallie before killing that little pooch I just gave you." His eyes gleam like molten coals although his voice is soft. It's his way of showing me that he is dead serious and fully in control. "Is that what you want?"

Trapped

My lips tremble when I shake my head, my heart clenched in an iron hold. This time, I don't fight him when he pulls me closer. Every part of me revolts as I am forced to do the deed, curling myself into a tight ball when I'm done. He leaves me alone for the rest of the day, not joining me in the bed even after it has gotten dark outside.

At some point, I must have fallen asleep, and I almost jump out of the bed when his hand strokes my hair. I blink at him as he looks down on me with this cruel grin on his face that is always present when he takes revenge. Just like the first night, he places a cup of steaming hot tea and a razor blade on my nightstand.

"Try to get some rest, honeybun. You have a big day tomorrow." His shoulders shake under his chuckles as he leaves me behind.

For the next hour, I sip the tea, my eyes fixed on the razor blade. Temptation is burning through my veins like it did the times when my dad took me to the candy store and told me I could have anything I wanted. I breathe in deeply, pain surging through me. My eyes fill with tears. This is too much. I can't handle this anymore. For the first time in my life, I just want to end it all. Death is the only thing that can ultimately take me out of my nightmare and kill those demons.

With a sigh, I pick up the razor blade and place it on my open palm. The sharp edges draw me in. My thumb is already reaching forward, my mind screaming for the impending pain. The relief that this will all be over soon is sweet. I imagine what it will be like to feel nothing. Peace at last—but only peace for me. If I do this, I will let everyone down. My mom and Luke will be heartbroken, Finn mad as hell that I couldn't kick the habit. I don't want to disappoint them again.

Reggie told us in therapy that we have to be honest to ourselves. The cutting kept me trapped, just as much as my memories and self-pity. It kills the pain, but also forces me to constantly relive a part of my nightmare to keep the pain alive, just so it can be killed again, which is nothing more than a vicious cycle. I am my own worst enemy, dragging me and everyone down with my victim role. It has to stop, not only for my mom and Luke and Finn, but mostly for myself. I don't want to blame everyone else for my unhappiness.

With a small smile, I place the razor blade back on the nightstand. Jed will not win this time. My hand automatically reaches for the light switch and soothing darkness falls over the room. I am done with this part of my life—there will be no more self-harming and inflicting more pain. The scars I have now will be hard to heal, but they will eventually fade. There is no reason to add more misery.

Chapter 20

The next morning, Jed summons us into the kitchen for Hallie's birthday breakfast—to "have a good time." As promised, he did get a birthday cake and sixteen candles burn in a circle.

"Let's sing," he announces and I reluctantly join in after a wicked glance from him.

Hallie sits rigidly on the barstool with a clenched jaw, her lips pressed together in a thin line. There are tears in her eyes. She seems numb, not even the slightest hint of joy on her face. I'm pretty sure she is mourning another loss. Sweet sixteen is one of those days that only comes around once in a lifetime. It's awful to have it ruined like this.

Maisie is rolled up in the crook of my elbow. She was on my bed when I woke up this morning. I could swear Jed put something in the tea to knock me out because I never heard him come in—neither to place the dog on the bed nor to remove the razor blade and the tea cup—and I am usually a very light sleeper.

I focus back on the birthday song and finish it with a forced smile.

"Make a wish," Jed shouts cheerfully.

Like a robot, Hallie bends forward and blows out the candles. Her eyes are squeezed shut. There could only be one wish on her mind and that is getting out of this hellhole.

Jed cuts the cake, keeping the knife at a safe distance from us, and locks it back into the drawer as soon as he's done. His face is almost mask-like—I cannot read his emotions at all. That makes him even more unpredictable than usual.

The next few minutes are dominated by silence. All three of us stare at different specks on the wall, deeply engrossed in our own thoughts while taking small bites from the cake. I chew automatically without tasting anything and remember my sixteenth birthday like it was yesterday. It was two months before my abduction. I had a big party and my parents had pooled their resources to get me a small car, a new Volkswagen Beetle Convertible. It was midnight blue, with cream leather seats, and I loved it—at least until I was taken. After that, it drew too much attention to me.

Jed is stirring his coffee absentmindedly, probably brooding over his next devious scheme. I wonder if he will force himself on me before Napoleon comes over later today—I sure wouldn't put it past him. Even he must have felt I was damaged and dirty after one of his friend's visits, because he wouldn't touch me for a few days afterward, every time it happened.

As if he can read minds, his gaze lands on me. "Napoleon will be over at six."

A gasp escapes Hallie's mouth. She cups her hand over her lips, her eyes wide with a pitiful glow.

I turn around under Jed's burning stare, carefully placing Maisie on the floor. Without a single word, I stroll into the bathroom. The door closes behind me with a loud bang when I give it a good push with my foot.

The solitude of the enclosed space fails to give me comfort when I break down, hugging my knees. I want to cry—maybe even rant and rage—but all emotions have vanished. The fighting spirit is extinguished. What would be the point? Jed will watch me like a hawk for the rest of the day, and I doubt I'll get another opportunity to be with Hallie outside. Attacking him is not an option—with his boxing skills, he will beat the crap out of me before getting rid of Maisie. He'd probably even make me watch when he slit her throat.

Trapped

I'm not sure how long I have been crouched on the cold floor when Jed knocks on the bathroom door. "Are you okay in there?"

He asks the dumbest questions at times. I choose to ignore him.

More knocking. "Can I come in?"

Again, I don't bother to reply.

The door opens with a low squeak and he pokes his head in. After a good once-over, he steps inside the room, lowering himself next to me.

"I know it sucks," he says.

"How can you pretend that you care about me and then have another man touch me?" My voice is getting shriller with every word. "You're such a coward."

He shakes his head with vigor. "No, that's not true." His hands enclose mine. He looks like prey, trying to hide from a hunter. "I can't fight him, honeybun. Trust me, I've tried. If I don't do what he asks of me, he'll kill you before coming after me. There's no way to fight him." His words are laced with utter fear and panic.

I realize it is not some act he's playing. "How the hell did you ever get involved with him? He sounds like a total psychopath."

He buries his face in his hands. "I've known him for a really long time. He didn't used to be this way, but ever since we took you the first time, he has gone totally mental." He pulls up his shirt, exposing a long slash alongside his ribs. "That's what he did after I let you escape. When I left town after the charges were dismissed, I didn't try to get away from the rumors, but from him." Wetness glistens in his eyes. "Last spring, he tracked me down and told me I had to return because he wasn't done with you. The dog leash, the spiders, the book—those were all his ideas."

I squint at him. "Oh, come on, Jed. He didn't force you to rape me and I saw how much you enjoyed torturing me."

"True," he concedes. "I wanted revenge, but after you got away, I was done. All this"—he swoops his hands around—"I didn't want."

"Then let's go to the cops together now and you'll tell them everything. They'll protect you, and if you cooperate, they'll give you a deal."

His eyes go wide. "I can't. Do you know what they do to rapists in prison?"

If it's anything like what Finn had suffered, he should be concerned, but that really isn't my problem. He brought this on himself.

"Look, Jed," I say calmly. "Sooner or later, you *will* get caught, and this time, you won't get off on a technicality. My stepdad is a lawyer and I promise you, he'll defend you and make sure that nothing will happen to you in prison. Just let us go."

He squeezes my hand, his face devoid of emotions. "I'm sorry, honeybun, but I just can't."

~~~~

For the rest of the day, he avoids striking up a conversation. Hallie is locked up in her room and when I ask if she could come downstairs to play with the puppy, he flat out refuses. When Maisie whines to go outside, he grabs her for a short stroll on the porch, and his sinister glare deters me from asking whether I can tag along.

With every passing minute, the tension in the cabin becomes more pressing, and by the time the clock chimes 5:45, the atmosphere is so explosive that a lit match would have caused mayhem.

Jed clears his throat. "It's time, honeybun. You have to get ready."

I cuddle my face into Maisie's soft fur, pressing a kiss on her with a soft "see ya later, girl." She whimpers when a sob runs through me and a stream of hot tears gets her wet behind her ear. With gritted teeth, I follow Jed into the bedroom.

He passes me a Victoria's Secret bag. "Put this on."

I stare at him. "You can't be serious."

His eyes are pleading. "Please, honeybun, just do what I tell you and don't fight me. I really don't want to have to hurt you."

My dignity gets the better of me and I lunge forward—I will not be some dress-up doll who will pander to Napoleon's whims. Jed, however, expects trouble and I run straight into his fist. The blow is not hard enough to knock me out but still floors me. I shake my head to get the fuzziness from my mind, black spots dancing in front of my eyes. Jed's fist gets ahold of a bushel of my hair and tilts my head back, which is about to explode.

"Why do you always have to be so difficult?" he yells, clutching my hair tighter until I scream in pain.

When he releases me, I close my eyes to get the buzzing out of my head. Nausea sits like a fat lump in the back of my throat and my whole body is covered in cold sweat. I lie still on the floor until my ragged breath calms.

Jed is towering over me when I squint at him, my head still a throbbing mess. When he probes me with his foot, I instinctively curl into a ball to protect myself from a kick.

His glare sends shivers down my spine. "Napoleon will be here any minute, so get changed. I swear if you give me anymore hassle, I'll knock every single one of your teeth out." His lip trembles slightly, but I'm not sure if it is anger or fear of his master. Whoever Napoleon is, he scares the living daylights out of Jed.

My hands are shaking while I fumble with the button on my pants until Jed loses his patience and pushes me on the bed. I don't fight him anymore when he slides off my pants and orders me to stand up so he can pull off my shirt. His fingers brush warmly over my skin when he unclasps my bra. His eyes stay on my breasts for a brief moment before he covers them again with the new lingerie. The panties are actually a thong that make me feel naked.

A blindfold soon covers my eyes, throwing me in a world of gloom. My tears are caught by the soft fabric. Ever since the last abduction, I'm terrified of complete darkness and my whole body shivers, competing with my chattering teeth. Yet the rushing of my blood in my ears is soothing. My heart beats strong, even if it is twice its usual speed. When my tongue runs over my lips, I taste the salt from the sweat, pearling on my upper lip.

I focus on my other senses, determined to learn as much as possible about Napoleon. This time, I will give Larouge something to catch that bastard with, and if I try hard enough, I might even be able to figure out his identity on my own. I will no longer be the helpless victim. Jed confirmed I know him. If I try hard enough, something will give him away.

When Jed starts to secure my arms and legs with cable ties, my body turns stiff. From prior experience, I know they are especially painful when I struggle, tightening to a point where my hands and feet become totally numb and I lose all feeling in my fingers and toes. They also leave nasty cut marks behind, the scars still visible from my last encounter with Napoleon.

Jed is just tightening the restraints around my left ankle when there is a knock on the door. "He's here," he whispers.

My heartbeat accelerates even more and a large stone fist pushes harshly on my chest. I open my mouth wide to suck in oxygen, feeling like a fish on land.

"Just don't fight him and it'll be over quicker." Jed's voice is hushed and drifts over from the door. A low click confirms that he must have left the room to greet his friend.

I lie perfectly still in the darkness, focusing on my breath and heartbeat. When my ears pick up a low scratching noise, my fingers instinctively curl—I can sense the presence of another person in the room. A cool draft floats in before the door closes, causing a shudder to run through me.

As footsteps approach, my heart races so fast that I fear it will jump out of my chest and fly away. More tears spill from my eyes and soak into the blindfold, which sticks to my eyelids and cheeks. My arms and legs automatically begin to fight the restraints as he walks around the bed. Only the burning pain of the plastic strap breaking my skin forces me to still again.

Goosebumps spread all over my body when his hot breath grazes my neck before he traces little kisses along my jawline. Every part of me transforms into clumps of ice, my stomach twisting in knots. I bite my lip to stifle a scream. His tongue probes and I grant him access, knowing that any resistance is futile. He used to squeeze my cheeks with his fingers so hard when I clenched my teeth—they worked just like pincers to pry my mouth open.

Don't be afraid, I tell myself over and over in my mind. *You've survived this before and can do it again.*

His breath becomes heavy when he presses against me, but I force myself to stay calm, thinking of Maisie and her warm round eyes as they gaze at me with trust. If I beg and cry like I did in the past, he might hurt her, or worse, kill her, to teach me a lesson. I have to stay strong. His fingers run alongside my body, teasing me. It takes all my effort not to gag. He doesn't need to know how much he disgusts me.

I sense him sitting up and staring at me. Holding my breath, I brace myself for more of his touch, but he gets up instead and moves away from the bed. By the time the door closes with a low thud, I am utterly confused. What the hell is going on? Where did he go?

Muffled sounds from a hushed conversation drift through the wall, and I prick my ears to make out the words and voices. It's to no avail. I can't even tell if one or two people are talking. There are rushed footsteps and someone storms into my room. Before I can even register what is happening, light stings my eyes when the blindfold is pulled off. I blink to find Jed's face just inches from my own.

"I'm so sorry, honeybun. I swear I didn't want this to happen."

My brain is scrambling to make sense of his words when a loud scream echoes through the house. The ice clumps turn into an avalanche that hits me full force, knocking all life out of me. Yet my willpower fights back with all my might and I twist in my restraints as sobs and loud pleas from upstairs open up the gates to my nightmare.

"He's with Hallie. I have to help her." My voice is shrill and pierces my eardrums.

Jed's hands wrap around my arms just below my wrists, his body almost entirely covering me to prevent me from tearing the skin off my bones in my restraints.

"Please, honeybun, calm down. You can't help her."

I wiggle to get him off me, spitting a colorful assortment of profanities in his face. His pocketknife finally frees me and my fists start pounding on his back. Hallie's continued screams and wails fuel my rage and give me more strength than I've ever experienced. My fingernails claw every part of Jed that is not covered by clothes until his arms wrap tightly around me like an iron rope, preventing further damage.

"Let me go," I shout at the top of my lungs. "I have to help her."

"You can't help her," he repeats, the calmness in his voice boiling my blood.

His weight knocks the wind out of me, and soon, my lungs sting from my efforts. Exhaustion overpowers my will to fight and my fury manifests itself in fresh tears.

While I weep in his arms, he starts talking softly to me. "Please, you have to stay here with me. He'll kill you if you ever see his face. Just stop fighting and I'll cut off the ties on your legs."

It's the first time that I realize I am still bound to the bottom bedposts. My ankles burn as if the cable ties were fiery bracelets, and the sudden pain causes a small whimper to run from my lips. More tears roll down my cheek as I desperately try to banish Hallie's continued shrieks from my mind, focusing all my remaining energy on my next rescue attempt.

As soon as Jed cuts the ties, I'm on my feet and leap for the door. He reaches me before I can close the gap, his embrace quashing my hopes. He pulls me back on the bed, spooning me tightly into his arms. Neither my pleas nor death threats rattle him; he holds me firmly in place while I continue to fight him, telling me over and over again how sorry he is.

When Hallie's cries finally die down, I'm close to insanity. My throat is raw, my lips a bleeding mess, and large parts of my body are bruised from my struggles. I can barely walk straight when Jed finally allows me to get up after the front door slams shut. Yet, my need to comfort Hallie prevents my knees from buckling.

At the door, I turn around and glare at him. "I swear I'll kill you for this."

A frown is his only response. He doesn't realize that, in my whole life, I have never been more serious.

Chapter 21

Hallie is curled up on the bed, her small frame shaking under her sobs. Her underwear was torn off and tossed carelessly on the floor. Napoleon must have cut the ropes she was tied with before he left. Her wrists are burned and raw, but not cut like mine from the cable ties.

I carefully slide the blindfold off her eyes, but she still shrieks, her body almost convulsing with fear until she realizes it's me. I notice the blood streaks on the mattress and bile rises in my throat. For a moment, I almost burst out crying, but I have to stay strong for her. She must feel incredibly dirty; I need to get her out of the bed and into the bathroom.

She allows me to guide her, her eyes staring vacantly into the distance. Half her face is beginning to swell, her lip bleeding from a nasty cut. There are red spots all over her body which will turn blue in a few hours. She whimpers with every step she takes, and I drape a blanket over her shoulders so that Jed won't get an eyeful of her nakedness.

My arm slides around her waist, supporting her while she stumbles down the steps. Once she slips and I almost drop her, but my fingernails dig into the rail at the last second. Pain throbs through my shoulder and robs me of my breath when my arm is almost pulled from its socket.

Jed is gazing up and opens his mouth, probably to offer his help, but I just shake my head. A male voice, no matter how gentle, will scare her and make matters worse. Obediently, he steps aside when we get to the bottom of the stairs—one wrong move or word and he will feel my knee in his groin. I'm done playing, even if that means he'll beat the crap out of me.

I lead Hallie into the bathroom and turn on the shower, ensuring that the water is warm but not too hot before allowing her to step into the tub. Mechanically, she applies soap to her skin, silent tears streaming down her face. Every move is robotic. No sound passes her lips and her eyes are totally blank.

I decide to give her some privacy and step into the kitchen after sliding into a bathrobe that is hanging on a hook by the door.

Jed stares at me with big round eyes. "How is she holding up?"

It takes all my effort not to slap him across the face. "What do you think?"

Walking over to the sink, I pour myself a glass of water, letting the cool liquid run down my raw throat before playing around with it in my mouth. My head throbs, and every time I move, my bleeding wrists and ankles shoot pain waves up my arms and legs. I glare at the inside of the glass, my thumb running over the rim. Anger, stronger than I've felt in a long time, takes a grip of me, a vicious devil hacking at my frayed nerves until they finally tear apart. With one swift move, I throw the glass against the wall with all my might.

"You fucking knew this was going to happen, didn't you!" My eyes burn into Jed's skull when he drops his gaze. If I had a gun, I would shoot him right in the center of that forehead.

"I didn't want him to touch you." His words are low and he pulls his head in between his shoulders like Luke used to do when he was little and scolded by his dad.

"So you set Hallie up?" My voice trembles with fury. "I mean, you made sure she was tied up and blindfolded, all ready for Napoleon when he decided I wasn't worth his effort."

His eye twitches under my glare. "Look, honeybun, your words really hit home when you said that I was a coward for letting someone else touch you." He gives me a pleading look. "I really like you and I couldn't stand the thought that he would rough you up. I knew he would turn away when you were submissive and didn't fight him—that's the kind of person he is." A slight blush colors his cheeks. "He joked once that he can't get off unless a girl struggles and he can hurt her."

What kind of sick bastard is Napoleon? With disgust, I turn my back on Jed, squatting down next to the shards of glass. With careful fingers, I reach to pick them up, but he is by my side before I can even touch the first piece.

"Let me get that for you."

I realize he's afraid that I will use the broken glass to cut myself though the thought hasn't even occurred to me. I'm doing well on that front. Hallie might be struggling, though, and I will need to keep an eye on her. I don't want her to fall into the same trap and repeat my mistakes.

With my back leaning against the wall, I hug my knees and watch Jed while he sweeps up the glass with a dustpan.

"You're really mad, aren't you?" he asks when he pours the leftovers in the bin.

Mad is the understatement of the century. "How could you do this to Hallie? She was still a virgin and it's her birthday." Not that it would have been any better on another day—losing one's innocence through rape is traumatic under any circumstance.

"I'll make it up to her, I promise," he mutters.

I gasp at his ignorance. "And how are you going to do that, Jed?" My eyes are challenging. "Get her a puppy?" My gaze wanders to Maisie, who is curled up on the chair, sleeping. "But let me tell you—whatever it is you're planning to do, you can never replace what Napoleon stole from her today."

His face twists like he was just punched in his stomach. "Don't you think I know that?" He tears the lid off the kettle with a sigh, filling it with fresh water.

I rest my chin on my knees, my glare stalking him as he walks over to the stove to heat the water. "I hope you feel like crap."

He slams the kettle down. "I already apologized to you a thousand times, so what more do you want?" His eyes have turned three shades darker, the vein on his forehead pulsing on his skull. With his outstretched finger, he points at the bathroom door. "I could've never saved her. If it didn't happen today, it would've been tomorrow or the next day. Napoleon never intended to spare her. It was just a game for him to see how far you were willing to go."

My jaw drops. "So it was never about me then? He wanted Hallie from the start."

Jed shakes his head. "No, it was about you alright. Napoleon is obsessed with you, always has been, but he likes the old Kelsey. The one who screamed and tried to fight him. He called you a wildcat he wanted to tame, but then you turned into this sulky girl who lost all her fire. That's when he brought me back to Stonehenge to help him shake things up a little."

The pieces finally fall into place. Napoleon's plan for me to fight back after Jed returned to my life backfired when I once again assumed the victim rule and mutilated myself to a point where I was admitted to the hospital. Then he probed and tortured me until I finally bared my fangs. Yet Hallie's virginity was the cherry on top—the one thing he couldn't resist. He's a despicable excuse of a human being and the mere thought that I actually know him sends chills down my spine.

Jed opens a cabinet and tosses a medicine bottle my way. "Take two and break them into powder. There's a butter knife in the sink you can use."

I look at the pack, but it's not labeled. "What are they?"

"Sleeping pills. I'll mix them with Hallie's tea. It will help her sleep and forget."

He really has no clue how rape works. The nightmares will still haunt her, even if she takes a whole bottle of that stuff. Since I don't feel like arguing with him, I take the knife out of the sink, my thumb testing the blade to ascertain whether it could be used as a weapon. It's duller than my fingernail.

I pour the tablets in my hand and let two of them roll onto the counter when an idea strikes. My eyes dart to Jed who is busy adding sugar to Hallie's tea. Two more pills disappear in the pocket of my bathrobe. With vigor, I begin to beat on the tablets on the counter with the handle of the knife until they turn into a fine powder. I catch the medicine with my open hand to add to Hallie's tea.

"Can Hallie stay with me tonight?" I ask Jed while he stirs the tea.

"I guess that's the least I can do."

I get on my tiptoes and brush a kiss on his cheek. "Thank you."

His eyebrows quirk. "What was that for? I thought you wanted to kill me."

"You explained to me how Napoleon ticks and there is no way you could've prevented Hallie from being raped. It's just something I have to accept."

There is huge relief on his face when I take the tea out of his hand. He is totally oblivious that I'm only stringing him along, already planning my next escape. Once he gets a literal taste of his own medicine, I can get the keys, Hallie, and Maisie, and then it will be "hasta la vista, baby"— until the cops arrest his ass.

Back in the bathroom, I help Hallie out of the tub and wrap her in a large fluffy towel. Her skin is reddened from all the scrubbing, but I know she still feels dirty and cheap. Her right eye is almost swollen shut and she has a fat lip, though the bleeding has stopped.

I run a brush through her hair. Her eyes are a little bit more alert. She hisses when her curls get entangled and I have to pull hard. After a few minutes, all the knots are out. I give her a cold cloth for her eye.

"Tell Jed you liked the tea," I say, pouring the contents of the cup into the sink. "Then yawn and claim you're sleepy."

She considers me with big eyes, then nods. With her gaze glued to the floor, she toddles behind me into the kitchen.

I set the empty cup into the sink.

"Was the tea okay?" Jed asked, giving Hallie a good once-over.

She stands frozen by the counter and stares at him, her lips trembling. Fresh tears pool in her eyes—she is about to lose it.

I quickly intervene before she gets us both into a sticky situation. "I'll take Hallie to bed now." I glance at the cup. "Could you maybe make me some tea as well?"

He beams at me. "Sure, honeybun."

Guiding Hallie by her shoulders toward the bedroom, she takes automatic steps forward. When we get to our destination, I rummage for sweats and a long-sleeved shirt, setting a pair of woolly socks aside.

"Put these on and get into bed. Pretend to sleep until I get you."

Like a well-trained dog, she obliges my every command. When she is securely tucked into bed, I return into the kitchen after switching off the lights. I can just hope she stays put or this could ruin my plan.

The kettle is just boiling and Jed pours the hot water into a fresh cup. The scent of mint fills the kitchen, making my stomach rumble. Since breakfast, I haven't eaten anything, my guts too knotted in anticipation of Napoleon's visit. My nerves are still shot, but my body demands fuel. I grab an apple from the fruit bowl, taking a big bite. "Aren't you going to have tea?"

Jed takes out the whiskey bottle and a tumbler. "I need something stronger. It was a rough night for me, too."

I almost shed tears—both of sarcasm and joy. The alcohol will work better with the sleeping pills and knock him out even quicker. Now I just need to find a way to distract him.

On cue, Maisie raises her head and whimpers.

"I think she needs to go to the bathroom."

Jed stretches. "I'll take her. I need a smoke anyhow."

He takes the keys to the front door out of his pocket and clicks his tongue a few times to get her attention. Maisie jumps down from the chair and shakes herself, her ears flopping from side to side. She really is the cutest pup.

Jed fumbles forever with the locks. My fingers drum on the counter and the ticking clock on the wall is driving me nuts, every fiber of my body on high alert. I will only have a few minutes. As soon as the door closes behind him, I spring into action, pulling the two sleeping pills from my pocket. The knife is no longer in the sink and I let out a small curse. Why are all the odds stacked against me tonight? My eyes dart around, trying to find anything that could be used to crush the tablets, but Jed has cleaned up and locked everything away.

In the end, I go for the tumbler. With shaking hands, I pour the whiskey back into the bottle, spilling half of it before slamming the pills with the glass. The booming *thump* scares me half to death. I still, my ears pricked for any sound from the outside, but only the howling wind rattles angrily at the shutters.

This won't work. I have to somehow muffle the sound. My eyes find the towels on the rack. I grab one, laying it over the medicine. The sound of the banging glass is now hardly audible. I work quickly, my gaze fixed on the door. Jed could be back at any second.

The pills are finally crushed and I sweep the powder into the glass. A good amount of whiskey is poured on top to make sure the taste is not noticeable. My hands fly while I wipe the remains of the powder and the spilled whiskey off the counter before tossing the towel into the laundry basket. With a small hop, I get back onto my barstool—just in time.

The door opens and Jed steps back in, his hair soaked. Maisie is in a similar condition, shaking herself and sending little water droplets flying.

"It's miserable out there," Jed says. "The snow has turned into freezing rain. The rate it's going, we'll have a major ice storm tonight. I should get the generator ready just in case the power lines are knocked down."

An ice storm could seriously hamper our escape options. If we don't take the van, we could freeze to death from hypothermia, yet the roads will be treacherous. Black ice will cover them within minutes, especially in a rural place like Tacoma Lakes.

I'm still tossing around different options in my mind when Jed brushes past me, his fingers briefly grazing my cheek. I close my eyes and take a deep breath, hoping the disgust won't show on my face. He takes a good swallow from his whiskey before his face contorts into a grimace.

"Yuk." He sniffs the drink. "I think I didn't rinse out the glass properly—this tastes like dish soap."

I drop my gaze when my cheeks begin to burn, cursing this new streak of bad luck. I never expected that his palate could pick up the taste of the pills that easily. To my horror, he pours the rest of the whiskey into the sink, the brown liquid twirling around the drain before disappearing into the pipe.

"Jed."

His head snaps around to look at me.

Somehow I need to keep his attention away from the sink. "I—I . . ." My mind is wiped of all thoughts—the only thing my brain registers is the residue of the powder which is clearly visible in the streaks of the whiskey that were left behind. If Jed notices them, he will immediately figure out that I tried to knock him out.

"Could you . . ." I start again.

A sweet smile plays on his lips. "Yes, honeybun?" He wiggles his brows, looking at me expectantly.

I hold my breath—my mind totally failing me. There is not even a hint of a useful idea to hide my sabotage attempt. Disaster is approaching fast and will hit me with the force of a bulldozer.

That's when his gaze turns back to the sink.

Chapter 22

I haven't experienced many moments where I felt that life was unfolding in slow motion right in front of my eyes, but this is one of those times. My gaze is fixed on Jed as his body swings around frame by frame, and at some point I squeeze my eyes shut, ready for the big blowout. I'm sure he will beat the crap out of me.

A sharp buzz startles me and I almost fall off the barstool when I jump a few inches in the air before I manage to grab onto the counter at the last second. A soft melody drifts through the kitchen—the intro theme of a TV show that my mom and Roy always watch—and I gather it is the ringtone of Jed's mobile. When I glance at him through hooded eyes, his back is turned once again to the sink. He holds up the phone to his ear.

"Yeah, what's up?"

The caller on the other end tells him something that causes a small frown to wrinkle on his forehead. "Is it really that bad?" He listens intently. "Well, let me go downstairs and check on the generator. I'm sure the power will be knocked out sometime tonight. Where are you?"

He walks off and I'm on my feet in an instant, dashing over to the sink. The water turns on with a small gurgle. I splatter it around with my hand until the whiskey and powder remains have vanished down the drain. When I'm done, I realize that my whole body is shaking. For good measures, I sprinkle water on my face to clear my humming head.

"What ya doing, honeybun?"

I spin around with another startle to find Jed leaning against the counter. If the night continues with these dodgy situations, I'll have a heart attack by morning for sure.

"Nothing." My eyes fall on the tumbler. "I was just rinsing out your glass so you can fix yourself another drink."

He stretches. "That was Napoleon. The storm is so bad that he barely made it home. I really shouldn't drink tonight in case the power goes out and I have to start the generator." He winks at me. "The basement steps are rotten and dangerous, even when you're sober. I'm sure you don't want me to break my leg, or you'll have to take care of me."

I would rather have him break his neck but keep that thought to myself. "I should go to bed. It's getting late and Hallie might need someone to talk to when she wakes up."

He steps closer and pulls me into his arms. "You're such a good friend to her." His face nuzzles into my hair. "She's really lucky to have you."

I go rigid when guilt washes over me—I blame myself for what happened to her. Though I know that I couldn't have saved her, the way it all went down was just horrific.

He pulls away and yawns into his hand. "I'm really tired, too. It was a stressful day for all of us." He glances at Maisie in the chair. "Even the damn dog is out cold. She will probably pee in the house because of the storm. You should have seen her out there shivering earlier. I was scared she would shoot off the porch when she slipped on the ice."

This is likely the worst night for an escape, but probably our only chance before Napoleon is back for more terror. Jed's pupils are dilated, so some of that sleeping aid must have gotten into his system. The window of opportunity is small but still worth the risk. Hallie could not go through the ordeal of being raped a second time without losing her mind—the hurt and distress was just too visible on her face.

"Well, good night, Jed."

He blows a kiss on my cheek. "Good night, honeybun. Don't let the bedbugs bite you."

That's what my dad used to say before my parents got divorced—I was only three. I quickly wipe away a loose tear. Since my mom married Roy, I hardly see him, but we usually get together over the holidays. I wonder about his reaction to the whole "I need a break thing" and my disappearance. Knowing him, he probably bought it—he has never really been attuned with my feelings.

Hallie is awake, staring at the ceiling, when I slide into bed. She lies perfectly still, taking even breaths like she's hooked to a breathing machine. Her glassy eyes give me the creeps. Hopefully, she will be able to keep it together during the escape.

I give it a good half hour during which we both lie in the darkness without a sound before I get up to check whether the coast is clear. Jed is curled up on the sofa under a thick patchwork quilt that looks ancient, Maisie resting in the folds above his feet. Her head rises as I approach. The echo of her whimper sounds magnified in the still house.

To quiet her, I pat her head, which only causes her to start licking my hand. Her small body wiggles around on Jed's legs. He stirs in his sleep, mumbling something. I quickly scoop up the puppy—she's going to ruin everything if she wakes him up.

Not sure what to do with the struggling dog, I take her to the bedroom and sit her down next to Hallie.

"I really need you to focus now and keep an eye on Maisie. I know you're hurting, but I'm trying to get us both out of here and I need your help."

Hallie seems to wake up from a deep slumber and a fire begins to burn in her eyes. "What do you want me to do?"

"Get ready. It's storming and freezing outside, so go through all the drawers and get everything imaginable to keep us warm. I'm going to get the keys and our coats and shoes."

"Why don't you just get Jed's phone and call the cops?"

That idea was crushed when I saw his cell tonight. "I have no clue where we are other than Tacoma Lakes, which is a huge area. He uses a really old phone, something that was popular maybe ten years ago, and I'm sure it doesn't have a tracking device. Even if they contact the network and do a search, it will be hours, if not days, before they find us. We can't wait that long. Once we're away from Jed, we'll call them."

Hallie nods and jumps out of bed, fully on board with my plan. The first drawer is pulled out, its contents dumped on the floor, before she starts rummaging through the clothes. I turn toward the door to get Jed's keys and phone.

His head hangs off the couch and he is snoring with his mouth wide open. I tiptoe closer. Squatting down next to him, my hands wander under the blanket. He sneezes and grumbles, rolling on his right side, facing the backrest. One of his jeans' pockets is now totally out of reach and I just pray that it's not the one with the keys.

I take a peek under the blanket to target the right area before my hand slides in his side pocket. My fingers hit a metallic object and I rejoice when my thumb runs over the edges of a key. Jed smacks his lips. I freeze, ensuring that his breath is even before continuing. My fingertips slowly work the keys into my palm. Finally, I manage to pull them out. I rise hastily. A floorboard squeaks under my feet when I take a step forward.

Jed wrinkles his nose, scratching it before blinking at me. "Honeybun, what is it?" His voice is thick from sleep—he is still in this half-asleep, half-awake stage.

My heart pounds in the back of my throat as my mouth dries up. "I just came to get Maisie." I give him my sweetest smile. "Go back to sleep."

He pulls the quilt closer around him and snuggles in. A minute later, he's back to snoring. A silent sigh of relief rolls over my lips. That was close. Taking careful steps, I dance across the floor into the bedroom.

Hallie is crumpled on the floor with her knees pulled to her chest, her shoulders trembling with silent sobs. I roll my eyes—we don't have time for this. I'm about snap at her, but then stop myself. What am I thinking? This had been me just a few weeks ago and I, of all people, should understand that this is eating at her very substance. I have to cut her a break. Telling her that this is not the time to mourn is the wrong thing to do.

I lower myself next to her and stroke her back. "What's the matter?"

In response, she lifts up a picture that has been lying face down on the floor. "I found this."

I take the photo and a cold chill runs down my spine. It's a close up of my younger self, terror and incredible pain in my eyes. Jed must have taken it during the first abduction. His words that he and Napoleon were taping me rings in my ears. I wonder how many more photos and videos are hidden somewhere. They probably get off watching me scream; a sickening thought that pushes bile up my throat.

"Why are they doing these things to us, Kelsey?" she asks with tears streaming down her face.

"Because they're sick bastards." I squeeze her arm. "I know it's hard right now, but we need to go. It's the only way to punish them for what they did."

"Do you think I'll ever be able to have a boyfriend?"

I remember what Finn told me. "It's up to you to fight for your happiness; no one else will do it for you. I lived for over three years in total misery and it took your kidnapping to wake me up. Don't worry, I'll help you get through this."

A tear rolls down her cheek. "I'm just so glad I'm not alone. I can't even imagine how hard it must've been for you when there was no one around who had your back."

This is not the time to wallow in self-pity. "Let's go."

She takes my offered hand and I pull her on her feet.

"Where's the phone?"

I grimace. "Jed was lying on it and there was no way to get it without waking him up. We'll call the police as soon as we're safe."

Her head points to the bed. "This is everything I found. Where are our shoes and coats?"

I curse myself. "I forgot. Jed almost caught me and all I could think of was getting back in here. Let's grab them on our way out."

The next minutes are spent to transform us into Artic explorers. We layer up on thermo underwear under two sets of jogging pants with several short and long-sleeved t-shirts covered by warm wool sweaters. I just hope I will still manage to get into my boots with the three pairs of socks I'm wearing.

I wrap a scarf around my neck which I can also pull up to cover my mouth and tie another one around my head like a bandana. Hallie opts for one of Jed's beanies and pulls it far over her ears. Her scarf is even thicker than mine and scratchy, her skin reddened when she can't stop itching her neck. Sweat pearls on my forehead; it's now stifling in the room.

"Ready?"

She nods and wraps a small blanket around Maisie. "Let's do this."

I peek my head into the living room, but Jed is back asleep, snoring like he's planning to tear down the house. We scurry over the floor like little mice and halt by the closet. It is locked.

"Damn it," I silently curse, starting to fumble with the keys. I get lucky, the third one fits. The door swings open with a loud squeak. Goosebumps spring up when my eyes dart to Jed, but he is just drooling in his sleep, oblivious to our latest scheming.

With trembling fingers, I slide into my boots, glad that I went for the unfashionable combat-style model which cost $300. My mom almost had a seizure when she saw the price and forced me to buy a larger size with room to grow. My socked foot slides easily inside. With fast fingers, I begin to tie the shoelaces.

Hallie is not so lucky and cannot get into her shoes which are flat ankle boots. Her feet will be frozen within minutes if she only puts on a pair of flimsy socks like she wore this afternoon. It was a miracle that she was even able to run that fast in the snow, but her boots are totally impractical on the ice.

I point at Jed's working boots. "Put those on. The van is parked right outside."

While she fastens the straps, I turn toward the front door, the last barrier between our prison and the outside. This time, I find the right key on the first try. When the door swings open, I brace myself for more squeaking, but the hinges must be oiled well. Only the howling wind greets us. A cold breeze floats in, heading right for Jed, who stirs in response.

My hand finds the light switch for the outside lanterns. I usher Hallie with Maisie in her arms outside, glancing one more time at my tormentor before pulling the door quietly shut behind me. The cold wind hits me full force as soon as I step out of the house's shelter and chills me right to the bone despite all the protective clothing. Freezing rain stings my face like little daggers, the downpour turning into ice right in front of my feet. I pull the scarf up so only my eyes are showing.

When I take a step forward, I land on my butt. Frozen in shock, I stare at the door, certain that the thump woke up Jed. When all stays quiet, I let out a sigh. "Be careful, Hallie. It's real slippery."

She hangs onto the banister, staring at me with wide eyes. "Do you think it's a good idea? It hasn't been this bad in years."

I roll my eyes. "Unless you want to go back inside, there is only one way out of here and that's down those steps."

My feet move forward slowly, making sure I have solid footing before shifting my weight to my other leg. Progress is slower than a snail on the worst of days. My knees are wobbly; in my mind, I'm back on the ice rink for the first time when I was little. I remember my mom's words—always find your center. After that, it becomes easier.

I get to the top of the stairs and slowly make my descent. The freezing wind hits me like a wall. I get down on my butt and slide from step to step until I reach the bottom. As I turn to tell Hallie to do the same, she loses her balance. With a small yelp, her feet fly toward me, her arms instinctively cradling the puppy into the crooks of her elbows for protection. When she hits the frozen snow pile next to me, pain spreads across her face.

"Are you okay?" I shout over the howling wind.

Maisie has freed herself and is shuffling around at the bottom of the stairs, trying to find a hiding place. I grab her and shove her inside my coat where her warm body wiggles around in panic.

Hallie tries to stand up, but her knees buckle. Her face twists in pain. "I can't put any weight on my right foot."

I slide my arm around her waist and drag her toward the van. With gritted teeth, she hops along on one foot, pain burning in her eyes. Luckily, the area between the steps and the van has been cleared before and is not as slippery as the rest of the way. Yet by the time we make it inside the vehicle, my legs are so numb that I can hardly feel them. Maisie is deposited on the backseat and goes into hiding.

Hallie leans back in her seat, whimpering. "I think my ankle is broken. It hurts like hell."

"I'll take you to the hospital and they can call the cops for us." I start the car. "Check the glove compartment. Some people keep painkillers in there."

Hallie pops the compartment open and grins. "Look what I found." She pulls my cell phone from the dark space.

Finally, something works in our favor. "Does it turn on?" I ask while shifting into first gear. The car rolls forward as soon as I release the emergency break, but I am careful not to accelerate too much because of the ice.

She shakes her head. "No, it's totally dead." She pops the back open. "The battery is gone. Jed must have taken it out."

I curse under my breath. "Check in the glove compartment. Maybe he stuck it in there."

My eyes focus on the road. It is dark inside the car, only the green digits of the clock on the radio cover the dashboard in a surreal light. It's just before ten. I am tempted to turn on the radio to drown out Maisie's whining in the back, which is nerve-racking. Hopefully she didn't get hurt as well, but I'm reluctant to ask Hallie to check on her. Every one of Hallie's moves is accompanied by a low hiss—she must be in a lot of pain.

"I found it," she suddenly announces.

I glance at her while she pops the battery into the phone. "Does it turn on?"

The van is having trouble climbing a hill and I accelerate, my full attention focused on the task. I remember Luke telling me that I need to gain momentum on an icy road when I drive up an incline or the car will stall and roll backward.

"What's your pin?" Hallie asks.

"Two, six, nine, two," I reply absentmindedly, my eyes squinting at the road ahead. It looks like there is a curve on top of the hill, but it's hard to make out in the headlights. To the right and the left of us, the woods lay in total darkness. The wind rattles the van, making it hard to drive straight. My wrists hurt from my tight grip on the steering wheel.

"Okay, I got in," Hallie says. "It'll take a few minutes to find a network."

I grumble something under my breath, my gaze glued on the road. The top of the hill is approaching too fast and I steer frantically to the right to make the curve. The van is not responding, heading straight for a huge snowbank at record speed.

In a panic, I yank at the steering wheel at the same time I slam on the brakes. The car swerves before turning into a spin. I lose all sense of direction as the van spins faster and faster until it is finally stopped by the force of a tree. The screeching sound of bending metal is painful. My eyes try to find a focus, but the forest keeps spiraling out of control. Dizziness twirls in my head. When the airbag blows, my face slams into the cushion, which isn't soft upon impact. Hallie's piercing scream is the last thing I hear before my head threatens to break into pieces. With the consuming pain comes the darkness which completely swallows me up.

Chapter 23

The coldness has soaked through every layer of my clothing when I try to pry my eyes open. A dull pounding in my head competes with the nausea in my throat; it is easier to drift back into the nothing than fight to stay awake. The cycle repeats itself, but I can't fight the cold darkness. It's like someone has stuck my eyelashes together with superglue.

When something wet and rough tickles my nose, I finally force my eyes open. Maisie is crawling around on my chest, busy with licking a sticky substance off my face. As her tongue swipes at my forehead, a sharp pain shoots through my skull. Probing with my fingers, I hiss—there is a cut just above my eyebrow, which is bleeding heavily.

I push Maisie away when she tries to lick me again and sit up. My chest hurts from the collision with the airbag though the pain doesn't worsen when I breathe in and out. I take it as a sign that my injury can't be too serious. Wriggling my fingers and toes, I let out a sigh of relief—the rest of my body appears to be intact. Maisie is panting and moving around without any effort. That only leaves Hallie.

My hand reaches over to her and gently strokes her hand. Her skin is freezing cold and for a second, my heart stills. "Hallie? Are you okay?"

A small moan drifts over from her side. "I'm alright, I think."

The air escapes my mouth with a sigh. Her speech is clear, which is good. With my shoulder, I push against the door but it doesn't budge an inch. I glance around as much as my stiff neck allows, but I can't make out anything in the darkness. Turning the key in the ignition, the radio clock springs to life.

It is just past midnight. We have been in this car for hours and will get hypothermia if we don't start moving soon.

My fingers run over the carpeted ceiling by the mirror until I find the switch for the interior light. I gasp when the extent of the damage registers. The tree has totally smashed the back seat. Several thick branches block my exit and the tree is at such an angle that I cannot climb out through the back. The fact that I am trapped once again makes me shudder.

"Hallie, can you get out?"

She cries softly as she pushes open the door before heaving herself out of the car with a low growl. A freezing draft blows through the van, but it has stopped raining. Light snow flakes fall instead. I push Maisie toward the opening, but she takes one whiff and decides to hide in the footwell. I curse under my breath as I crawl over the seat—not that I blame her. It's dark and miserable out there.

My head hurts with every move and warm blood trickles down into the collar of my coat. With every passing second, the soreness in my body worsens. I clench my teeth and push on, though I'm uncertain how long I will be able to continue without collapsing. The exhaustion of the last twenty-four hours is settling in; the adrenaline rush I felt during the escape has evaporated into thin air. All I want is to lie down and close my eyes. In a fleeting moment, the memories of my mom's hot cocoa and lullabies stifle my breath before I remind myself that I have no time to wallow in nostalgia.

When I finally make it outside, I'm greeted by a gust of wind, the force almost knocking me off my feet. My teeth chatter uncontrollably and shivers battle my body. Hallie is half leaning, half holding onto the van, balancing herself on one foot. Wetness glistens in her eyes as she regards me with a clenched jaw—I can tell she's in a lot of pain. The van is totaled.

My gaze wanders aimlessly around in the darkness. What are we going to do?

"Where's the phone?" I ask her.

She pulls it from her pocket and hands it to me.

No signal.

"Damn it!" If there's truly a guardian angel up there, he and I need to have a serious chat.

I use the light from the phone to find my way to the back of the van and open the door. Jed's tool box is right in front of me. I snatch a flashlight that could be used as a weapon before grabbing a crowbar. After a good shake, the flashlight flickers to life, casting the area around the van in a bright glow.

Directing the beam at the road, I scout out the path that winds through the forest. If it wasn't for the cold, it would be a magical winter wonderland, but with the storm, nature is as big an enemy as Jed and Napoleon.

My gaze returns to the road we just came from and I ponder whether we should try to walk back toward the cabin in hopes of getting a signal closer to the lake. We could hide under the porch if things get too bad. Even being with Jed might be better than freezing to death.

The path ahead ends in darkness—it could be miles to civilization. Yet it's the route to the main road, and at some point, the phone should pick up a signal. I shine the light in Hallie's face, who is paler than a ghost—she won't make it far without breaking down. We could hide in the back of the van until the storm eases, but that could take hours. At some point, Jed will also come looking for us.

I sigh. No matter what I choose, every option looks dire. Finally, I decide to go with my gut feeling—move forward and put more of a distance between us and Jed. Squatting next to the passenger door, I lean in to scoop up the struggling puppy. Maisie kicks when I shove her back into my coat, sending throbbing stabs down my side and temporarily stealing my breath.

"We need to get out of the forest to get a signal," I tell Hallie, handing her the crowbar. "Let's go."

She wraps her arm around my shoulders and I support her by her waist as we begin our journey. The cold night air bites at my exposed body parts. My fingertips lose all feeling within minutes. I don't complain and just grit my teeth. The newly fallen snow crunches under our boots, giving us a firmer grip than before.

We make little progress and Hallie leans into me, putting more and more weight onto my shoulders. I drag her along, but my knees are getting weaker, my arm numb from her tight grip. Just as I'm about to suggest a break, my eyes fall onto the pillars of a driveway, hidden under the snow—finding shelter in an abandoned summer cabin might be the best solution. Hallie still has the crowbar and we could break open a door or smash in a window. Even if the owners are assholes and press charges, there must be some type of extenuating circumstances to breaking and entering in a time of crisis.

With a jerk of my head, I motion to the driveway. "Let's go inside and call the cops from there. Even if the cell doesn't work, they might have a landline."

Relief is written across Hallie's face; she's close to collapsing. "Good idea. I also really have to pee."

The log cabin is tiny and surrounded by trees with a small porch in the front. I drive the crowbar in the gap between the door and the frame right under the lock and lever it in a way I once saw on a cop show. To my surprise, the door pops open. There is neither a deadbolt nor a chain nor an alarm. This is Maine, after all, and people here still trust their neighbors.

I take Hallie straight to the bathroom before setting Maisie down in the middle of the floor. She is probably thirsty and I rummage through the cabinet to find a bowl. When I turn on the water, all that comes out is a gurgling sound. Either the water pipes froze or the power is out, which makes the water pump useless. I try the lights, but the cabin stays dark.

"There's no power," I say when Hallie hops out of the bathroom.

She grimaces. "I noticed when I tried to wash my hands. Get some snow from outside which we can melt. That way, we at least have some water."

It's a good idea, and I grab another bowl, filling them both up with snow before placing them on the kitchen counter. The cabin is surprisingly warm, a hint of orange and cinnamon still lingering in the air. When I walk over to the open fireplace to start a fire, I notice glowing ashes. Whoever owns this place must have just recently left. Maybe a family who sought some peace and quiet from the usual Christmas turmoil but decided to return home before they get stuck in the storm.

Matches are right on the mantle and several candles are scattered throughout the cabin which I light to preserve the battery of the flashlight. I get to work on the fireplace next, stacking the logs in a circle with kindling in the middle. Soon, I have a blazing fire going.

Hallie finds a seat on the couch and takes off her boot and socks to inspect her ankle. It's swollen quite badly. I find a towel in the cabinet and wrap some snow inside as a cooling pack. When she presses the pack carefully against the sore spot, her lips twist in pain.

"Okay, let's see if we have a signal." My hand slides in my pocket where I stored the phone but find nothing. I check the other side, again, to no avail. The cell is gone.

"Shit. I think the phone fell out of my coat when I got Maisie out of the van."

I scan the cabin for a phone, but the equipment is absolutely basic. Even the fridge is a bit of a dinosaur.

"What are we gonna do?" Hallie asks as she gazes into the fire. The flames dance in her eyes—she seems to have aged a decade in the last day. Her youthfulness and innocence has been replaced by so much sadness and bitterness that it makes me cringe. I know this look too well—having stared into the same eyes for the last three years in the mirror.

"I'll go back to the van and get the phone. It isn't far. I should be back in half an hour."

Hallie frowns. "You can't go out there on your own. It's too dangerous and the storm is still raging. Maybe we should wait until the morning."

I shake my head. "We only drove a few miles and Jed will be able to find us. We have to get out of here as soon as possible."

"Then let me go with you."

"No. You stay put." I add more logs to the fire. "You can't walk on that foot and will just slow me down. I'll be back in no time."

As soon as I step outside, the freezing wind penetrates my Artic explorer outfit and chills me to the bone. With my hands buried deep inside my pockets, I trudge through the snow, my chin and mouth covered by the scarf. The snow is now a few inches deep with the ice buried beneath it, which gives me good traction. My strides are steady and I walk along at a good speed. My efforts keep me warm and sweat forms on my back when my steps turn into a jog.

I can already make out the van's shapes in the distance when a voice startles me. I take cover behind a tree. My eyes squint at the silhouette barely visible in the flickering glow of a flashlight, instinctively knowing that it's Jed before muffled words drift my way. He is talking on his phone.

"Look, this is the last message I'm leaving you. They're both gone and the van is totaled. I have no clue where they are. I got rid of all the DNA evidence and wiped the cabin down for prints like you asked me to, but that's it for me. I'll pack up my stuff and disappear tonight, probably cross over into Canada. You better pray the cops won't catch me, or this will turn ugly. Like I told you before, I'm not going to jail alone."

With a growl, the phone is tossed against a nearby tree before he turns away from the van and stomps down the hill until his frame is totally swallowed up by the darkness.

This is my chance. I sprint toward the van, ignoring the burning stitch that rages in my side. The mist from my breath almost obstructs my vision. Squatting down next to the passenger door, I lean inside the van, fumbling around the area where Maisie was hiding. My fingertips run over the smooth cover of the phone and I fist pump.

As I rise, I notice the signal is back—not strong, but enough to make a call. There must have been a network disruption from the storm earlier. With trembling fingers, I dial 911, waiting for the ringtone. My heart is racing in my chest while I hop from foot to foot, mumbling "Come on, come on, pick up" to myself.

"Hang up the phone, honeybun." The cold words chill every fiber in my body and beat the freezing wind tenfold.

I slowly turn around and stare at Jed just as the operator's voice fills my ear.

"911—what's your emergency?"

I swallow hard, my eyes fixed on the blade of the hunting knife in his hand. It would slice through my throat like butter.

"Hello, is anyone there?" the operator asks.

Jed waves the knife around, his face contorted in a menacing frown. There's no doubt that he will attack me as soon as I mutter the first word. With my thumb, I push the red button to end the call.

"I always knew you're smart," he says, grinning. "Toss the phone over to me."

I oblige, my fists instinctively balling tightly. I purposely miss and the cell lands in the snow just in front of him. As soon as he bends down to pick it up, my foot flies forward. The tip of my boot finds its mark square on his chin, knocking him down. He shakes his head, his eyes unfocused. I kick at him again, this time in the general direction of his stomach.

Just as before, his reflexes are fast—trained to perfection from years of fighting in the boxing ring. He catches my foot midair, both his hands wrapping around my ankle and twisting hard. I scream and lose my balance before my back hits the ground. The snow softens the impact, but it is still enough to take my breath away. I'm temporarily paralyzed, pain burning in my lungs and all down my back.

Jed's boot comes to rest in the center of my chest. "Do you know that I could just crush you like a cockroach?" He grins. "Though I wouldn't mind having a little bit of fun just one last time."

I gaze at him through teary eyes. "You're a nobody, Jed. How does it feel having to force yourself on a woman since there's no girl who can even stomach being with you otherwise?"

"Truthfully, you're not even worth freezing my ass off out here." A wicked smile plays on his lips. "Napoleon and I, we'll find your friend Hallie since she can't be far. She and that mutt are probably hiding in a cabin nearby." He wiggles his brows. "And when we find her, I'll make her pay for your smart mouth. I'll tell Hallie it's because of *you* when she screams for her mommy before I cut her throat."

Anger swells inside me like a volcano and my fingernails dig into the fabric of his jeans. He applies more pressure in response. I'm totally helpless, only able to whimper as I gasp for air.

He tilts his head. "You know, honeybun, I'm not going to make this quick. I want to see the light go out in your eyes." With a lazy flicker of his hand, he tosses the knife away.

When he takes the boot off my chest, I seize the opportunity, my legs arching to push myself to my feet. I can't find traction, my shoes slipping in the snow. It is just like treading water. By the time I'm able to lift myself inches of the ground, he is already on top of me.

His hands wrap around my throat, his mouth right by my ear. "Rest in peace, honeybun."

As his breath warms my neck, cold chills blast through me. He starts to squeeze. With my oxygen supply cut off, my legs start to kick at the same time my fists pound on every available part of his body. A vicious grin is frozen on his face as his grip tightens more and more around my throat.

My mouth opens and sucks in much-needed air, but I'm unable to transport any of the oxygen to my lungs. My eyes seem to bulge from their sockets. The dancing black spots in front of me multiply, the only sounds a steady flow of blood rushing in my ears that is soon overpowered by my racing heartbeat. A metallic taste floods my mouth as I continue to struggle for air.

I have read that just before you die, your whole life replays in front of your eyes. It's a chilling thought since I sure don't want to be a witness to my own rape before departing from this earth. Yet what bothers me the most is that I will never find out who Napoleon is.

As my strength dwindles, utter rage seethes inside me. My mind wants to live and finally take revenge, but my body is just not cooperating. I am weak, unable to fight the opponent who has tormented me for all this time. I feel myself going limp under Jed's weight, and as the black spots dance faster and faster, I finally realize that this might be the end. That's when my life starts rolling backward—just like you see in the movies.

Chapter 24

The bang echoing through the night sounds just like a broken exhaust pipe. Jed freezes. A gurgle erupts from his lips as he opens and closes his mouth, gasping for air. The pressure on my throat eases, and my own mouth opens wide, sucking in a deep breath.

As another bang breaks through the darkness, Jed falls forward. His heavy body crushes me, knocking out the little bit of oxygen my lungs managed to absorb. I push against him, my legs kicking, but I'm so weak that he doesn't move an inch. To my horror, something warm runs down my side. When my fingers brush over it, I realize it's blood.

A yelp escapes my throat and I struggle harder to free myself. Jed's body seems to weigh a ton. His face is buried in the snow, his hair grazing my cheek, and the touch sends chills down my spine. My shrieks grow louder. Jed's chest doesn't move and I am trapped underneath him. The thought that he might be dead spreads in my head like wildfire. I fight the building nausea in the back of my burning throat, my shrill screams tearing through the tranquility of the night the only sound to overpower my thumping heart.

Finally, the heavy burden is pulled off me and through my blurred vision, I find Finn staring down at me. My tears start to flow freely as soon as he wraps his arms around my shaking body.

"He is dead," a voice mutters next to me.

The words make my head snap sideways and I gaze right into Jed's glassy eyes. My stomach heaves. I clutch my hand over my mouth to keep the bile from spilling out before I meet Marcel's gaze, who is squatting next to Jed's still body. His hand runs over Jed's face and forces the eyelids shut. I am grateful—though those lifeless eyes will still haunt me.

Marcel rises. "I'm gonna call the cops."

He fishes a cell from his back pocket and steps away, giving Finn and me some privacy.

"Did Marcel shoot him?"

Finn shakes his head. "No, Luke did."

It's the first time I notice a third figure in the darkness, leaning against a tree. I try to get up and go to him, but Finn holds me back. "Give him a few minutes."

I wiggle out of his grip. "He's my brother and he needs me."

My steps are heavy as I walk over to him. Luke's face is streaked with tears and his lip trembles. He looks like he is about to faint. A rifle is by his feet.

We embrace without uttering a single word and I guide him away from the gun, away from the dead body. In the sanctuary of the trees, I finally break the silence.

"Thanks for saving my life."

His face is barely visible in the darkness. "I can't believe I killed him." His words break when a sob shakes his body.

"It was either him or me. You shouldn't blame yourself."

"I know." His voice is laced with despair. "But I can't help it. It feels wrong."

"Luke."

I reach for him and he finally snaps out of his trance. With the back of his hand, he wipes the wetness from his face before stroking my cheek. "How are you?"

My whole body is sore, my throat on fire and my head pounding, but I don't want to give him any more grief. "Alright, I guess." A thousand questions zoom in my head. "How did you find me?"

"Marcel has this GPS device that can track phones, and a few hours ago, he got a signal. He came up straight from Portland and picked Finn and me up. Luckily he drives like an absolute maniac or we probably wouldn't have gotten here in time."

In that moment, sirens and lights break through the forest as five patrol cars slowly make their way toward the crashed van and Jed's dead body.

"We should talk to the cops, Luke."

I tug at his sleeve when his body goes rigid, his lips pressed together. He pushes himself to follow me as I walk back toward the crime scene, the cops already talking to Finn and Marcel.

"Officer, there's a second girl who has been abducted," I say. "You need to send a car to get her."

The cop pulls out his walkie talkie. "Are you Kelsey Miller?"

I nod.

"What's the other girl's name?"

"Hallie Garvey." I hop from foot to foot, avoiding to look at Jed's figure in the snow, while he is talking to someone on the radio. "Please, officer, hurry. She's all alone and hurt."

He waves at one of his colleagues. "Can you tell him where she is?"

I chew on my lip, trying to visualize the way in my mind, but my memory fails me. "She is at a cabin, but I honestly don't know how to get there. It was dark. I can't even remember if we passed any driveways. Can I please come along?"

The two cops exchange a look. "But we need you back here for your statement. In the meantime, please confirm that none of these three men were involved in your abduction?" He swings his arm in a big circle, which could include every cop on the scene, but I am pretty sure he's talking about my three heroes.

"These guys saved my life, officer. They deserve a medal."

His eyebrows crease as his gaze travels to Marcel, who glares back at him with his arms folded across his chest.

"I told you I had nothin' to do with this. It was self-defense and I wasn't even the shooter." His chin points at Luke. "Ask him. He's the rich white boy with the clean record, so I suppose you can trust *his* word."

All eyes land on Luke who shuffles his feet under the attention. "It's true, officer. I shot Jed, but it was self-defense."

The officer rubs his chin. "Okay, I'll take this for now. I need all your statements before you leave here tonight, and you need to remain within the state while this investigation is pending." He turns to his colleague. "Ms. Miller will show you where Hallie Garvey is. She is the minor who went missing just before Christmas. I'll call the FBI team so they can close this out on their end."

I trot behind the young cop to one of the patrol cars, wondering what just happened. For me, this matter is crystal clear, but the police don't seem to share my opinion. The way the officer looked at Marcel almost gave me the impression that he thinks that Marcel is the criminal here and Jed the innocent victim.

Still mulling over this injustice, I hardly notice that the car has started to move and is slowly driving down the forest path.

"How far is it, ma'am?" the cop asks.

I focus on the road. Walking in the dark, it seemed like an eternity but to my surprise, we pass the pillars to the driveway after only a couple of minutes.

"It's right there." A prickling sensation spreads at the nape of my neck. Now I wish I hadn't left Hallie behind. I know it is stupid since the cabin provides good shelter and she was too hurt to wander around in the snow, but my mouth still dries up like sandpaper. With every yard the car edges closer to the cabin, more muscles in my body tense.

I jump out as soon as the car has come to a halt and storm up the steps to the porch, ignoring the cop's warning shout. With one strong push, the door flies open. I stare into an empty room. Surprisingly, the lights are on, but there is no sign of Hallie or Maisie. A bowl of water is on the ground and the blanket that covered her is still warm from her body heat. The fire has been extinguished but for some glowing ashes.

My gaze darts around the cabin, trying desperately to find a sign of her. "Hallie!" I rush to check the bathroom, but she isn't there either. My fingers run through my hair, my mind not wanting to accept the horrific thought. What if Napoleon got her?

Every part of me shakes in cold sweat when my knees give way and I reach for the sink to balance myself. Guilt washes over me, slicing into my heart. I should have never left her. If something happened to her, it will be my fault. Images of her being raped and screaming for my help twirl in my head, causing my stomach to twist. It takes all my effort not to break down and cry.

I force myself to return to the living room where the cop is talking on the radio. With a raised finger, he quiets me. I stare at the ashes in the fireplace, replaying my earlier visit to the cabin. I should have checked the bedroom and made sure she was safe before I left. Hindsight is a wonderful thing, but no matter how often you wish you can turn back the clock, it never happens.

"Okay, I put a search out for your friend"—the cop interrupts my sullen thoughts—"We'll have roadblocks within the hour. With the storm, it's the best we can do."

I give him a crooked smile—he has no idea who he is dealing with. In an hour, Napoleon will have slipped through the cracks. I fall onto the couch and bury my face in my hands, hot tears caught by my fingers. My head feels heavy, my body aching every time I flinch a muscle. I would love nothing more than to lie down and allow for exhaustion to take over, but my mind is racing at a hundred miles per hour. I am tired, buzzed, and utterly miserable, all at the same time. With my legs and arms tingling painfully, there is no way I could go to sleep.

"We should go back," the cop says.

When I stand up, the room starts to spin and my knees buckle.

The cop is by my side and lowers me back down on the couch. "Watch it there, ma'am." He frowns, observing the cut on my forehead. "That looks pretty bad. You might have a concussion. How did this happen?"

For a second, I'm taken aback. Didn't he see the crash site? Then I remember I was with Luke in the woods when the police first arrived, so he probably didn't make the connection. "I was in a car crash." I lean back, fighting the nausea in my throat that seems to be getting worse the more I talk.

"Are you in any pain, ma'am?"

I gaze at him through hooded eyes. "I couldn't tell you one part of my body that doesn't hurt." My hand clutches over my mouth when bile rises, but I manage to force it back down.

He clicks his tongue like it's my fault that he didn't ask earlier, mumbling something under his breath before raising the walkie talkie to his lips. "Ten fifty-seven to my location."

There is a brief crackle. "Ten four, over."

I can't help but chuckle. The whole scenario reminds me of some bad police soap. A sharp dagger stabs me right in between my ribs in response, warning me to stay put.

"I called an ambulance."

I feel obliged to acknowledge his efforts with a smile— after all, it's not his problem that I feel like total crap, and he just tries to be helpful. In silence, we wait, the ticking grandfather clock on the wall counting down the minutes. The monotone sound stretches my frazzled nerves to the limit.

Finn and Marcel arrive at the same time as the ambulance.

"Where is Luke?" I ask while the paramedics carry me out on a stretcher.

"They took him down to the station," Finn hurries along, his fingers entangled with mine.

"Why? Did they arrest him?"

Another horrific scenario unfolds in my mind, this time of Luke in jail for murder, his whole life destroyed. Roy told me when Jed got off that it doesn't matter if someone is guilty or innocent—the courts only care about what the prosecutor can prove. What would happen if no one believes that Luke only shot Jed to save me?

Finn's thumb brushes over the back of my hand. "Don't worry about it. It's routine, I think." The forced grin on his face is neither comforting nor convincing.

"Can you call his dad? I'm sure he wants to go down there as his lawyer."

He squeezes my hand. "Already done." When the paramedics lift me into the ambulance, his voice pleads, "Can I ride along?"

The guy squints at him. "Are you two related?"

Finn grimaces as he shakes his head.

"Sorry, dude, can't allow it."

Finn steps aside and lets go of my hand. "I'm right behind you," he mutters.

While the ambulance rolls through the night with roaring sirens, I answer basic questions about my age and medical health. As I list the names of all the medications I am on, fear crunches my chest. I was strong these last few days because of Hallie, but will I be able to continue on my own? What if the cops don't find her, or worse, they find her broken body? I won't be able to cope and there is a strong possibility that the urge to cut myself will once again take over my life.

A cold gust greets me when I arrive at the hospital. The storm is still not done with us, freezing rain hitting my face as they wheel me inside. The lobby is filled with cops who huddle around another patient. When I catch a glimpse at her, my heart skips three beats.

"Hallie!" I wipe my eyes, making sure she isn't a hallucination.

She squeals. "Oh my god, Kelsey. They told me you were okay, but still . . ."

When our eyes interlock, a heavy burden lifts off my chest. I exhale, letting all my worries escape together with the air that is pushed through my nostrils.

The nurse stops my trolley right next to her wheelchair and my hand reaches over to touch her, ensuring she is real. "How did you get here?"

She points to a guy who is talking to a few cops with his back turned to us. "He's the owner of the cabin and returned after you were gone. He had forgotten his phone at home, so we couldn't call the cops, but he had a car out back and brought me here."

When he turns around, my eyes narrow. "That's Jackson, my brother's cousin. What was he doing out by the lake?"

Hallie shrugs. "He said he had a fight with his parents and wanted to be alone. When the power cut off, he went out and was working on the generator in the shed, so he didn't hear us when we broke in. You should have seen his face when he first saw me." She giggles. "He thought I was a ghost."

My gaze stays on him as the prickling sensation in my neck returns. All this is way too convenient. I will ask Larouge to check him out.

"Has Jed been arrested?"

Hallie's question tears me away from my conspiracy theory. "No, he's dead."

She gasps. "How? Did you—"

My lips twist in pain when I imagine his grip on my throat and my fingers instinctively run over the sore spots on my neck. "My brother shot him as he was strangling me."

Her gaze is intense. "Did he tell you Napoleon's identity before he died?"

I hesitate before answering her. "No, he didn't."

We stare at each other, her eye twitching. I'm sure she's thinking the same thing as I am—as long as Napoleon is still out there, we will never be free.

Chapter 25

"Kelsey, your friend is here!" my mom shouts from downstairs.

I poke my head around my bedroom door. "I'll be right there, Mom."

She mumbles something to Marcel and gets a pleasant "yes, ma'am" in return. I chuckle. My mom loves him and both Roy and I have neglected to tell her that he is a gangbanger.

As soon as my bullshit letter had been discovered by Luke, Finn got a rather unpleasant visit from my brother, who accused him of making me run away from home. After that, Marcel and Finn took charge of the rescue operation, and apparently, every criminal in Maine was looking for me on top of the police. For Mom, Marcel is my knight in shining armor.

I slump back into the chair and grin at Hallie's face on the Skype chat. "Okay, I'm ready to go. I'll see you in about an hour."

Excitement glistens in her eyes. "I can't wait." Since our rescue a week ago, she has been tied to the house. Her ankle was broken and her sister insisted on her taking it easy. The storm knocked the power out in the entire state for two days and with New Year's and the aftermath of our kidnapping, we only got to chat on Skype. I asked her a few times whether she has been cutting and she reassured me she wasn't, but I couldn't shake the feeling that she might be lying. I want to see her arms with my own eyes to make sure.

I logoff the computer and snap my fingers at Maisie, which only gets me a lazy yawn.

"Come on, girl," I coo. "Time to get out of the house."

Her tail wags hesitantly when her eyes wander to the window. It's like she is debating whether she really wants to venture outside in the freezing cold.

I click my tongue. "Treaty."

That gets her attention and she jumps off the bed, her tongue sticking out with a little drool as she looks up at me.

I roll my eyes. "You are the greediest dog in the entire state." I grab the box with the little housetrain treats and offer her one, which she gulps down without one chew. At least she is alert now and trots behind me after I grab my coat and purse and head downstairs.

Marcel is chatting with my mom, his fingers clutched tightly around a coffee cup. The truth is he's just listening—her words pelt down on him without mercy. When she is in the mood, she manages to talk up a storm without taking even one unnecessary breath or giving her dialogue partner a chance to reply. The topic they are discussing really has her going, her face twisted in a big frown. She's probably telling him about the injustices that Luke is suffering.

He tosses me a desperate eye and I decide to rescue him. "We gotta go now, Mom. Hallie is waiting."

She looks torn. If it was up to her, I wouldn't be leaving the house anymore until I'm past my retirement age. "When will you be back?"

I plan to spend the entire day with Hallie. "Not till tonight."

Marcel flings his arm around my shoulders. "I'll take good care of her, Mrs. Franklin. No need to worry."

That gets me off the hook and she grudgingly agrees to let me go without further hassle. Marcel brought the big SUV and slides behind the wheel. I hop into the passenger seat after luring Maisie into the back. He seems preoccupied, his eyebrows knotted together when he starts the car.

"Thanks again for playing chauffeur for the day. You don't know how much I appreciate it."

"Don't mention it." A beaming smile appears on his lips. "Like I told you on the phone, I had some business in Lewiston, and Stonehenge is just a couple of miles out of the way."

"Yeah, but you have to make the extra trip tonight."

"It's really not a big deal. Driving relaxes me." With his thumb, he switches on his navi. "Where to?"

I give him Hallie's address and he enters it on the screen.

"What 'bout Finn?" he asks. "Is he coming, too?"

I purse my lips, though I anticipated his question. "Not today."

He glances over his shoulder before pulling out of the parking bay. "Any particular reason?"

I don't want to tell him that his friend is one of my Napoleon suspects. "I'll tell you later."

"Okey dokey."

My thoughts drift to Finn and a dull ache spreads in my chest. For the thousandth time, I question why I'm even accusing him, but no matter how hard I try, Jed's snide remark that he and Finn used to work on cars together always eats at me. My gut instinct insists that he was just trying to upset me, but my rational mind reminds me that I can't exclude him. After all, why did Finn never mention that he knew Jed when we had talked about my abduction? His love for history is another strike against him.

Marcel breaks the silence when he merges with the traffic on the highway. "So your mom tells me that they charged your brother with murder."

I cringe when I picture Luke in a cell at the county jail. "Yeah. My stepdad thinks it's not going to stick when it gets to the grand jury, but I'm really worried."

"It totally sucks. Have you spoken to him?"

"There's a waiting period before friends and family can visit. I'm planning on seeing him tomorrow."

The highway has been cleared from the snow and the car picks up speed when we head toward Portland. It's one of those crisp winter days with a bright blue sky and frosty winds, but the warm sun shining through the window onto my face is very pleasant. I almost doze off when he breaks the silence again.

"They will subpoena us to testify in front of the grand jury, and I'm telling you now that Tyrone will have a real problem with that. He doesn't want me involved anymore."

"But you still picked me up today."

"Yeah, but that's on my own time."

We continue our journey in more silence, my eyes fixed on the trees rushing by. The car seems to be flying and I just hope we won't hit a patch of ice. Marcel stares straight ahead, chewing on his lip, his mind lost in another world. I wonder what drug dealers like him think about.

When we pass the Gray exit, I take another stab at a conversation. "Can I ask you a question?"

He grumbles something which I take as a yes.

"Why didn't you shoot Jed?"

"Your brother beat me to it, plus I probably wouldn't have smoked him anyhow. Prison would've been so much worse for him."

I don't like his answer. Jed damn near killed me and the thought that Luke might have acted hastily doesn't sit well with me. I nevertheless decide to probe further. "So you think there were other options?"

He doesn't respond right away, his attention focused on a car he is passing.

"Jed didn't have a weapon," he finally says. "I was just going to pull him off you and beat the crap out of him." His fingers brush over my arm when I tense. "Don't get me wrong.

I think Luke did what he thought he had to do. In those types of situations, the majority of folks act out of instinct, and I sure won't complain. That bastard deserved it."

I continue to stare out of the window, my mind drifting in all kinds of directions. I can see his point, but I'm still not willing to criticize my savior. Luke killed Jed for me and I will owe him for the rest of my life.

Hallie's house is in a little side street close to downtown. A few elementary-school-aged children play in front of the gates when Marcel and I pull up. They eye him with suspicion as he gets out of the car before moving their game three doors down. Their small faces are twisted in anguish—they seem afraid of him.

Marcel pulls a packet of cigarettes from his pocket. "What time should I pick you up?"

I frown. That isn't part of my plan. If Hallie and I want to successfully track down Napoleon, we need his help. "Aren't you coming inside?"

He considers me with calm eyes. "I work for Tyrone and you really shouldn't hang out with people like me."

I twirl a strand of my hair around my finger. It's time to fess up. "You're the only one I trust at the moment, Marcel, and I really need your help. My other abductor is still out there and Hallie and I want to find him."

"And y'all thought *I* could help you?" His eyes sparkle with amusement. "I'm a criminal, not a detective."

"Well"—I give him my best puppy dog eyes—"technically, you're a private investigator and you managed to track my cell phone. I'm sure you can give us some pointers."

"It's not gonna work. Business will pick up again and I already got a job."

I pout. "Come on, Marcel, just for a few days. If it's money you're worried about, I'll pay you."

He laughs. "I doubt you can afford me." He lights a cigarette and takes a deep drag, letting the smoke escape through his mouth and nose while studying me intently. "Sorry, kiddo, but you guys are on your own here."

In that moment, the front door opens and a young woman steps outside, huddled into a warm winter coat. Her face looks just like an older version of Hallie. That must be her sister.

She walks over to us with a small smile, her eyes glued on the cigarette in Marcel's hand.

"Are you Kelsey?"

"Yes. You must be Donna."

"I am." She tears her gaze off the cigarette. "It's really nice to meet you. Hallie told me what you did for her and I can't tell you how grateful I am. She'd probably be dead if it wasn't for you."

My cheeks burn; I don't deserve her gratitude. If it wasn't for me, Hallie would likely not even have been abducted. "We helped each other. I'm just glad we got out." I nudge Marcel's shoulder. "And he deserves all the credit since he was the one tracking us down."

Donna gives him a good once-over before her focus returns to me. "Well, Hallie's waiting for you. I have to quickly run to the store to get some milk." Her eyes wander back to Marcel. "And smoking is not allowed inside the house."

He flicks his cigarette away. "Don't worry, I'm not going in."

"Okay then." There is relief on Donna's face.

The awkward silence that follows is interrupted by Maisie's howl from the car. She probably feels neglected or has to use the bathroom. As soon as Marcel opens the back, she dashes out, shaking herself before jumping up on my legs, her tail wagging at a hundred miles per hour.

Donna crouches down and rubs her behind her ears. "And you must be Maisie." Her words are soft and Maisie eagerly licks her hand. "Yeah, you're a good girl."

Marcel clears his throat. "You wanna ride to the store? The sidewalks are still really slippery."

She regards him through narrow eyes, but when a cold gust of wind hits her and almost knocks her over, she gives in. "Sure, I'd appreciate that."

With his best gentleman manners, he opens the passenger door for her. "Here we go." He gives me a wide grin, motioning with his head toward the house. "Get inside and out of the cold, girl, before you get sick."

I quirk an eyebrow. What's his game all of a sudden? "Sure thing. Pick me up at five." That will give Hallie and me enough time to make a suspect list and maybe I can change his mind about helping us when we drive back to Stonehenge.

Hallie's house is small but cozy, her room not much larger than our family bathroom. Movie posters are pinned to the wall—*Hunger Games, Divergent, The Maze Runner*. She must really like dystopian. Other than her single bed, there is only a small desk and a chair, which becomes my home for the next few hours.

Hallie is stretched out on the bed with her laptop, her cast elevated and Maisie curled up next to her. She is one content puppy; it only took a good poop and half the treat box to bribe her inside the house. Two large glasses of soda are on the nightstand next to a bag of gummy bears.

"Before we start, show me your arms?"

Without hesitation, she pushes up the sleeves of her sweater. Other than some fading scars, there is no sign of cutting.

"Now you."

It's an amazing feeling that I can show her my arms without any fresh cuts. Our eyes interlock; we're both on the right track.

With that out of the way, we are ready to start with our suspect list.

"Okay, who do we got?" Hallie asks after opening a new document.

I lean back in the chair. "So there's Drake, since the police always suspected him, and he's at least worth checking out. Justin is a definite—and Finn." The last name barely rolls off my lips. "I know you think Jackson is a real straight-up guy, but it's odd that he was at the lake the day after Christmas."

I remember the few Franklin family get-togethers I attended with Roy and Luke. That family takes clingy to a new level. "Luke's family is close knit and I just can't see Jackson leaving, even if he had a fight with his parents."

She pecks away at the keyboard. "What about Jed's family? I read that family members often conspire in crimes like kidnapping."

I didn't think of that. "As far as I know, the only one left is his sister who lives out of state. His parents are dead."

"Okay, so that's a cold trail. Who else?"

I chew the inside of my cheek, afraid to tear open fresh wounds, but our mission is too important. "I know it's hard, but do you remember anything about Napoleon when he was with you?"

She nods eagerly. "Yeah, I already told the police. He smelled like Irish Spring. I only noticed it because it was my dad's favorite and he used it all the time." Tears rise and she quickly wipes her eyes. "He reminded me of my dad, which made it worse."

I cannot hold her gaze, the horror of her words settling in. It will make it even harder to forget. "Come to think of it, Roy uses Irish Spring shower gel."

She squints at me, the tears forgotten. "Your stepdad?"

"Yeah." I never thought of Napoleon as an older guy, but I sure wouldn't bet my life on it. "I think we should consider every possibility."

The front door opens and Donna's laugh drifts upstairs. "You want another coffee?" she asks.

"Sure thing." A nervous chuckle follows Marcel's words.

Their voices are muffled when they move their conversation into the kitchen.

Hallie stares at me. "What's that all about? I thought you said she didn't like him."

"That was my first impression. Maybe she warmed up to him when he gave her a ride to the store."

"I doubt it. She's probably just trying to be polite. She hates drugs and gangs."

Who doesn't? For the first time, I realize that just a few months ago, I wouldn't have given Marcel the time of day. If I hadn't seen this different side of him, when he helped me without hesitation, he would just be a lowlife criminal to me.

A few hours later, we have located Drake's whereabouts through the Internet and decide to focus on him and Justin first. The topic of how to best approach them, and even more so, how we're going to exclude them, is ignored for now. Ultimately, the only way to be positive is for them to drop their pants—something I don't even want to imagine—so I'm relieved when any further decisions are postponed to another day. Hallie looks exhausted and I feel a slight headache coming on. With nightfall approaching, I should be getting home or my mom will freak out.

Trampling steps echo through the house when someone runs up the stairs. Marcel pokes his head into the room.

"Ready to go?"

I stretch my stiff limbs. "Yep. Just finishing up."

Without an invitation, he steps inside, closing the door behind him. "And what have y'all been up to?"

Squatting next to the bed, he grabs a handful of gummy bears, tossing a few into his mouth.

"We made a suspect list."

He munches on the gummy bears. "Let's hear it."

Hallie reads out the names.

With a vacant expression, he stares into blue light of dusk before stuffing more gummy bears into his mouth. "What about Luke?"

I gasp. "He's my brother. What are you implying?"

He chews with a sullen look. "He's your stepbrother, and statistics show that if a girl is abducted by someone they know, it's often a person close to them."

The thought sends a shudder down my spine. "He killed Jed."

"And effectively eliminated the only one who could have pointed the finger at him." He throws a gummy bear in the air and catches it with his mouth. "Sorry, Kelsey, but you have to think like a criminal here. In my books, he's on top of the list."

I glance at Hallie, who grimaces. "I hate to agree, but Marcel is right."

With a sigh, I allow the air to dramatically escape through my lips. "Okay, okay, I see your point. Put him on." My arms fold in front of my chest when I squint at Marcel. "Does your sudden interest mean that you'll help us after all?"

His lips twist to an apologetic grimace. "Sorry, I can't. Tyrone is pissed at me as it is since he feels I don't have my loyalties straight. I can't get into anymore hot water or there will be repercussions."

I try to hide my disappointment. "I understand," I claim with slumped shoulders. It would have been so much easier to convince someone to drop their pants with him around.

He chews in silence until he all of a sudden stops and stupidly grins at Hallie. "Say, does your sister have a boyfriend?"

Hallie's smile is smug. "No. Why are you asking?"

"No reason." He shoves the last gummy bears into his mouth. "We should go. We have to make one more stop before I take you home."

I shoot him a quizzical look. "Where?"

"Finn's house." The jest is wiped off his face. "He'll either be cleared today or going to jail."

My heartbeat accelerates when I realize the full impact of his words—this has been standing between Finn and me ever since the night Jed was killed. He deserves to know why I've been avoiding him, yet the thought of confronting him twists my guts into tight knots. If he truly is Napoleon, I don't think I will be able to trust anyone ever again.

Chapter 26

My mind works in overdrive the whole way back to Stonehenge, imagining the terrible scenarios which could be lying ahead. Finn could be Napoleon, but even if not, he might hate me for accusing him in the first place and refuse to speak to me ever again. Best-case scenario, he will still be pissed. After all the things he did for me, it's a horrible way to repay him.

He is just leaving the house when we arrive, a duffle bag hanging off his shoulder. I frown, wondering what he is up to. Marcel must feel equally puzzled, his hand wandering under his jacket as he approaches his friend.

"Hey, Finn, you and I need to talk."

Finn's eyes dart from Marcel to me. The light from the street lamp illuminates his face and I notice that his cheeks are red and puffy like he has been crying.

With a sigh, he tosses the duffle in the back of his truck. "Now is not a good time, guys."

Marcel squints at him, his shoulders shifting. "Where're you going?" Both his voice and eyes emit the same type of coldness as they did the day he confronted Justin in the coffee shop.

Finn throws up his hands. "Look, bro, if you want to shoot me, shoot me. Everything else will have to wait until I come back."

Before Marcel can pull the gun, I step between them. "Now, let's just all take a deep breath, alright?" I grab Finn's arm. "What's the matter? I can tell you've been crying."

He pulls from my grip. "It's my brother. I have to go and get him."

There's a desperation in his eyes that I have never seen before. Whatever happened to his brother must be really serious—he is worried sick about him.

"What happened?"

His shoulders slump, wetness making his orbs shimmer in the darkness. "Cameron called and said that he couldn't take it anymore. He threatened to kill himself if I don't come and get him."

The tremble in his voice summons a deep wrinkle on Marcel's forehead. "Sorry to hear that, bro. You got a piece?"

I blink at him. Sometimes, this gang slang is too cryptic for me.

Finn, on the other hand, doesn't seem troubled. "No way. If the cops stop me, I'll already be in big trouble for leaving the state while on probation. No need to add a firearm violation to that."

Marcel kicks the tire of Finn's truck. "You'll never make it to New Haven in that. I'll drive you."

Finn is hesitant. "You sure? What 'bout Tyrone?"

"He'll get over it."

Both men turn toward Marcel's car, leaving me standing in the middle of the sidewalk without a further glance.

"Hey, what about me?" My sudden panic at being left behind in the dark is camouflaged by an evil glare.

"Get in the back," Marcel says. "We'll drop you home on the way."

I shake my head. "If you go on a road trip, I want to come." There is at least an equal chance that Finn is not Napoleon and the thought of my tormentor still being out there while they are both out of town scares me to bits.

The two exchange a glance.

"Your mama would kill me," Marcel declares and I secretly have to agree, but she won't be able to stop me.

"Leave her to me." Hands on my hips, I force my chin into the air. "I really want to come."

Marcel and Finn debate under their breath while I stare at them, my foot tapping. My mind is scrambling to come up with more arguments that could convince them to bring me along if they don't buckle. For a second, I even consider threatening that I will call the cops and squeal on Finn for leaving Maine, but I discard the idea. Stabbing him in the back like that is unforgiveable.

"Well, alright then," Finn finally mutters.

I squeal, relief washing over me. Only Marcel's frown stops me from hugging them both. Not once do I consider what I've just signed up for.

~~~~

It is already almost 11:00 p.m. when Finn wakes me from a deep slumber. After a brief but loud fight with my mom, which ended with Marcel calming her down, I fell asleep right around the time we crossed into New Hampshire. I've always had trouble keeping my eyes open on long car rides, the monotone hum from the engine and soft bouncing of the SUV working better than any sleeping pill.

We end up somewhere on the southern side of New Haven in an area that is even more rundown than Tyrone's. Some houses are so rotten that they look like they will fall apart at any second, the sidewalks dimly lit by flickering streetlamps. A few vicious dogs bark furiously as we drive by, reminding me of Roxy before she attacked Jed. Those hounds might not guard treasures, but I sure wouldn't try to convince them of that. Poor Maisie would probably be torn apart in a heartbeat—yet she eagerly yaps back with a wagging tail, oblivious to the danger. The bliss of the innocent.

Trapped

Finn guides Marcel through the night, his voice laced with hoarse anxiousness. We finally arrive in front of a small two-story house in a quiet street off the main road, a rusty old car parked out front. The trashcans are overflowing—mostly with pizza boxes and beer cans—and the fence has several holes in different places. It looks like someone has repeatedly kicked it.

Marcel's eyes scan the area with a frown and stop on the house across the street where several guys lean out a window, smoking a cigarette. From the way they eye the car, they are just itching to give us a hassle.

"Are they who I think they are?" Marcel asks Finn.

Finn lets out a sigh. "Looks that way. They must have moved in since I left. A mom with six kids used to live there."

That mother probably figured out what kind of predator resided in the neighborhood and ran for the hills before her kids met a fate similar to Finn's and his brother's. I still can't believe that Finn's mom is so ignorant and allows that type of abuse to go on under her roof. I would have kicked out that boyfriend a long time ago.

Marcel and Finn don't get out of the car, but glare at the men hanging out the window. They have been joined by a few others who stare back at the car.

"Who are these guys?"

"Blood Dragons. They're Tyrone's competitors."

I read that gang rivalries could get messy.

"Are they going to attack us?" My question sounds silly, and the glare I get from Marcel is a clear indication that now would be a good time for me to shut up.

"What are we gonna do?" asks Finn.

Marcel rubs his bald head. "Get the gun out of the glove compartment and leave the talkin' to me." He turns around. "Whatever you do, don't say a word or we'll all be dead."

I swallow hard and cower low into my seat when Finn and Marcel slide out of the car. At the same time, three guys approach from the house across the street. Their leader walks a few steps in front but is closely flanked by his two cronies. I feel like I'm part of the movie set for *Boyz 'n The Hood.* My teeth frantically work the tip of my fingernail at the same time my heart pounds harshly against my ribcage—the tension in the air seeping into the car is almost killing me.

The leader smirks. "What's up?" His eyes stay on Marcel, who casually hooks his thumb into the front pocket of his jeans.

"Yo, we ain't looking for trouble." Marcel's chin points to Finn's house. "We're just here to pick someone up and be gone in a few minutes."

"Cameron? He sometimes runs errands for me." The man's eyes dart to Finn. "You his brother?"

Finn nods but keeps his mouth shut.

"You look just like him," the man remarks. "Where're you taking him?"

Marcel shifts his weight as his fingers move closer to the hem of his pants. "You ask a lot of questions." His voice is icy and gives me the chills.

I crawl further into my seat, ready to drop to the footwell of the car if Marcel decides to pull the gun. Why of all days did I have to put on my big-girl panties tonight instead of staying home?

"Like I said, he runs errands for me," the guy tells Marcel, his tone just as cold. "He's like family."

A smile spreads on Marcel's lips. "Well, he ain't your little bitch, so don't fuck with me. He's coming with us."

For a moment, they glare at each other. I bite my thumb so hard that I taste blood. Maisie is whimpering in the back. Even she can sense that the air is explosive. If someone lit a match under those guys' noses, the whole street would blow into pieces.

I will probably never understand the rules of the street—not that I truly want to—but Marcel must have said or done something that told the others he is higher up in the food chain. The three guys back up—slowly—without taking their eyes off him or Finn. As soon as they disappear in the house, his head snaps around.

"Let's go, Kelsey."

My eyes travel from his face to Maisie and back to him. "Can't I wait in the car?"

"Nope." He opens the trunk and shoos the dog away before lifting up the carpet to take out a rifle. "They'll come back for you if we leave you out here alone."

I gaze at my puppy, who watches me with big brown eyes. "What about Maisie?"

"She'll be fine."

Doubt claws at me, but he gives me a reassuring smile. Finn bobs his head up and down in agreement and I grudgingly concede defeat. Maisie might actually be safer in the car than with me. After all, who knows what types of danger await us in Finn's house. Judging from his tense face and Marcel's tight grip on the rifle, they must be expecting trouble.

The front gate opens with a low squeak. Finn signals us to follow him around to the back of the house. We pass by a lit window and the muffled sounds of a television drift through the decayed wooden frames. A strong smell of urine irritates my nostrils as we approach the backdoor, which mixes with the leftover stench of alcohol the closer we get to a mountain of booze bottles piled up next to the steps.

Finn peeks through the small window in the door. "Damn, my mom's in the kitchen." He squints to get a better look. "But she's passed out." His fingers turn the doorknob at the same time his shoulder presses gently against the door. It pops open and he squeezes inside.

The odor of garbage and burned candle wax lingers in the air as soon as I step into the kitchen. My eyes dart around, absorbing the dirty dishes in the sink together with the food leftovers on the counter that are already partially molded. Finally, they land on a woman who is curled up on the floor, a glass pipe and a spoon next to an unlit candle by her side. Her face is partially hidden by stringy raven hair. In her youth, she was probably very pretty.

"Bro, I didn't know your mama was a crackhead," Marcel mutters under his breath.

Finn wrinkles his nose. "Her boyfriend deals on the side and hooked her to shut her up."

I can't hold his gaze when I notice the pain in his eyes. What a terrible life he must have had under her roof, which makes Cameron's situation even more horrifying. How can a mother do that to her kids?

I tiptoe around her, but she is out cold and doesn't even flinch, drool running out of the corners of her mouth. There is a stupid grin on her face that, together with her raspy breath, creeps me out. I notice several scabs and bruises all over her arms. Blisters swell her lips in some spots and cracks are visible in others—she's an absolute mess.

Finn ushers Marcel and me down the hallway and we quickly make our way to the other side of the house. The ceiling light is broken, but the gleam from the kitchen prevents me from tripping. A dim glow shines through the gap between the door and the floor when we get to the stairs. Like silent ghosts, we scamper upstairs.

I find myself holding my breath when Finn pushes a door open, halfway expecting to find the boyfriend with Cameron in the bed together. Marcel must have had a similar idea. The gun rests firmly in his hand when he steps around me.

The boy is alone, stretched out on the bed with headphones stuffed into his ears, his head bouncing slightly. When he notices us, his eyes widen. Finn places his finger over his lips with a slight hiss. He only speaks after I close the door behind me.

"Get your stuff, Cameron. Take only what's absolutely necessary."

The boy hesitates. "What about mom?"

A shadow crosses Finn's face. "What about her?"

"I can't just leave her here." The words are laced with a stubbornness that reminds me of Finn when he is hardheaded.

Finn sighs. "Look, Mom's a grown woman and can take care of herself. Besides, she never cared about what Oshin did to us and only worries about getting high and drunk. She'll never leave him. Think of yourself for once and let's go."

The struggle is all too visible on Cameron's face, but the need to remove himself from the situation prevails in the end. He jumps from the bed and gets a backpack, stuffing random clothes inside.

"Shit." Marcel, who has been keeping an eye on things outside, stiffens. His initial concern is followed by a whole shower of colorful curses, some of them pretty creative.

I'm just about to ask him what got him so wound up when a voice breaks through the night.

"Attention, this is the New Haven Police Department. Anybody who is inside 2395 Crane Street, come out with your hands up! I repeat—this is New Haven PD. Anybody inside 2395 Crane Street, come on out with your hands up."

Chapter 27

In the deadly silence that follows the police announcement, my eyes dart from Finn to Marcel. "What are we gonna do?"

Finn looks terrified, probably imagining being beaten up in jail again, while Marcel is surprisingly calm. "We need to make sure that Finn gets out without being arrested, or his probation will definitely be revoked. The cops have surrounded the house, so we need to create a diversion."

I bite my lip, my skin prickling with excitement. "What type of diversion?"

Marcel rubs his chin. "Good question." His gaze falls onto the bed. "Get the pillowcase and wipe down the guns. We'll plant them here and distract the cops at the back door. That way, Finn can slip out."

I frown. It doesn't just sound dangerous but illegal, too. What the hell have I gotten myself into? Nevertheless, I strip the pillow of its cover and run it over the offered rifle.

Loud banging echoes through the house. "Police. Open up."

The demand is answered with some loud cussing from downstairs, followed by the flushing of the toilet.

"Your mom's boyfriend is getting rid of his stash. We need to hurry. They'll bust down the door any minute."

I frantically wipe down the gun. "Why haven't they come in yet?"

"They likely have no warrant." Marcel grabs the pillowcase and cleans off his gun before tossing it on the bed. "Take those to your parent's bedroom, Cameron."

The boy is frozen, his lips twisted into a pout. "I want to go with Finn. I'm not staying here." For the first time, I realize how immature he still is. He has no clue about the seriousness of the situation.

Marcel shakes his head. "That could compromise his escape. You'll have to surrender when I tell you to."

Cameron looks like he is about to cry. "They'll put me into foster care." His gaze moves to Finn. "Don't let them do this, Finn. Please."

Finn grabs his brother by his shoulders. "It's the end of the line, bro. If they catch me, I'll go to prison for at least ten years." His voice is insistent. "The best you can do is to come clean. Tell them the truth about Oshin, that way, at least he can't do that stuff to you anymore. I'll come back for you as soon as I can."

"But, Finn—" he pleads.

"No, Cameron." Finn's voice is firm. "Do what Marcel says." When his brother still hesitates, he hisses, "NOW."

Still pouting, Cameron grabs the rifle and the gun with the help of the pillow case, and disappears down the hallway.

Marcel signals me to follow him. "Stay close behind me."

We rush through the dark house—the banging has stopped. Cold sweat pearls on my forehead. I expect the front door to be kicked in at any second. If that happens, I'll drop to the ground like they do in the movies.

Finn's breath is grazing my neck. He's breathing much heavier than usual, probably scared out of his mind. In a sense, I should be, too, but somehow, this seems like a piece of cake in comparison to my abduction. Back then, the stakes were much higher. The worst that could happen today would be for me to get arrested, and I'm sure that Roy can get me off.

We pass by the bathroom where Oshin is still flushing the toilet, threatening whoever sent the police after him in between loud and colorful curses. If he gets himself out of this mess, I'm sure that he and the guys across the street will have some serious words—if he doesn't shoot them straight away, that is. I catch a glimpse of his wide frame from the back. He has a neck like a bull and an undefined waist. His strawberry blond hair is drenched in sweat, his muscle top sticking to his back. There are still four large bags of white powder next to him on the cabinet. It will take ages to get rid of it all. Secretly, I hope he won't make it.

Finn's mom is still passed out in the kitchen, oblivious that her house is under siege. Marcel scopes out the backyard, careful to stay hidden behind the curtains.

"I can see four cops." He and Finn exchange a glance. "Just walking out of here won't work."

My knees begin to wobble and my fingers wrap around the backrest of a chair. I'm having second thoughts. It all sounds like a really bad idea. Horrifying scenarios unfold in my mind— from getting shot to being abducted and raped by the guys across the street. I chew my lip, uncertain how to tell Marcel that I would prefer to just surrender to the police.

Before I can thwart the plan, Cameron appears in the doorway. His face shines from his tears. When he sees his mother, he squats down next to her, gently shaking her shoulder. "Mom. Wake up."

Marcel clicks his tongue. "Leave her. She'll be better off in jail. At least, she won't be able to smoke any crack."

Cameron tosses him a dark look. "Who the hell are you anyway, bossing me around?"

Marcel's eyes narrow. He's about ready to give the boy a piece of his mind when I intervene. "Let's just focus on the problem here."

Cameron and Marcel continue to glare at each other until Marcel reclaims his leadership position. "Okay, this is what we gonna do. Kelsey and Cameron will make a run for it while I'll let the cops in through the front. There'll be enough screaming and commotion for Finn to disappear."

My jaw drops. "Are you crazy? They'll shoot us if we run."

Marcel's lips twitch. "These are cops, Kelsey. They never shoot without a warning, especially not at a girl and a kid. Just trust me here."

I squint at him, full of doubt, before I grudgingly admit that he is kind of the expert here. My gaze lands on Finn, who has swallowed his tongue, his face paler than a ghost. He fought my battles with Jed and went to jail because of it, now it's time to repay him.

All fired up, I glance at Cameron, who slowly rises when Finn throws him a pleading look.

Marcel is all business. "Take off in different directions; that will be the most effective." He turns to Finn and they fist bump. "Good luck, bro." Sucking in a deep breath, he glances around our little group. "Let's do this. Count to thirty and run." With that, he disappears into the darkness.

I never realized that half a minute can be so short. When I was raped and beaten, I totally lost track of time. When you lay still, all tied up in bed and uncertain what will happen next, the passing moments can seem like an eternity. Now, I wish I could extend the seconds—at least in my mind. I want just one chance to think clearly, one opportunity to object to this wacky plan.

Sweat trickles down my temples, my breath shallow. I've never been in trouble with the police and my mom will totally freak. The all-too-familiar crushing of my chest returns as oxygen slowly drains from my lungs. Everything around me turns surreal.

When there is a loud bang in the hallway, Cameron takes off. My legs turn to jelly, but I force myself to step into the open doorway. When the cold night air hits me, my instincts kick in.

I draw in a deep breath, and with a long jump that would make a cheetah proud, my legs begin to pump. I don't know where I'm running to and can only hope that Marcel was not mistaken about the cops not shooting fleeing suspects.

Loud yells surround me—he sure was right about the commotion—and I push forward until my attempts are thwarted by a heavy body tackling me to the ground. I land on my stomach, pain shooting up my side. When I struggle to get up, my face is pushed into the soft grass at the same time as my arm is bent backward. Cold metal wraps around my wrist.

"You have the right to remain silent." The second handcuff closes around my other wrist. "Anything you say can and will be used against you in a court of law." I'm pulled to my feet and stare into the face of a young cop. "You have the right to an attorney, and if you can't afford one, the state will provide one for you." He shoves me in the direction of the house where one of his colleagues has secured Cameron. "Do you understand your rights as I have just told them to you?"

I nod, my eyes darting around for Finn, but he is nowhere in sight. Hopefully, he managed to escape. I catch a glimpse of his mother; a paramedic is attending to her. Loud hollering comes from the hallway. Oshin is bitterly complaining about the raid on his home. There is not a peep from Marcel, but since no shots were fired, I figure he should still be alive.

Five minutes later, I am loaded into the police cruiser. With screeching sirens, we take off. I lean back into my seat, staring at the bars that divide my section from the front. I can't help but grin, feeling like a badass. Yet it's definitely not an anecdote I wish to share with my kids.

~~~~

They put me in with the general population, but jail is nothing like you see on TV. The other women ignore me and no one is trying to steal my shoes or start a fight. The jumpsuit fits me perfectly and actually doesn't look that bad, though it is not something I would choose for my casual wardrobe. The only authentic moment was my smudged fingers when they took my prints, and I wonder if I will get to keep my mug shots. In my excitement, I forgot to ask for a phone call.

In my cell, I get comfortable on a cot, mental exhaustion replacing my pounding heartbeat. It must be already after midnight and everyone else is sleeping, or at least not making a sound. The bright neon light in the hallway keeps me awake, my muscles still twitching from the adrenaline surging through my veins. Worry for Finn and Maisie is settling in, though I don't consider my situation dire.

They come for me when I'm just about to doze off; I would have growled if the cop had not been so intimidating. He's a tall dude and I barely reach his shoulders. Surprisingly, he is not wearing a uniform. He ushers me down the hallway into a small office. An older guy is seated like a king behind a desk. Marcel is standing by the window, staring into the blackness of the night. He seems unharmed, which is a relief.

"Take a seat, Ms. Miller." The tall cop points at a chair across the desk.

I sit down and fold my hands in my lap, trying to show that I fully intend to cooperate.

The older guy takes over. "Ms. Miller, I'm Agent Walters with the DEA. Do you know what that stands for?"

I clear my throat when he glares at me, my voice failing me. For the first time, I realize that I might be in bigger trouble than I thought.

"Yes," I finally mutter. "It's for Drug Enforcement Agency."

"Great." He smiles at me. "Then we're on the same page." His eyes travel to Marcel by the window. "You wanna take it from here?"

There's a moment of silence; he hasn't once turned around. "Yeah. Could you just give us the room?"

I squint at him, noticing that he neither wears a jumpsuit nor handcuffs.

Walters rises and signals the big agent to follow him. The door closes behind them before Marcel finally turns around.

I gasp when I see his bruised face. "What happened to you?"

He leaves his place by the window, plopping into the chair that was just occupied by Walters.

"Okay, what I'm telling you now needs to stay in this room. If you spill any of this to anyone, I will most likely get killed. Do you understand?"

The spit dries in my mouth as I nod.

"I work for the DEA as an undercover agent and have been investigating Tyrone for the last three years. Thanks to our little road trip, things are about to fall apart. That is, unless you help me."

I struggle to comprehend the words. In a way, I'm not surprised. He has never acted like a criminal, at least not in front of me. "What do you need me to do?"

He lets the air escape through pursed lips. "Finn got away, just as planned, but he'll want an explanation on how we got out of jail. I'm gonna claim that the cops beat me up, and when they couldn't pin the drugs or guns on me, they let me go to avoid being sued. If you confirm that story, he is more likely to believe it. Just tell him that you saw them roughing me up when we first got to the station because I gave them a hard time during booking. You being a witness will also explain why they let you go."

I'm puzzled. "Why don't we just tell him the truth? He's your friend."

Marcel chuckles with bitterness. "You don't really have friends in this line of work. Finn saved my nephew's life in juvie, and when he moved to Maine, we started hanging since he didn't know anyone else in the state besides his uncle. Ultimately, he doesn't owe me anything and he hates the police with a passion. There's always a chance he'll let it slip to Tyrone as an entry ticket to join the organization. Since he could also be Napoleon, I'm not sure how far I trust him. The less people who know, the better." When I remain silent, he adds, "Look, I'm not expecting you to do this for me for free. In return, I'll help you find Napoleon."

I gaze up at him from under my eyelashes. "Are you sure?"

"Yeah. It's like a business deal." He shrugs. "You do something for me, I do something for you. That way, we're both invested to hold up our end of the bargain."

The idea is growing on me. "What about Finn? If he gets involved in Tyrone's business, are you going to arrest him?"

"That really depends on his involvement. So far, he's clean. He never concerned himself with Tyrone other than buying some weed for personal use when he came by to visit me. Cameron finally talked to a social worker, so the sexual abuse charges can be challenged, but he still almost killed Oshin O'Grady. It's ultimately up to his lawyer to ask for a new trial." He sighs. "Look, Kelsey, Finn seems like a nice guy, but helping him tonight was total insanity and got me into a lot of trouble with my boss. I almost got fired." His eyes are pleading as he watches me with slumped shoulders.

I remember how he helped me with Justin, his boyish smile when he dallied with Hallie's sister. He's the only one I explicitly trust at the moment, and not only because he is a cop. "Okay, I'll help you."

I drown the few doubts nagging at me by convincing myself that it's the right thing to do. Finn's life may have been a bunch of crap, but if he is a criminal, he deserves to be punished, just like anyone else—and if he is Napoleon, I hope Marcel will kill him.

Chapter 28

The visitation area of the Androscoggin County Jail is a small room the size of our storage closet. A metal stool is bolted to the floor in front of a bulletproof glass window that is several inches thick. I chew my lip as I stare at my fingernails, waiting for Luke to appear on the other side of the glass. There is no sound and after a while, I automatically start humming to break through the nerve-racking silence.

When the door behind the glass finally opens, the man crossing the threshold has barely a resemblance with my brother. His face is covered with stubble and dark circles underline his eyes. The few days he has spent behind bars has easily aged him by ten years. His tan from the summer has totally vanished, his skin shining ghost-like under the bright neon light.

His lips spread into the widest grin when he lowers himself onto the stool across from me. His palm comes to rest on the glass. Tears fill my eyes when I raise my hand to mimic the gesture. The glass feels cold and Luke appears miles away despite our closeness—the separation tears painfully at my heart. A few hot tears spill from my eyes and roll down my cheeks. There is nothing in this world I want more than to touch him.

He grimaces, picking up the phone, and signals me to do the same. As soon as the receiver touches my ear, I hear his voice.

"Hey, sis, what's up?"

I know he is trying to make this experience easier for me and I wipe the tears off my face with the sleeve of my jacket. Snuffling, I make a mental note to bring tissues next time.

"I'm hanging in there." I don't want to ask him how he is—afraid of the answer—giving him my bravest smile instead.

He takes the lead, volunteering what I need to know. "I'm okay, really. It's nothing like you see in the movies. Most of the guys in here are actually alright, though the food is terrible. We get to watch TV almost all day and are even allowed to go to the gym."

"You have a gym?" I ask with surprise.

"Yep. They even let you use an exercise yard for some fresh air when it's not too cold." He pats his stomach. "I think I've been losing weight, which isn't necessarily a bad thing. You'll see, by the time I get out of here, I'll be in top form."

My smile is crooked; his efforts to cheer me up only bring new tears to my eyes.

"So, what have you been up to?" he asks.

I ponder whether I should tell him the truth about my recent endeavors and decide to play it by ear. "I've been hanging out with Hallie a lot."

"That's good." His words don't match his reserved smile; he must not think it's a good idea.

My fingers wrap tighter around the receiver. "We have been playing detective, trying to find Napoleon."

His eyes narrow. "Don't you think you should let the police handle that?"

I have seen the expression on his face a hundred times before—it's his typical big-brother protective look. Wanting to ease his mind, I feed him some more information. "Marcel has been helping us. You really don't need to worry."

He snorts. "He's a drug dealer. I really don't think he's the right person to hang with, Kels."

It's my turn to frown—after all, he helped him find me— and it is rather hypocritical to judge him.

"Don't get me wrong," he adds. "I appreciate what he has done for you, but those types of guys attract trouble like a magnet. Sooner or later, he'll pull you down."

I almost chuckle when I remember our road trip to Connecticut. Luke has no idea that he and Finn already totally corrupted me. If Marcel wasn't a cop, I would probably be sitting in a similar jail cell in New Haven.

"I just don't think this case is a priority for the police," I admit. "As long as Napoleon is out there, I'll always have to look over my shoulder. I refuse to live like this for the rest of my life."

"I understand."

My gaze drops when I notice the pain in his eyes.

"I guess I just want to be the one helping you," he says. "It drives me nuts, sitting in here, terrified that Napoleon will snatch you again and I won't be around to protect you." His face softens. "I hope you understand."

My hand moves over the glass again. "Of course I do, and I wish you were here with me, too." My voice is trembling and I swallow down the lump building in my throat. "Did your dad say what'll happen next?"

"The DA will present the case to the grand jury, and if I'm lucky, they'll drop the charges after that. The state really doesn't want to pursue this, but they fear that people will scream favoritism because my dad is a hotshot lawyer. He said they're just going through the motions and that I shouldn't worry. I just hope he's right."

That makes two of us. "When's the grand jury?"

"Not sure. They'll subpoena you to testify, so you'll know."

"Well, I will tell them that your act was nothing but heroic." I smile. "You saved my life, Luke."

He lowers his gaze. "Just make sure you stay safe."

I'm just about to tell him not to worry when the door behind him opens with a low squeak.

"Time's up, Franklin." The guard glares at him without even the slightest bit of sympathy.

The wetness in Luke's eyes betrays him; this is so much harder than he lets on. "I love you, Kels."

My bottom lip trembles when our palms connect over the glass one last time. "I love you, too, Luke. I'll be back in two days."

My heart is torn from my chest when the guard leads him away and the door closes behind him. The silence envelops me, sucking the little bit of restraint right out of me. With my face buried in my hands, I weep, wanting to find Napoleon more than ever. He has destroyed my life in every way imaginable and I will not rest until he is the one behind the glass.

~~~~

An hour later, I meet up with Finn at the coffee shop. Though he hasn't been officially cleared as Napoleon, I figure I'll be safe in a public place. My initial apprehension has been slowly dwindling away after I started to convince myself that he couldn't possibly be my tormentor. He had plenty of opportunities to abduct me during our night on the town. And beating up Jed and risking a lengthy prison term, just to cover potential future tracks, makes no sense.

He grins when he squeezes into the seat across from me, his eyes lively. He certainly is in a much better mood than me.

"My uncle went down to Connecticut to get Cameron," he informs me after mumbling a "Hi" and signaling the waitress to bring him some coffee. "Social Services cleared him as a temporary guardian after I agreed to move out until my lawyer can file a motion to vacate my conviction for sexual assault. I'm not allowed to be around Cameron for now, but at least he's safe and won't be in foster care."

I frown, fearing the worst. "Where're you gonna stay?"

My suspicion is confirmed just moments later. "I think I'll crash at Marcel's for a while. Tyrone has a big house and I could even help out, earn some extra cash."

The waitress places the coffee in front of him and gives me a refill. I wait until she is out of earshot before I cut into him. "I think that's a terrible idea."

If he is living there, he'll get caught up in Marcel's undercover operation. Marcel had just told me this morning that the DEA will be moving in soon to make the bust since a huge deal with some South American drug cartel is about to go down. "Tyrone's a criminal and you're setting yourself up for trouble. Your probation officer will probably violate you if he finds out you're living there."

He sips his coffee slowly, glaring at me with knotted brows. "You know, I'm really surprised to hear this. If it wasn't for Marcel, you'd be dead." He tries to keep the trembling anger from his voice, but fails. "He's my friend and has always been there for me. I hope you won't make me choose, because let me assure you, you'll lose."

The thought of giving him an ultimatum had crossed my mind but is quickly discarded after his words. "Hey, I don't wanna fight. I'm just worried you'll get yourself into more trouble." I grimace. "This gang business is new to me and I don't really feel comfortable around Tyrone. He creeps me out."

"I guess he can be scary, especially for some country chick like you. Sometimes, I forget you grew up in Stonehenge. You stood your ground like a real street kid out there in New Haven." He laughs. "You were kickass."

Sal Mason

"Yeah, I suppose." My smile is slow, uncertain whether to take this as a compliment. The fact that he grew up around crime and drugs makes me question his values at times. I now understand why Marcel mistrusts him to a certain degree—I'm not sure if I would put my life in Finn's hands if I was a cop.

It was almost too easy to sell him Marcel's story. After we had gotten the car from the impound yard and had checked on Maisie, who had temporarily found a home with one of Marcel's DEA buddies, Marcel called him and picked him up from the Greyhound bus stop where Finn had been waiting for a bus back to Maine.

As soon as Finn saw Marcel's face, he immediately presumed that Marcel had hired some legal heavyweight and gotten himself released with the threat of a lawsuit. Convincing him that his assumptions were right was a piece of cake after I confirmed Marcel's detailed account of how the cops had managed to screw up the entire case. I just explained how they retaliated with brutal violence right in front of me after he had given them a smart lip.

A giggle from the door distracts me when two new patrons enter the coffee shop.

"There she is," Cynthia mutters to Justin, loud enough for the whole diner to hear.

I frown—why can't those two can't just leave me alone? The gossip in town has been booming since Luke's arrest and I have suffered under the constant stares and whispers of anyone I passed on the street.

Justin slowly strolls over to me. "Nice pictures you posted on FriendBook. I have to admit, you're hot." He kisses Cynthia's cheek when she nudges him in the side. "But of course not as hot as you, babe."

That causes her to giggle hysterically.

I roll my eyes. "I have no clue what you're talking about. I haven't been on my FriendBook account in years."

"Oh yeah." His eyes fall on Finn and he smirks. "Dude, those pictures are dynamite. Your girlfriend seems great in the sack. I'm just sorry that it's with another guy."

Finn glares at Justin. "She just told you she doesn't know nothing about it."

Justin lazily fishes his iPhone from his pocket, tapping around before holding my FriendBook profile under my nose. "Here we go."

All color leaves my face. My profile picture has been changed to a topless photograph of myself. Underneath, there are dozens of pictures of me having sex with Jed. I clutch my hand over my lips as a gurgle builds in the bottom of my throat.

"I—I didn't do that." My mouth is so dry that I have trouble swallowing. Every breath is agonizing, the all-too-familiar feeling of oxygen being squeezed from my lungs with an iron fist spreading across my chest. I gasp, the diner spinning. Jed's lustful eyes burn in my mind; his groans echo in my ears and mix with my pleading yelps for him to stop.

A sharp pain pulls me back before the panic spirals out of control. I find Finn's eyes, his fingernails clawing deeply into my skin. His message is clear—"Keep it together."

"Get lost," he hisses at Justin and Cynthia. "If I were you, I wouldn't share these photos, or you might regret it."

Justin throws me a vicious look. "Too late. Kelsey's profile is public, so the world can see those pictures. They've been on there for hours. Everyone knows."

Tears fill my eyes as the full impact hits me. There is no way to get every single one of the photos deleted—they will be on the Internet forever. Napoleon must have broken into my FriendBook account and not only posted them, but set my profile to public.

Anger flares, and in my rage, I turn on Justin. "You probably remembered my password and uploaded these. Hell, for all I know, you were the second kidnapper. I'll talk to the cops and have you arrested."

For a moment, he stares at me, and I triumph, thinking I actually scared him. Then he starts laughing.

"You're totally crazy." Tears sparkle in his eyes as he continues to snicker. "Cynthia and I weren't even in the country over Christmas. We went to her family's vacation home in Barbados and didn't come home till last night." He nudges my shoulder and I recoil. "You are hot, but not enough for me to go through the trouble of kidnapping you." He takes a deep breath, his chuckles finally dying down. "Boy, that's the funniest thing I've heard in ages."

For the first time, I notice that they are both covered with a golden tan, Cynthia's face full of freckles that usually fade in the winter. He must be telling the truth.

Finn's eyes narrow. "If you touch her again, I'll break your jaw, and then you won't be able to laugh for a while. What kind of sick person makes jokes about stuff like that?"

Justin pushes out his chest with a smug expression on his face. "You two aren't even worth my time." His arm comes to rest around Cynthia's shoulders and he smiles sweetly at her. "Let's go, babe. The movie starts in ten minutes and this is our last week before you go back to college."

He winks at me as he whisks her away, my gaze following them with a sullen expression. Of all the people on my suspect list, I would have loved seeing him in jail. He's such a douchebag.

Finn signals the waitress and pulls out his wallet. "We need to get those pictures off FriendBook. Let's go to your place and take care of it."

I hesitate—there won't be anyone at the house. My mom and Roy have gone to Augusta for the day to meet with one of Roy's friends who is supposed to help with Luke's case. My mom had only agreed to go when I had sworn to return straight home after my visit at the jail.

"I'd rather be alone for a while," I claim, my shrewdness competing with my mounting need to have a friend by my side.

He pulls out a five-dollar bill, placing it on the table when the waitress takes her sweet time. "There's no way I'll leave you alone and risk you cutting yourself. This is a prime situation to relapse."

It is time to fess up. "Finn, you can't come. I don't want to be alone with you."

His forehead wrinkles in confusion. "Why's that?"

How do you tell your friend that you suspect him of being a rapist? I nibble on my lip—feverishly thinking of something to sugarcoat the inevitable message. My mind comes up blank. This may be one of the hardest things I'll ever have to do. "Because there's a chance that you could be Napoleon."

He looks like someone just cut his chest open with a machete as all color leaves his face. Confusion, pain, and the utter sense of betrayal are written in his eyes, making me feel like a despicable human being. How could I have ever doubted him? I want to take back the words—apologize—but he doesn't give me the chance.

With a sigh, he slides the wallet back into his pocket. "Take care of yourself."

As he strolls out without another glance, I can't shake the feeling that I will never see him again. That's when my heart shatters into a thousand pieces. It's the moment I realize how much I actually care for him. Though I know that I owe it to myself not to take any chances, my stunt likely screwed up my one chance at happiness. Yet this time, there is no one else to blame but myself.

Chapter 29

The diner in the center of Bangor is the old-fashioned type where waitresses still wear uniforms that were popular in the fifties and the menu has dozens of different milkshakes on offer. I slurp the double chocolate Oreo kind, my eyes fixed on the small window behind the counter where the kitchen staff places the completed orders. So far, no sign of Drake Whitmer, though I'm sure he works here.

"Wanna try some of my brownie?" Hallie asks, pushing the plate closer to me. Her eyes are filled with concern.

My mood has been on a constant decline ever since Finn departed from my life a little over a week ago, and I have been more than a bit snappy. The brownie looks delicious, but my appetite is lacking. "No, thanks. I'm good."

She shifts with a small grimace. I can tell her cast is bothering her. "Any word from Finn?"

"Nope." My gaze wanders to Marcel, who is right outside the diner, talking on his cell. He told me that Finn had moved into one of the spare bedrooms at the house, but so far, has not involved himself in any criminal activities. The bust is only days away and I hope that he doesn't end up in handcuffs.

"What do you make of Marcel?" Donna asks. She has squeezed herself into the booth right next to Hallie and the crutches. When we told her we were going to Bangor, she insisted on coming. "I mean, he seems really sweet and all, but do you think he would change for a woman? He asked me out on a date the other day, but I'm not sure if that's what I want. One day, he'll probably end up in jail and I'll be left with a whole lot of problems."

I would love to tell her the truth about him, but I swore complete secrecy. Even the Maine police don't know about

Marcel's undercover operation since the DEA suspects that a few of the cops are on Tyrone's payroll. The risk of exposure is just too high, which would not only blow the operation but could get him killed.

"I think you should give him a chance," I say. "He's obviously trying to turn his life around, otherwise, why would he help us? He has proven himself a good friend. After all, he rescued your sister."

Donna puckers her lips and I'm not sure if she is convinced. In that moment, Marcel glares at us with a menacing frown. He sure is wearing his best drug runner impression, which doesn't help. With swinging arms, he continues his conversation—whoever is on the other line is making him angry.

"Can I get you anything else?" the waitress asks.

"Yes." I beam at her. "I heard an old friend from high school is working here—Drake Whitmer. Is he around?"

"He works in the kitchen. Do you want me to get him for you?"

I glance at Marcel. I would prefer him to be around, but this might be my only chance to lure Drake out. "That'd be great. I just want to say hello."

She disappears and I signal Marcel to come in, but he ignores me. My fingers drum on the table, not sure what to do if Drake shows up. My eyes keep darting to the kitchen entrance, then back to Marcel—he now has his back turned to me, and I have no clue how long his phone call will take.

Drake looks just like I remember him—he has always reminded me of a beaver with his two big front teeth that constantly seem to tug on his lip. He pushes his glasses up when he realizes it's me, his eyes wide in panic. His gaze moves to the door and I'm sure that flight is one of the options he's considering.

With a sigh, he finally trots over to our table, his arms folding over his chest when he comes to a sudden halt three steps away. "What do you want?" A stick could have competed with his rigid, straight body.

I decide not to beat around the bush. "Closure. I need to know if you were one of my kidnappers."

His jaw drops; he apparently didn't expect such an honest answer. "I swear I had nothing to do with it and I already told all that to the police. Anything else?"

"Like you would really tell us if you did," Hallie mumbles. "You have to do better than that."

His eyes narrow. "And who the hell are you?"

His reaction to Hallie is very convincing. He shows not the slightest indication that he knows her.

"Well, my second kidnapper had a scar on the inside of his thigh." I grin, not really eager to see that part of him. "No scar and you're off the suspect list for good."

He snorts. "No way. You better leave, or I'll call the cops and tell them you're harassing me. You can't just go around, making these types of allegations."

"Sure we can." Marcel finally finished his phone call and strolls up behind Drake. I have to admit, his timing has always been impeccable. "Now, man, we can either do this the hard or the easy way"—he cracks his knuckles—"and trust me, it makes no difference to me."

All color leaves Drake's face as he slowly backs up. "Stay away from me, dude." He glances at our waitress. "Call the cops, Liz. This guy is threatening me."

Marcel clicks his tongue. He is done playing. "Let's go." Grabbing Drake by the collar of his shirt, he drags him toward the bathroom. Halfway there, he halts, squinting at me. "Coming, Kelsey? Wanna make sure I look in the right place."

With much hesitation, I get on my feet, facing the inevitable. At least I will know afterward for sure if Drake is my tormentor.

I have never set foot in a man's bathroom before and the first thing I notice is the stench, reminding me of chlorine and pee. There are five urinals against the wall next to a couple of sinks and two stalls. Luckily, no other patron is using the facilities and the room is empty.

"Okay, drop your pants," Marcel demands, his hand coming to rest on the grip of his gun.

Drake's eyes go as wide as saucers; for a moment, I'm afraid he'll wet himself as his stare stays on the gun in Marcel's waistband. The gangbanger glares at him with an even expression. If I didn't know him, he would scare the shit out of me.

With trembling fingers, Drake begins to fumble with the button of his jeans. It takes him forever to get the zipper open. I squeeze my eyes shut when the pants drop.

Marcel clears his throat. "Kelsey, where do I look?"

"Top of the left inner thigh, right next to—you know." I peek a little when there is shuffling beside me, but drop my gaze at the sight of Drake handling his private parts.

This might have been a sixty-second affair if the door had not been pushed open, another customer toddling in. He halts in his tracks when he sees us, his eyes laced with shock at the sight of a pantsless Drake.

Marcel smirks. "You're welcome to join the party."

The guy's cheeks color crimson red and he turns on his heel, storming out.

"That's our cue to get out. Someone is bound to call the cops and I sure don't feel like explaining what we've been doing." He cups Drake's head and pulls him closer, his mouth only inches from his ear. "Now listen, man. It'd be best if you forget this ever happened. If anyone called the cops, tell them it was just a silly prank. If not"—he chuckles softly—"you can imagine what I'll do to you."

Drake stutters an "Okay" and Marcel lets go of his head. It's amazing how well he plays the part of the bad guy. He can be absolutely terrifying, and I'm sure Drake got the message. I actually feel a little guilty. After he has been cleared of being Napoleon, he sure didn't deserve being hassled like that, though it's his problem that he just disappeared while the first investigation was still ongoing. He could have volunteered to be eliminated as a suspect years ago as Larouge suggested, but his lawyer objected on the grounds that such an invasive procedure violated his human rights. Since there was never any real evidence, the cops dropped the ball after that.

Pressing silence hangs over the diner when we step out of the bathroom, but it's not only Marcel and I who have caused a ruckus. Hallie is sobbing silently at the table while Donna mumbles to her, stroking her back. When our eyes meet, I know something terrible must have happened.

"More drama is all I need," Marcel mutters under his breath. With a small huff, he places fifty dollars on the counter, not waiting for his change. Scooping up Hallie into his arms, who is too stunned to protest, he departs.

I shrug—that was the practical solution. It would have probably taken ten minutes to calm her down. Donna grabs the crutches and follows him, and we almost collide at the door. For once, I can't wait to get back to Stonehenge, sure that I won't visit this diner again.

Hallie is still crying when Marcel takes off with screeching tires. He must have watched too many movies and be imagining he's driving a getaway car. As he speeds along to get some distance between us and the diner, Donna fills us in.

"Someone broke into Hallie's FriendBook account, too, and uploaded these nude pictures after she was raped. A friend from school messaged her and that's when Hallie totally lost it."

"I hope you didn't delete them," Marcel says, shooting me a dark look.

I've been lectured on and off after deleting mine since they are considered evidence of a crime. Apparently, it's harder for the police to track who uploaded them once they are off my timeline. Detective Larouge was able to find a few downloads to aid in the investigation, but so far, all trails have gone cold.

"Why is this guy doing this?" Donna rubs Hallie's arm and she slowly settles down.

"It gives him a certain control over his victims and keeps them afraid of him." Marcel makes a sharp right turn and the seatbelt cuts into me. "It's like 'Hey, I can torture you whenever I want' and also implies that sooner or later, he'll try to snatch them again."

He hit the nail on the head—that's exactly how I feel. It's like I'm still trapped in my own nightmare.

"Do you really think this guy is that dangerous?" Donna asks with a frown.

"Yep, he's a total psychopath." Marcel honks his horn when the car in front of him doesn't move at the light that just turned green. When he passes at high speed, he glares at the driver. "Old folks really shouldn't be driving." The words are mumbled to himself but still make me wonder why he is acting like a maniac all of a sudden.

He calms down a little when he gets to the highway but still keeps the speed ten miles over the limit.

"Are we in a hurry?" I ask, my hand clutched to the seatbelt.

"That was Tyrone earlier." He glances at Hallie and Donna in the back, but they are engrossed in a hushed conversation and don't pay attention to us. "He's mad as hell that I keep disappearing without an explanation. The process server stopped by earlier and served the grand jury subpoena on Finn, so I have to get in touch with him for mine. Tyrone doesn't want me to go."

Roy said his testimony is crucial if Luke wants to get off. "You have to go. It's my brother's life we're talking about."

"I'm really sorry, Kelsey, but things are turning into a mess. I can't risk it. When all this is over, testifying at trial is not an issue, but Tyrone will freak if I disobey him again."

I pinch the corners of my eyes to suppress the tears. "Please, Marcel, this one last thing. I wouldn't ask you if it wasn't so important."

He grumbles something inaudible. "I'll think about it."

I stare outside the window with blank eyes, the thought that the grand jury could indict Luke unbearable. After that, he could actually get convicted of murder and go to prison for the rest of his life.

"Well, we can at least knock Drake and Luke off the suspect list," Marcel remarks as he speeds up again to pass a truck. He glances at me with a grin. "That's something less to worry about."

I frown. "Why are you all of a sudden excluding Luke?"

"Well—" He curses when a car pulls out in front of him and he hits the brakes hard.

I'm catapulted forward, saved by the seatbelt, but Hallie yelps "Shit" from the back seat after spilling half her water bottle. Maisie howls for good measure, likely to remind us that she's still here.

Donna glares at Marcel. "I'd appreciate if you don't kill us. I just got my sister back and would like to keep it that way."

"Sorry." He slows down a little, his eyes fixed on the road. "So, like I was saying, I don't think it's Luke. He was arrested on the spot after Jed's death and didn't have time to conspire with anyone or pass along the photos to an accomplice. Inmates don't have access to a computer at the jail, so he couldn't have uploaded the pictures himself."

His words make sense and make me feel a little better.

"Couldn't someone have gotten them from Jed?" Donna asks.

"Nope." Marcel honks his horn again when the car in front of him seems to crawl. "Jed's computer was confiscated the night he was killed, and the police would have told you if they had found pictures like that on his hard drive. Hallie's pictures were also just taken the night Kelsey and Hallie escaped, so the window of opportunity was as good as nonexistent. Truthfully, I think Napoleon took Hallie's pictures without Jed's knowledge as a trophy. Those types of mementos are private, and people usually don't share them."

Silence follows his words, then Donna laughs. "You know, you almost sound like a cop."

He bites his lip before forcing a chuckle. "I guess all those private investigator classes are starting to pay off. I feel like a real detective."

He winks at me, and I smirk, imagining Donna's reaction if she knew that she was actually right. The two could really be good together and I ship them. Maybe when this is all over, things will work out for the best. I have no idea how this will impact Marcel's job but can't shake the feeling that he is growing tired of the gangster act and being undercover all the time.

My eyes stare blankly out the window, relief flooding through me that Luke has been cleared by Marcel. Ever since he was added to the suspect list, this nagging voice has been taking little stabs at me. My mind was always able to reason them away, but that didn't alleviate my qualms. I even thought of confronting him once during a visit to the jail, but after Finn's reaction, the fear that he could take it the wrong way glued my lips together. Losing him is an unbearable thought.

Marcel drops us off in front of the Stonehenge police station, so Hallie can file a report about the FriendBook pictures with Detective Larouge. He has managed to hold onto the case by pulling jurisdiction over Portland once the FBI departed. She is still really upset that she can't delete them yet, but most of her friends have pledged their support and told her how appalled they are. The jealous sting burns. For once, I wish I was in her shoes, having people who really care about me. With Finn not around and Luke in jail, it can get quite lonely.

"I'll figure something out with Luke," Marcel promises before he speeds off.

Though this has been a productive day, I still feel rotten. Anytime I make a step forward, it seems like I'm pushed three steps back. Napoleon is winning, and in that moment, I fear that he will be the one coming out on top.

Chapter 30

I barely sleep the night before my grand jury testimony, my worry about Luke keeping my mind occupied. I had hoped that Roy would be there, but neither he nor Luke will be part of the procedure, which stinks. The proceedings are informal and Roy explained that it's usually not very hard to get an indictment. Jurors only decide whether a potential crime was committed and the self-defense argument won't come into play until the trial, which could be a year away.

The thought that Luke might have to remain in jail until then terrifies me. So far, he hasn't missed any of his classes, but his college will start back up next week. The topic of law school has been avoided, but I overheard Roy telling my mom that Luke will have problems with his bar admission even if he wins at trial. Apparently, any arrest has to be disclosed and lowers the chances of becoming a lawyer. I feel terrible that my brother may not fulfill his lifelong dream because he saved me, and my mood has been accordingly sullen.

Roy drops me off at the courthouse. "Keep your chin up, Kelsey, and whatever you do, tell the truth. You won't help Luke by lying."

I grimace, not sure what I could be lying about. Luke is a hero, and the sooner people realize that, the faster we can all move on with our lives.

When I lower myself on the bench by the jury room, my fingers twist together and I realize how sweaty they are. To distract myself, I study the stucco decorations on the ceiling, checking my watch from time to time. The subpoena said my testimony is scheduled for eleven, but it is already eleven fifteen and no one has come for me yet. At eleven thirty, I'm about to complain to the clerk when a woman turns the corner and steers right toward me.

"Ms. Miller?" she asks with a polite smile.

I nod, my mouth too dry to respond.

"I'm Deborah Gibbons from the district attorney's office. Mr. Hutchinson would like a word with you before your testimony."

I remember Hutchinson; he was the DA who handled Jed's case. I bawled in his office when he informed me he was dropping the charges because of the screwup with the warrant. I have held a grudge ever since. The fact that he is now prosecuting Luke makes him even less likable.

I nevertheless follow behind her as she ushers me into the annex that houses the district attorneys. Hutchinson's office is on the third floor and he's alone when I enter. I am not sure if I should talk to him without Roy and reluctantly take a seat in the visitor's chair across his desk. Gibbons grabs a chair behind me by the wall and I feel ganged up on.

Hutchinson is ancient, pushing close to sixty. He has always reminded me of a walrus with a gray mane, though I have always wondered if the hair is real. Every word he mutters is accompanied by a low wheeze and his teeth are yellow. He either drinks loads of coffee or is a heavy smoker.

"Ms. Miller, we got some new evidence this morning that would indeed suggest that your brother was allowed to use deadly force in defending you."

All of a sudden, I want to hug him.

"As you know, my office is not eager to proceed with this case, given Jed Edwards extensive criminal involvement in the kidnapping of you and Ms. Garvey," he continues, which puts a stupid grin on my face. "However, he is a victim like everyone else, and I need to justify if I do not move forward on a criminal charge."

I'm not really sure what he is getting at. "What do you want me to do?"

"Well." He and Deborah exchange a glance. "This morning, I got a rather unexpected visit from Mr. Brown, who disclosed that he is working for the DEA."

I swallow hard. What the hell did Marcel do? This could jeopardize his whole mission.

"I have since confirmed his assignment with his superior, and therefore, I am inclined to rely on the new evidence he presented."

Hutchinson's eyes drill into me and I twitch under his glare as confusion settles in. If this is the case, what does he want from me?

He takes a clear plastic bag from a drawer that contains a switchblade and places it on the desk in front of me. "This, Ms. Miller, is the new evidence. Mr. Brown said that it was Jed's and he was just about to slit your throat when Luke shot him. That, of course, would be a clear affirmative defense to your brother's actions. However, you previously said that Jed only choked you, so I need you to confirm Mr. Brown's statement."

I almost blurt out that there was no knife—I distinctly remember Jed tossing it away—but stop myself at the last second. Truthfully, I don't remember anything about the last moments before the shot went off and Jed could have had a second knife. Yet it is odd that Marcel never mentioned it before.

"It was dark and I was about to pass out, so I couldn't even tell you, but I'm sure that Marcel wouldn't lie. He is a highly decorated federal agent." I have no clue if this is true but figure that someone who works that deep undercover must have received some recognition throughout his career.

"I guess that's good enough." Hutchinson gives me a fake smile. "I won't proceed with the grand jury indictment, and I will let Roy know that he can collect Luke from the jail later today. It will take a few hours to process him out."

My jaw drops. "That's it?"

"Yes. I think this outcome is in everybody's best interest. Jed was a criminal and I guess he got his justice in the end. I never wanted to charge your brother in the first place, but like I said, my hands were tied."

I'm thrilled that all my worries were for nothing. With a wide grin, I thank him and even shake his hand when I bid him goodbye. There is so much relief and all I want to do is call Marcel to tell him how grateful I am.

He doesn't answer his phone, so I leave a message. Determined to wait for Luke to be the first to congratulate him on his release, I stop by in the new coffee shop across from the jail and get a white chocolate latte and a lemon muffin. Opening up my Kindle app, I scroll through my library until I find the book I'm reading—*Ferocious* by Leigh W. Stuart.

It's about this girl who gets these warnings from her kidnapped dead friend and feels lost because everyone thinks she is crazy. I can relate—having felt similarly these past years—though luckily, no ghost has ever spoken to me. The last thing I need is for Jed to come after me from his grave. The book still disturbs me a little, unleashing painful memories, but I'm determined not to let this bother me. After a while, I almost find the read therapeutic. She fights back, just as I did in the end.

I lose track of time and the ringing phone startles me. Marcel's number flashes on the display. Eager to talk to him, I push the connect button, but it's Finn on the other end of the line.

"Kelsey, please don't hang up. I have no one else to call." He sounds frantic. "Marcel got beaten and is really hurt."

I gasp, feeling like I just collided head on with a truck. "What happened?" Crazy things shoot through my head. Tyrone probably found out who he is working for and is out to kill him.

"Tyrone sent a few men after Marcel to teach him not to disobey his orders again. He disappeared a few hours this morning and missed a delivery, so Tyrone was really pissed." A sob drifts through the receiver. "Kelsey, they cut off his ear."

My stomach turns at the news. "Did you take him to the hospital?" My breath is heavy, and I can hardly think straight.

Finn snuffles, his voice almost incomprehensible. "He refuses to go. There's so much blood and I don't know what to do."

I pinch the bridge of my nose, fighting off the panic. "Where are you?"

"In a warehouse down by the docks on Commercial Street. I can ask Marcel for the exact address."

My eyes scan the road for a cab. "I'll be there in less than an hour. Text me the address." Luckily, my mom gave me a prepaid credit card for Christmas, which has $500 on it. That should be plenty.

When I slide into the backseat of the taxi, my eyes fall on the front door of the jail where Roy is just about to enter. Luke will be fine without me—getting Marcel help is more important. He risked everything for me and now it's time to repay him.

~~~~

He is in a worse state than expected, and I almost run out of the warehouse screaming when I see the puddle of blood around him. He's huddled on the floor with his back against the wall, a soaked towel pressed to the side of his head. Even though his eyes are closed and he's controlling his breathing, I can tell he is in a lot of pain.

His face is bruised with several cuts, his shirt torn. They really didn't spare any part of him. Tyrone wanted the message delivered and his men beat the crap out of their leader. Marcel never had a chance.

I crouch next to him on the ground. "Hey, can you get up?"

He groans. "I can't go to the hospital. Tyrone will kill me."

"I know." I rub his shoulder to comfort him, but when he flinches, my hand flies back. "We have to get you some medical attention. You're losing too much blood." Out of the corner of my eyes, I glance at Finn, who is leaning against the wall a few feet away before dropping my voice to a mere whisper. "What about the DEA? Maybe they can keep it under wraps?"

"That's against protocol and they will pull me off the case." His lips are barely moving before they contort to a painful grimace. He hisses, his head falling backward against the wall.

Tears fill my eyes when I realize how much he is suffering. I gaze at Finn again, who is paler than a ghost.

"Maybe we can take him home," he suggests.

"No." The anger roars inside me—I will not give Tyrone the satisfaction of seeing Marcel like this. My mind races through my options. I can't take him to Stonehenge since Roy will call the cops and I don't know anyone who is a doctor.

And then it hits me—Donna. She is an ER nurse and must be able to bandage him up.

"Where's your truck?" I ask Finn.

"Up the road."

"Get it." I focus on Marcel. "Do you think you can make it to the truck?"

He finally opens his eyes, which are almost swollen shut. "Where are we going?"

"Donna's."

He groans again, this time more out of desperation. "She'll be so mad."

"Well, it's either her or Tyrone. Take your pick."

My arm slides around his waist when he tries to stand, and he yelps in pain. With unsteady feet, he stumbles forward and every so often, we take a break. His face is twisted in agony and a few times his knees almost buckle. Blood drips from the towel to the floor, leaving a little red trail behind us.

Finn reappears and takes over. "Get in the truck. I got him."

He manages to heave Marcel into the passenger seat and I slide into the back. As soon as the engine starts, I text my mom to let her know I'm okay. I will still be in trouble for just disappearing without checking in with her first, but if I tell her it was an emergency with Marcel, she'll get over it.

It's not far to Donna's house; I just pray she is home. A sigh of relief rolls over my lips when she opens the door.

All color leaves her face. "Oh my god!" She stares at Marcel with wide eyes. "What the hell happened to you?"

Marcel tries to produce a faint smile but fails when a moan shakes his body. "I had a little disagreement with my boss. No biggie."

I could have slapped him for trying to pull this macho act.

Donna frowns before taking over. "Get him into the kitchen."

With Finn's aid, Marcel climbs onto a barstool. Donna puts on the kettle and disappears, returning with a stack of towels. Hallie is right behind her, hopping in on her crutches.

"What's going on?" Her hair is sticking up and her voice is hoarse; she must have just woken up.

"What does it look like?" Donna growls. "Your friend's work finally caught up with him."

I grimace. Though we have never talked specifics about Marcel's job situation, her suspicion that he is involved in gang activities always hung in the air like a dark cloud whenever he was around. I hate that this incident proves her right, even though the reality couldn't be further from the truth.

Furiously, she scribbles down something on a notepad. I glance at Marcel, who is slumped on the barstool in total misery. He was right—she is absolutely pissed. Now I wonder if we would have been better off taking him to Tyrone. This stunt might have cost him his one chance with her.

She hands Finn the page from the notepad and 2 twenty-dollar bills. "Go to the drugstore down the road and get me this." Her chin points to Hallie and me and then to the door. "You two wait upstairs. I get nervous when people stare at me while I work."

I glance at Marcel with sympathy before following Hallie into her room with slumped shoulders. Twenty minutes later, Finn joins us; he has been banned from the kitchen as well. We talk with hushed voices, trying to listen to the noises from below.

A few muffled curses drift up on occasion, but otherwise, it stays quiet. Marcel must still be pretending to be tough and eating up the pain. I watch the clock on Hallie's nightstand as the minutes pass by. My phone vibrates a few times in my pocket, yet the worry about my friend prevents me from picking up. It can only be Luke or my mom, who will want me to come home, but I'm not ready to leave Marcel until I know he'll be okay.

It's already getting dark when Donna comes upstairs. "He's sleeping now. I stitched him up and it will take a few days, but then he should be almost as good as new."

I can't even imagine how he will look like without his ear, though I know firsthand, since the incident with Jed and Roxy, that there are reconstructive surgeries for this type of injury.

Finn gets up and stretches. "I'd better get going. Thanks for everything, Donna." He grabs his jacket off the chair, not even glancing at me. "Marcel is a really nice guy. What happened today was not his fault."

Donna grumbles something that sounds close to "He's still a criminal."

My eyes follow Finn as he strolls out. I want to call him back and ask him to take me home, but the words refuse to leave my mouth. While we were waiting, Hallie had told him about Drake. It would have been easy for him to get exonerated right on the spot. He didn't offer and I didn't push the subject.

Instead, the conversation went from awkward to dead, the atmosphere growing more pressing as the hours passed by. In the end, it was painful to be cramped together in the small room. Every time I glanced at him, my heart threatened to tear apart. Only Hallie's forced chit chat kept me halfway sane, though it also prevented me from reaching out to him. Not that I would have known what to say, so it was probably for the best. We might have gotten into another argument if I had opened my mouth.

With a sigh, I pull out my phone and dial the familiar number of the one person who has always bailed me out as long as I can remember.

Luke answers on the first ring. "Hey, Kels. I was worried about you. Where are you?" He tries to sound calm, but there is a panicked undertone.

"I'm in Portland at Hallie's house and need a ride." I step to the window and watch as Finn gets into the truck, taking off with too much speed. A part of my heart goes with him. I wonder if we'll ever put our stubbornness aside and work things out between us.

Luke's voice shouts in my ear. "Kels, are you still there?"

I swallow the building lump in my throat. "Yeah."

"What's the address?"

A few tears spring loose and I allow them to drop off my chin. With a last-ditch effort, I pull myself back together. "112 Chestnut Lane."

"I'll be there as soon as I can." He cuts the line and I stare out in the dark, trying to will Finn to come back.

When I turn around, Donna is gone, but Hallie stares at me with sad eyes. "It's gonna be okay. As soon as Napoleon is captured, you and Finn can kiss and make up."

I want to cry again, but I'm simply too exhausted. The events of the day have utterly worn me out and I long for just one ordinary day in my life—a day where I don't have contact with a law representative, don't see any blood, and don't worry about rape suspects. That would really be nice for a change.

Chapter 31

Marcel stays at Donna's house for a couple of days before quietly disappearing, probably trying to salvage whatever is left of his career. He doesn't contact me and I leave him and Finn alone, determined to give them their space. Marcel has already done plenty, and I am mad at Finn for not valuing our friendship enough to get himself exonerated. How hard can it be to drop your pants for a few minutes to put matters to rest once and for all?

Hallie and I focus on our ultimate mission to find Napoleon, zooming in on Jackson next. He has been hitting on Hallie since the night he found her in the cabin, texting her almost daily and asking her out on dates. Personally, I have never liked him after he dropped a frog in my shirt during one of Luke's family barbecues when I was thirteen, which also elevated him to the top of my brother's shit list. In Jackson's defense, he was nothing more than a boisterous eleven-year-old, but the memory of squealing hysterically in front of everyone until Luke rescued me is too horrific to just ignore.

When Hallie gets a walking cast, we are ready to strike. In my book, he is the most likely suspect since I find his presence at the cabin too odd a coincidence. Yet Hallie likes him, so I keep my opinions to myself, especially after Larouge couldn't find any connection to the kidnappings. According to him, they are still checking him out, which is police code that Jackson is not a prime suspect in their book.

I'm surprised how well Hallie copes with the rape. Not once does she try to kill her pain by cutting; as a matter of fact, she never talks about it. Instead, she tells me how cute guys are and that she wouldn't mind having a boyfriend. Dr. Stromberg told me that everyone deals with trauma differently and that she's probably suppressing the memory. It still makes me bitter since I've struggled so much over the years—her nonchalance slowly drives a wedge between us.

"Jackson, this is Hallie Garvey," she coos into the phone. "I got your flowers and just wanted to call and thank you. They are totes amazing."

I roll my eyes at her suggestive laugh.

"Guess what, I got a walking cast." She listens to Jackson's response and giggles. "Yes, that's why I'm calling. I'd love to go to dinner with you."

She giggles again. "Friday night sounds great. And yes, I love Italian."

She certainly sounds convincing, and he eats it up, promising to be at her house at seven.

She beams at me after she hangs up. "That's set. Now who is going to accompany you on the stakeout?"

The plan is to lure Jackson to the restaurant and pull a Drake on him by ambushing him in the bathroom. Since he will likely not be too cooperative, a little help from a guy couldn't hurt. Otherwise, I will be on my own.

Hallie refuses to reveal that she is in on the plan, afraid that this will ruin her chances with him once he is cleared. After my friendship with Finn was destroyed in the exact same manner, I can relate to her fear.

"I think we should ask Marcel," she says. "He owes us since my sister bandaged him up."

Marcel is out of the question. If he was still interested in helping us, he would have called. "Let's ask someone else. He might still be too hurt to be of use."

"True." Hallie wrinkles her nose. "Are you sure you don't wanna ask Finn?"

It irks me that she constantly brings up his name. "Yes, no Finn." The only other person is my brother. "I'll ask Luke. I'm sure he'll help us."

Later that night, I visit Luke in his room. College started back yesterday and he's sorting through his new textbooks, a pen firmly tucked in between his teeth. He freezes when he notices me, giving me a stupid grin.

"Hey, Kels."

The words sound funny with the pen in his mouth and I snicker. "I need to ask you a favor." Flinging myself onto the bed next to him, I gaze at him with my best puppy dog eyes.

"Oh, oh, I don't like where this is going." He pulls up a chair. "I only get this look from you when you're trying to get me to do something, so spit it out."

I grimace; he really knows me too well. I feel awful getting him entangled in this. "As you know, Hallie and I have been playing detective."

"Yes, and as *you* know, I think it's a really bad idea. That's what we have the police for."

"The cops aren't doing jack shit." I twist my lips into a pout which makes him laugh. "Come on, Luke. If you don't do it, I have to go alone and I'm sure you don't want that."

He twitches and I know I got him. "Okay, what do I have to do?"

After I fill him in on the plan, he has second thoughts. "I don't know, Kels. This sounds a little farfetched. Jackson is still my cousin and kidnapping someone doesn't compare to planting a frog in your shirt. Besides, I have plans with Rhonda on Friday night."

I frown. "I thought she broke up with you after your arrest, because she couldn't be bothered with a boyfriend in jail."

"She did, but we've been trying to reconcile. Friday night was supposed to be our first official date. She'll be mad if I cancel."

Ever since Rhonda abandoned my brother in a time of crisis, she has been on *my* shit list. "I really think you shouldn't just give her another chance. She acted like a total bitch."

After some more desperate puppy dog eyes, he grudgingly agrees to postpone his date. Everything is set for our trap. If Jackson turns out to be innocent, only two names will remain at the top of the suspect list—Roy and Finn—and I will be forced to make some pretty big decisions.

~~~~

Luke and I go grocery shopping on Friday afternoon—if we're going to have a stakeout, we want to do it in style. After the mandatory soda and water bottles, six different flavors of potato chips get added to the cart, together with an assortment of gummy bears, caramel popcorn, and tons of candy bars. At the checkout, I throw in a pack of gum. If we're already going to indulge in a sugar revelry, we could at least watch our dental hygiene.

"How did Rhonda take it?"

"She threw a hissy fit and told me she never wants to see me again. I don't think we'll work it out."

I snort. "You don't look very heartbroken."

He flings his arm around my shoulders, pushing up his chin. "Who needs a nagging woman when you can spend a night with your sister, eating junk food in a cramped truck while watching a couple eat in a romantic restaurant with binoculars? This will be epic."

I laugh, just about to tease him, when my phone rings. I realize it's Marcel and an immediate prickling sensation spreads across my scalp, making me edgy.

"Hello."

"Kelsey, it's Marcel." He pants like he has been running, his voice no louder than a whisper.

I step to the side of the beeping cash register, sticking my finger in my other ear to hear him better. "What's the matter? Are you okay?"

"Yeah." There's a moment of silence. "Listen, it's going down tonight. You have to get Finn away from here, or he's gonna be screwed."

I nibble on my lip, uncertain how to convince Finn to come up to Stonehenge. "He might not wanna come."

"Kelsey, I don't think you realize what's at stake." I can hear him breathe heavy on the other end. "If Finn gets caught up in this, he'll go to jail for a very long time. This thing is huge and Tyrone will point his finger at anyone in his organization to get himself a good deal. Finn is still on probation and the DA won't even plea bargain. Under the federal sentencing guidelines, he'll get twenty years just by mere association. He can't be in Portland tonight, period. You're his only hope."

With his sex-offender conviction, Finn wouldn't survive a year in prison. "Okay, I'll figure something out to get him up here."

"He needs a solid alibi," Marcel stresses.

"Yeah, okay, I got it." The prickling in my scalp is getting stronger. "I'll take care of it. You better worry about yourself. I kind of like having you around."

He chuckles. "Don't worry about me, kiddo. In the meantime, stay safe. Once this bust is over, I'll promise we'll catch that jerk who raped you, but I need you to stay put until then."

He cuts the line before I can object. I trot over to Luke, my mind on Marcel's instructions. This is getting complicated. I'm not sure if a stakeout will count as a solid alibi, even with Luke in the picture, and maybe we *should* just wait for Marcel to join the hunt. He is an expert after all.

"Who was that?" Luke asks.

"Marcel. We have to change our plans for tonight."

"Why? What's going on?"

I give him a crooked smile. "Sorry, but I can't tell you."

His eyebrows rise, deepening the creases on his forehead. "You're keeping secrets from me now?"

"It's not that." I start to load the purchases onto the belt. "It's a promise I made to Marcel."

A shadow crosses his face. "I told you before, I don't like the guy. He'll just end up getting you into trouble. You should stay away from him."

I hardly listen, pondering how to get Finn to Stonehenge. "Marcel got you off, didn't he? Without his statement, you would still be in jail."

Luke goes rigid before exhaling with a huff. "That's the problem." He glances around. "The DA told my dad what he said, Kels, and it was a lie. There was no knife."

I stare at him—Marcel is a cop. If he lied about the knife, he could be dirty. "Are you absolutely sure?"

He nods. "Positive. I mean, I'm thrilled I got out and don't have to go to trial, but what he told Hutchinson was definitely untrue. Jed was choking you and I panicked, so I took the shot. Marcel had a much better handle on things. He knew it would've been enough to pull Jed off you. He took me aside that night and told me he had my back. Not sure why. Truthfully, I think he's got a crush on you. That's probably why he's helped you all this time. Hell, for all I know, he could be Napoleon."

"Now that's ridiculous. I didn't even know him when I was abducted the first time."

"It's a small world, Kels." He fishes the wallet from his pocket and hands the cashier his credit card. "I know it's unlikely, but he could've been friends with Jed back then and kept his identify a secret because that's what career criminals do. I mean, have you never wondered why a man who is almost ten years older than you is helping you like that?"

The credit card slip is placed in front of him and he signs while I muse over his theory. Marcel's behavior has been a little odd, though I always thought he helped me because of the deal we made in Connecticut. He's never even so much as flirted with me, but maybe that doesn't mean anything.

Yet none of this helps me with Finn. Absentmindedly, I dial Hallie's number to inform her about the change in plans.

She is more than miffed. "What am I supposed to do all night? I was really looking forward to getting out of the house."

I smile when an idea begins to form. "Why don't you call Finn and ask him to bring you up here? If you tell him he owes you for Donna stitching up Marcel, I'm sure he won't blow you off. We could all catch a movie with Luke, and later on, go to the house and eat junk food. You could even sleep over. It'll be fun."

She likes the idea and I kill two birds with one stone. With his sense of loyalty, Finn will feel obliged to repay Hallie for Donna's help while he would flat out refuse to come to Stonehenge at my request. Hell, he might not even answer the phone if I call.

I fill Luke in while we are loading the groceries into the car and he agrees with a grunt.

"I hope you're not expecting me to be nice to Finn."

I slap him on the back of his head. "Behave. He's my friend."

With a chuckle, he opens the door for me. "Are we at least gonna share the popcorn like we used to?"

I smile fondly at the memory. He and I haven't been to the movies in ages. "We sure are."

This would be at least as much fun as the stakeout, if not even more, and maybe I will even get a chance to work out some things with Finn. If I apologize and don't push the subject, he might volunteer to prove his innocence in front of Luke. My brother will probably have a heart attack if he has to inspect Finn down there, but afterward, we can all laugh about it.

"I'll drop you off at home," Luke says when he starts the truck. "I have to quickly run over to the library and pick up a book for class. Shouldn't take longer than an hour or so."

I mumble my agreement—that will give me some time to get ready. Since we are going to a restaurant and the movies, the sweats I was intending to wear won't cut it. It will be painful to pick a nice outfit, but with Finn coming, I have the urge to look at least halfway decent.

Hallie calls a few minutes later and confirms that Finn will pick her up at five thirty to take her to Stonehenge after she stirred his guilty conscience. Her plans with Jackson have been postponed to next weekend, and by then, Marcel will have returned to the team.

Unless . . .

I don't finish the thought, determined to confront him the next time I see him. He's easygoing enough not to take it the wrong way when I share with him Luke's Napoleon theory, and he will have some serious explaining to do about the knife. I hope Luke is wrong with his suspicion and that Marcel will turn out innocent in all respects—because if he doesn't, I fully intend to take him down.

Chapter 32

Hallie and Finn arrive just before seven and we decide to take Luke's truck over to the shopping center in Lewiston since it has a bigger cabin. Hallie claims the passenger seat because of her cast, forcing Finn and I to squeeze into the back. The ride is more than uncomfortable, both of us trying our best to keep our knees from touching while silently staring out opposite windows.

Luke pops in a CD and the first verses of an old Meat Loaf song drift through the truck before he strikes up a conversation with Hallie about school. I listen with one ear as they discuss some history assignment about Hitler, a hot debate soon erupting about whether the Internet would have made any difference back then. After a while, Finn butts in, and I realize that they are all history buffs. Figures.

The shopping center is packed and we only find a space in the lowest level of the parking garage, which is almost deserted. Our steps echo in the empty space, mixed with Hallie's giggles. She has her arms around Finn's and Luke's shoulders, clumsily walking along in her cast while the two guys keep her balanced. I trot behind with slumped shoulders, envious that she is the center of attention. Finn laughs as they almost stumble, his eyes sparkling with happiness, yet he cringes every time he looks at me. Maybe this joint night out wasn't such a good idea after all.

The others decide on pizza at Antonio's without consulting me, and even though I usually love Italian food, I object for good measure, just to be told that the majority rules. Once inside the restaurant, I get stuck with the seat facing the wall despite Luke knowing that I hate sitting with my back to the dining area. It makes me feel naked and exposed.

They order a large pizza to share with plenty of garlic bread—again without asking if I like any of the toppings—and ignore me during their vivid conversation, this time about Roman culture. I feel totally left out and have no clue how ancient history could even capture anyone's interest.

Hallie is like a magnet for compliments and distributes her little flirtatious remarks evenly between Luke and Finn. She laughs with that typically high-pitched teen giggle, throwing her head back, which I find totally annoying but seems to mesmerize the guys. I can't believe her behavior. She has totally changed and is acting like a slut.

Luke gawks at her almost the entire time, only glancing at me every so often with a stupid grin on his face, while Finn avoids eye contact altogether. I nibble on my garlic bread, trying to toss in my five cents at times, but whatever I try, I can't break into the conversation.

Longing for the only friendly voice I can think of, I decide to check on Marcel, but when I look in my purse, my phone is missing. It must have fallen out in the truck on our way over.

"Hey, Luke, can I have the car keys? I left my phone and want to get it."

He searches through his jeans pockets and pulls out the key. "Are you okay on your own, or would you like me to go with you?"

I'm so mad at him for ignoring me that I would probably bawl him out the second we leave the restaurant, and I don't want to cause a scene. "No, I'm good. It'll only take a second." After all, I am in a mall with tons of people around. It's safe.

Pushing my way through the crowds, I head for the elevator. When the doors open, my gaze falls on Justin, Cynthia, and a few of their friends. I frown; this is the last thing I need.

Justin bows deeply. "Milady. May I have your autograph?"

Everyone starts laughing as my cheeks begin to burn.

The anger seethes faster than I can control it, and my hand rises and slaps him across the face before I can even take a breath. "You measly jerk. After everything I had to deal with, I'm so tired of your fucking shit."

That kills the laughter, and all eyes turn to Justin. He rubs his cheek where I left a nice clear handprint, his free arm sliding around Cynthia. "Come on, honey. She's totally crazy."

Yet as he pulls her away, she meets my eyes. To my surprise, I find nothing but admiration.

One of his friends winks at me. "Good for you. Take care of yourself, Kelsey."

I give him a feeble smile as he trails behind them. My fist balls in victory. It feels good to finally stand up to my ex and I won't let him torment me any longer. I'm so done with all of them.

I walk swiftly across the parking deck, cursing Luke for parking far away from the elevators. The truck unlocks with a low beep. I open the driver's door, fumbling under the seat for the phone, but come up empty handed. Glancing around the truck, I finally locate it in the middle console with no clue how it could have ended up there.

When I notice a missed call from Marcel, I push the recall button without another thought. It rings for a long time, and I'm about to hang up when I hear his voice on the other end. "Yo, what's up?"

There's chatter and music in the background.

"Marcel, it's Kelsey. You called me?"

"Yeah." His voice is light and cheering erupts next to him. When the shouts settle down, he delivers the news. "It's all over, Kelsey. We made the bust and Tyrone is in jail. Me and the guys went out to celebrate. I can't tell you how relieved I am."

I should be thrilled for him but can't hold back the tears. "That's great, Marcel." I choke on the words and take a deep breath to stop my voice from trembling. "I'm so happy for you."

The noises in the background fade until they disappear completely. "What's the matter? You sound like you're about to cry."

Tears roll down my cheeks and I sniffle. "I'm not having a good time tonight, and Finn is still really mad at me. I guess that upset me."

I sit down in Luke's seat with the door open, telling Marcel all about the drive over and how left out I felt in the restaurant. My sentences are interrupted by sobs as more tears stream down my face. I feel absolutely silly for ruining his big night with my drama.

There is silence when I'm finished.

"Where are you?" he asks. "Your voice is echoing." The lightness in his tone is gone; instead he sounds worried.

"I'm in the parking garage at the Lewiston Mall."

He sucks in a deep breath. "Where are the others?"

My laugh is hollow; he is beginning to scare me. "Upstairs in the restaurant. Why?"

"I want you to walk back into the mall immediately." His words have a sense of urgency. "Stay on the phone until you're back in public."

I glance around. He is making me paranoid. I nevertheless start walking toward the elevator, my eyes darting around the empty deck. "Marcel, talk to me. Why are you so worried?"

"It's probably nothing, but I don't want you to walk around alone in deserted places at the moment."

My steps accelerate, but the elevator seems miles away. The few sounds in the garage are drowned out by my racing heartbeat; I wish Marcel would say something.

Cold sweat pearls on my back when tires boom on the ramp. A car pulls into my deck. I glance at Luke's truck, wondering if I should go back and hide, but I'm already halfway to the elevator. My steps turn into a jog, my eyes fixed on the silver doors. A van shoots past me and comes to a screeching halt right between me and the elevator.

"Marcel, there's a car that's blocking my way."

He takes in a sharp breath. "What type of car is it?"

"A red van."

"Can you see the plates?"

It's facing sideways and I'm not even sure it's from Maine. "No."

"What about the driver? Can you describe him to me?"

I squint at the van, but the windows are tinted. The interior is totally obscured. "No, it has tinted windows."

"What's the van doing?"

"It's just sitting there with a running engine." My knees turn to jelly. "Marcel, I'm scared."

"Go back to your car."

I spin around, rushing toward the truck.

"Do you know how to drive?"

I glance back at the van whose driver accelerates the engine with a roar in the park position. "Yes, but I haven't driven since I was sixteen, unless you count totaling the van at Tacoma Lakes."

"Don't worry, it'll be fine."

With quick steps, I approach the truck. It's getting closer. Fifty feet maybe, possibly less.

The van takes off with screeching tires, heading right for me. I start to run, the phone almost slipping out of my hand.

"Marcel, he's coming for me."

He lets out a curse. "Stay calm, Kelsey. Can you make it to your car?"

Trapped

The truck seems to have moved farther away, the van almost at my heels. The driver engages in a cruel game—slowing down until I gain momentum, then speeding up again. A thousand little needles sting at my thighs while I run. Luke's truck gets closer and closer. I stretch out my hand, almost able to touch it.

And then I fall. I'm not sure if I stumble over my own feet in my haste or whether there is something on the ground, but I hit the floor hard, falling flat on my stomach. The impact knocks the wind out of me. Dark spots start to dance in front of my eyes, a sharp pain stabbing at my spine. I try to move but am paralyzed. My fingernails scrape over the floor to find the phone.

"MARCEL," I scream with my last strength. I try to get some control over my body, but nothing seems to work. My limbs are totally useless, numbness immobilizing my muscles.

The van stops next to me. Someone jumps out, quick footsteps approaching. I try to turn to face my attacker, but before I can heave my body around, a bag is pulled over my head. The rope closing around my neck almost chokes me. Two arms enclose me and I'm lifted up on my feet. When I'm unable to stand, my attacker drags me along like a ragdoll. The tips of my sneakers scrape over the rough ground before cable ties wrap around my wrists. A shove transports me headfirst into the van. The door slams shut, and a few seconds later, we take off.

The car swerves a few times, making me sick to my stomach. I can barely breathe under the bag, the scent of rough cotton stinging my nostrils. Blood soon swooshes in my ears, blending with my racing heart, which pounds so hard against my ribcage that I'm scared it will burst from my chest.

When the van makes a sharp left turn, I'm thrown into a corner. Something cuts through my coat into my upper arm. I cry out in anguish and fear. The warm blood is soaked up by the fabric as pain throbs through my arm from my shoulder to my fingertips.

In the next curve, I'm tossed to the other side, my back colliding with the metal. I whimper, more pain soaring through my body. My head spins and the swooshing in my ears is getting louder. My fingers fumble around for something to hold onto, but with my secured hands, I come up empty.

When the van abruptly stops, I am catapulted forward. This time, it's my head that crashes into the back door and my skull almost splits in half. I yelp. A metallic taste floods my mouth as I try to shoo the darkness away. It's a losing battle. The blood in my ears turns into a rushing vortex that sucks me down into a bottomless abyss, tearing with it my pain, sorrow, and most of all, my incredible fear. Three strikes and you're out. There's no way I will come out of this situation alive.

~~~~

When I regain consciousness, I'm lying face down on a hard floor, the bag still over my head. Soft music fills my ears and the scent of orange and cinnamon overpowers the smell of the cotton. My winter jacket has me roasting, more heat emitting from a source to my left. When I strain my ears, I can make out the crackling of wood. All this adds up to a cabin, and given the familiar scent, my guess is it's Jackson's.

I stir, trying to determine if someone will notice. A foot prods me in response, the tip of the shoe digging straight into my wound. I cry out, my body shaking with pain. I wish he would talk to me, finally tell me who he is. I can't stand lying here on the floor, totally at his mercy.

My arms are pulled backward, which allows the restraints to cut deeply into my wrist. The sharp pain drives tears to my eyes. I'm lifted up onto my feet and pushed forward, but this time I decide to fight. Just as I learned in my self-defense class, I spin around while leaping forward, leaning into his body before pulling up my knee. He must have expected the attack and pushes me away before I can cause any harm.

His punch hits me square in my stomach. I double over, gasping for air. When I stumble forward, my knees buckle before hitting the floor. His next blow is directed at my ribs. Something inside me breaks when his fist connects, sudden piercing pain stealing my breath. I suck in oxygen through my mouth and nose to prevent myself from passing out again. My only hope is that I will be able to outsmart him.

He grabs me by the collar of my jacket and tosses me into a chair. I twist around, kicking forward with all my might, but my feet hit nothing but air. His laughter freezes my blood.

When the bag is pulled off my head, I stare straight into Napoleon's smirking face. I'm stunned. My brain refuses to process the information, but when the truth finally sinks in, my world stops turning.

Chapter 33

Ever since I was abducted almost four years ago, I have prayed every day to learn Napoleon's identity. It had become an obsession, taking over every aspect of my life. I knew I could never move on—never heal—without that knowledge. It was just like a deep cut requiring stitches. Without them, the wound would always ooze a little.

Now, I feel differently. I want to close my eyes and be transported back in time, back to the restaurant or maybe even the grocery store. Drop my search for Napoleon and walk away with the knowledge that there is still one person that has been there for me as long as I can remember—that one person that I have always trusted with my life.

Yet that person is gone—and in his place is a monster that looks just like him but no longer resembles the boy I once called brother.

"Luke, it's you." The words are painful, and in that moment, my heart is torn from my chest.

He laughs like he used to on my birthdays, stretching out his arms. "Surprise!"

There is a giggle from the couch in the corner, and for the first time, I realize he isn't alone. My jaw drops when I realize it's Hallie, whose phone is hiding part of her face.

"Her reaction was priceless, babe." Her tone is mocking. "That'll be a great addition to our Kelsey library."

Bewilderment and curiosity fill some of the void that has been left behind by Luke's betrayal. "I don't understand. What are you doing here?"

Luke laughs again and squats next to my chair, his eyes level with mine. "I guess we owe you an explanation, honeybun."

I cringe at the memory of Jed's nickname.

That gets such a snicker out of her that she almost chokes on her spit.

"You see, we played you, Kels." Luke's lips twitch, his eyes filled with amusement. "Hallie's abduction—that wasn't real. It was all just a test to see how far you'd go to save her, and you walked right into our trap."

His words crash over me like a wave of freezing water, my whole body trembling. I struggle to understand what he is saying; it's almost like a foreign language that I can't comprehend.

"Why?" I whisper. "I thought you loved me."

His face scrunches in a grimace. "That's exactly the problem, Kels. I love you, but not in a way a brother loves his sister. You have driven me crazy from the moment I accidentally walked in on you in the shower when you were thirteen. I just knew I had to have you, but you rejected me, over and over again with your sister act." His eyes glow like those of a madman. "And then you dated Justin. He was gonna score with you sooner or later, and I wasn't gonna have that. You are *mine* and I was gonna be the only one to turn you into a woman."

Hearing this from his mouth robs me of the little bit of sanity I have left. In a sudden rage, I tear at my restraints, but when the plastic edges cut into me, I still. The throbbing in my arm has turned into a dull pounding; I try to breathe evenly to lessen the pain.

Luke squeezes my shoulder, and for the first time, I feel disgusted by his touch. His fingers run down my arm before gently tracing my wound, which is met by my hiss. When his thumb applies pressure, a scream escapes me, the pain eating into the marrow of my bone. Tears blur my vision. When he lets go, I clench my jaw with all my strength to stop my teeth from chattering.

His eyes are full of cruel lust, and I can tell he's relishing my pain. "This last time will be so great. I'm gonna make you beg for your pathetic life, but when I'm done with you, you'll wish you were dead." A wicked smile curls his lips. "And since I love you, I'll even put you out of your misery."

The implication that he finally revealed himself to me breaks through the surface. He is going to kill me. Yet if he thinks I'm going to go quietly, he has something else coming. His eyes are still in another world, and I seize the opportunity. My feet kick forward, finding their mark. This time, I have the element of surprise. I get him good, right in his groin, and he doubles over, gasping for air.

I jump up and leap for the door but didn't account for Hallie coming at me from the side. For someone who struggled walking in her cast just a few hours ago, she has made a rather speedy recovery. Her head functions as a battering ram and hits me square in my cracked ribs. I am thrown against the wall, the pain taking my breath away. Like a lioness defending her cub, she goes after me again, grabbing a fistful of my hair. With one jolt, she spins me around. I fly across the room and would have fallen into the fireplace if the coffee table hadn't been in the way.

It breaks in half from the sudden impact. As I hit the floor, my insides scream in agony. I shake my head, trying to get rid of the fuzziness, but before I can move out of the way, Hallie is next to me. She raises her arm. In the last second, I realize that she is holding the fire poker. I instinctively roll into a ball, but before she can strike me, Luke's voice stops her.

"That's enough. I don't want her to lose consciousness again."

When I gaze up, her face is twisted in rage, but she allows Luke to take the poker out of her hand.

He tosses it into a corner before he pulls me up with both hands. "That was really stupid of you."

One good shove throws me back into the chair. Every muscle in my body aches, my head about to explode. Only my will to live prevents me from passing out.

Luke points furiously at me, his eyes spitting with anger. "You brought this on yourself, Kels. You should have stayed away from guys and agreed to come to California with me, but no, you had to fall for Finn." He catches my chin and forces me to look at him. "I can't stand you being with someone else. I'd rather see you dead."

I glance at Hallie; turning her against him is my last hope. "What about Hallie? Don't you love her?"

His lips twist in a mocking grin, and he reminds me of one of those creepy clowns they have in horror movies. "Hallie and I have an understanding. She knows that there will always be other women in my life. She's okay with that."

I stare at her, but she doesn't flinch, totally under his spell. Since she doesn't seem to mind when he beats her, she's probably into this bondage shit. Her words from therapy ring in my ears—she only feels alive when she's hurting. After her parents' deaths, feeling only numbness has always been her biggest problem.

When he grabs my arm just below my wound to get me to cooperate, I know my time is up. As more pain waves shoot through me, I grit my teeth to prevent the tears from falling. He guides me toward the bedroom as I stumble forward. My muscles convulse when I step over the threshold. This is not how I envisioned the last minutes of my life.

The door is closed with the back of his heel before he stands me in front of the bed, facing a camera.

"This will be a nice memento. I'm really gonna miss you, Kels."

Alternating hot and cold flashes rage through my body and my teeth chatter again, despite my effort to show no fear. I don't want to give him the satisfaction. I will not beg or show him how hurt I am. He will not get what he's looking for from me.

After the camera is rolling, he fumbles with the buttons of my blouse, taking his time to open them one by one. He is practically drooling, keeping his lips moist. His eyes are glued on the task. With a knife, he cuts my sleeves open to avoid loosening the cable ties. After my blouse drops, he runs the dull side of the knife over the wound. I hate myself when I cannot suppress the tears. As they roll down my cheeks, he takes a step back, soaking in the sight.

"God, everything on you is perfect." His voice is thick with desire. "You're a beautiful woman, Kels."

I spit at him. "You're sick, Luke. No normal man gets off by raping a woman."

The force of his backhand throws me onto the bed. He swings himself on top of me. Sitting upright on my hips and thighs, he playfully slides the blade of the knife under the strap of my bra, cutting first the left side, then the right. The knife is tossed into the window frame. He has no more use for it until he's done with me. With shaking hands, he peels off my bra. His fingers stroke teasingly over my bare skin, drawing little hearts on my belly.

I turn my head, sick of his lustful gaze. When his thumb presses into my wound, I whimper. My eyes squeeze shut to keep control of my tears.

"Look at me, Kels."

When I refuse, the pressure increases. The pain soars through me like a burning layer of lava, robbing me of my breath. Unable to handle the agony, I find his eyes.

"Good girl." With a smirk, his hand slides back onto my stomach. "Just play along."

I would love to spit in his face again but have to preserve my energy. In the seconds before he reaches his high, he will be most vulnerable. That's when I intend to strike.

His index finger finds its way into my jeans. It runs alongside the waistband until stopping under my button. With a low chuckle, he pops it open and unzips the pants.

"Don't you want to fight me, Kels," he whispers. "I would really like that."

I want to tell him how much he disgusts me, but remember the night at the cabin when I didn't fight him. I won't give into his cruel games, which will hopefully get him to lose interest in me faster. It's at least worth a shot.

His face hardens when I remain quiet, and he presses two fingers into the cut. This time, I scream, my whole body shaking in agony when he finally lets go. While I gasp for air, a sadistic smile plays on his lips—he's enjoying this tremendously. There is truly nothing left of my brother.

When I kick at him, he catches my ankle and slowly twists until I still. My boots are quickly removed before he pulls off my pants, my panties the only thing left in his way. He shakes out of his sweater. His body is still gaunt from the jail food. I realize the toll this has taken on him, but for the first time, I don't feel sorry. There is no longer any doubt in my mind that he shot Jed deliberately to cover his tracks. I'll be his second kill, and this time, he probably won't even blink.

When he drops his pants, my eyes automatically search his skin for the scar. I have to squint to see it; it's really not more than a tiny red line on his pale skin all the way at the top of his thigh. Even loose-fitting swimming trunks would have hidden it completely.

He follows my gaze. "Yeah, the one flaw in my plan. Truthfully, it happened such a long time ago that I had totally forgotten about it until you brought it up to the police. Blindfolded, your sense of touch must have been heightened for you to even pick it up." His fingers run over the small slash. "You can't even feel it unless you really pay attention."

I'm surprised that he was able to hide an injury like that for all those years, but then again, we were not a family that was very uninhibited. Even my mom never changed clothes in front of me. I can't recall a single time when I have seen him naked. "How did it happen?"

"Playground accident when I was little. My mother was so embarrassed that I don't think she even told my dad. They were already fighting for custody back then. A couple of months later, she disappeared from my life, and I had bigger problems than crying over a little scratch. Not having a mom like all the rest of my friends really sucked."

His mother had moved to Spain and broken off all contact. When our parents got married, this was the one thing that had quickly bonded us together. My father had shown very little interest in me, and both Luke and I felt abandoned, placing even more significance on our sibling relationship. Now all this was blown to pieces by his deranged obsession with me.

"Well, you're not going to get away with this. Marcel knows that I was taken. He and Finn will put two and two together and come after you. You'll end up in prison where you belong."

He cracks a smile. "I accounted for that. When Hallie and I planned this tonight, we were going to blame it on Jackson, but after you changed their dinner plans, Finn became the perfect fall guy. He didn't even get suspicious when we lured him away from the restaurant, and knocking him out was a piece of cake. The cops will find a nice murder-suicide scene, starring you and Finn as the main cast. Even the van can be tied back to him. I took it this afternoon from his uncle's shop. Everything will add up nicely. The cops won't suspect a thing."

My hopes slowly dwindle away; he thought of everything. He kneels in front of the bed, sliding off my panties, his tongue running over his lips. When I lie totally naked in front of him, he cocks his head sideways, studying me intently. His hand strokes the inside of my thigh, the closeness of our bodies turning my stomach in repulsion. That smile that used to give me comfort sneaks onto his face—it's now just as vile as his secret.

"This will be so much more fun now that I can actually see the pain in your eyes."

Chapter 34

The chuckle that follows his words is the most evil and sickening laugh I have ever heard. A fireworks show of emotions dances in his eyes. There is wickedness, excitement, and most of all the satisfaction that I am once again totally at his mercy.

"Now, before we turn to the good stuff, let's get you in the party mood." His pout is mocking. "You look miserable, Kels."

I turn my head as the nausea rises in my throat, unable to hold his vicious gaze.

He jumps up and strolls over to a small gym bag. "Hmm, what should we start with?" He snaps his fingers. "I know." He pulls out a small bag holding several dice. With a smug smile, he waves it in front of my eyes. "What color would you like?"

I scramble into a corner of the bed, pulling my knees up with a stubborn frown. "Screw you, Luke." If he gets any closer, I will give him a good kick.

His lips split to a wide grin. "Now play nice, Kels, or I'll have to tie you down completely." He regards the dice in the bag. "Let's take the red one. I know it used to be your favorite color before you got all sucked into this black stuff, and it reminds me a little bit of your blood that night I took your virginity."

The tears burn fiercely as the words resonate in my head like a bullet trying to find its way into my heart. A part of me is still screaming that this is all a big mistake, but the pain and disgust are slowly taking over. He used to cradle me in his arms and let me cry on his shoulder after one of my self-harm episodes. The thought that this probably aroused him turns my stomach to tight knots.

He rolls the dice and it lands on four. "Hey, that's a good one." He beams. "Let's make this the remaining hours of your life." With his thumb, he sets the stopwatch on his phone before setting it next to me on the nightstand, so I can see the display.

A breath is caught in my throat when the minutes start to wind down. The seconds seem to fly. When the first minute is up, I finally tear my eyes off the screen, my gaze returning to Luke. He has been watching me intently, a small smile playing on his lips.

"Okay, let's find out how often we'll have sex in those four hours. Personally, I hope for a six." He shakes the dice inside the hollow of his hands before he rolls it again. "Oh, a five. Well, I guess that's close enough."

This time, tears roll down my cheeks when I glance at the stopwatch. My eyes dart back to him. With a chuckle, he starts to stalk me like a predator—every step feels like an agonizing stab to my soul. There is so much sadistic lust in his eyes that I wish I was blindfolded again.

He lowers himself next to me on the bed, his fingers playing with strands of my hair. "You know I like it rough, but I wouldn't mind taking it easy a couple of times, so you, for once, get something out of this, too." His thumb traces my trembling lips. "It's really up to you, Kels."

"You're a monster." The words are so painful that fresh tears well in my eyes. I hate myself for showing him how much I'm hurting.

He wrinkles his forehead like he's considering my point. "Yeah, maybe you're right." A cruel laugh resonates from the depths of his throat, penetrating my aching soul. "But truthfully, I don't think so. Most people have these fantasies, secretly craving dominance. There cannot be pleasure without pain—only with great pain and suffering can you truly appreciate and feel complete pleasure and joy. The past should have taught you that."

I suppress a sob, sucking in a deep breath to refocus. The last few minutes, I've played right into his hands. He wants me scared and trembling. I have to find a way to turn the tables on him.

When he gets up and strolls back over to the bag, lightning strikes. The answer is Jed. It must have bothered him at least a little bit that he had to share his prized possession with another guy.

"You know, the last few days over Christmas, Jed and I really connected." I close my eyes, forming the words in my head to force them out. They're sickening, but the only way to get to Luke. "Sex with him was amazing."

He freezes, spinning around. "You're a fucking liar." His finger points at me, his face twisted in rage. "He swore to me he never touched you then."

I snort. "And you believed him? You really *are* stupid." It's my turn to gloat. "You can even ask Hallie. She knows."

He squints at me and I high-five myself. I got to him. When his face turns into an ugly grimace, every muscle in my body flexes. I'm ready for him. I know him well enough that he's about to have one of his rage fits, a leftover from his wild days. In those moments, he acts spontaneously and usually has his guard down.

When he joins me on the bed, I blink at him innocently, which enrages him further. With a growl, he tries to straighten my legs, probably to tie them down, and I know that this will be my last chance. I kick him in the center of his face with my heel, trying to distract him long enough to make it to the window.

He shouts out in pain and clutches his nose. Without a second thought, I'm up on my feet, darting toward the window.

If my wrists hadn't been secured, I would have probably made it. A kick to my back catapults me into the wall. I wince when my sore side collides with a shelf, the pain making me gasp. I try shooing the black spots that dance in front of my eyes away, but before the room comes back into focus, Luke's breath grazes against my neck.

"That was really stupid of you, Kels."

When he spins me around, his body pins me against the wall. His eyes are deadly. "On second thought, I think the worst I can do to you is actually make you come. Have your body beg for my touch and ache with pleasure."

I stare at him, stunned by the deviousness of his plan. "I'll never come for you," I mutter, though I'm not sure if there aren't ways for him to bend me to his will. One of the girls in group therapy told us that her uncle used to do this to her when he molested her. I remember her tears when she thought it was all her fault because he always claimed she wanted to be touched. It was the ultimate degradation.

He spins me around and his arms enclose me from the back. I kick but he tightens his grip. When the pain from my ribs gets to be too much, I finally still and allow him to carry me back to the bed. This time, he secures my legs with ropes from his gym bag. I am back in a semi-spread-eagle position, ready for his malicious games. I clench my jaw, trying to control the tremble in my body when his lips blow little kisses on the inside of my thigh. As his mouth travels north, I hold my breath, determined to fight him until the very end.

~~~~

"Hey, asshole." The words hang over the room like a dark cloud. Only the cocking of a gun breaks through the sudden silence.

Luke closes his eyes, exhaling with frustration. "You're like an annoying brat who doesn't know when to give up."

Finn smirks. "And you're a fucked-up rapist who should've gone to jail a long time ago. Get away from her." He waves with the gun to underline his point.

Luke slowly backs up. "I suspect this is the gun from my glove compartment. It only has one bullet in it, so use it wisely."

"Bullshit. No one keeps a gun in their car with just one bullet."

It's Luke turn to smirk. "I use it to play Russian roulette with Hallie. It's fun."

My jaw drops, but Finn just clicks his tongue. "You're really sick, man. You should be in the nuthouse." He glances at me, pulling the knife out of the wood by the window. Without taking his eyes of Luke, he cuts the rope that holds my legs in place before freeing my hands. "Check the drawers for something to wear. It's freezing outside."

I find a thick wool sweater in one of the closets and pull it over my head, the rough fabric irritating my skin with an instant itch. For now, it'll have to do. A shudder still runs through me when a light breeze flows in from the open window. My pants and boots are next, my fingers closing the buttons and zippers in desperate haste.

When I'm done, my eyes find Finn. "I'm ready."

"Climb through the window." Finn's full attention is focused on my brother. He leans lazily against the wall, yet his eyes are alert, dominated by a vicious glow. I know he's just waiting for an opportunity to attack. His cold gaze sends a shiver down my spine—he really is a monster. How could I have ever trusted him? Tears rise in the back of my throat when I realize that I lost my best friend forever.

My mind is still weeping from the betrayal when I jump out of the window, landing hard on the frozen ground. A cry escapes me from the sharp pain that shoots up my arm, my side throbbing mercilessly. I almost fall when I stumble forward, waving my arms to keep my balance, which makes matters worse.

A single shot breaks through the night. I freeze before an uproar of conflicting emotions throws me into a frenzy. My instincts tell me to drop to the ground while my mind orders me to run. Yet my heart prevails in the end, demanding I check on Finn. I turn toward the window. An utmost relief washes over me when I stare right into his eyes.

His face is twisted in pain. I notice blood dripping from his nose, but before I can offer my help, he is next to me on the ground.

"Run."

The word releases adrenaline into my bloodstream. The muscles in my legs begin to flex automatically as I trail behind him toward the tree line. It's dark, but the moon shines with a milky glow that helps me find my way across the lawn. As soon as we enter the forest, the shadows swallow us up. I stub my toe and curse, stumbling forward. Only Finn's hand enclosing my wrist prevents the fall. He pulls me along as we chase through the night.

"We need to keep moving." His breath mists the air in front of him.

I stay close behind him while our steps pound on the forest path, my mind ignoring the burning pain that has spread to every part of my body. Angry thorns grab at my hair and sweater, scraping exposed skin on a few occasions. I pant, the fog from my own breath like a wall of comfort to keep me warm. My back is covered with sweat, the wool sweater now heavy and slowing me down.

When I fall behind, Finn's fingers entangle with mine and speed me along. I focus on my strides, trying to find an even rhythm, but my racing heartbeat drowns out all the other noises, and trips me up. I feel dizzy as I chase through the woods, avoiding fallen tree stumps and trying not to stumble over weeds. Everything around me becomes blurry. I'm sucked into a surreal world in which nothing exists but my breath, my heartbeat, and this incredible will to live.

When we get to a clearing, Finn pauses. I double over, gasping for air as I try to calm the stitch in my side. Loud trampling and the snapping of twigs is right behind us in the forest—Luke can't be far.

"What happened?" I ask between yappy breathes.

"He attacked me as soon as you jumped out the window and the gun went off in the struggle. I punched him in the head, but it must not have been enough to knock him unconscious."

I grimace. "For someone who's supposed to be kickass, you sure act like a wuss."

He playfully nudges my shoulder. "I promise if we get out of this alive, I'll take karate lessons." His face turns serious when the noises in the woods get closer. "We need to keep moving."

"Do you know what happened to Hallie?" After her fighting performance at the cabin, we can't be too careful.

"When I snuck in, she was blasting the music on her iPod. I didn't want to knock her out since any noise could have alerted Luke. I'm sure that her cast will slow her down, even if she ran after us."

With the snow patches and ice on the ground, her cast would be a serious hindrance. For now, Luke is the only enemy. My eyes dart across the field. I have no idea where we are. We could be heading toward the lake or the main road. Best to keep heading opposite the approaching noises.

I push myself forward when Finn takes off, racing behind him through the knee-high grass. There are still a few patches of snow which I avoid by hopping around them. Finn takes long even strides, his arms and legs pumping in perfect unison. He's a hell of a sprinter. Watching him, he makes it look easy, like a gazelle dashing across a veld. It spurs me on and I find my rhythm, flying across the clearing. The tree line on the other side is getting closer. We have almost made it.

A shot ricocheting through the night kills my false sense of security. Something hot grazes my arm, a stinging burn making me gasp. Another shot almost splits my eardrums—I feel like prey in the open. Swaying from left to right, I try to avoid being an easy target, like a rabbit averts the hunter. *Keep moving* is the only thought on my mind.

A figure steps out of the forest on the other side. A sudden panic paralyzes me, and if my body wasn't on autopilot, I would have probably fallen or peed my pants. The moon is behind him, throwing a long shadow onto the clearing, which makes his frame appear gigantic. I can't see his face, only the gun in his hand. The metal gleams menacingly in the moonlight.

When he lifts the gun, I stare at Finn, who keeps moving in his direction.

"Over here," the figure shouts, and I realize it's Marcel. Once again, the cavalry has come to my rescue.

I slow down when I reach him and turn back to my pursuer. "Be careful, Marcel," I mutter, gulping down large mouthfuls of air. "Luke is Napoleon."

Fog from my rapid breath distorts my vision, and it takes me a second to realize that Luke has stopped, gazing at us from about thirty yards away. A rifle is pointed right at the middle of my stomach.

"Drop the gun, Marcel, or I'll shoot her." His voice is calm and composed; there's no doubt that he is serious.

"That won't be necessary." Marcel's gun swings around, zooming in on Finn. "Sorry, bro, but I'm with Luke here. Game's over."

Chapter 35

For the second time that night, I'm stunned that someone I have trusted explicitly could betray me like this. My lips tremble and I'm about to tell Marcel what I think of him when Finn seizes the opportunity.

"What the hell!" His voice is laced with utter bewilderment. "I got a text earlier that you and Tyrone—"

A pistol whip to the back of his head silences him. Marcel aims directly at me. "Wanna run your mouth off, too?"

With a clenched jaw, I shake my head. Tears burn in my eyes, but for the first time tonight, it's not from pain or fear. It's rage. If I was the one holding the gun, Marcel would be dead. His betrayal stings almost as much as Luke's—he played us all for a damn fool and we blindly trusted him.

Luke lowers his rifle. "What do you want, Marcel?"

"What everyone wants." Marcel smirks. "Money."

Luke glares at Finn's figure on the ground. He is out cold, but his chest is moving evenly. At least he is alive and isn't bleeding. Maybe Marcel's blow wasn't as bad as it looked.

Luke's gaze travels back to Marcel's face, whose dark, cold eyes freeze the fibers in my bones. This is the look of a killer.

"How much is it gonna cost me?" Luke asks.

"A lot." Marcel hisses when I twitch, his head shaking with a warning. "My boss ran into some legal troubles that prevent him from further employing me. I need to disappear. Make it a hundred grand and I'm out of your hair."

Luke whistles. "That *is* a lot. What makes you think I got that type of money?"

Marcel's dry laugh is like a bark and makes me sick to my stomach. "Don't play games, pretty boy. We both know your daddy has been pulling strings in the background. It won't be the first time he's paid someone off."

I gulp, refusing to accept this new revelation. "Roy knows about this?"

Marcel clicks his tongue. "You're so naïve, Kelsey. Do you think your bro here could have pulled this off by himself?" With a smug smile, he glances at Luke. "Tell her, man. Open her eyes that she never had a chance to find justice."

I realize that this goes far beyond what I imagined. Almost everyone I know seems to have their fingers in the pie.

Luke chuckles. "Who else do you think tipped Jed off when the police came to arrest him that night without a warrant? His old friend Larouge kept him in the loop when they couldn't find a judge fast enough in the middle of the night to sign the paperwork, and it only took a couple of phone calls to set things up with the tape. My dad is so obsessed with me becoming a lawyer that he'll do anything to make this go away."

Only howling wind follows his words. I'm totally numb, the world crashing down on me. I was denied justice—not because of some screwup—but because the people around me are vicious liars. All Roy's ranting and raging about Jed getting off was just a show, a well-orchestrated scheme to protect his son.

I shake my head, trying to focus. "But you beat up Jed!"

"Those beatings were warnings to keep Jed in line." Luke beams, probably thrilled that he can finally reveal the truth. "After we sent you the book, he wanted out. He has always been a coward, and it was only a matter of time until he would've opened his big mouth. Shooting him was the only way to permanently quiet him." The satisfied smile twitching on his lips is plain evil.

Marcel prods Finn with his foot, who responds with a moan. "He'll wake up soon. Let's get this over with."

Luke's eyes cut into me when he raises his rifle. "Sure thing."

I want to squeeze my eyes shut but can't get myself to tear my gaze off him. We glare at each other before he smirks—that same wicked grin that he had when he raped me tonight.

"On second thought—" His rifle swings around. A boom breaks through the night as it discharges. It takes me a second to realize that the bullet misses me—hitting Marcel instead straight in the chest.

In slow motion, I watch him fall backward, his body crashing to the ground. My mouth opens, but the scream is stuck in my throat. In that moment, my survival instincts take over. I dive forward, my eyes fixed on Marcel's gun.

Without a second thought, my fingers clutch the grip. I whirl around, pointing the barrel in Luke's direction. My eyes squeeze shut as I pull the trigger. Pain tears my shoulder apart. It feels like I've been kicked by a horse as the backward momentum from the gun pins me to the ground.

When bright light replaces the darkness, I actually think that I've been hit, and this is the end. I expect to float up and see my own body or walk through a bright tunnel to get to my ultimate resting place, but instead, loud voices echo around me. I cup my hands over my ears, refusing to listen, too afraid of what I might hear.

Someone pulls me to my feet and shakes me. "Kelsey, are you alright?"

I squint at Detective Larouge, trying to make sense of his question, before my eyes dart around to assess the situation. The mouth of the forest path and the clearing are filled with cops. A couple are crouched next to Finn, who is sitting up with an icepack resting against the back of his head. He is talking and seems fine. My eyes find Marcel, who lies motionless on the ground. A few officers huddle around him, one zipping his jacket open.

"He'll live, sir," she mutters. "The bullet went straight into his vest. Luckily, he wore a plate and it was only a twenty-two."

My head is spinning, and I clutch Larouge's arm when a bulky cop slaps the handcuffs on Luke. My brother can barely keep himself on his feet, blood spilling from his shoulder. His whole face is contorted into an ugly grimace. He struggles against the cops who pull him toward a waiting stretcher, yelling at them with a flood of colorful curses.

As he passes me, his eyes interlock with mine—they glow with so much venom that every part of me recoils. "This is not over," he shouts in my face and I flinch backward. "I'll get out of this, and when I do, you're fucking dead. You'll pay for this"—he tears on his handcuffs—"and you, too, Marcel."

My lips form a response. I want to tell him to rot in hell for eternity, but no sound leaves my mouth. The momentary relief that Napoleon can't hurt me anymore is replaced by an agonizing pain—my heart wails that I lost my brother for good.

"Are you alright?" Larouge repeats, his hand softly stroking my back.

I stare at him, my mouth dry like it's filled with cotton wool. "I—I don't know." I glance around like a lost and scared animal—terrified of what the future might hold. Just as my knees are about to buckle, I'm pulled into a tight embrace, which prevents me from falling.

Finn's face nuzzles into my hair. "Don't worry, we'll get through this. I'm here for you."

I want to believe him and shout at myself that everything will be alright, but when the tears begin to roll, the terrible fear that I will never feel whole again traps me. Of all the possibilities, why did my tormentor have to be Luke?

Chapter 36

Just like the night of my first rescue, the blanket around my shoulders doesn't provide any comfort. My insides are frozen to ice, and every time I flinch, my sore body aches in protest. What is different, though, is that I am alert despite the late hour, my mind racing at mega-warp speed. I still refuse to come to terms with the events of the last hours as my eyes stare blankly at the wall.

The hospital went by in a blur. They bandaged my arm and torso, gave me a bunch of painkillers, and told me to take it easy when I refused to stay. Luke was being attended to in the next room, and I couldn't stomach being anywhere near him.

Finn has not left my side, holding my hand through the entire ordeal and allowing me to cry into his chest when a new wave of sorrow sears through my soul. I am glad. Since my days of cutting are over, I desperately need a friendly face in my corner.

"Hey, how are you two holding up?" Marcel asks from the doorway of the small office they stuck us in, studying us before closing the door behind him. I'm still utterly confused about his role in all of this, but judging by the fact that he is still walking around a free man with his DEA badge dangling around his neck, he must somehow fall into the category of a good guy.

The look Finn gives him reflects my mood—he is thoroughly pissed at his friend. "Bro, you better start explaining why you knocked me out." He rubs the back of his head. "First, Luke, then you. My head is about ready to explode." His gaze travels to the badge. "And what's with the dog tag? Don't tell me you're some damn cop."

Marcel smirks. "Sorry." He plops into the chair behind the desk, propping up his feet. "You were just about to spill that I was supposed to be in jail, which would have raised Luke's suspicion. Didn't mean to hit you so hard."

Finn doesn't look convinced, and neither am I.

"So this was something like a setup?" I ask.

"Yep." Marcel shifts his weight in the chair with a twisted face. He seems to be in a lot of pain. "I suspected Luke already while we were all searching for you. He was a little too nonchalant for my taste, like he wasn't really worried. Even tried to convince me once that you might've just needed a break and I should let it go."

I frown. Why didn't he tell me this before?

"The night he shot Jed, I knew I was right," he continues. "But Larouge couldn't pin him down. Luke was slick, always putting his father into play whenever he got himself into a tight spot during the interrogation. At some point, he refused to cooperate altogether. That's when Larouge threw him in jail. He thought Luke might break under the pressure, but no, he hung in there. Eventually, he would have walked on the self-defense claim, and if he was found not guilty after a trial, double jeopardy would have prevented us from ever charging him for Jed's murder again. That's when we made up that story about the knife. Larouge needed more time to investigate."

Finn lets out a low chuckle. "So let me get this straight. You and the cops—tonight was all part of some grandiose thought-out plan?"

Marcel grimaces. "Unfortunately not. We didn't think he would grab Kelsey again without Jed—too risky. There was clearly an accomplice, but I thought it was his dad. Roy is a corrupt lawyer, but no kidnapper, so I never figured Luke could have a helper. It was stupid on my part. I should have known something was up with Hallie when Donna voiced her concern about her odd behavior. After her arrest tonight, she gave a full confession. Luke and her started dating when they met while he was taking you down to Portland for your therapy sessions. She's totally obsessed with him and would've done anything he cooked up in his deranged mind."

Finn rubs his head again. "She sure is a conniving little bitch. They lured me out of the restaurant, claiming they had this surprise for Kelsey. When they got me to the van and I noticed it was my uncle's, Luke jumped me from behind while she gave me this angelic smile. Luckily, she wasn't a Girl Scout—she couldn't tie a knot worth shit."

I jump to my feet, unable to breathe. All this conspiracy with me as bait doesn't sit well with me and I long for some fresh air. I head for the door. The two guys don't stop me, probably knowing that I will take Marcel's head off if he gets in my way.

It's still dark when I step outside, the chill of night freezing me to the bone. I stare into the sky, wondering how this could be justice. In one night, my brother, my stepdad, and my friend are gone from my life. What did I do to get the losing end of the bargain?

With chattering teeth, I rub my arms, hissing when I accidentally touch the bandage. The pounding pain is quickly overpowered by surging rage—the whole world has been fooling me. My balled fist hits the wall, accompanied with a loud "Arghhh" shouted into the darkness.

"I guess you're mad."

Marcel's voice startles me, and I punch him in the shoulder, which makes him cringe.

"Careful there, Kelsey. I'm already damaged enough."

"Why?" I snap. "You could have told me the truth the night we were arrested in New Haven. I could have died tonight if Finn hadn't been there."

He fishes a pack of cigarettes from his pocket, offering me one. I shake my head, done with everything that could harm my body. After lighting the cigarette, he takes a long drag. His eyes close when he allows the smoke to escape from the corners of his mouth. For the first time, I realize his hand is shaking slightly—his nerves must be shot.

"Truthfully, Kelsey, when it came to Luke, I wasn't sure where your loyalties lay. You were so dead set on trusting him that I was scared you would let it slip eventually." His eyes drill into mine. "Believe it or not, this case was more important to me than Tyrone's, and even though I had some pretty selfish motives, I do care about you." When I frown, he laughs. "Not like that, just as a friend. Despite what everyone might have been tellin' you, you're a really strong woman, which I admire. I know you'll pull through this eventually, even though it might take some time."

I search his face for a sign of insincerity, thinking he is just trying to smooth things over, but he openly holds my gaze. He doesn't even break eye contact when he takes another drag, and it is me who finally ends our staring contest.

"So what were your motives?"

"Simple really." He flicks the ashes away before taking another drag. "I wanted out of the DEA, but no police department would touch me with a ten-foot pole. You see, before I became a cop, I was really in a gang." The drags are more frequent—this is hard for him.

"How did you get out?" I ask when he remains silent.

"When I was sixteen, I shot an FBI agent during a raid and put him in a wheelchair. They were gonna lock me up for a really long time, but he intervened, making me a deal. If I turned my life around, he would make sure my case stayed in juvie court, and eventually, he'd get my record expunged." He lights another cigarette with the butt of the first, tossing it away with a little too much force.

"So I agreed"—he blows the cigarette smoke toward the sky—"but police agencies who hire transfers still have access to your file and know about these things. No one wants a former thug on the team unless it's for undercover work, and Larouge actually laughed in my face when I inquired if there were any jobs. He told me to get lost. In his eyes, I was nothing but a criminal."

I click my tongue; that's so typical for Larouge. He's third-generation detective and undoubtedly looks down on guys like Marcel. What he doesn't realize is that not everyone is born with a silver spoon up their behind.

"So Larouge said if you give him Napoleon, he'll hire you."

"Pretty much. Your abduction case was one of the few he hadn't been able to solve, and it looked bad on his record. Yet he didn't only want Napoleon, but also the guy who tipped off Jed. His department looked terrible after the warrant incident and he wanted blood. After we zoomed in on Luke, Roy was the most likely suspect, but with his reputation and pull with the bar association, we needed hard evidence. And the only one who could give us that was Luke."

Now the pieces finally come together. Larouge wanted the full package, handed to him on a silver platter, and since I was already messed up and Marcel his pawn, he didn't care what would happen to us as long as he could make his arrest.

In a sense, he had done me a favor, since otherwise, there would have probably never been enough evidence against Roy. And knowing my stepdad, he would have found a way to get his son off. I would have been denied justice once again—now, I at least have a chance.

"Look, I'm sorry I deceived you," Marcel flicks away the second cigarette butt, lighting a third. He inhales deeply, staring into the darkness. "If it's any consolation, they tracked you pretty quickly after Luke snatched you tonight, and we were about to move in when Finn and you escaped. If you hadn't been so quick after he took me out, they would have shot him in the head."

It doesn't exactly make me feel better, but it will help me to look at Larouge without constantly imagining how best to strangle him. I study Marcel, pondering if we can still be friends. He looks pitiful as he hops from one foot to another to stay warm with this guilty expression on his face. Though he was way out of line, at least he had a good reason.

"Are you in a lot of pain?"

"Yup."

"Good." I glare at him. "You know that's your punishment for fooling me."

"I know." He glances at me with a goofy grin and I'm almost ready to forgive him.

"What about your ear?"

"That'll heal. Donna did a great job and the doctors say they'll be able to reconstruct most of it. I got hurt on the job, so the government will foot the bill."

I smirk to myself. "You know, you should take this as an opportunity to grow some hair. I think it'll suit you."

"Yeah, maybe." His eyes glow mischievously as he flicks the next butt away.

When he's about to light another cigarette, I stop him. "And you should stop smoking. Girls like Donna don't like that."

He shoots me a dark "who made you my mother" look but stuffs the pack back into his coat pocket. "So are we cool?"

His eyes are just like Maisie's when she begs for a treat, and it strikes me that he is actually quite lonely. The people he hangs out with are criminals he intends to betray, and as far as

I can tell, Donna is the closest thing he has to a girlfriend. After what happened tonight with Hallie, she might turn her back on him. He can use a friend as much as I could.

Yet I'm not ready to let him totally off the hook. "You're not out of the dog house, Agent Brown, but you're getting there."

"Good." I can tell he is dying for another cigarette, but he fights the urge. I hold his pleading gaze, wiggling my eyebrows to show him I mean business.

The door behind us opens and a young cop sticks his head out. "Excuse me, Ms. Miller. Your mother is here and would like to see you."

Crap. They probably arrested Roy and she is freaking out.

"Do you want me to talk to her?" Marcel asks.

I shake my head. This one, I have to do on my own.

~~~~

Four hours later, I tuck my mom into bed at our house after the doctor prescribed a strong sleeping aid for her to rest. She took the betrayal and loss of her husband and stepson worse than I could have ever imagined, forcing me to step up to the plate and take care of her for once. Before I switch off the light, my eyes rest briefly on Maisie, who has curled up on my mom's feet. Her eyes are wide with a hint of sorrow—even she can sense that nothing will be the same after tonight.

For the longest time, my mother wept in my arms, asking me questions over and over again I had no answers to. Finn finally pulled her off me and managed to halfway calm her down when he noticed I was close to collapsing. Bravely, I swallowed down my own tears, though I'm dreading the next few days. The emotional drain of the night is about to bubble to the surface and I have no clue how to cope with it.

Finn is fighting with the coffee maker when I get to the kitchen. Glancing at me, he mutters, "You should lie down. You look absolutely exhausted."

I slump onto the barstool, burying my face in my hands. "I don't think I can go to sleep." Every time I close my eyes, I see Luke and his vicious grin. A sob runs through me when I remember that less than twenty-four hours ago, he and I were in this very kitchen, devouring my mom's pancakes and making plans for the evening. I can still hear his laughter—now it's making me sick to my stomach.

"Damn it, I can't get this thing to work." With a huff, Finn chucks the kitchen towel on the counter. "You need a college degree for this."

The coffee maker is one of those fancy Italian designer machines Roy got my mom for Christmas. I never used it and am no help to him. With my chin propped up on my palms, I watch him as he rummages through the fridge for something else to drink. It occurs to me that I have never even asked how he's doing. "How is your head?"

"Alright," he grumbles. "Doctor gave me some painkillers."

"And the rest of you?"

He peeks around the fridge door with a frown. "What do you mean?"

"I want to know how you feel, Finn. About everything."

His head disappears in the refrigerator again. "Honestly, I don't know. I'm still pissed at Marcel, and I'm totally confused about everything else. All I know is that I want to be there for you because whatever I'm feeling, you must be feeling a hundred times worse." He slams the door to the refrigerator closed, banging the orange juice container on the counter next to me.

"Easy there, tiger." I smile. "I'm not gonna clean up after you if you spill the juice all over the floor."

There is a moment of silence before he explodes. "This whole situation is totally fucked up."

Tell me about it. "It is what it is, Finn. There's nothing I can do to change it."

The truth that I lost almost everything in just one night hits me like a bulldozer. My chest is tight as my eyes dart around the kitchen. My mom will likely have to sell the house and go back to work without Roy's income, though I don't really want to spend another night here anyways—not in the place where I was once happy with my brother. There will probably be a trial and I will have to look Luke straight in the eyes when I tell the jury what he did to me.

Suddenly, I'm terrified of the future. The tears spill before I can control them, and a sorrowful sob resonates from the depth of my soul.

"You know you'll get through this," Finn says, turning my chin to force me to look at him. "You ain't that girl anymore that I met back at the hospital nine months ago. Sometimes, your strength almost scares me."

I blink at him through my tears—he and Marcel should form a fan club. With a feeble smile, I wipe the wetness off my cheeks with my sleeve. "What if I can't do it?"

He squeezes my hand. "You have no choice. That's what life is all about—we have to keep pushing no matter what is thrown our way. You can't let life slip through your fingers by living in the past."

More tears roll down my cheeks—this time because I'm thankful to still have him in my life. Whoever said that you can't fall hard as long as there is someone to catch you sure knew what they were talking about.

Epilogue

"Please sign right here, Ms. Miller."

With a smile, my pen scratches over the receipt before the woman behind the counter hands me my brand new passport. My thumb runs over the smooth emblem of the United States of America. I can't wait to use it.

"Oh, hi, Kelsey. How are you?"

I spin around with a small frown, but my face relaxes when I recognize the older lady who is standing right next to the card display by the counter. "Hello, Dr. Stromberg." I force a smile on my lips—my motto for the month is to be more approachable.

Her eyes fall on the passport. "Going somewhere?"

This time, the smile is sincere. "Yeah. My mom gave me one of those plane tickets to go around the world as a present for finishing my GED, so I'll be traveling this next year. I'm leaving for London in a few days. It's so exciting." Traveling has been one of my lifelong dreams, though the trip is mostly designed for me to figure out what I want to do with the rest of my life.

"I bet." Dr. Stromberg's eyes search my face. "Are you going alone?"

I grimace—that is the only setback in the plan. "Yeah, unfortunately." Marcel and Finn's cheers of "You can do this" ring in my ears. Without them, I would have discarded the whole crazy idea from the start. They even agreed to help my mom out with Maisie by taking her on daily walks. After that, I had run out of ammunition.

"Well, that's admirable." A fond sparkle glows in her eyes. "You know, Kelsey, you're one of my success stories. There was a time I thought you'd let the past destroy you, but you proved us all wrong. I'm really proud of you."

My gaze drops as my cheeks begin to sting. I suck at handling compliments. "Thanks, Dr. Stromberg."

"Are you still in therapy?"

I shake my head. After Luke's arrest, I had severed all ties with my old life, which included dumping her and finding a new therapist. It was actually Cameron's social worker who recommended a woman not much older than me who specializes in sexual assault trauma. Since she is also a former victim, I was able to connect to her much more easily and have thrived under her guidance. Just last week I got my official stamp that I'm now capable of dealing with life's hurdles on my own.

"And how is your mom?" Dr. Stromberg continues to pry.

A mess but hanging in there—something I don't share with strangers. "She is doing alright."

Dr. Stromberg nods. "That's good. I followed the trial of your brother and your stepdad closely. It's really tragic what happened to your family."

I stifle a sigh, sick of everyone's sudden concern. "Well, justice was served in the end."

At least on the surface. Roy got a couple of years after accepting a plea bargain and will be out on good behavior by the end of the summer. If he had testified against his son, he could have even gotten away with probation, but he stayed loyal to Luke till the end. Disgraced in all respects, he lost his law license, and my mom is divorcing him. It will be awkward to see him walk around Stonehenge again, and I secretly hope he'll move away.

Luke is a whole different story. The judge threw the book at him after he insisted on a trial, and with Hallie's testimony, the jury convicted him of premeditated murder of Jed.

Hutchinson held off on the rape and abduction charges at Marcel's request. My friend felt that forcing me to relive my nightmare and Luke's betrayal for the whole world to see could be too much for me.

At first, I fought him, determined to have Luke convicted for raping me, but after a while, I was thankful. Having to tell in open court every detail of his atrocious acts was a terrifying thought. When he ended up with a life sentence without the possibility of parole, he was out of the picture for good. Finn let it slip to one of his old friends who was doing state time that my brother was nothing but a nasty rapist, and Luke has suffered at the hands of the other inmates accordingly. It's painful to imagine, even though he deserves it.

I tear myself back from the events of these past sixteen months—I still can't believe how much my life has changed since I stood in that field the night Luke got arrested. "Well, I'd better run. A friend of mine is getting married today and I still have loads to do."

"Sure, it was so nice seeing you again." She extends her hand and I shake it. "Tell your mom to give me a call if she ever needs to talk."

"Will do." I escape the post office and unlock my bike. Driving is still a drag for me, something I'm planning on tackling as soon as I return from my trip.

Ten minutes later, I stop my bike with screeching brakes in front of the small two-story my mom has been renting ever since she sold the house. The bouncing of a basketball attracts my attention, and I lean the bike quietly against the garden gate and squat down next to it to stay invisible.

Laughter erupts when Finn scores a basket, which is met by a low cuss from Cameron.

"It's nine to eight, bro," Finn says, briefly doubling over to catch his breath. "One more and I win."

Cameron scowls. "You're so full of yourself. I'm not gonna lose to an old geezer who smokes. You're going down."

I suppress a snicker when he elbows his brother in a slick side maneuver to get closer to the basket to score. With his fifteen years, he's still scrawny, yet this gives him great agility. It's only a matter of time until he outgrows Finn both in height and muscle strength, and after that, Finn will have his hands full—not only on the basketball court, but also in the girl arena. Cameron can be quite the charmer when he wants to be.

The court has allowed contact ever since Finn's sexual assault conviction was vacated a few months ago, and the two have been spending a lot of time together. This also brought Andrew, their uncle, into our lives which has been a really good thing for my mom. There have been a few stolen glances and smiles that give hope for a happy ending after all.

I remain crouched to the ground and watch them shoving each other boisterously to get the upper hand. It's a warm and mild morning, and the wind plays with my hair. Maisie is rolled up in the grass next to them in a deep slumber, her ears only twitching from time to time. I sometimes envy her that she can just sleep her life away. Haunting nightmares still torture me from time to time, making sleep still the hardest exercise.

Finn has slipped out of his shirt and the sweat is glistening on his bare torso. He's still pale from the winter, which doesn't take away from his six-pack and his firm chest muscles. I try to ignore my racing heartbeat and the warm tingling in my stomach that lately seems to be present whenever I look at him, reminding myself that we are just friends. Healing takes a long time for people who are as damaged as us.

He finally notices me and gives me a goofy smile, which earns him an eye roll from Cameron. The boy whispers something under his breath; Finn, in response, knocks him on the back of his head. "Hey, behave."

Trapped

My legs ache from kneeling down on the hard ground. After I rise, I hop up and down to get the circulation going, realizing how silly I look when the boys' lips begin to twitch. I pout in response, giving them my best evil eye, which makes it worse. Finn's laughter is catching and grows the more I pretend to be infuriated.

"Stop, Kelsey, please," he splutters in between chuckles. "You're too funny."

I swallow a sarcastic remark when he stretches, a breath caught in my throat as his muscles flex. He follows my gaze, which is fixed on his chest, and clears his throat. Awkward silence falls over our little group.

"I told you she's drooling over you, bro," Cameron remarks dryly.

That gets him another slap on the back of his head. "Oh, shut up." Nevertheless, the widest grin is on Finn's face when he slips into his shirt. For a second, our eyes interlock and he winks at me. That sends a hot flash to the pit of my stomach. I drop my gaze with burning cheeks.

Luckily, my embarrassment is cut short when my phone dings with a message signal.

"*HELP!!!*" the text reads.

"Who is it?" Finn asks when he notices my frown.

"Marcel." I show him the message.

"Sounds serious." He digs the keys from his pocket. "I'll drive." His eyes zoom in on his brother. "Go home, Cameron, and get ready. I'll pick you up at two. Andrew got your dress pants and shirt from the cleaners and I expect you to wear a tie."

Cameron grimaces. "Can't I just wear jeans?"

"NO!" we both shout, our horror reflected in this one word.

"It's a wedding," I remind him. "Loads of girls will be there, so you want to look nice."

He sticks out his tongue at me. "Girls are gross."

I remind myself how childish he can be. My mom said it's common in emotionally neglected kids—it takes some of them much longer to grow up in some areas.

"For once, just do what you're told, or you'll be in trouble." Finn's voice is firm, trying to sound authoritative.

"Yeah, yeah." Cameron waves him off, but I know he won't disobey. There are times you just don't mess with Finn and this is one of them. It's something I have come to appreciate over these past months because it makes me feel protected.

For a moment, my heart clenches. I will miss him during my trip. It will be odd to go for such a long time without seeing him, and I can only hope that when I come back, he's still around and has not forgotten all about me.

I push the dull thoughts from my mind when a second message flashes on the display of my phone.

"ARE YOU ON YOUR WAY?!!!"

Someone is getting anxious—and for today, he'll get all of my attention. That's the least I can do for my second best friend on his wedding day.

~~~~

The small apartment that Marcel and Finn share is in total shambles when we arrive. Open boxes filled halfway with random stuff are scattered throughout, and a pile of clothes I'm not sure is clean is spread on Marcel's bed.

He stands in front of the mirror with desperate eyes, already dressed in his tux pants and dress shirt. His fingers fumble with the band that's supposed to become a bow tie, and I immediately know that this is the big drama that got him all wound up. Marcel can be so silly at times, getting upset over nothing.

Pages upon pages of printouts of bow-tie suggestions are lying on the dresser in front of him. He curses in frustration as he tears the band open once again. "I can't figure this out."

I grab his hands. "Marcel, look at me."

He lets out a dramatic sigh as he takes his gaze off the mirror. I search his eyes to determine if this is really all that's bothering him. Over the last year, he has been able to fool me less and less. In a way, it has become a game to figure out his thoughts and feelings. After he has been hiding his real self for so long, it is still hard for him to trust anyone.

I guide him over to the bed and sit him down. "Now why don't you tell me what's really wrong?"

His fingers run over the short coarse hair he managed to grow. "What if she doesn't show up?"

My eyebrows arch in surprise. "Why wouldn't she? Donna loves you."

"I dunno." He chews on his lip. "Girls do that sometimes."

A snort escapes me. "This is not some cheap remake of the *Runaway Bride* with Donna standing you up at the altar. You shouldn't worry about it."

He doesn't look convinced, falling back on the bed with a loud huff. "She was really upset earlier."

That gets my attention. "And why was that?" I nudge him. "Did you do something to her?"

He sits up like a rocket. "Hell no." He avoids my eyes when he gets on his feet and walks back to the mirror. "It's Hallie. They won't allow her to come because she was caught lying again, so Donna was in tears. As you know, Hallie is her only family left."

I let the air slowly escape through pursed lips. Hallie's condition has been a constant concern in Marcel and Donna's relationship. The DA worked out a deal with her in return for her testimony against Luke, which only resulted in a juvenile conviction, though they could have easily charged her as an adult for the kidnapping.

The court still locked her up in a mental institution until she's at least nineteen, claiming she is a threat to society without proper treatment. Ultimately, I had to agree and just hope she will be able to pull herself together. Lately, she hasn't been doing as well as everyone had hoped.

"What did she lie about this time?"

He grimaces. "You're not gonna like this. Apparently, she convinced one of the janitors to smuggle out a letter for Luke. The prison caught it, but when the therapist confronted her, she said it wasn't hers. *You* were trying to frame her to get her into trouble."

I roll my eyes—we have been here before. Though I have written her a long letter forgiving her for her involvement, she is still convinced I hate her. "That's ridiculous."

"Yeah, I know." He fidgets again with the bow tie. "Worst thing is that she can't help it. Being the pathological liar she is, she actually convinces herself that her lies are true. People like her can trick out lie detectors."

It's one of the reasons why she could so easily trick me with the staged rape at the cabin. In her mind, it really happened. Add real tears and fear, and she actually convinced herself that she was a kidnap victim like me. Otherwise, she might have sabotaged our escape or accidentally prattled away their plan. Coupled with her severe fear of abandonment, she had been a powerful weapon under Luke's spell. After her parents' death had pushed her over the edge. She was so afraid of losing him, too, that she would have done anything to please him.

Ultimately, I hope she'll get her act together. "Do you want me to talk to Donna?"

"Would you?" He looks like a little boy with big pleading eyes. "I'd really appreciate that."

I check my watch. "Okay, I'll swing by the hotel before going home to change. My mom should be there, too. She promised Donna to help her get ready."

He lets out a sigh of relief. "Thanks." The tension is gone—it doesn't take much to make Marcel happy.

"But before I go, we'll figure out this bow tie."

That puts a wide smile on his face. "Have I ever told you that you're the best friend anyone can ask for?"

I divert my gaze. "Don't try to smooth-talk me, Officer Brown. It won't work."

He snorts. "Smooth-talking is not my area of expertise." He winks at me. "I'll leave that to someone else." My cheeks flush when I start on the bow tie while his eyes stay on me. "You know he likes you, right?"

I quickly glance at his face, not in the mood to talk about it. It's too early to think of Finn as anything but a friend. Maybe once I come back from my trip, things will be different—but not now.

~~~~

Four hours later, I'm standing in the chapel as Donna walks down the aisle, looking prettier than ever with the happiest glow on her face. Having dealt with plenty of blows in her lifetime, she got over the fact that her sister couldn't be there rather quickly. Donna is a practical woman that way. Why cry over something you can't change—life is too short for that.

She is beaming when Marcel takes her hands. As they exchange vows, I wipe a few tears away. Of all people, they deserve to be happy. Yet my eyes return more and more to Finn, standing next to the groom and looking absolutely stunning in his tux as Marcel's best man. When our eyes interlock, a smile curls his lips. That alone gets me so distracted that I almost miss the wedding kiss.

The reception is at Stonehenge's only hotel, and it seems that half the town has been invited. Marcel has built a good reputation and his career as a police officer is thriving. He's often seen having a heart-to-heart with some of the local hooligans, which usually gets them to straighten up. Kids practically stand at attention when he walks by and there is not one who has ever tried to mess with him.

At first I was afraid that Tyrone would seek revenge when Marcel moved with Finn to Stonehenge, but I learned that the DEA maintains the covers of their agents in case they ever have to plant them again in that same group. For Tyrone, Marcel was being held in a different part of the jail until being shipped off to a federal prison in another state. Tyrone actually snitched on Marcel to get a better deal, and the DA cut a few years off his sentence to make it more believable. In the end, Tyrone still got twenty years, which makes the streets a hell of a lot safer.

The food is divine and the only downer is that I cannot sit next to Finn during dinner. He is huddled around Donna and Marcel with the rest of the wedding party. To my delight, he isn't paying any attention to the maid of honor—Donna's best friend since kindergarten—though she's trying her hardest to flirt with him.

Right after dinner, he excuses himself and drags me onto the dance floor. When the upbeat music changes into a slow song, he pulls me closer, nuzzling his nose into my hair.

"You know, I'm gonna miss you."

I snuggle against his broad chest, taking in a whiff of his cologne. "Me too. I wish you could come." For a moment, I close my eyes and get lost in his embrace, wishing to hold onto this moment forever.

Marcel clinks his knife against the water glass and kills the mood and the music; with a small frown, I turn to hear yet another speech. There were already at least a dozen during dinner, and I'm getting sick of them.

When I try to hide behind a pillar to play with my phone, Marcel catches me red handed. "Kelsey, Finn, could you please come here for a second?"

I gaze at Finn, wondering what this is all about, and his big smile almost cuts his face in half. A prickling sensation spreads at the nape of my neck—I can't help but think that this is a big conspiracy.

Marcel clears his throat melodramatically when I stand next to him. "First off, I'd like to make an announcement. My beautiful wife"—he beams at Donna—"told me a few weeks ago that she's expecting. We are very excited about this, but we have decided that going to Hawaii for our honeymoon might be a little much, so we're staying closer to home."

I almost strangle him. For months, he has been whining about his fear of flying, and it is so typical that he takes Donna's pregnancy as an excuse not to go. He will be in a boatload of trouble when I get him on my own.

"Since this frees up quite a lot of travel funds, Donna and I want to make a little present of our own today." With a sheepish smile, he squeezes my hand. "As y'all know, we wouldn't even be here today if it wasn't for this young lady. She is planning a trip around the world—alone—and since she tends to get into a lot of trouble, we thought she'd be better off with a chaperone." He nudges Finn, whose eyes are fixed on me with a rather anxious expression. "So my best man here will tag along, as long as that's cool with Kelsey."

My jaw drops. "You mean . . ."

Both Marcel and Finn nod in unison.

Tears pool in my eyes when I find Donna's face, who grins just as widely as the guys. Without another word, I pull Marcel into a hug. "Thanks." A few tears are soaked up by his tux, and I'm ready to scream when happiness bubbles inside me.

Finn whisks me away under the applause of the other guests. My head is spinning, the truth that I won't have to conquer the world on my own after all still sinking in. In the shadows of the rose bushes, I finally catch my breath. My mouth opens to scold Finn that he kept this a secret, but he places a finger over my lips to shush me.

We just gaze at each other as the music starts back up. A light evening breeze warms my skin, but it is nothing in comparison to the heat that surges through me when he bends forward. When our lips connect, my racing heartbeat is the only noise in the world. I close my eyes, and this incredible pain seeps out of me, more and more as the kiss intensifies.

When we break, wetness glistens in his eyes. "I think I love you, Kelsey."

Just this morning, those words would have scared me to death. I would have been convinced that it could never work— that I could never let go of the past enough to open my heart to a man and trust him with my soul.

Now, it all makes perfect sense. We cry together, we laugh together, and we give each other strength. It is time to cross a new bridge and kill off those remaining demons that trapped me for too long—time to give love a fair chance. That's what I owe to the both of us.

Here's a FREE GIFT to you!

WAR ORPHAN

A TOMÁS ARAYA STORY

Life has been a struggle for Tomás Araya. Orphaned after the execution of his parents by the new regime of Malaguay, he elbows his way up the ranks of the national army. At nineteen, his life looks bright. A fast-track career beckons in the military, his sweetheart carries his child, and his music is to lift him to the stratosphere.

But the higher you rise, the deeper you fall.

As Tomás's life explodes, he needs to act.

Fast.

One wrong turn, and it's game over.

Get War Orphan as a free download when you sign up to my mailing list at
www.salmasonauthor.com

Sal Mason

If you enjoyed Trapped, you'll be able to join Kelsey and the crew when they return as neighbors of Aeree Cahill, heroine of Survive.

Survive

To survive, Aeree Cahill has to stay one step ahead of the flying bullets.

When an idyllic weekend getaway to the Green Mountains turns into a deadly trap, Aeree and her fellow campers find themselves hunted by a ruthless sniper. Now a prime target, she must race against the clock to discover the killer's identity.

As a web of lies begins to unravel, dark secrets will be exposed and some will stop at nothing to protect the evils of their past. For Aeree, evading the bullets is only the beginning. With danger and deception around every corner, there can only be one rule.

To get out alive, trust no one.

Continue for an exclusive sneak peek at Chapter 1 of Survive . . .

* Please remember that reviews help other readers find books. I appreciate all reviews, whether positive or negative. *

Survive—Chapter 1

"Paper or plastic?" With my best fake smile, I gaze at the old lady in front of me, my fingers drumming on the small ledge next to the cash register when she doesn't respond. My eyes wander to the line of customers behind her and I sigh—so much for the extra bathroom break I so desperately need.

"What did you say, dear?" She fiddles with the small plastic hearing aid behind her ear.

"Do you want paper or plastic?" I ask a few octaves higher, hoping my words get through this time.

"Oh, paper, dear." Her lips split into a toothless grin. "Plastic is bad for the environment."

This time, my smile is genuine—someone her age who is concerned about the pollution future generations will have to endure totally rocks. My attention turns to Ricky, our bagging clerk, and I give him the thumbs-up, our sign for paper bags. He nods, but I'm not sure if he understands or just bounces to the music blasting through his earplugs.

He grabs a paper bag and I start to scan the first item. One by one, the groceries move forward on the belt, a low metallic beep indicating I'm doing it correctly. The lady is a health nut, buying mostly salads, fruits and vegetables, and lean chicken breast. The only sin is a small box of chocolates.

"That will be forty-two sixty-five," I say when I'm done.

"Can I get a lottery ticket, please?"

I point to the customer service desk. "Sorry, we don't sell them at the register anymore. You have to go over there."

It takes her forever to count out the money, the line growing with every penny she places on the small space in front of me. I peek into her wallet and see an extra ten dollars, but she insists on giving me the exact change. After that, she is on her way.

I turn to the next customer with my fake smile, but the voice of Mr. Hill, the store manager, stops me before I can get started.

"Aeree, a word, please."

Usually, he is friendly enough, but this time, he looks like he just choked down a glass of lemon juice. His lips are pressed together in a thin line as he regards me with a sullen expression.

My eyes dart from his face to the long line of customers and back to him. "Now?"

"Yes." He signals for Tammy from the customer service desk to come over.

"Finish here," he hisses before shooting me a nasty glare.

Somehow, I can't shake the feeling I'm in trouble, though I can't figure out what I could have possibly done wrong. I'm always polite, on time, and never have any cash shortage in the register. This is an entry-level job at the supermarket and hard to screw up.

He ushers me into his office and, to my surprise, closes the door behind us. The hairs on my neck rise in alarm—I'm not comfortable being around men on my own, especially those I don't know well. My body tenses when he gives me a curt smile that doesn't hit his eyes and points at the chair in front of his desk.

"Sit down."

I oblige with hesitation, lowering myself on the front edge of the chair with my feet firmly planted on the ground. I measure the distance to the door—five, maybe six steps—too far to make a safe escape. If he tries anything, he will taste blood.

"Well, Aeree, it has been brought to the shop's attention that you lied on your employment application."

This earns him a frown. "Excuse me, what are you implying, sir?" Playing ignorant might be my only chance to salvage my job. Not that it's a great job, but with my rocky past, my options are severely limited.

"We received information that you have a criminal record you did not disclose."

Busted. I force a sweet smile. "Well, don't they always say people deserve a second chance? I'm an outstanding employee—that should count for something."

"You still lied. Store policy is clear that, in an instance like this, I have to let you go."

"Don't you at least want to hear my side of the story?" The desperation in my voice makes me cringe. I swear to myself that I will not resort to begging like the last time—screw him and his job.

"It's a little late for that. If you raised this in the interview, I would've been more than willing to listen, but not now." His face is stern; he reminds me of the judge who sentenced me four years ago when all that shit happened.

"Okay." I hate how timid I sound.

"You have fifteen minutes to clean out your locker. Your last paycheck will be available on Friday." He makes a sour face and scribbles something on a piece of paper before waving his arm, apparently his way of dismissal. "I'm sorry it has come to this. You can go now."

"Fine, your loss." I jump to my feet and storm out, my heart screaming about another injustice. There's no way the prick would have hired me if I had been truthful. People with felony convictions don't make good employees, no matter what they say. It's a fact of life I have learned the hard way. My chances of ever finding a decent job are nil.

I purposely bang the door of the locker against the wall a few times to blow off steam, but it doesn't help, even when I kick against it and leave a good dent. The result is only a sore toe. Cussing under my breath, I stuff my phone and lunch box into my backpack, glancing around the staff room one more time. The job sucked anyway. I don't need this. My husband earns enough money and will take care of me for the rest of my pitiful existence. Screw these people and their judgmental attitudes.

Chin held high, I march out of the shop without bothering to say goodbye to anyone. Mitch can pick up my paycheck or they can mail it—I don't intend to ever set foot into this hellhole again. I swallow down the lump in my throat as the automatic doors slide open. Only the cold, harsh world waits on the other side.

As I walk to my car, a tingling sensation spreads along my scalp. I gaze around. It almost feels as if someone is watching me. The parking lot is empty except for a woman and her kid who mind their own business. I squint at the windows of the supermarket; no set of eyes gawks back. An empty soda can rattles and holds my attention as the wind carries it over the smooth asphalt, which glimmers from the heat of the midday sun.

I tear my gaze off the can and continue my way to the car. The feeling of eyes burning into my skull persists. By the time I slide into the small convertible that Mitch got me for Christmas, my body screams from the tension, and I'm covered in cold sweat.

I try to ignore the prickling feeling in my scalp when I start the car and pull out of the parking lot. The heat is probably driving me crazy—nothing a cold drink can't fix. On my way home, I stop at another supermarket and pick up a few cans of zero cola and a six-pack of beer for Mitch. Slurping the ice-cold drink, the liquid runs down my throat with a tingle, taking off the edge. The prickling is still in my scalp, but I'm probably just getting paranoid. There is no one watching me—my life is way too boring for that.

Enjoyed this little sample?
If yes, don't forget to sign up to my newsletter at
www.salmasonauthor.com
to stay up-to-date with the latest news of the Hide & Seek
Series.

Special Thanks

So I guess now it's the time to thank all those who have supported me on my writer's journey. There were many, and if I forgot anyone, feel free to yell. I'll make sure to add you in the next edition.

Before I start, I have to apologize to my kids for all the burned pizzas, piles of laundry, and the millions of "just a sec" they got to hear while this story was a work in progress. Thanks, guys, for being patient with me.

My next special thanks goes out to my editor, Nicole Ayers, who fought her way through the plot and made it so much better. Thanks for answering my many annoying questions and for the great pointers you gave me. Editing is a painful process, but you made it bearable.

Next on the list is Lucy who happens to be an amazing cover designer. We all know we shouldn't judge a book but its cover, but we all do, so thanks for making the cover of *Trapped* stand out.

Also a very special thanks to Elle Davis, Leigh W. Stuart, Lina Hanson and Elicia Hyder who helped me tremendously during all or parts of this book. Oh, and not to forget Julie Clarke who was my guinea pig during my early stages of writing.

Another thanks to Audrey Jean who cast a final eye on the finished manuscript to get rid of the last, pesky mistakes we all overlooked.

Of course, I can't forget my launch team who helped me to get *Trapped* off the ground. Couldn't have done it without you—thanks:

Aastha, Alba, Amanda Rojas, Ana Simons, Anna, artkissez, Baylee B, Bhavadharani, Brenda, CheyAnne Deatherage, Clabastian, Cookiescupcake1, Courtney, D. L. Schroeder, Denise Denney, Destiny Shania Dale, Detta Drake, Dominica Luna, Elle Davis, Elicia Hyder, Em Ralph, Faith Ratliff, Farah, George Johnson, Hailey Williams, IcyBee, IsaMarie, Jasmine, Jessie Hazel, Juliet Lyons, Kaitlyn Tucci, Katherine Stein, Kayla Zarate, Khansa Jan, Leigh W. Stuart, Leja Rosé, Lina Hanson, M Greenhill, Maithilee, May Freighter, Melanie, Melody Hall, Melody Veen, Nahomy, Nathan James, Nina, Ortiz, RK Close, RealOriginality, Remedythe Williams, Safia Nayeem, Solina Piani, Tainted Ortiz, Tatum McPadden, Tiana Izawa-Hayden, Tjarda, Wendei Stoltie.

And finally, I want to thank all my readers on Wattpad for your support. Without your encouragement, the story would likely be nothing more than an idea in my head. You guys are simply the best.

Made in the USA
Lexington, KY
21 March 2019